DANNY BOY

A moving tale of love and survival...

Rosie's family doesn't have much money, but she's rich in other ways and when Danny Walsh asks her to walk out with him, it's a dream come true. Soon they are married, but Danny's young brother runs away to join the uprising of Easter 1916, and Danny has no choice but to find his brother and bring him home. Before he can be released, Danny must swear to take his place. He takes Rosie and their daughter to Birmingham, where Rosie takes a job in munitions. Little does she realise the danger she is in...

DANNY BOY

DANNY BOY

by

Anne Bennett

Magna Large Print Books
Long Preston, North Yorkshire,
BD23 4ND, England.

British Library Cataloguing in Publication Data.

Bennett, Anne
    Danny boy.

        A catalogue record of this book is
        available from the British Library

        ISBN   0-7505-2466-9

First published in Great Britain in 2004 by HarperCollins Publishers

Copyright © Anne Bennett 2004

Cover illustration © John Hancock by arrangement with
P.W.A. International Ltd.

Anne Bennett asserts the moral right to be identified as the author of
this work

Published in Large Print 2006 by arrangement with
HarperCollins Publishers

Magna Large Print is an imprint of Library Magna Books Ltd.

Printed and bound in Great Britain by
T.J. (International) Ltd., Cornwall, PL28 8RW

To my only son Simon, with all my love.

ACKNOWLEDGEMENTS

When I suggested the idea of this book to Susan Opie, my lovely editorial director, so many months ago, she advised me to 'run with it'. At first, I could barely crawl with it, for the facts were so difficult to find. It is hard to credit today, when sometimes it appears you only have to sneeze for someone to write a thesis about it, but things were not documented back then in the same way at all. The Irish uprising itself was: there are books and websites and songs and poems about it, and the same can be said for the battles of the First World War. However, trying to find out what life was like for the ordinary Dubliner that Easter in 1916, or what a soldier earned once he'd enlisted in the British Army and when the carnage was over, what he was given in unemployment pay, was like asking for moon dust.

These were times when I could go no further because I couldn't find the information I needed. I did manage in the end, largely due to the help often perfect strangers gave to me. I am always staggered when this happens and I take great pleasure in thanking those people now.

The little village of Blessington, where the book opens, for those who don't know, is situated just outside Dublin in the county of Wicklow and even today is still a local beauty spot. The great people who live there like nothing better than to talk of old times, as I found out when I visited in April 2003. But they have gone one better, for the members of the Blessington Local and Family History Society have compiled a book, *Blessington Now and Then*. Without this book, my life might have been far harder.

Ken Finlay's website depicting Dublin 'in the rare old times' was particularly good too. And, as well as information and photographs, he would answer any question I threw at him. Surely a saint of a man?

But there were others, like the young girl at the National Library of Ireland who found, photocopied and sent me old maps of Dublin and especial thanks must go to Molly Staunton, who lives in Tallaght and who carried out research about the Blessington to Dublin steam tram for me in her own time and out of the goodness of her heart. Then there was the girl in the Terenure Library. Terenure had been the old terminus of the steam tram, and a librarian there spent her lunch hour finding out the routes of the two electric trams that had gone into Dublin from there, which I had been unable to find anywhere else.

The people at the harbourmaster's offices in Dun Laoghire astounded me (pre-1918 this town was called Kingstown). When they heard I was unable to get hold of a book detailing the history of the port by a man called John de Courcy, they not only photocopied the book, but also bound it beautifully before sending it to me.

Sincere gratitude must also go to Sister Barbara Jefferies. Sister Jefferies is the archivist at St Mary's Convent in Handsworth, (Sisters of Mercy) who supplied me with literature and the history of the order. In the same way, the Catholic Archdiocese of Birmingham helped find out about the Catholic churches and schools in the area at that time.

Handsworth Historical Society was able to supply me with facts about local history and old maps as did the compilers of *Astonbrook - The History of Aston,* which has had support and input from Carl Chinn. He has given me, and continues to give me, immeasurable help in anything to do with old Birmingham.

The website, 'The Home Front. Britain During The First World War', was informative as to the woman's role in that Great War, but for many particular things I had to contact individuals – thank God for e-mail!

Thanks, therefore, go to Chris Baker and Andrew Jackson. Andrew has compiled a moving and emotive site about Accrington Pals and it is well worth a visit. It reduced me to tears. In search of this important information, I also contacted the War Research Society and was put in touch with Nick Frear (Nick@Nickintime. co.uk) who gave me help, answered questions and supplied me with other material and facts that could form the basis of another book or two. Thanks Nick.

Then there was Paula Biddlestone, the lady in Birmingham Social Science Library, I told you this list went on and on. This terrific lady searched through the archives and unearthed pages and pages of papers relating to National Insurance records for the relevant periods and marked the photocopied pages to make life easier for me before sending them on.

While I was searching for information about life on the canals at that time, I came upon a site called, 'Up the Cut' about the boats on the Birmingham canals which again helped tremendously.

There was one book, too, which gave me valuable material and that was a book called *Up the Terrace – Down Aston and Lozells*. It was written by a man called Donald K Moore and he'd recounted the reminiscences of his grandfather, who had been a child at the time of the First World War. I have tried to contact Mr Moore personally, for the book was a pleasure to read and very helpful, but have been unable to find him, so here I would like to extend my heartfelt thanks.

I have great respect for the thousands of people who spend hours compiling and adding to various sites on the internet to help keep history alive and pass on their knowledge and that of others. I'd like to feel I do my bit and try to give accurate information in the novels I write, but my work would be harder without the internet and also without the people who have helped me and if I have forgotten anyone, I am very sorry.

My family's unfailing support is also a great encouragement to me, from my four children, Nikki, Simon, Beth and Tamsin, my son-in-law Steve, my daughter-in-law Carol and mother-in-law Nancy Bennett, to my lovely husband Denis, who I would be lost without.

Thanks also to my dear friends, Ruth Adshead, Judith Kendall and Judy Westwood, who in various ways helped to make this book a reality.

But especial and immense gratitude must go to the most marvellous team at HarperCollins who work with me: my editorial director, Susan Opie, and equally my editor, Maxine Hitchcock, my valiant agent, Judith Murdoch, Ingrid Gegner, my publicist and last, but by no means least, Peter Hawtin, the Midlands' sales director. I owe them all so much.

Thanks a million times to each and every one of you.

ONE

Rosie McMullen never thought much of the beauty of the countryside she lived in, like the verdant green hills to each side of the farm. These were speckled with sheep and dotted here and there with cottages very like her own and had rivers that shone like silver ribbons in the sun trickling down them that fed into the large lake beside Blessington village.

She lived with her parents Minnie and Seamus and her two younger sisters, Chrissie and Geraldine, on a small, but prosperous farm just over two miles from the village in County Wicklow, a county that was often dubbed 'the garden of Ireland'.

She took it all for granted like she did her home, that squat, whitewashed, thatched cottage, with the cobbled yard in front of it, full of strutting hens pecking at the corn and grit. There was a barn to one side of the cottage, a byre to the other, a midden at the back and a spring well in the first field. The cottage itself had a large kitchen with a curtained-off bed, in the corner where Rosie's parents slept. There were also two other bedrooms, the first and largest one, which opened directly off the kitchen was used by Rosie and her sisters and at the end of that room another door led into a smaller room, which remained unoccupied until Rosie took it over for her first ten years.

From the cottage window, Rosie could see the winding lane leading up to the road with cultivated fields to one side of it and the pasture land to the other side, where the cows stood placidly chewing the cud.

However, Rosie's childhood was a harsh one, even in this idyllic place and came to an end entirely by the time she was just ten, when in October 1907 her mother gave birth to a baby boy she named Dermot. Rosie's sisters were eight and six, and from the moment Dermot let out his first newborn wail, it was as if they'd all ceased to exist.

Neither Minnie or her husband had ever been particularly demonstrative with their affections towards the girls, and Minnie especially, was always quick to find fault. She would fly into a temper for little or no reason and smacks, or strokes from the strap was a regular feature of their childhood. They never questioned this, it was just how things were. But, Dermot, they were soon aware, had a totally different kind of upbringing.

At only twenty inches long, Dermot ruled the house and all in it. Neighbours trailed to the house to offer their congratulations and catch a glimpse of this marvellous child, as if Dermot McMullen was the first child born to the family. Seamus's hand was shook over and over. He was stood drinks at the pub by the men, while the women brought gifts for the baby and cakes and other fancies for the family. The three girls were mostly ignored, but if they were noticed at all, it was only to be asked if they weren't delighted altogether by their wee brother?

18

Strangely enough, Rosie was. She had no argument with the small baby and she often stole away to gaze at him. He looked so vulnerable. He had a dusting of light silky hair and his skin was a creamy colour, his eyes the milky blue of the newborn. She was enchanted by his tiny flexing fingers with minute nails and his podgy little feet, which would kick out in freedom when he was released from his bindings. No, Rosie couldn't blame the wee baby for the changes in the house, but as time passed, she blamed her parents and particularly her mother more and more.

Minnie was unaware of how her eldest daughter felt. In fact she seldom thought of her at all, now that she had her son. She would have said, if asked that her daughters were not neglected, they were fed, warm and kept clean. Rosie, if ever she'd given voice to her feelings, would have said that, though their basic needs were attended to, they were never given a kind word or shown a warm smile. Rosie would have liked her mother's eyes to soften when she looked at her daughters sometimes, the way they did when they lighted on Dermot and to be spoken to in the soothing, gentle way she reserved for the baby.

She never discussed these things with her little sisters, but resentment began to burn inside her and she promised herself that she'd never make a daughter of hers feel so unwanted, however many sons she might have.

Dermot's eyes eventually turned bluey/grey, but his skin stayed fair and he developed dark blond curls. The three McMullen sisters all looked totally different to their brother. They all

19

had large, dark brown eyes with a dusting of freckles beneath them and across their pink tinged cheeks and the bridge of their snub noses. Their hair was as dark as their eyes and fell in natural waves down their backs.

Each Saturday night, Seamus went into one of the pubs in Blessington village and the girls would have their weekly bath. Minnie would help bring the bath in before the fire and help fill it and then they'd be left to their own devices. It was Rosie who lathered her little sisters and washed their hair, remembering to use the water from the rain barrel outside the door for the last rinse, so as to give their hair extra shine.

It was Rosie who helped her sisters from the bath and dried them and towelled their hair to stop it dripping before attending to herself. And later, when they were all bathed, the water emptied pan by pan into the gutter in the yard, and the girls dressed for bed, Rosie would plait all their hair, so that it would be wavy for Mass in the morning.

And the next morning, while her mother attended to Dermot, Rosie would see to her sisters, brushing their hair and checking that they were tidy and that their boots were fastened correctly and they had a clean hanky up the leg of their bloomers and the collection farthings secure.

Chrissie and Geraldine accepted Rosie as their substitute mother without complaint and so possibly felt the lack of a mother's love and attention less than Rosie did. And Rosie felt a sort of fierce protective love for her two little sisters and took a pride in their appearance.

When they stepped out for Mass dressed in their best clothes with bonnets tied beneath their little pointed chins, and their boots shining with polish, they looked lovely. All three girls were dressed the same for Mass, but though many of the neighbours smiled at the girls, their attention was all for Dermot.

Wasn't he the little dote? Hadn't he grown so? Wasn't he the best baby in the world, so good, so contented? Surely Minnie didn't know she was born with such a child and with three daughters to help her rear him.

In truth, the girls seldom got a look in where Dermot was concerned. Minnie seemed to either be nursing him, or cuddling him most of the day. She'd instruct Rosie from the chair before the fire in frying rashers and eggs for Sunday breakfast after Mass and later Rosie would cook the meal.

Rosie learned fast. Nothing enraged her mother more than vegetables burned onto the pan, lumpy gravy or inadequately drained cabbage and she had no wish to inflame her mother's temper. So, without complaint, she learned also how to make soda bread, barnbrack and apple pie.

She'd always been used to helping. It had been her lot for long enough anyway, particularly as she was the eldest. She knew it was what most girls did and that it would stand her in good stead when she married. But, just sometimes, she would have liked to hold the baby, to feel his warm little body against her and see his eyes looking into her own.

Minnie however, guarded him jealously, only letting Seamus hold him grudgingly. Babyhood though, doesn't last forever and as Dermot began to crawl, and then pull himself up to stand and walk, he wasn't content to be cuddled all the day. He loved all his sisters, who were always willing to stop what they were at to do his bidding, but Dermot's favourite in the house was Rosie and he was devoted to her.

Dermot began at the County School in Blessington the September before his fifth birthday. Rosie and Chrissie had both left school by then and Geraldine, who had been eleven in June had just one year left, so it was her job to take Dermot up to the school while Rosie and Chrissie helped wherever they were needed, on the farm, the house, or the dairy.

Rosie had settled well in to the mundane life, although she often missed the company of the girls at school and as she neared fifteen she noticed changes to her body she could have done with advice over, things that she could hardly discuss with a younger sister. There was no-one she could think to ask and she often wondered if thinking about it too much could be construed as a sin.

Then, one dreadful day, she'd gone to the privy outside, driven there by severe stomach cramps and found she was bleeding from her bottom. She came in, her eyes swollen, her body weak from crying for hours, for she was convinced she was dying.

Even then, she could hardly bear to tell her mother, but fear eventually overcame her embarrassment. 'You're not dying,' her mother told her brusquely. 'It's what happens to every woman, every month.'

Rosie's eyes opened wide in astonishment.

She'd never heard of such a thing. Minnie Mc-Mullen was hazy about why women had periods and the workings of a human body – it wasn't something a good, Catholic woman should know about she felt. But, she knew the monthly periods were connected somehow with having a child, and this was what she told Rosie.

Rosie looked at her in horror. She knew very little about sex and what you did to have a baby, but from the odd snippets picked up in the school yard, she knew you had to 'do' things with a man and she knew that to do those things before you had a husband and then to go on and have a baby, was just about the worst thing in the world. She'd be like Cissie Moriarty who, people said, had been expecting when she was but a young girl and there had been no boyfriend in sight. Anyway, whatever the truth of it Cissie was sent far away from her home to a place for bad girls so the rumours went and she was never seen or heard of again.

Rosie, gripped with desperate fear cried, 'But, I'm not having a baby. I don't want to have a baby.'

'I didn't say you were, you silly girl,' Minnie replied sharply. 'And I trust you won't think of having a child until you are respectably married. This other thing is just part of being a woman, so that you can have a baby when you're ready.'

Rosie was relieved beyond measure that she was normal and she wasn't dying, but there were still things she needed to know and she decided to ask her mother now, while they were talking of intimate matters. 'Mammy, how do babies get into you?'

Minnie's lips pursed. 'There is no need to know those things, or even ask about them until you're married. Then, all will come clear to you.'

How? Rosie wondered, but she didn't ask. One look at her mother's face convinced her it would be a waste of time. Maybe, when she married, her husband would tell her. She hoped to goodness he knew something about it, or they'd never have a child.

She spent a lot of time as she reached her mid teens thinking about boys, wondering who she might marry and whether it would be someone around them, like Larry Sullivan the son of the blacksmith, or Rory McCabe, whose family owned a farm similar to their own, or even Dessy Finnegan, though when she thought of him she had to smile, for the boy was so small she stood head and shoulders above him like most of the other girls.

However, none of these boys attracted her in any way. In fact, they irritated her more often. Perhaps feelings change as a person gets older she mused or maybe she'd be swept off her feet by someone else entirely. She wondered what it would be like to fall in love, how it would feel to have a man's hands upon you. Of course, that verged on impure thoughts and then would have to be confessed to Father McNally and yet she could scarcely prevent thinking of such things when she was in her bed at night.

Really though, when she thought deeper about it, she wondered if she'd ever have a boyfriend. She'd had to do so much with her sisters since she'd been ten that she'd seldom had time to think of her own appearance. She brushed both her sisters' hair a hundred times each before plaiting it for bed, but her own waves got a cursory brush and she'd spent so long seeing that Chrissie and Geraldine were neat and tidy for school or Mass, that she scarcely had a minute to think of herself.

She examined her face and body critically in the mirror in her room and could see she had little to recommend her. Her eyes she felt were as dull as her hair, her skin sallow and while her body was thin enough, it had no shape to it at all.

She had few to compare herself with, for she saw her contemporaries only at Mass or the village, if she went in on Saturdays. There was a social in the church hall once a month for young people over the age of sixteen, but Rosie didn't think she'd ever be allowed to go. She knew her mother didn't approve of such goings on. Rosie didn't mind too much for she had nothing to wear, the serviceable day clothes and outfits for Mass were not the sort of clothes to wear to a dance. She knew too, the possibility of her mother spending money to get her new clothes, especially the things suitable for a social, was as likely as her flying to the moon, and she had no money of her own.

But, despite all this, there was a boy, a man almost, Rosie liked and his name was Danny Walsh. She was the same age as his younger sister Elizabeth, while Sarah his other sister was another two years older and he had a younger brother Phelan, who was the same age as Geraldine. The girls had all been at school together and when she talked to them after Mass, she had ample time to study their older brother, Danny.

He was a well set up and muscular young man, and from being out in all weathers his face was always bronzed. As he was the eldest son he was set to inherit the family's farm and he carried that assurance with him. His mouth turned up at the sides as if he was constantly good humoured, his chin was determined and strong and his sparkling eyes were as dark as the mop of brown curls he sported.

Rosie knew that nobody as handsome as Danny Walsh would look the side she was on, and she kept her thoughts about him to herself and only dreamed about him in her bed at night when she was tucked in beside her sisters. However, Danny Walsh had noticed the young girl with the deep brown eyes and hair that shone in the sunlight, but he also knew how old she was and he was no cradle snatcher.

In the spring of 1914, Rosie was sixteen and a half and Danny's feelings for her had deepened, though he had no idea how she felt about him. He was no flirt and didn't give his heart freely and that Sunday morning he decided it was time to see if Rosie liked him enough to step out with him and he dressed with extra care. The McMullen family came out of church and Minnie and Seamus stopped to speak to some neighbours just a little way from the porch.

It had rained in the night and dampness still lingered in the air and Geraldine and Chrissie had Dermot between them and they were jumping him over the puddles. Rosie was standing a little way apart watching them, a smile playing at her mouth at the squeals of delight from Dermot and was unaware of the figure beside her, until he spoke.

'It looks as though the afternoon might turn out nice after all,' Danny Walsh said to Rosie and she, certain Danny couldn't be talking to her, looked around to see who he was addressing.

Danny laughed. 'It's you I'm speaking to Rosie McMullen,' he said. 'And I'd like to take a walk with you this afternoon, if you are agreeable?'

For a moment or two, Rosie was unable to speak, both from astonishment and pleasure and her face flushed with embarrassment.

She didn't know quite how much the flush suited her and how the blood pumped through Danny's body at the sight of her pretty, fresh face. He felt his heart soar with joy for the blush and tentative smile told its own tale.

'I must ... I must ask my parents,' Rosie stammered at last, when she'd recovered enough to speak. 'If ... if they have no objections I'd be pleased to walk out with you. What time did you have in mind?'

Danny shrugged. 'Half past two/three o'clock. Whatever you prefer.'

'Either would suit me admirably,' Rosie said.

Minnie and Seamus had no objection to a relationship beginning between Danny Walsh and their daughter. The Walshes were known to them, their farms were nearly adjoining, though they were over two miles apart by road and they knew them to be a respectable, and a good, catholic family.

'And he's the eldest,' Seamus said. 'Going on for twenty-one now and set to inherit all.'

'Aye,' Minnie said. 'Course Rosie is young yet.' And a grand help to me, she might have added, for she knew she'd miss that greatly.

'Old enough to marry,' Seamus said. 'Sure, she'll be seventeen in September, and you were just eighteen when we wed.'

'Aye,' Minnie said with a sigh, knowing her willing helper would not be with her much longer. But then Geraldine would be leaving school herself in the summer and Chrissie would still be at home, time to lick the pair of them into some sort of shape.

And so, a courtship began between Rosie and Danny Walsh. Each Sunday afternoon through that long and glorious spring and summer, Danny would call for her and they would go from her home sedately enough until they were out of sight of the farm, whereupon Danny would clasp Rosie to him and kiss her, until she felt she had no breath left in her body.

They would walk hand in hand by the side of the lake and just the touch of Danny's hand in hers sent heat pounding though Rosie's body and when he turned to look at her and smile, she felt as if her heart had actually stopped beating.

Rosie regularly visited Danny's parents, Connie and Matt, and found she liked them very much and knew they liked and approved of her. Phelan, though he liked Rosie, was not above teasing her. On her second visit to the farm he had a grin on his face as he grumbled, 'Danny's making me do all the work, since he met you.'

'You cheeky young pup,' Danny cried, cuffing his brother, lightly on the side of the head. 'Bout time you pulled your weight. Anyway, it's only the evening milking I've asked you to do.'

'Aye, so far.'

'Your turn will come, boy,' Matt told his younger son. 'Danny does his share and more, so lets have no more talk about it lest we embarrass our Danny's young lady.'

Rosie was anything but embarrassed. She loved the teasing and ribaldry between the family, never having experienced anything like it. As she helped Connie clear away the things from the meal one evening, while the men had a smoke by the fire, she gave her a brief account of her life and the cooking and washing and dairy work she'd done since she'd been a child.

Connie knew some of it of course. She knew too about the baby boy born to the McMullens after three daughters and at first she'd been as pleased for them as any of the neighbours, knowing most farmers wanted a son. Made the work all worthwhile if their own flesh and blood was to inherit all they'd worked for but though she'd been delighted herself to have two boys, she fiercely loved her daughters too.

She could talk to her daughters, far more than to her sons and she took pleasure in their company and she'd always hoped that Danny and Phelan would choose women who would fit in with the family, when they took a wife. She was delighted with Danny's choice and knew she would get on a treat with Rosie and told Matt this later that night when Rosie and Danny had set out for a walk.

'Mind you,' she said. 'I don't like the set up in that house at all, and that's not so much from

29

what Rosie said, but more from what she didn't. And didn't Danny tell you when he was invited up for a meal, that the wee child was served even before his father and that he held court over the conversation at the table and all had to be quiet and listen to him?'

Matt gave a brief nod. 'Aye, he did right enough.'

'God, but they'll have him ruined,' Connie said. 'Do him no good in the long run.'

'Aye, don't I know that?' Connie said with feeling. 'Course Minnie has always been daft about the boy and never has a good word to say for the girls and from what Danny says is far too free with her hands. Rosie herself let slip that Minnie had used the strap on her more than once.' She shook her head. 'I can't understand the woman at all. Rosie, at any rate, is a daughter I'd be proud to own and I'd welcome her here tomorrow.'

Danny somehow talked Minnie into letting Rosie go to her first social, to show her off he said and Minnie relented enough to buy Rosie a dress when she said she couldn't go, for she hadn't suitable clothes. Minnie wouldn't want the Walshes to think her mean. Rosie didn't care why the dress was bought, she was just glad it was for she was wild to go and let her friends see the fine man she had. Several girls were already jealous of Rosie's luck in landing such a grand catch, but Rosie didn't see Danny as a catch, but as a good and kind man whom she loved with all her heart.

Shay, Danny's best friend still footloose and fancy free, teased Danny about settling down so young that night at the social. He had noticed a change in his friend over the last few weeks and knew Rosie had captured his heart. 'Sure, isn't there plenty of time and the whole world full of women?'

'Aye, but it's just the one woman I want,' Danny said. 'You'll know one day. You'll fall for someone and it will hit you like a ton of bricks and nothing will do you, but marry them.'

'Well, I wish you joy of it. I'm in no hurry myself.'

'Just wait until it's your turn,' Danny said and he left Shay and went over to claim his sweetheart, who was surrounded by a group of girls. 'Excuse me ladies,' he said. 'I need to have a dance with my lovely Rosie.'

Rosie missed the looks of resentment and envy on many of the girls' faces for she had eyes only for Danny and he took her by the hand and led her to the dance floor and they made up a set for the Dublin Reel with young people like themselves. 'Enjoying yourself?' Danny asked, as the music came to an end and the partners bowed to one another.

'Ever so.'

'Well, it won't be the last time you go to a dance I promise,' Danny said. 'You shouldn't be stuck away in some farmhouse all the time, for just to look at the beauty of you would brighten anyone's dull life.'

'Oh, Danny, you say such silly things.'

'True things,' Danny said and Rosie was unable to answer for she was swung away by another man, as the music changed to a polka. The man had his arm tight about her waist and the pace was such that there was little time or breath to talk and she was glad to take a rest at the end of it and hang onto Danny's arm and accept the glass of home-made lemonade he had ready for her for she was out of breath. It was a wonderful, magical evening and later in bed that night she went over Danny's words again and again, as she did after every date and they warmed her very soul.

In fact, she thought about Danny nearly every waking minute and dreamed of him every night. With every passing hour and day, she loved Danny Walsh more and knew she would do anything in the world to please him.

One Sunday afternoon in late June, they climbed the Wicklow Hills. They'd been before, but never so high and eventually, Danny called a halt, hauling Rosie up to join him. They stood and looked about them, the lake shimmering blue in the sunshine that lit up the hillside. 'Have you ever been up there?' Danny said, pointing his hand way into the distance. It was a clear day and they could see for miles.

'Sugar Loaf Mountain?' Rosie said, recognising its distinctive granite summit where it was said nothing grew at all, although it was miles away. She shivered. 'No. I'd be afraid. They say the Devil walks there at will.'

'Jesus, Rosie, you can't believe that?' Danny cried. 'It's a tale put about to frighten the weans. Shay and I always promised ourselves we'd go there one day and stay the night, just to prove there was nothing to be scared of, but we never did get around to it.'

Rosie liked Shay Ferguson. The Walshes and Fergusons were good friends and Shay and Danny had been inseparable since their school days, just as Shay's brother Niall was with Phelan now. 'We used to get up to some high jinks as lads,' Danny said. 'We even had a den. Don't know if I could find it now, if it's still standing that is. It was an old shepherds' shelter, but we thought it a grand place. We became blood brothers together there, slicing our fingers with our pen knives to mingle the blood.'

Danny gave a short laugh at the memory. 'Little wonder we didn't bleed to death, or get an infection.'

He put his arm protectively around Rosie. 'There's no need though for you to fear anything any more, Rosie McMullen for I will never let anything harm you in all your life.'

'Oh Danny.'

'Do you love me, Rosie?'

'Oh yes, I haven't enough words to tell you how much.'

Danny sank to the ground and Rosie was glad to sit beside him on the springy turf, for her legs had begun to tremble. They lay together clasped tight and when Danny began kissing Rosie, she felt those strange yearnings beginning in her body which she barely understood. Danny fumbled at her top until her breasts were partly exposed and as his tongue gently parted her lips, she felt such excitement and pleasure, she could no more tell him to stop, than she could prevent the sun from shining.

Dear God! She knew right from wrong, but never knew about this, this passion that could rise up in you. When Danny's lips began to nuzzle at her breasts, she pressed him closer her whole yearning for him. Yes. Oh yes, and she pushed her fist in her mouth to prevent her saying the words aloud.

But she couldn't help the cry escape her when Danny slid his hands between her legs. She felt she'd died with happiness and she cried. 'Go on. Oh Danny, please go on.'

And how much Danny wanted to. God, he loved Rosie so much it hurt and he knew now, this minute, she would stop him doing nothing and that she wanted for them to be truly together as much as he did.

He pulled away reluctantly, though his groin ached with desire. He had to be strong and sensible for both of them. He was four years older than Rosie, and he had to be the one to put on the brakes, for she seemed incapable of it. He didn't want her disgraced, her family dragged through the mud with her, the wedding rushed and baby born a scant six months later and all claiming it was premature. He'd seen that enough times and didn't want it for his Rosie.

After that though, their courtship became more ardent and their lovemaking more and more intimate, until there were few places on Rosie's body Danny hadn't explored. Rosie, with Danny's urging, had touched him too, feeling his strong muscles move beneath her hands and she had even felt the throbbing hardness of his manhood.

Each time, Danny would pull away from Rosie with difficulty and she would return home frustrated and filled with desire. She didn't know what it cost Danny to resist, for he was burning up himself.

'Oh God, Danny,' Rosie said breathlessly one evening at the farm gate, as Danny pulled away from a passionate embrace. 'Christ, I can't stand this much longer.'

Danny too felt they had waited long enough. 'Rosie, do you love me, as I love you with all your heart and soul?'

'I love you with all my being,' Rosie told him earnestly. 'Danny, I'd need a lifetime to show you how much.'

'Then you'll have a lifetime,' Danny said emphatically. 'Rosie, will you marry me?'

'Oh Yes. Yes. Yes. Yes. A thousand times, yes.'

'Then my darling, we'll talk to your parents tomorrow evening,' Danny promised.

But, despite Minnie's indifference to her daughter, she had seen Rosie come home flustered time and enough and knew what ailed her. She hoped Danny Walsh had respect for Rosie and that Rosie had worn her sensible head when she was with him, for she knew well enough what could happen to young couples allowed out alone. So she was relieved and pleased that Danny came to see them and asked for permission to marry Rosie and readily gave their permission. Connie and Matt weren't averse to this either, for they weren't fools and had seen the way things were going for some time and the wedding was set for October 1914, a month after Rosie's seventeenth birthday.

Rosie began sitting by the fire each evening that she didn't see Danny, sewing things for her bottom drawer. Geraldine was an accomplished seamstress and helped her, but Chrissie had no interest in it at all. Rosie looked at the cobbled mess Chrissie had made of the sheets she'd offered to hem and knew she'd have to unpick the stitches and begin again. She knew Chrissie had tried though and said nothing to her.

Not so their mother. 'Who in God's name would marry a woman who barely knows how to thread a needle?' she demanded, giving Chrissie a cuff across the head so hard that it knocked her from the stool. Chrissie's face burned but her eyes remained dry. She said not a word to her mother, but once she'd left the room she whispered to her sisters, 'Am I worried? I don't think so. There are more ways of satisfying a man than sewing a button on his shirt.'

'Chrissie,' Rosie cried shocked. 'Take care, Mammy would take the strap to you if she heard such talk.'

'That's why I'm not telling her,' Chrissie said, with a defiant toss of her head and the three girls giggled together.

But, although Rosie had help with the basic sewing, she embroidered the night gowns and pillowslips by herself, for she had a knack for it and eventually a week later, with her wedding only days away, she said with satisfaction, 'No-one could have a better bottom drawer than me.'

Chrissie had watched Rosie finish the last rose-bud on the neck of the cambric gown, and snip off the thread and said, 'Aye, it's a fine nightdress right enough. And now, with all the work you've done on it, don't you let Danny tear it from your back. Tell him to go slow.'

'Chrissie!'

Chrissie paled instantly. She'd not heard her mother come into the room and now she watched her approach with dread. The first slap snapped her neck back, but the second on the other cheek with the back of the hand, scored a line down Chrissie's cheek from Minnie's rings. 'We'll have no more of that sort of dirty talk. You can just be thankful your father is out.'

Chrissie's face with the scarlet handprint on one cheek and the other oozing blood from the deep graze had wiped the smiles from Rosie and Geraldine's faces. Rosie wondered if she should say something – intervene, but in the past when she had tried that, it had only made things worse.

She wouldn't risk it and waited till her mother left the room again before reaching for Chrissie's hand. 'I don't care,' Chrissie said defiantly as tears she wouldn't let fall, glistened in her eyes. 'I hate her! She's a cow.'

'Hush, oh hush,' Rosie said putting her arms around her distraught sister. 'Never say things like that, Chrissie. Think them if you must, but never say them. Mammy would kill you if she heard. But I'll tell you what,' she added, hoping to turn the subject from their mother, 'Danny can remove the nightdress in any way he chooses and if he's too slow, I'll help him, so I will.'

Chrissie's smile was tremulous, but it was at least a smile and both Rosie and Geraldine were glad to see it. Rosie gave her sister another hug and returned to her seat before her mother should come in.

Connie had offered Rosie the loan of her wedding dress, to save the young couple money and when Rosie had seen it, shimmering satin with an overdress of lace and a large train, she felt her eyes fill with tears at her generosity. A neighbour woman ran up dresses of white satin for Rosie and Danny's sisters on her treadle sewing machine and they were decorated by Sarah and Elizabeth with beads and little pink and blue rosebuds.

Then, Minnie announced she was going to Dublin to buy clothes for Seamus and Dermot. 'The trousers on the suit your father wears for Mass have worn thin. They're always shining on the knees and don't hold the crease for five minutes and the jacket is downright shabby.'

Rosie knew she was right, but she worried at the expense of it, what with them already paying out for the reception although it was being held at Danny's house as it was bigger. 'Oh Mammy, Daddy will be fine in what he has,' she protested. 'Don't be spending money like this.'

'Och, sure aren't you the first to be married?' Minnie said and a rare smile touched her lips for a moment. 'We'll do the job properly or not at all.'

'But Dermot, Mammy. He's just a wee boy. What does he need?'

'I want him in a sailor suit,' Minnie said. 'In the paper it said they were the talk of the place in England. Won't he look a little dote in one. Of course you'd get nothing like that in this town, but I'm sure to find something in the fine shops in Dublin.'

Rosie knew then why her mother was making

the trip. It wasn't for her father's suit at all. The material could have been bought at the drapers' in the town and run up by a seamstress the way it was always done, but, Dermot had to be dressed as a wee sailor on her wedding day. She said nothing, she had no wish to argue with her mother now and anyway there was little point. Her mother was blind and deaf to reason where the child was concerned.

Dermot didn't care whether he had a sailor suit or not. He didn't even want to go and see his Rosie marry a man who would be taking her away and he said so forcibly and shed so many and such bitter tears that Rosie felt immensely sorry for him. So little had been denied Dermot in his young life that he thought he just had to say that he didn't want Rosie to go and she wouldn't. It was a shock for him to realise that Rosie was going ahead with her plans, regardless of what he thought. 'Don't you love me any more?' he asked plaintively.

'Dermot, of course I love you. I'll always love you.'

'Not as much as you love Danny Walsh.'

'I love you differently,' Rosie corrected. 'It's all part of growing up, getting married and leaving home. Nearly everyone does in the end and I'll not be far away. You can come and visit as often as you are let.'

Dermot scrubbed at his wet cheeks with the sleeve of his jersey. 'It won't be the same.'

Rosie, moved by the sadness in Dermot's face bent down and put her arms about him. 'I know it won't and I can't do anything to make that

39

better, but I want you to remember something always.'

'What?'

'That you are very, very special to me. My own wee brother and wherever I am you will always hold part of my heart.'

Dermot was only slightly mollified by Rosie's words, but he did at least begin to see that whatever he did or said, would change nothing and the days rolled by one into another.

The day before the wedding, Rosie felt herself looking around her home, seeing her room, her sisters, her parents and little distressed Dermot in a new light, knowing soon she was leaving them behind her. She loved Danny and oh without a doubt she longed to be with him, longed to be his wife, longed for fulfilment and to be loved with intensity, but it was a big step nonetheless, whereas for Danny, little was changing. He'd have a wife certainly, but he would still be living at his own house and with his family still around him. It wouldn't be the same wrench for him at all.

It wasn't that Rosie disliked Danny's parents or siblings and they'd gone out of their way to make her welcome in their home. It was just that she was nervous of leaving. Her home had never been a bed of roses and since Dermot's birth, it had been liberally strewn with thorns, but it had been familiar and she knew she would miss her sisters greatly.

Minnie didn't help her daughter's unease at all, when she spoke to her the night before the wedding. She chose to talk to her after her sisters and Dermot had made their way to bed and Seamus was doing one last round of the farm before turning in. 'There are things about marriage that women don't talk about,' she began.

There had been no lead up to the conversation. Rosie had stared at her mother slightly appalled and a little embarrassed. It was too late for this type of discussion.

Evidently, Minnie didn't realise this, for she went on. 'You must let your man do as he pleases once you are married. It's what you'll promise to do before the priest and congregation tomorrow. You don't have to enjoy what he does, most women don't, but you must endure it. He may hurt you at first, this fine husband of yours, but even if he does, you must let him have his way, for this is what marriage is all about.'

It seemed an eternity that Rosie sat before the dying fire that night after her mother's words, looking into the turf settled into the grate with a hiss and lick of orange flame, while the wind gusted around the cottage, trepidation and fear of what was before her, driving away tiredness. And then, her father came in, the door torn from his grasp by the wind, so it slammed against the wall with a crash. He brought in with him the cold of the autumn night and Rosie, unable to sit any longer and make inane conversation, after the declaration her mother had made, took herself off to bed.

TWO

The next day, Rosie awakened to a silent house. The morning was a dark one but the clock said it was half past seven and she knew her father would have been up a few hours or more, milking the cows. Guiltily, she pulled herself away from the warmth of her sisters curled up together, and began to dress.

Her mother turned from the fire before which she was sitting as Rosie came in. 'That was good timing,' she said. 'I was just about to call you.' The plate she laid before Rosie almost took her breath away – there were rashers, an egg, fried tomatoes, potato cakes, white pudding and fried bread.

Rosie couldn't remember the last time her mother had cooked her breakfast, never mind a feast like this. 'Mammy, this is marvellous.'

'All brides should have a good breakfast on their wedding day,' Minnie said. 'Sets you up for the day and Lord knows when you'll ever have one so good again.'

'It's like giving a condemned man one last request, the way you put it,' Rosie complained, but with a smile. However, when her eyes met those of her mother's and she saw her tight-lipped, an icy thread of apprehension trailed down her spine.

It vanished at the church when she saw Danny waiting for her at the altar beside Shay Ferguson, his best man. She walked slowly down the familiar church on her father's arm, her four bridesmaids coming behind, when really she wanted to fly into the arms of her beloved.

The church was full of neighbours and friends of the young couple and Rosie heard feet shuffling in the pews and a few coughs or sniffs as women sat dabbing at their eyes with handkerchiefs. She wanted to say, 'Don't cry, I'm happy, I've never been so happy.'

But, of course, she said nothing. She reached the altar at last and gave her bouquet to Chrissie, slipping her arm from her father's to stand beside Danny. He turned to look at her, and she felt her heart nearly stop and gave a short gasp at how handsome he looked. As for Danny, he thought he'd never seen a girl so beautiful. He knew in Rosie he'd met his soul mate who he would love till the end of his days, and at that moment vowed never to do anything that would hurt her.

Rosie came out of the church later, blinking in the rays of the October sun, on the arm of her husband and as she smiled at the crowds milling around them cheering the young couple Rosie felt warmed by their good wishes.

The wedding breakfast was laid out in the farmhouse. Trestle tables with benches had been borrowed from the church hall to seat people. Rosie sat at the end table with Danny, their parents either side of them, and looked at the spread put on and knew Connie and her daughters must have worked for days and days to provide for so many. Though her parents had paid for the food, Rosie knew her mother had not done a hand's turn to prepare it.

The two-tier wedding cake had been a present from the baker in the village. 'You keep the top tier for the christening,' he'd said, with a nudge to Rosie's ribs and then laughed uproariously as her face flamed with embarrassment.

It was fortunate that the day was dry and warm enough for the dancing to take place outside, and this gave Connie and her daughters time and space to clear away the dirty things. Rosie's offer to help was waved away. 'Not on your wedding day, bonny girl,' Connie said. 'Away and dance with your man.'

And Rosie did dance with him. She was seldom off her feet as the accordion, fiddle and banjo played the familiar reels and jigs and polkas while the bodhran beat out the steady rhythm.

It was a wondrous, tremendous day, and when the revellers eventually made their way home – and not all of them terribly steady, either – Danny and Rosie stayed outside while the velvety darkness closed about them. Danny had his arm around Rosie and she leaned against him in absolute contentment.

'Are you happy, Mrs Walsh?' Danny asked her.

'Deliriously so, Mr Walsh,' Rosie replied with a smile.

'Shall we go in?'

Rosie, remembering her mother's words, couldn't stop the slight shiver that ran through her. Danny guessed immediately what she was nervous of. 'Don't be scared,' he told her. 'Not of me. I'll not hurt you. Trust me.'

And she did trust him, of course she did, this

was Danny, her Danny, who she'd lay down her life for. 'I do trust you, Danny,' she said. 'It was the night air causing me to feel chilly, that's all. Let's go in.'

Danny knew it was no night air but he kissed Rosie on the cheek, took her arm and led her indoors, where he found everyone had prudently taken themselves to bed.

Rosie knew that they would be living with Danny's family for a while, maybe for years, until a house of their own could be built near to the farmhouse. Connie guessed Rosie might find this strange and could well understand it. She had put her arm around Rosie's shoulder one evening a few days before the wedding and said, 'I don't want you to feel that this is someone else's house you are living in when you come here. From now on, this will be your home.'

'Thank you, you're all so kind.'

'We should be thanking you,' Connie had said, 'for making our son such a happy man. In you I really feel I have gained a daughter. We must decide what you are to call me, for I know it has been awkward at times.'

Rosie had blushed. She had not known what to call Connie. Mrs Walsh sounded too formal and Connie too familiar, but she hadn't been aware that the woman had known of her dilemma. Connie had gone on, 'It was the same with me and my mother-in-law at the start, yet in a way it was easier for me: my own mother was dead and so I just called her Mammy.'

Rosie had thought of the love she'd experienced in this house in just the few months she'd been coming there, more by far than she'd ever had in her own home. She couldn't ever remember her mother putting her arm around her the way Connie did with ease. Even Matt would catch hold of her hand or pat her on the shoulder as he passed and she realised these good, kind people were better parents to her than her own would ever be. She had turned to Connie and had said, 'I would love to call you Mammy.'

'You would?' Connie had asked. 'You don't think your own mammy will mind it?'

'I don't think she will give a tinker's cuss for anything I do,' Rosie had replied bitterly. 'It used to upset me, but now I have Danny, a new home and a new life and to an extent a new family. To call you Mammy will just be part of it.'

Danny was pleased his mother and Rosie got on so well together for he knew if there was any sort of friction between them, living in such close proximity would be untenable and there was no-where else he and Rosie could live for the present, although he was doing his best to give them a private bedroom at least. As in most farmhouses, the main bedrooms led straight off the kitchen-cum-living room. The first one was the room that Elizabeth and Sarah shared and you went through that to reach the one Danny had previously shared with Phelan, just as it had been in her own home while Connie and Matt had the one room in the loft, up the stairs to the back of the kitchen.

Underneath the stairs was another room that had been used for storage and that was the room Danny had chosen. He and his father had worked hard before the wedding, moving all the

46

junk to the barn and making sure the place was watertight and damp free.

Now Rosie stood at the threshold of the door and looked around in delight as Danny lit the lamp.

Connie and Matt had bought them a new iron-framed bedstead and mattress, and Rosie looked at it made up with the sheets and blankets she'd brought with her, the embroidered pillowcases visible where the sheets were turned down, and one of her nightdresses draped over the coverlet.

She saw Connie had been busy. There were pictures on the walls and bright rag rugs on the stone-flagged floor, and the Sacred Heart of Jesus above their bed. Rosie and Danny had bought a new bedroom suite from a catalogue, but Rosie hadn't seen it until now because it had been delivered to the Walshes' farmhouse only a few days before the wedding. Now, Rosie saw someone had hung her clothes in the dark wood wardrobe and her personal things were laid out on the matching dressing table.

'Oh Danny, it's beautiful!' she cried.

'So are you and I can't wait much longer,' Danny said huskily, wrapping his arms around his young wife. 'Oh God, Rosie, how I've longed for this moment. I love you and want you so much.'

The love in his voice melted Rosie's apprehension and she allowed Danny to strip the wedding dress from her and let it fall in silken folds at her feet, her petticoats, corset and bloomers following as he laid her on the bed and removed her boots and stockings. She lay beneath the sheets, naked as she hadn't been since she'd been a wee child,

47

for she'd always been taught to dress and undress beneath her nightdress.

Suddenly, Danny, in his haste to divest himself of his clothes, kicked the chamber pot beneath the bed and the ringing sound reverberated throughout the house. Rosie put her hand across her mouth to still the giggles.

'Shut up,' Danny hissed, laughing himself. 'This is no laughing matter, madam. Please conduct yourself with proper decorum.'

'Aye, Mr Walsh, I will,' Rosie said, gazing at her husband as she spoke and realising she was seeing a naked man for the very first time in her life. Danny snuffed out the light and slid in beside her.

After her mother's words she'd imagined herself lying rigid in the bed in her pristine nightdress while Danny did unmentionable things to her that she had to submit to now that she was his wife. She imagined it hurting her so much she'd cry out and everyone would hear.

But it wasn't a bit like that. Danny held her close and caressed her gently, while his tongue, darting in and out of her mouth, sent sharp shafts of desire flowing through her whole body as she let her hands explore his body too. When she came upon his hardened penis, she gave a gasp. Danny was nuzzling at her breasts and she cried, 'Oh, Danny, please, please hurry.'

Danny smiled. The passion in both of them could be denied no longer and he carefully entered his young wife. She did feel pain, but it was overridden by waves of exquisite joy which engulfed her over and over again, until she felt she could die with happiness. She couldn't help the cry that burst from her lips, and as Danny, spent at last, lay on top of her, she felt tears of joy seep from under her lashes and trickle down her cheeks.

She felt loved, desired, wanted, as she'd never truly felt in her life before. But none of her earlier life mattered – now she had Danny and he more than made up for her parents' indifference.

When Danny discovered Rosie was crying he was horrified. 'Don't cry. Oh God, Rosie, don't,' he implored. 'Did I hurt you? Oh God, I'm sorry.'

Rosie's smile was watery but her voice firm as she said, 'Are you not the finest eejit, Danny? Don't you know women cry from happiness as well as sorrow? Don't ever apologise for what we did tonight, for I wanted it as much as you and it was wonderful so it was.'

Danny knew he'd found a treasure, a woman who'd love him all his life and who enjoyed their lovemaking. He wrapped his arms tightly around her. 'I love you, Mrs Walsh,' he said.

'And I you, Mr Walsh,' Rosie replied happily. She snuggled against him and the two slept entwined until the cock crowed the next morning.

Connie got on well with Rosie. She liked the girl for herself and also because she made her son happy. She'd known it from the first morning. Connie had heard the cry Rosie had given the previous night and knew what they were about and prayed that it was a cry of joy and not pain. She hoped her son had had the patience to take

Rosie gently, for she knew she would be a virgin, and later the stained sheets she stripped from the bed gave further evidence of this.

But when she saw the two of them together the next morning, she knew that whatever way Danny had approached their first nuptial coupling, it had pleased his young wife, and that was all that mattered. She saw the way their eyes met and the secret smiles between them, the way Danny found ways to be near Rosie, putting his hand around her shoulder, touching her arm, catching her suddenly around the waist and pulling her close. Rosie delighted in these exchanges, even as she coloured in embarrassment. They were happy and at one together and Connie was content.

Rosie had wondered how it would fare with so many women in the one kitchen, but she needn't have worried. Danny's eldest sister, Sarah, had been working as a seamstress in Blessington village since Elizabeth had left school and was able to help her mother. Now, with Rosie to take on that role, Elizabeth was anxious to follow her sister, who assured her there was plenty of work. 'Do you mind?' Rosie asked Elizabeth. 'I'd not like to think I was pushing you out of your own home.'

'You're not,' Elizabeth told her. 'I've been dying to go. Sarah has fun there with the other girls and after I left school I found the farm a bit stifling and lonely – you know how it is. It's different for you, you're married now and you'll probably have your own babies soon enough, but I want something for myself before I tie myself down.'

'Well, if you're sure?'

'I am,' Elizabeth said, and suddenly, impulsively, gave Rosie a kiss on the cheek. Rosie was pleased but surprised. 'What was that for?'

'Oh nothing,' Elizabeth said. 'Just to say welcome to the family. We're all glad you're here, Danny especially – he's like a dog with two tails.'

There was a lot of talk and laughter around the Walsh table in the evenings. They found humour in many things and were not averse to poking fun at one another. Rosie was included in this from the start and it only took her a short amount of time to be able to come back at them in the same teasing vein.

Connie knew that Rosie hadn't been happy at home and she also knew, like most of the village, that the main problem in the house centred around the fuss made of the wee fellow Dermot.

It didn't help that Dermot looked so angelic, with his fair curls and his large blue eyes and elfin face. He looked remarkably like the statues of the cherubs in the church in Blessington, except that he didn't have the angels' chubby frame. Dermot was slight and fine-boned, and Minnie called him delicate yet the child seldom ailed. 'She'll not let the wind blow on him because if it,' Danny said with a snort whenever Connie spoke of him. 'The child's no more delicate than I am.'

'I agree with you,' Connie said. 'Phelan was a bit like that when he was younger and now look at him.' Phelan had sprouted that year and was continuing to grow, and while Danny was six foot in his stocking feet, she thought Phelan might even exceed that eventually. 'No,' Connie concluded. 'There's not a lot wrong with that wee boy – I'd just call him wiry.'

'Call him wiry, delicate, or whatever you like,' Danny said. 'I'll tell you one thing, I'm almighty glad Rosie is out of that unnatural atmosphere.'

Connie agreed with Danny, and yet she encouraged Rosie to visit her old home once a week. After all, it was no distance at all over the fields, even if they were too muddy to cross and she had to use the roads, it was only just over two miles away, not that far at all.

Rosie was glad to go, for kind though Connie was, she missed her sisters and young Dermot too, for all he was a wee tyrant. But as the days shortened she seldom saw her brother for she always left the house before he came in from school so she could be back home before the dark set in. As the weather got colder, she often thought if it wasn't for Connie urging her to go and the genuine welcome she received from Chrissie and Geraldine, she'd often not bother to leave the Walshes cosy farmhouse to fight with the elements to reach her old home. Her mother didn't seem to care whether she was there or not; she never showed any interest in her new life, her marriage, the Walshes and how she was treated, and though Rosie had expected little else, she was still hurt.

Chrissie and Geraldine, on the other hand, were interested in everything, and Chrissie was particularly interested in sex and what it was like. Remembering her own ignorance over periods, and how it had caused her such distress and made her think she was dying, Rosie told her sisters about what would happen well before it should.

Chrissie had been grateful to Rosie when she began her periods the previous year, but in talking about it, Rosie had set a precedent for talk of intimate things.

So on Rosie's first visit home, Chrissie, on the pretext of leaving her down at the farm gate, had asked her as soon as they were away from the house, 'Have you and Danny done it yet?'

Rosie turned to face her sister and replied sharply, 'That's none of your business.'

'Oh, please, Rosie,' Chrissie pleaded. 'You're the only one I can ask.'

'Why should you want to know?'

'Well, just because I'll probably do it eventually myself, won't I?' Chrissie said. 'I mean, most women do and I'd be scared, if I didn't know what to expect.'

'It's natural to be a bit scared,' Rosie said. 'I was.'

'I just can't imagine letting any man do that to you,' Chrissie said. 'It seems such an odd thing.'

Rosie hid a secret smile as she remembered the longing and passion that had almost taken over her reason when she'd been courting Danny. Chrissie had not yet had those feelings, but she was bound to have them one day and maybe it would do no harm to tell her a wee bit in advance. 'The other girls talk about it,' Chrissie went on. 'Josie Clancy said her sister bled like a stuck pig the first time and it hurt like hell then and got no better. It's just something you have to let men do. Is that the way it was for you?'

'Far from it,' Rosie said.

'Do you bleed?'

'Aye,' Rosie said, 'the first time. It shows that you're a virgin.'

'And does it hurt?'

'Aye,' Rosie said. 'Again, just the first time, but you don't notice it.'

'I'd notice it, if someone hurt me.'

Rosie laughed. 'Look, Chrissie, I'm not going into details, but there are things a man can do to a woman that means you're as willing as he is. You have to let your husband make love to you, however you feel about it – it's what you promise on your marriage, but if he is kind and patient and loving it can be that you will want it and enjoy it as much as he does.'

Chrissie still looked doubtful and so Rosie went on. 'One day there will be someone who'll make you feel just the way I've described and you'll want to do things you know are wrong and he may promise you the moon if you'll let him do as he pleases. When that happens, Chrissie, remember what I've told you and wait for the ring on your finger.'

'Don't fret yourself,' Chrissie replied with meaning. 'No man will get within a yard's length of me I'm telling you. It seems a lot of fuss for little return and I want no part of it.'

Rosie remembered when she had felt the same about the vulgarities of sex. Any thoughts she had about boys had been romantic and very chaste – the position Chrissie was in now. But she said nothing else, and hoped when the time came, Chrissie might remember her sister's words and that they might prove helpful to her.

She kissed Chrissie at the gate and made her

54

way home, going over the conversation in her head. 'I'm a fine one to talk about my words helping Chrissie,' she told herself. 'There are not words written that would have helped me with Danny. I just thank God he was good enough to make me wait.'

The Walsh family walked together to Mass early on Christmas morning. The milking was done but there had been no breakfast cooked for no one was allowed to eat or drink before taking Communion. Rosie was glad to hang on to Danny: she felt light-headed and her empty stomach growled in protest.

It was better in the lovely church, everything white and gold and shining and she listened to the Latin words and let the familiarity soothe her. The sermon was short, the priest taking pity on his hungry parishioners, some who'd come far greater distances than the Walshes.

Afterwards, around the churchyard, Rosie glimpsed her own family and Dermot, catching sight of her before anyone else, came hurtling across and threw himself at his sister, nearly tipping her over. Rosie felt sorry for the boy – though she'd visited her home every week, she'd always had to leave before Dermot arrived home from school and so she hadn't seen him in ages. She also knew Dermot hadn't been told that Rosie had visited on these occasions because her parents were well aware of the fine rage the child could work himself into if ever he was thwarted in anything. To Dermot it must have seemed as though Rosie had abandoned the whole family.

They'd never even met at Mass, for Rosie and Connie attended the one at half past seven, with Danny too if he was through milking in time. Occasionally, she'd glimpsed her father in the congregation and have a brief word, but she knew her mother, sisters and Dermot would attend the children's Mass at nine o'clock.

So now, when Dermot pulled himself away from his sister's embrace and said accusingly, 'Why haven't you been to see us?' she knew he had a point.

However, before she was able to reply, Dermot continued, his voice high with excitement, 'Santa's been to our house, and I got an orange and pencils, a tin whistle and a bar of chocolate in my stocking.'

'Well, aren't you the lucky boy?'

'Aye, and that's not all,' Dermot continued, almost breathless with the thrill of it all. 'I've got a train set too – it's all set out on the floor in the kitchen.'

Rosie's mouth dropped open with astonishment. Her questioning eyes met those of her two sisters who'd followed Dermot to speak to Rosie and it was Chrissie who nodded and added wryly, 'Aye, he does – a big one. It's clockwork.'

'You wind it up,' Dermot boasted. 'And I've got two big engines and lots of carriages and goods wagons and two tracks that wind together and a bridge and a tunnel and a station.' He hopped around with exhilaration. 'Come and see,' he urged. 'You can play with me.'

'Not now, Dermot,' Rosie replied. 'I must go home and help cook breakfast and then Christmas dinner for us all. I'm coming to see you tomorrow.'

'Promise?'

'Aye, I promise,' Rosie assured him.

Back home at the Walshes' house, after they'd eaten, there were presents for everyone. Rosie's were small for she hadn't much money of her own, but she had bought lace hankies for Sarah and Elizabeth, a bottle of perfume for Connie, socks for Matt and Phelan and a new shirt for Danny.

She was overwhelmed by their gifts to her: a hat, scarf and glove set in dark red from Matt and Connie, and a blouse from the girls which they'd made in their free time at work. It was peach and the material had a shine to it, and the girls had embroidered flowers in pale blue and white on the collar. Rosie was able to declare truthfully that it was the prettiest thing she'd ever owned.

And then Danny gave her his presents. The first was a thick woollen coat in navy blue, the cut of it the height of fashion and the hem falling just to the top of her boots. She put it on and spun around in the kitchen in absolute delight and said she felt like a queen, and all the family had laughed at her fondly. Then Danny presented her with a little box. Inside it, set in tissue paper, was a brooch with an amber stone, surrounded by a filigree of blue and white that he'd chosen especially to go with the blouse his sisters had told him about.

The gifts, selected with such care, brought tears to Rosie's eyes and she suddenly thought of her parents' house, where a wee boy had a train set and numerous other presents and his sisters would barely be wished a 'Happy Christmas'. But she wouldn't let the unhappiness she was feeling for her sisters spoil her own magical day.

After a wonderful dinner, neither Rosie nor Danny was let near the sink. Sarah would wash, Elizabeth would dry, and a reluctant Phelan would put away. 'Don't even try complaining about it,' Elizabeth told her scowling young brother. 'It's Christmas Day and it's a mortal sin to argue on Christmas Day.'

'It is not.'

'It is so,' Elizabeth told him emphatically. 'And on Christmas Day, all big sisters have the right to beat the head off younger brothers who won't do as they're told.'

They all laughed so heartily that even Phelan had to smile, and Danny ruffled his brother's hair as he passed. 'That's it,' he said. 'Give in gracefully.'

'And what will you do?' Connie asked Danny. 'Will you come up to the fire?'

'No, I don't think so,' said Danny, with a glance over at Rosie. 'I have a mind to go for a walk with my pretty young wife.'

'The wind would cut you in two out there,' Matt told him.

'Och aye, for old bones maybe,' Danny said.

'It's not you I'm thinking of, it's Rosie,' Matt said.

'With her warm coat on and her new hat and gloves covering her head and hands, her scarf tucked around her neck and my arms about her, what chance has the wind to even blow on her,'

Danny said to his father. 'What d'you say, Rosie?'

She would say she'd follow this man to the wilds of Siberia and so she hurried from the room to dress for her walk.

They took the path down towards Blessington Lake, where they'd spent so many hours of their courtship. The cold was intense and the wind fierce, the sky leaden grey and yet Rosie was content to be by Danny's side.

Blissfully happy at spending their first Christmas together as husband and wife, she nearly told him about the baby she might be carrying, but she couldn't be sure until the New Year so decided to told her tongue. She knew what Danny would do if she was to give him a hint of it – he would run home and broadcast it to his family, friends and anyone else who'd listen.

She was even more glad she'd kept her news quiet when they arrived home to find that friends and neighbours had popped in with things to eat and drink and with a fiddle and an accordion player too. The rugs were lifted and the furniture shifted to make more room for dancing.

'Your mother said nothing of a party,' Rosie said to Danny, as she took off her things in the bedroom.

'Everyone knows it's open house here on Christmas evening,' Danny replied. 'Put on your new blouse, then let's go out there and see the envious eyes of every man in the place.'

'Oh Danny,' Rosie admonished him, but she put the blouse on, to please Danny's sisters as much as Danny himself.

Most of the people were known to her and many

had been to the wedding and were delighted to see Danny and Rosie already so settled and happy together. Rosie had her hand shaken by many a man there and was hugged by the women. She felt surrounded by the love and best wishes exuded by the crowd and nearly danced her feet off.

During the evening, other people called in and the eating, drinking and jollification went on so late Danny said it was hardly worth seeking his bed at all that night for he'd be up in a few hours for the milking and that maybe it was a good thing Christmas Day came just once a year.

For all that, they did eventually snuggle up together as the house grew quieter. Rosie leaned against Danny and felt his big muscular arms enfold her, and wondered if it were possible to die from happiness.

THREE

On Boxing Day, Rosie and Danny were greeted grudgingly by Minnie and Seamus and received only a scant thank you for the slippers Rosie had bought her father and the shawl she'd chosen for her mother.

Chrissie and Geraldine, though, were delighted by the jumpers Rosie gave them. She'd spent many hours in the evenings knitting each jumper, one in blue and the other in lemon. She'd used the softest, fluffiest wool she could find and both girls were almost speechless with pleasure.

But it wasn't the presents that mattered. Many people would have had no presents that Christmas, for there'd be no money for them, but for all that there'd be love and laughter and enough to eat for the couple of days at least. It was hard to see her wee brother surrounded by such a wide array of toys while her sisters had obviously received nothing.

Rosie had bought Dermot a monkey on a ladder that could be made to go up and down and do various other antics, as Dermot soon realised, by pressing the button on each side of the ladder's base and despite all his other toys, he was enchanted with the one Rosie had chosen.

It had begun snowing as Rosie and Danny had set out for the McMullens', but it had been fine, just a dusting on the ground and they had still cut across the fields. 'The ground is rock hard,' Danny had said, 'and it will take some time for the snow to be thick enough to take hold.'

He was right, it had been easy to walk the fields, even pleasant, Rosie thought, cuddled against Danny and dressed in her warm clothes with the snowflakes drifting down on them.

However, by the time the meal was eaten, the snow lay over everything like a white blanket, gilding the trees' stark winter branches and icing the tops of hedges. When the dishes had been washed, dried and put away, Danny suggested a snowball fight.

There were cries of agreement from Dermot, but Chrissie and Geraldine looked first towards their parents for permission. 'You're both too old for such nonsense,' Minnie said irritably, but Danny cried,

'Not today. No-one's too old for anything at Christmas.'

Minnie was unable to find a suitable response and so the girls went to get ready.

Like the children they still were, Chrissie and Geraldine leaped outside and into the snow without further ado, dressed in their shabby top coats and bonnets. Neither had gloves, Rosie noted, and she was determined to remedy that as soon as she could. She was a grand one with the knitting needles now.

The snow was thick underfoot and a watery sun, peeping from the clouds, spread the last of its scarlet rays upon them as they pounded each other with the soft snow.

At last, they stopped for a break, gasping and

laughing. Danny suggested making a snowman, the biggest and best snowman in the whole country, and Dermot could barely contain his excitement. The snowman eventually stood tall and proud, with pieces of turf for his eyes, a carroty nose and an old cap of Seamus's on his head. Dermot leaped like a young colt in front of him before running into the house and dragging his parents to the door of the cottage to see their creation.

Later, walking home in the pale moonlight which shone on the snowy fields and road and lit their way home, Danny said, 'I feel sorry for your wee brother, Rosie, because for all the toys he has, he's never really played with anyone before today.'

Rosie agreed with Danny. On one hand her young brother had everything and yet in another way she sensed a loneliness in him, for no young ones lived nearby and he seemed to spend a lot of time on his own. But there was nothing to be gained by talking about it for she couldn't change the situation and so she snuggled against Danny and his arm tightened around her as they ploughed through the snow together.

Connie already knew Rosie was pregnant before she told her. She often looked quite pale and strained in the morning, though she'd recover her spirits as the day went on. But she decided to say nothing and let Rosie tell her in her own time.

When Rosie did eventually say, Connie showed little surprise and so Rosie asked her, 'Did you know?'

'I didn't for sure,' Connie said. 'But I guessed.'

'How?'

'Well, for one thing, you've not used any of the cotton pads from the press.'

'Of course.'

'It's not only that, though,' Connie said. 'It's a certain something about you – a look. Oh, I don't know how to explain it, but you're different in some way.'

'I suppose you've heard me being sick too.'

'Aye,' Connie said. 'But though it came as a shock to me, I'm still delighted. What did Danny say?'

'He doesn't know yet.'

'Och, girl, he should have been told first,' Connie chided gently. 'When d'you intend to tell him?'

'Today,' Rosie said. 'I wanted to be absolutely sure first. None of my family know either – the weather has been too bad for me to make it to their house since Christmas.'

'Well, lose no time in telling Danny.'

Rosie nodded. 'I will, as soon as he comes in.'

Danny, Phelan and Matt had gone up to the hills with the two farm dogs, Meg and Cap, to collect and bring the sheep down to the lower pastures where it was easier to feed them the bales of hay which they relied on for the winter. Nearer to the house it was also easier to keep an eye on the pregnant ewes too, for some of them were due to give birth within the month. They'd been gone a couple of hours already, for it was a tidy tramp, and Danny told her the odd sheep often got into difficulties which they needed to sort out.

Rosie didn't envy them: the cold was intense. It was almost too cold to snow, though there had been a sprinkling in the night and this had since frozen solid and lay sparkling on the yard. Rosie rubbed her hands against the misty kitchen window and looked out. The world seemed hushed and still, the empty fields dressed with a covering of snow, and icicles hung like silver spears from the window's edge.

She turned with a shiver and Connie said, 'Aye, it's bone-chilling cold, all right. They'll all be glad of the stew I'll have ready for them when they come in. Put new heart into them.'

'Aye,' Rosie said, rousing herself. 'I'll get some water in to wash the potatoes. They might be back soon.'

'Are you all right, girl?' Connie asked. 'I can get it.'

'Don't fuss now!' Rosie admonished. 'I'll not have you treat me like an invalid because I'm expecting.'

'No danger of that,' Connie said with a laugh. 'You fetch in the water then, and I'll make us a drink.'

Rosie picked up the galvanised bucket from beside the door and went out into the wintry afternoon. The skies were heavy, grey and snow-laden, and the bitter chill caught in her throat and made her teeth ache. She wished she'd thought to lift her coat from the peg. As soon as Rosie stepped out onto the slippery cobblestones her feet began to slither. Gingerly, she made her way forward, but didn't notice the sheet of ice that had

65

formed around the pump where some of the water had dribbled out and frozen solid. As she stepped onto it she felt one leg slide from beneath her.

In a panic, she fought to try and regain her balance, but as she did the other foot skimmed across the icy cobbles and she lost her footing completely. She fell awkwardly and clumsily, the bucket clattering beside her as her head slammed heavily against the ground.

Connie was beside her in seconds. 'Oh dear God!' she cried. 'Are you all right?'

It was obvious Rosie was far from so. The very breath had been knocked from her body and she lay on the frozen yard and felt as if every bone had been shaken loose.

Dear God, Connie thought, if Rosie was to lose this child before Danny even knew he was about to become a father! That would be dreadful altogether. But then, she chided herself, there was no need to look on the black side of things: the girl had had a fright, that was bad enough, and anyone would be in pain after falling in the yard. A hot drink and bed, that was best.

She helped Rosie indoors, supporting much of her weight. The kettle had already begun to sing over the glowing turf and she sat her before the hearth.

'You need tea with plenty of sugar to steady you after a shock like that,' Connie said, pressing Rosie down gently in the armchair. 'And then it's bed for you.'

She filled the teapot and while it brewed she lifted two air bricks from the back of the fire with tongs and wrapped them in flannels. 'I'll put these in the bed to warm it for you,' she told Rosie as she hurried from the room.

Rosie didn't answer. She was feeling light-headed and muzzy, but her overriding fear was for the child she carried. She put her arm protectively on her stomach and groaned.

Connie heard her as she came back in and her heart contracted in pity, but one of them at least had to stay positive. 'Come on,' she said, handing Rosie a cup of tea, which she'd also laced with a drop of whisky. 'Drink this while it's hot.'

Rosie obediently took the drink, glad of its warmth for she felt chilled to the marrow, and Connie, aware of her trembling, gave the fire a poke to release some of the warmth. She wished Danny was there to fetch the doctor, for the white-faced girl in front of her worried her half to death.

Rosie was too weary and sore to undress herself, so Connie gently removed the clothes from her as if she were a child and then slipped a white cambric nightgown over her head before helping her between the warmed sheets and tucking the blankets snugly around her.

Rosie gave a sigh of thankfulness to be lying in the semi-dark in a soft warm bed and Connie sat beside the bed, waiting until Rosie's closed eyes and even breathing told her she was asleep before she left her.

The men came in, stamping their boots on the mat and bringing the cold of the fields in with them. 'By, that smells good,' Matt said. 'You need

67

something to stick to the ribs today.'

Connie scarcely heard her husband. Her eyes were only for her son. When she'd left Rosie's side she'd rehearsed over and over how to tell Danny that his beloved wife had hurt herself and maybe the unborn child he knew nothing of yet would be lost because of it. 'Where's Rosie?' Danny demanded, seeing the anxious look on his mother's face.

'She ... she's had a bit of an accident,' Connie said. 'She slipped in the yard. I've put her to bed. I thought it was best. She was asleep when I left her.'

Danny was across the room in three strides, but his mother's hand was on his elbow before he opened the bedroom door. 'Danny, wait!' she said. 'It's best you know it all. Rosie is expecting a baby.'

The grim-set expression on Danny's face changed to one of incredulity. 'A baby?' he repeated.

'Aye,' Connie said, and then, because she knew her son would rightly think he should have been told first, she went on. 'She didn't tell me until after she'd had the fall. She intended telling you today.' That made Danny feel better and, when all was said and done, however he was told, his wife was expecting their first child. 'Go easy now,' Connie cautioned him. 'Let her sleep while she's able.'

Danny gave a mute nod and opened the door as quietly as he could and stood transfixed in the doorway. Rosie's hair, released from its fastenings, was spread out on the pillow, her pinched face as white as the sheets she had tucked around her and her breathing so shallow that her chest barely moved. Danny turned an anguished face to his mother. 'Oh, Ma. She looks...'

'She looks as if she's sleeping, which she is,' Connie said firmly, giving her son's arm a shake. 'She needs a doctor, Danny. You'll have go to the village and fetch out Doctor Casey.'

'Aye, aye,' Danny said, glad to be doing something practical at least.

Matt was beside his wife and son and looked in on the girl. 'Do you want me along with you, son?'

'No, I'll be fine,' Danny said. 'I'll ride in on Copper. He can go like the wind when he has a mind and is not pulling a cart behind him.'

As the door closed behind Danny, Connie gave a sigh. 'There goes a worried man.'

'Aye, and little wonder,' Matt said. 'For the sun rises and sets for Danny with that young lassie. Dear God, I hope no harm has come to her, or that child she's carrying.'

Connie crossed to the pot simmering above the burning turf and said, 'Will I get you a bowl of stew?'

Matt shook his head. 'It would choke me,' he told Connie. 'Though my old bones would welcome a drop of tea.'

Even Phelan shook his head. 'None for me either, Mammy,' he said, for he was worried about Rosie and the stillness of her that he'd glimpsed as Danny stood in the doorway. He liked her a great deal, she always made time to talk to him and he thought she had more patience than his own two sisters.

Dr Casey, in his pony and trap, followed Danny on horseback to the farm, and barely had they reached the yard before Danny flung himself from the horse leaving his waiting brother to help the doctor from his carriage. He gave no greeting to his mother who was bent over the fire, but went straight to the bedroom. Rosie lay as still as she'd done when he'd left her and he felt flutters of alarm beat against his heart as he approached the bed and kneeled beside it.

His relief when Rosie opened her eyes slowly and painfully, as if they weighed a ton, was immense. 'Hallo, Rosie.'

Rosie didn't reply but Danny didn't care. She was alive and that was all that mattered to him. He took her hand gently and kissed it. 'You'll be grand now, Rosie,' he said, wondering why people always said such inane things in times of crisis. 'The doctor is here to see you and he'll get you better in no time.'

The doctor had followed him into the room and Danny turned to him now. 'Will she be all right?'

'How can I possibly answer that till I've examined the patient?' the doctor said impatiently. 'Out of my way. In fact, out of the room altogether. Let me get on with my job and you get on with yours.'

Usually, Danny would never have let a man speak to him like that, but he knew they had need of the doctor's skills and so he said nothing. 'I'll be back,' he promised Rosie. 'I'll be just outside.'

Danny didn't need to tell Rosie where he'd be, for she heard him giving out to his mother as the

70

doctor's gentle hands probed first the gash on her head and then her stomach.

'What were you thinking of, letting her go out for water in this?' Danny demanded. 'The whole place is covered with ice, that yard is like a death-trap. Well, it's got to stop, especially now Rosie is expecting. I'll bring in the water in the morning. If necessary I'll buy a couple more buckets while I'm about it, but I'll not have Rosie go out and carry in heavy buckets of water.

'And she's not to lift heavy clothes from the boiling pan to the rinse pail, either – they're too heavy,' he went on. 'Nor is she to pound the clothes in the poss tub, or do the churning.'

Neither Connie nor Matt said a word. Connie watched her son walk agitatedly from one side of the room to the other, knowing Danny wasn't really blaming her, he was just worried and felt helpless.

So she didn't come back at him and ask Danny if he had any idea of how many buckets of water were needed for Monday's washday and how was she to do all this herself and the work in the dairy too.

Instead, she poured Danny a cup of tea and put it into his hands. He gulped at the scalding liquid almost immediately, his eyes never leaving the bedroom door. Under her breath, Connie began to pray to the Blessed Virgin Mary who knew what worry was all about.

When the doctor left the room he found four people in the kitchen staring at him. 'How is she?' Danny demanded.

'Badly shaken up,' the doctor replied. 'She has

a nasty gash on her head which I've bandaged, and her back will probably be badly bruised by tomorrow, but there are no broken bones.'

'What of the baby?'

The doctor shrugged. 'We must just wait and see. I'd advise at least a week of bed rest. If she starts to lose the child, send for me and I'll come.'

He wasn't reassuring, but Danny knew it was all they were going to get. 'Can I see her?'

'You can, but try not to disturb her,' the doctor warned. 'I've given her a draught and she'll sleep soon. Sleep's the best healer.'

Danny went into the bedroom and pulled a chair up to the bed. He sat beside his wife, whose eyes were already closing, holding her hand and talking softly to her. He told her how he loved her and how worried he'd been. He didn't mention the child. He'd barely come to terms with the fact that he was to become a father before he thought that this might be taken from him. Would he be distraught if that happened? he asked himself. He had to admit now that he wouldn't be. He'd be upset, of course, but Rosie was the one that mattered to him. They could have other children.

He bent and kissed her cheek, his whole being consumed with love for her, and then he returned to the kitchen to tell his mother he'd spend the night and maybe many nights on a shakedown on the bedroom floor. He'd not share a bed with Rosie in case he should inadvertently hurt her, but neither would he leave her alone and go back to sharing the mattress with Phelan.

'If that's what you want to do, then we'll sort it

out later,' Connie said. 'Now will you all sit up to the table and have a bowl of stew. You've not had a bite past your lips for some hours.'

When the girls came in from work and there had still been no sound from the bedroom, Phelan was all for going across the ice-rimed, rutted fields with the aid of a lantern to tell Rosie's parents about her fall. Connie told Phelan he wasn't to go. For one thing he'd likely break his neck, she said, and for another thing, he'd worry Rosie's parents and sisters unnecessarily, going over in the dark night. It wasn't as if the girl's life hung in the balance. 'I'll trot over myself, tomorrow,' Connie promised her son, and with that he had to be content.

Rosie awoke in the middle of the night and once her eyes had adjusted to the darkness, she saw the mound of her husband on the floor beside her. She was glad he was there, but would have preferred him in bed with her, his arms wrapped about her tight while he assured her everything would be all right.

She'd wanted to believe this, oh she did, but her back ached and her head throbbed and there were drawing pains in her stomach that caused her to pull her legs up. The doctor had told her that she must keep to her bed if she wanted to save her child, and then he had given her something for the pain that made it float away as she fell into a deep sleep.

Well, she wanted the baby all right. No question of it, and she vowed if that meant she had to stay in the bed, then she would. Anyway, she

73

thought with a wry smile, Connie, who'd been so pleased about the baby, would see she stayed there. She blessed the fact she was living with such caring people, and secure in that knowledge she let her eyelids close again.

However, despite Rosie wanting to do nothing to damage her baby, she found lying in bed irksome, particularly after a few days when the aches and pains had begun to ease. Connie was kindness itself, but had little time to spend with Rosie, working single-handedly, and the men were always busy.

She was delighted one day, therefore, to see her sisters at the bedroom door, for Connie had informed them the day after the fall as she'd promised Phelan.

It was a Saturday and Danny had gone into the village with produce to sell, and taken his mother and Sarah and Elizabeth to do a bit of shopping. Rosie was finding the day especially long. 'Tell me all the news?' she begged.

'What do we ever get to hear?' Chrissie objected. 'We never see a soul from one week to the next. No one visits and we never go to town.'

'Why don't you?' Rosie asked, knowing she loved nothing more than a morning shopping and gossiping in Blessington village. 'You're well old enough now. Would Mammy object?'

'I expect so,' Chrissie said. 'Doesn't she object to most things we say or do? But what is the point of us going into Blessington when we have not a penny piece to spend?'

When Rosie was at home she'd had no money

of her own either. But once she'd married Danny, the money got from the egg sales was split between her and Connie, with sometimes a percentage of the butter they made up in the dairy. Rosie liked the feel of her own money in her pocket. It meant she could buy the odd trifle for herself without asking Danny all the time.

She said to Chrissie. 'Have you thought of taking a job?'

Chrissie shook her head. 'Mammy would never stand it. Anyway, what could I do?'

'As well as the rest, I suppose,' Rosie retorted and then went on, 'Elizabeth and Sarah are working as seamstresses.'

'Well that's out,' Chrissie said. 'D'you remember my efforts at sewing?'

'I wouldn't mind a job either,' Geraldine said. 'But just because Sarah and Elizabeth Walsh have work, it doesn't mean there'd be anything for us.'

'Aye, but that's just it,' Rosie said. 'Danny's sisters have been working there a while now and they were mainly doing the fine work, the embroidery, or sewing beads or some such on to clothes and doing buttonholes, the fiddly things, but at the moment they're run off their feet.'

'Why's that?'

'Because of the war,' Rosie replied. 'The few machines they have in the workroom have been added to and they're making uniforms by the score. They need people both to operate the machines and to sew on the buttons and any other sort of decoration.'

'Well, I'm glad to see some are gaining from this war,' Geraldine said. 'There are plenty from

75

this village in the thick of it.'

'Aye,' Rosie agreed, 'couldn't wait to join up, many of them, like it was all some big adventure.'

'Well, it was supposed to be over by Christmas,' Chrissie reminded her.

'Danny never believed that,' Rosie said. 'But somehow, living here, it's hard to believe that awful things are happening not all that far away. I mean it will really only hit home if we hear of people we know dying, or being dreadfully injured. At the moment it barely touches us.'

And it didn't of course, but those men who had answered the call and were still answering it would all need uniforms and someone would have to make them, Chrissie thought. It wouldn't hurt surely to make a few enquiries.

When the Walshes came home in a flurry of noise and bustle a little later, everyone was in a grand humour for all the eggs and butter had been sold and Chrissie took the opportunity to speak with Danny's sisters about their jobs. They weren't so keen on doing the uniforms, they told her: the material was coarser than they were used to and there was less chance of finding a remnant to make up something for themselves, but the money was good and the work would continue at least as long as the war went on.

Rosie's sisters returned home after sharing a meal at the Walshes', with Chrissie determined to speak to her parents about getting a job of her own. She wanted the company of other girls and money in her pocket. With keep tipped up to her mother each week to sweeten her temper, just maybe it would work.

Minnie needed that sweetener, for at first she forbade Chrissie to even think of such a thing. She fanned her temper to full-blown fury and slapped Chrissie when she continued to plead her case. 'Be quiet, girl!'

'Do you want to make me a laughing stock?' Seamus asked. 'Have people saying I can't afford to keep you and that I had to send you out to work?'

'Matt Walsh doesn't think that way,' Chrissie pointed out, holding a handkerchief to her bleeding nose. 'He has two daughters at the factory.'

'Don't you dare answer your father back,' Minnie said, bouncing up before her. 'By God, I'll take the strap to you.'

Chrissie quailed inside, but outwardly showed no fear. 'There's no need, Mammy,' she said soothingly. 'I'll pay keep into the house.'

Minnie thought about it. Money would be useful, she decided. And there was still Geraldine at home – she'd have to do. 'All right,' she said grudgingly. 'We'll try it for six months. And,' she said, pointing her long bony finger at Geraldine, 'don't you get any ideas, miss, for the whole of the work will fall on you now.'

Geraldine didn't risk saying anything, and even her sigh she suppressed, but she shot her sister a baleful look and knew for her the future was now set.

FOUR

Rosie recovered from her fall with no after-effects at all, and after that she sailed through her pregnancy. There was no need for Danny to caution his mother about not letting Rosie do anything too strenuous, or carry anything heavy, for Connie was just as anxious as he was for a healthy grandchild. Sometimes she would let Rosie do so little she felt like screaming in frustration. She never lost patience with Connie, though, for she knew the fall she'd endured at the beginning had unnerved her.

As soon as Rosie had risen from her bed and the weather had allowed it, she'd resumed her weekly trip home. Her parents seemed unconcerned with her pregnancy, but Dermot, once he knew, was enraptured with the news and watched Rosie's growing stomach with great interest. She never saw Chrissie on these trips for, although as the nights lengthened she was able to stay until the schools closed so she could see Dermot, Chrissie had secured a job in the clothing factory with Sarah and Elizabeth. She began to come to the farmhouse on Saturdays to see Rosie and sometimes the two girls would go into the village together. There was usually someone from the farm going in, but if not the girls would begin to walk, though they were often picked up by a neighbour on the road.

'I don't tell Mammy what I earn,' Chrissie told her as they walked along one day. 'She'd have nearly every penny off me but you'd not believe the wages, Rosie, two pounds a week, sometimes two pounds and ten shillings. Of course, the hours are long to earn that type of money, but none of us mind that. I tell Mammy I get a pound a week and she lets me keep two shillings of it. I share what I have left with Geraldine and she saves it in a handkerchief in her drawer. D'you think me awful?'

Rosie considered this. 'Honour thy father and mother,' the Bible and the Catholic Church taught all children, and lying to one's parents was showing them no honour at all. Yet, Rosie had known for some time that the future for her and her sisters was totally in their own hands. Neither of her parents would lift a finger to help any of them. Dermot would inherit all and the girls would have to look out for themselves. So she said truthfully to Chrissie, 'I don't think you awful and I don't blame you either. But take care, for if Mammy sees you buying too much for yourself she'll tumble you're getting higher wages than you say. Geraldine will have to be even more careful.'

'Oh, she knows I give Geraldine something out of what she allows me to keep,' Chrissie assured her. 'I've asked if she can go with me to town a time or two to see if she wants to spend it, but Mammy won't let her, she says she has duties at home.'

'Well how do you do it?'

'I told Mammy if I'm working all week and

paying my way, I need free time,' Chrissie said, and didn't add that the first time she voiced this the resultant slap had knocked her from her feet, and the second time she had been thrashed with the strap. But she refused to give up and kept asking until her mother eventually gave in.

'You're a stronger character than Geraldine, though,' Rosie said. 'I always realised that.'

'Aye,' Chrissie agreed, and added almost fiercely, 'But I'll tell you one thing, Rosie, going to work in the factory was the best thing I ever did and I'd not give it up for a pension. Those sisters of Danny's are nice girls. I knew them from school of course, but they were much older and weren't friends then. But Elizabeth and Sarah have been really helpful. They've shown me all the fancy work they're back to doing now there are more girls working on the uniforms. They wouldn't let most of our lot near the work they do, but they're not snooty or anything. They give us tips on how to make the best of the clothes we have, like how to do up a shabby hat really cheaply, or how to spruce up a dress by adding a collar and cuffs, or maybe getting a belt and accessories to wear to make it look a bit different. I tell you, Rosie,' she said, giving her sister a friendly push, 'I will cut quite a dash at the socials when I'm allowed to go. Roll on sixteen.'

Rosie laughed with her sister, knowing she would be sixteen in August and glad to see her so happy, and then she said, 'Sarah's begun walking out with a young man, hasn't she?'

'Aye, by the name of Sam Flaherty,' Chrissie said. 'The silly fool nearly got himself arrested the other day.'

'Oh!'

'Aye, the recruiting officer was in the town, you know, and the band were playing and all, and we ran to the door to watch. He'd been to some places already and a heap of young men were already marching behind the soldiers. Sam was in the village and began shouting. He said they were being led like lambs to the slaughter and where was their sense; that Ireland needed their young men and why should they throw their lives away for a nation that had invaded them and always kept them down.'

'I suppose he has a point,' Rosie said. 'Danny feels the same.'

'Aye, many do,' Chrissie said. 'But it's a point it's not sensible to share. The Guards came out and it was only the threat of being locked up that stilled Sam's tongue in the end.

'Sarah gave out to Sam later,' Chrissie went on with a smile. 'He was waiting for her when we left the factory and she told him that he'd be no good to Ireland, or any other damn country, if he ended up behind bars. She gave it him straight. Said there was to be no more of it and from now on he'll keep a civil tongue in his head or he'll have her to deal with.'

'Oh, I think I'd take my chance with the Guards rather than Sarah on her high horse,' Rosie said with a smile, knowing the power of her sister-in-law's temper.

Chrissie laughed. 'From the look on Sam's face, he felt the same,' she said. 'Anyway, he never said a word back to her and they went off together.'

'Aye,' Rosie said. 'Well, Sarah will keep him in line if anyone can. But let's hurry now, I've a lot to buy today, mainly things for the baby's arrival.'

'Not that much, I hope. We'll never carry big parcels.'

'Could you see Danny allowing that?' Rosie said. 'He left early this morning to give Shay and his dad a hand with thatching their roof. Rain came through it during the winter and Danny said neither Shay nor his father were ever any good at the thatching. He told me to wait in Kilpatrick's Hotel when I'm done and he'll be along to fetch me as soon as he's able.'

'Come on, then,' Chrissie said, catching Rosie's hand and attempting to pull her along.

'Chrissie!' Rosie said, in mock indignation. 'I'm a married woman now, about to become a mother. The times for skipping through the town like a wean are past. Put your arm in mine and we'll walk with decorum.'

And, laughing like children, they went arm in arm along the main street.

Rosie's pains began on 14 July. All day the sun had shone from a sky that was a brilliant blue except for the odd fluffy white cloud scudding across it, helped along by the warm breeze.

Rosie had been uncomfortable for days: it was really too warm for her and everything she did was an effort, and so when she felt the first twinges, she thought fervently, 'Oh, thank God.'

She said nothing at first: the pains were no more than monthly pains and she'd already been told by Connie that the first baby usually took a while to come. 'Baby doesn't know what to do, see. But don't you worry, I'll be with you, and to be on the safe side I've asked Abigail Mehan to lend a hand. She's helped at many births.'

Rosie knew Abigail and was reassured. Now she lived alone, her man being dead and her children scattered, but she always had a cheery word. And though her hair was steel grey and her face brown and creased, her brown eyes still sparkled with life and she was kindly and softly spoken.

When Rosie picked at her tea later, only Connie noticed. Danny and his father were concerned about the milk yield being down because of the heat and Elizabeth was entertaining the family with some amusing incident in the factory, while Sarah had one eye on the clock for she was meeting Sam at half past seven. All missed the grimace of pain that crossed Rosie's face.

It was as they were gathering the plates after the meal that Connie snatched a quiet word with Rosie. 'Have you got pains?'

'Aye,' Rosie said, 'not so bad yet, though.'

'Still, I'll take Elizabeth and make up the bed. Then if things get worse, we'll be ready.'

Rosie nodded and went on collecting the pots until a sudden contraction caused her to double up in pain and the plates fell from her hands, clattering back onto the table.

'Oh dear Lord! Leave the pots. Go and sit by the fire while I see to this bed,' Connie urged.

'God, Mammy, I've no need for a fire, one thing I'm not is cold.'

'Well, sit anyway,' Connie said. 'That last one was big enough. It might not be so long after all.'

It was as Connie was helping Rosie to a chair that Danny and Phelan came in the door, each with a bucket full of water they'd got from the pump in the yard. There was only their mother and Rosie in the kitchen: Elizabeth was helping Sarah get ready for her date and their father was sitting on the wall outside, having a smoke. Danny took in at once the grey pallor of Rosie and sprang forward. 'What is it?' he immediately demanded.

Rosie was unable to answer for another wave of pain washed over her and Connie said, 'Nothing is wrong. It's just that she's about to give birth to the child she's been carrying for months, a day you knew would come.'

'Oh God,' Danny cried and he fell to his knees before Rosie. 'Are you all right?'

The pain had passed and Rosie smiled at Danny seeing his face creased with concern and nodded. 'I'm fine,' she assured him.

'What can I do?' Danny asked his mother.

'Nothing but wait,' Connie said. 'It's all in hand. Phelan, you run up to Abigail Mehan's house now and tell her Rosie's time has come. She knew it would be any day now and will probably be ready to come straight down with you.'

Phelan set off without a murmur. It would be different having a baby in the house, he thought, and he was glad to be doing something to help. As for Danny, he'd got to his feet and could barely stand still. His nerves were jangling inside him and Connie said, 'For Heaven's sake, Danny, will you relax. Sit down by your wife and keep her company while I make up the bed with Elizabeth.'

Danny sat obediently, but could think of little to say. But Rosie had no need of words and was just grateful to have a hand to hold. The pains were a lot stronger now, but, though it showed in her face and eyes and she gripped Danny's hand tight, she didn't utter a sound. When Connie told her all was ready for her, she followed her mother-in-law gladly and sank onto the bed with a sigh of relief.

Danny sat in the chair Rosie had vacated. Around him, life went on. His father came in. Phelan had told him the reason for his errand as he had left the house and Matt knew what Danny would be feeling, for he'd felt it himself. They had no need of speech and sat in a companionable silence.

When Phelan returned with Abigail she gave the briefest of greetings to the two men before hurrying to the room Phelan directed her to.

Sarah, dressed for her date with Sam, went in to see her sister-in-law and wished her all the best, and Elizabeth said she'd be on hand if she was needed. Danny felt useless and said so to his father. 'That's the way of it, son,' Matt said. 'Sure, don't all fathers feel the same, especially when it's the first?'

Danny couldn't imagine any other potential father being as worried as he was, but he was glad of his own father sitting with him, and even of Phelan whittling at a piece of wood while Elizabeth got on with washing and drying the dishes.

Later, there were groaning sounds from the bedroom and it was only his father's hand on his that stopped Danny from leaping up and into the room to find out what was happening. 'Let them get on with it, lad,' he advised more than once. 'This is women's work. Rosie will be as right as rain. Sure, isn't she in the best of hands?'

She might have been, but there was no way Danny would sleep that night, with it all going on just yards away. When Phelan was eventually driven to his bed with weariness, Matt sat on with his eldest son. Matt had been relieved they'd had no further children after Phelan. They had two fine sons by then and two beautiful daughters and he had no wish to see the body dragged out of Connie with a child every year. Yet, he was a normal man and Connie a sensual woman and she'd never refused him, but luckily there had been nothing to show for it since Phelan's birth.

Life was strange right enough, he thought, as he gave the fire another poke. All around them there were families of ten – even twelve or fourteen weren't uncommon – and Matt knew many men found it hard to earn the money to feed and clothe so many. There was a sudden strangled scream from the room and Danny, unable to remain still any longer, leaped to his. feet. 'Easy, lad,' Matt said, standing up himself and putting his arm round his son's shoulder. 'I'll brew up a pot of tea and put a wee tot of whisky in it, shall I? That'll put you right.'

Danny wanted no tea, laced or not, yet he knew it would help his father to do something and so he gave a nod. 'If you like,' he said, and then with a glance at the closed door, asked, 'How much bloody longer?'

'God, lad, could be hours yet,' Matt said,

pressing his son back into a chair and pulling out the kettle to rest above the glowing peat. ''Specially with the first. Dear God, always worst with the first.'

Danny said nothing. His insides were tied in knots through fear and worry. Matt made the tea and Danny drank it without tasting it and still they sat. Eventually, Danny noticed his father trying to cover his yawns with his hand, and immediately felt guilty for keeping him up. 'Go to bed, Da. You'll need to be up for milking in a few hours.'

'Aye,' Matt said, getting to his feet relieved. 'I won't say I'm not weary.' And then he leaned across to Danny and said, 'See if your mother and that Abigail would like a sup of tea, and Rosie too. None of them have had anything for a few hours now and God knows it's already been a long night.'

'Aye, I will,' Danny agreed, knowing he wouldn't sleep either. 'And I'll make the tea, don't worry. Go on to bed.'

Later, when he knocked on the door to tell them he had a cup of tea ready and his mother came out to take the tray, he asked anxiously about Rosie. 'She's fine, Danny. Dozing between the contractions now.'

'Does it... Is it normal to take so long?'

'God bless you, Danny, it's been no time at all yet.'

'I hate to think of her in so much pain.'

'And Rosie, like many before her, will forget it as soon as she holds that wee baby in her arms.'

Danny doubted that, but returned to his seat

before the fire and settled himself again for the long vigil.

He was dozing when his father came down the stairs for the milking a few hours later, but stirred when he heard him making tea. He rubbed the sleep from his eyes with his knuckles and struggled to his feet. 'No, lad,' Matt said. 'Stay and rest yourself, Phelan will give me a hand.'

'Daddy, I'd be better doing something,' Danny said.

Connie came out of the room carrying the tray at that moment and at the enquiring look from her son she shook her head. 'Nothing yet.'

Danny sighed. He was glad to follow his father to the byre. A little later, with his forehead leaning on the cow's velvety flanks and hearing the hiss-hiss of the jets of milk hitting the pail he felt more at peace. The rhythm of milking the soft, gentle cows, who stood so placid throughout with only the barest flick of their tails, often had this effect on him.

Back in the bedroom there was no such peace. Rosie was now in agony. She bit her lip to prevent the screams from spiralling from her, but she couldn't help the gasping sobs and the strangled yelps.

She was glad she wasn't alone, glad of Connie's hand in hers, unaware that her nails had scored that hand often through the night. She thrashed on the bed, trying to get rid of the pain inside her that threatened to break her in two. 'Hush, pet. Lie still,' Abby said again and again. 'Soon be over.'

How soon? Dear God, Rosie thought, this pain

has been going on for hours already. No one warned me it would hurt like this.

Abigail tied a towel to the head of the bed. 'Pull on that when the pain gets too bad,' she said. 'Many find it helps.'

Rosie glared at her. When the pain gets bad! 'Every pain is bad, you stupid bugger,' she wanted to cry, but the throes of agony took all of her energy and this time she tugged on the towel so hard she threatened to bring the bedhead on top of her.

And so it went on, hour after hour. Connie never left her side, for Rosie seemed to gain comfort from her presence and she continually wiped the sweat from her face, telling her she was a good girl and doing just fine.

Sarah and Elizabeth called in before they left for work and took in the situation in one glance. They felt sorry for Rosie: she was so ravaged by pain, her eyes glazed and sweat lending a sheen to her pale skin, for all Connie's efforts.

'We'll see to breakfast,' Sarah told her mother. 'Shall I make something for you?'

Connie looked across at Abigail, who gave a brief nod. 'Best have something,' she said. 'We have to keep our strength up if we're to help the girl.'

But suddenly Rosie arched in the bed and Connie knew they'd soon be too busy to eat or drink anything. Rosie let out a long low scream just as Danny was coming in through the cottage door. He felt as if his heart had stopped beating. 'What is it?' he asked his sisters. 'Dear God, what's up with Rosie?'

'She's fine,' Sarah said, closing the door firmly behind her, knowing it would do no good at all for Danny to catch sight of his wife now.

The breakfast was eaten to a background of groans and cries and the occasional scream or shout and Sarah and Elizabeth were glad to leave the farmhouse. Phelan too found many duties that kept him outside.

By eleven o'clock, Rosie was visibly tiring and Connie and Abigail became concerned. 'I'm going to have a wee feel about,' Abigail said. 'But first I'll scrub my hands. Seen too many women die because of infection.'

There was a pot of water hanging on the fire in readiness for this and Abigail poured some of it into the basin, and added cold from the bucket by the door. She began washing her hands thoroughly, glad the men, especially the girl's husband, were out of doors.

'Now,' she said, returning to the room. 'Let's have a look.'

She lifted the bedclothes up and bent Rosie's knees and felt gently inside her. Rosie was too far gone to know or care what Abigail was doing and Abigail nodded confidently. 'I can feel the head. It's nearly there. She must push through the pain now. Rouse her, Connie, for it's time for her to help us along.'

Rosie didn't want to be roused, and certainly didn't want to push. What was Connie talking about? The pains tearing through her body took her breath away, especially now there was such little space between them. 'I can't push,' she said mutinously.

'You can and you must,' Connie said firmly. 'Take hold of me and when the next pain comes, push with all your heart and soul.'

Rosie pushed but when that almighty effort yielded nothing, Connie said, 'All right, Rosie, now rest yourself until the next one.' Rosie wanted to scream at her, tell her to shut up, only she hadn't breath to do so.

Then Abigail, at the foot of the bed, suddenly cried, 'Come on, bonny girl, the head is nearly out. Let's have another gigantic push.'

Rosie gathered her strength and pushed and then felt such an extreme ache between her legs that she screamed and cried in pain, fearing she was going to be ripped in two.

And then it was over. The baby's body slithered out and its wails filled the room. In the barn, Danny, who had been sawing logs for something to do, lifted his head at the sound and then threw the saw down, overturning the stool in his haste to get indoors.

The door was still closed but he heard movement and above it all the wonderful sound of a child crying. Connie, coming out with soiled linen, saw her son pacing and smiled at him. 'It's all over,' she said. 'You have a beautiful wee daughter.'

'Oh Jesus Christ!' Danny said, relief coursing through him. He felt ten-foot tall. 'Can I see Rosie?'

'You'll see them both when they're fit to be seen,' Connie said. 'Just bide here a wee while longer.'

She left her son and went into the room to see

Rosie already suckling her daughter, as if it was the most natural thing in the world. Rosie's eyes met those of her mother-in-law and she asked happily, 'Can I see Danny?'

Connie smiled. 'You'll see him in a minute when we have you tidied up and before he wears a channel in the stone floor.' She stroked the down of hair on the baby's head gently with one finger and said, 'Have you a name for her?'

'Aye,' Rosie said. 'Danny and I discussed it for hours. She's to be called Bernadette Mary.' She didn't go on to say she would call the baby after no set of parents, for then her own might insist other children she might have be called after them. After the life they'd led her, she would not afford them that honour. To choose an independent name seemed safest.

If Connie was surprised the child was not called after her grandmother, or even herself, she made no comment on it. Abigail also looked at the baby. 'Doesn't matter how many times it happens,' she said. 'Always seems like a miracle. I love helping in homes such as this one where the children are wanted and not seen just as a burden and yet another mouth to feed.'

When Danny was allowed in a little later, Rosie scanned his face for any sign of resentment or disappointment that their firstborn was not a son. She saw none, but she had to be sure. 'You're not disappointed that it's a wee girl we have?' she asked anxiously.

Danny was mesmerised by the child. Rosie had removed her from her breast, but still held her close, and Danny noted the milky grey-blue eyes as they blinked trying to focus, and was amazed at the perfection of her, this perfect being he'd created with Rosie. 'Disappointed?' he said. 'Not a bit of it. I'm thrilled to bits.'

He was going to add maybe they'd have a son next time, but he stopped himself. He didn't know whether he'd want to put Rosie through all that pain again. But then again he was a normal man with normal needs and everyone knew that in the Catholic Church it was wrong to plan your family – you had to take whatever God sent.

Added to that, Rosie didn't look as if she'd suffered over-much from the ordeal. Her eyes were sparkling and her mood almost euphoric. Rosie was discovering what veteran mothers had told her was true: the trials and rigours of childbirth were instantly forgotten once you'd given birth to a healthy baby.

'Could you eat a wee bit of something now?' he asked, knowing she hadn't eaten for hours, and Rosie laughed. 'No, I could eat a great lot of something,' she said. 'I've done a hard job of work and existed on cups of tea since yesterday dinner. I'm famished now.'

'That's grand,' Danny said, glad there was something practical he could do for his young wife. 'I'll see to that straight away,' and he kissed Rosie and planted a kiss on the baby's cheek before leaving them.

FIVE

Connie complained good-naturedly that the path from the road would be worn away with the people who came to visit Rosie Walsh and her new baby. They came bearing gifts and good wishes. Even her parents came – Rosie guessed only because it would have been remarked upon if they hadn't. They certainly paid scant attention to the child and, on hearing the name chosen, Minnie snapped out sourly, 'What kind of outlandish name is that? She should be named for members of the family. That's how it's done. It shows respect.'

'Danny and I like the name Bernadette,' Rosie remarked calmly.

'Like! Like! What's there to like in a name? It's what you're called and that's an end to it.'

'Well, our baby is to be called Bernadette Mary,' Rosie said firmly. 'We've already spoken to Father McNally about it. He liked it and gave me a wee book about St Bernadette to read to the baby when she's older.'

That was that then. If the priest had put his stamp of approval on the child's name there was nothing further Minnie could say.

They didn't stay very long after that and although Connie said nothing in Rosie's hearing, she remarked to her own daughters that the woman was mean-spirited and miserable. Her

94

daughter and first grandchild were there together and she barely gave them the time of day and would not even stay long enough to take a sup of tea. God, what a woman!

Rosie's sisters made up for the lack of attention she and the baby had received from her parents, picking Bernadette up and cuddling her, crooning to her and telling Rosie how grand she was and how proud they felt.

They brought knitted coats and as Chrissie handed hers over she said, 'It's not great, Rosie, but I did my best.'

Rosie unfolded the little jacket and noticed the odd hole and dropped stitch, but said nothing. She knew Chrissie was no hand with either a knitting needle or a sewing needle, but it touched her that she'd tried.

Geraldine's little jacket was better, and Rosie thanked them both and showed them her other gifts. Pride of place were the two dresses Elizabeth and Sarah had given her, both in brilliant white satin and with smocking so fine and beautiful that Geraldine said, 'They're lovely, Rosie, both of them. Is Bernadette being christened in one of these?'

'No,' Rosie answered. 'Mammy – Connie, you know – has the family christening gown. It's beautiful and kept between layers of tissue paper in a trunk in the loft. She's washed it to freshen it up and it looks like new. It would so please her for Bernadette to wear it.'

'I love the cradle,' Chrissie said, tipping the rocker gently with her foot.

'It's beautiful, all that carving on the side,'

Geraldine said. 'Is that a family heirloom too?'

'Aye, but Danny did it up, you know, and gave it another coat or two of varnish. Mammy has spent the last weeks hemming cot sheets and nappies from a bolt of soft cotton she bought, and she's bought the softest woollen blankets too.'

But of either of the families, the one totally besotted by the child was Dermot. He'd spend ages just looking at her. The first day the girls called was a Saturday and Bernadette was four days old and he had insisted on coming with them. After that, he prised money from his piggy bank and went after school and chose the best rattle in the shop for his little niece.

The following Saturday they called again and Dermot had the rattle with him and waved it from side to side above Bernadette's head, but gently so as not to startle her. He was delighted when Bernadette's reflexes caused her to clasp his fingers and Rosie, watching him, thought it would have been the making of him if he'd not been the youngest in the family.

'Would you like to hold her, Dermot?' she said.

'Can I?'

'Surely you can.'

'I'll not drop her, Rosie.'

'I know you won't. Sit you up on the bed and open up your arms.'

Even Chrissie and Geraldine smiled at the awe on the young boy's face as he held the baby close to him, and so did Connie when she came into the room with refreshments for them all.

'Are you excited about tomorrow?' Chrissie

asked Rosie, biting into one of the biscuits.

'A bit. Are you?'

'No, I'm scared to death.'

'You only have to do the responses,' Rosie said. 'It's all written down and Sarah can go first if you like.'

'Oh I'll probably be all right when I start,' Chrissie said. She and Sarah were to be Bernadette's godmothers, and Phelan the child's godfather, for the baby's christening the next day. It was to be a lavish affair, with a large party afterwards in the Walshes' house. With the help of her daughters when they were home, Connie had been baking and cooking almost since the day the child was born.

Rosie was pleased at the fuss being made, although she protested that Connie was doing too much. The next day, as she stood before the altar of the church with the sun shining through the stained glass in the windows to send a myriad of coloured lights dancing in front of them, she felt such peace and contentment. Here she was, beside the man she loved, welcomed so warmly into his family. Her own were in pews behind, together with neighbours and friends, and Rosie felt tears of happiness in her eyes.

She wouldn't let herself cry, though, not at her own child's christening, and she passed the baby to Sarah as the priest indicated. If Sarah noticed Rosie's over-bright eyes she knew she would make no comment about it, for her own voice had been a little shaky when she made the responses.

Rosie wasn't aware straight away that Sarah was

raging about something. She was too busy showing off her baby and accepting the praise and presents of all those friends, neighbours and relatives who'd crowded into the Walshes' house after the christening.

Bernadette eventually went to sleep and Rosie took her into the room away from the noise and laid her in the cradle. It was on coming out again that she caught sight of Sarah's face and knew she was in a temper then right enough, for Sarah's feelings were always portrayed in her face.

The looks she shot across the room to her Sam, who was drinking deep of the beer Matt had bought and talking earnestly to Shay, should have rendered him senseless on the stone-flagged floor. 'Lover's tiff?' Rosie enquired lightly.

'No,' Sarah hissed back. 'It's that pair, on about the war and places none of us have heard of – Wipers and Gallipoli – and how over two hundred thousand have died now and a good percentage of them Irish men and boys. It's not the time or place to discuss such a thing, if there is ever a suitable time. I told them straight, but God, there's no stopping them when they get together. You'd think they were planning a revolution. They'll be at Danny next, you see if they're not.'

'They can try,' Rosie said. She remembered the conversation she'd had with Danny when war had been declared, just two months before their wedding. In no time at all recruiting officers had toured Ireland, gathering up zealous volunteers and Danny had assured Rosie that he was one man who had no intention of joining that war, or any other war come to that. 'Why should I help

England?' he'd said. 'They've gone to the aid of Belgium because Germany has invaded them, taking over their country and oppressing the people. It would be laughable if it wasn't so tragic, for isn't that the very thing that England have been doing to Ireland for years? If I ever took up arms it would be to gain Ireland's freedom. And I have no reason to do that, for Ireland will get Home Rule in the end. It's there, ready to be implemented, and is only postponed because of the war. Eventually, Ireland will be a united country and hopefully without a shot being fired.'

So Rosie was able to say categorically, 'Danny will never be tempted that way. Particularly now that he's a family man.'

'It's good to be so sure of him,' Sarah said. 'And you're right, of course, Danny has too much sense. At this minute I want to walk up to Sam and hit him across the top of the head with something heavy.'

Rosie laughed. 'Och, Sarah, don't mind him. Isn't it just the beer talking?'

'I wish it were just that, Rosie,' Sarah said. 'But he goes on the same way when he's stone-cold sober. Of course, Shay encourages him too.'

Connie, who'd been keeping a weather eye on Rosie, for she was still officially lying in, came up to her at that point. 'Don't be doing too much now,' she warned. 'Or your milk will dry up.'

'Aye, I know,' Rosie said. She did feel weary all of a sudden and so she said, 'I do feel a bit wobbly now you mention it. I'm away for a lie down, if that's all right.'

Danny saw Rosie detach herself from his

mother and sister and followed her into the bedroom. 'You all right?' he whispered, mindful of the sleeping baby as he sat down on the bed beside Rosie.

'Aye, I'm grand,' Rosie said. 'Just a wee bit tired.'

'Bed's the best place then,' Danny told her. 'You get tucked up and I'll bring you in a plate of goodies and a wee drink.'

Rosie was almost too weary to care about food, but she knew Danny would like to do something for her and with Connie having gone to so much trouble she felt it would be churlish to refuse. 'Aye, that would be nice,' she said.

Danny looked at his daughter snuggled in sleep and traced a finger gently across her cheek. 'Wasn't she a star today?' he said. 'Not a peep out of her. Even when the priest poured the water over her head, she just looked surprised.'

'Aye,' Rosie agreed and went on with a smile, 'One of the old ones told me they should yell their heads off in order to release the devil inside them.'

'Huh,' Danny said. 'Some of those old ones should have their mouths stopped up! Glad to see you're too sensible to take any notice of it.' He got to his feet and said, 'You get yourself into bed, pet, and I'll be back shortly.' He kissed Rosie on the cheek and left her.

Rosie ate some of the food Danny brought her without much enthusiasm, though she was grateful for the hot sweet tea and then she settled down for a sleep.

She had dropped off and slept for an hour or

so, when she was roused suddenly. She lay there for a moment as the last threads of sleep disappeared. She peered around the darkened room and saw the door swinging: someone must have stumbled against it and made the latch jump. The baby was mewling in the cradle, obviously awakened by the same thing. She wasn't crying yet, but she would, Rosie knew. She would be too hungry to go off to sleep again.

As she lifted her she became aware of a conversation just outside the door and groaned as she recognised Sam's voice. 'You've seen nothing like it, man, I was there on the dockside in Dublin and one of the hospital ships was in harbour. The stretcher cases were already gone, but the rest... God, Danny, it would sicken you. There were fellows twitching with shellshock and others stone-blind being led along by a comrade. There were those in wheelchairs with missing limbs, or with their lungs eaten away with gas. 'Course, they were counted as the lucky ones, for now there will be Irish bodies littering France, Belgium, and now bloody Turkey. Left to rot they are, to be eaten by the carrion crows.'

'Lord, Sam, no one pretends war is pretty,' Danny said. 'Everyone knew some of those valiant men marching behind the British Army would not come back and others would be maimed and crippled. That's the way of it. You don't begin a war and expect no casualties.'

'I know that,' Sam said. 'I'm not stupid. What angers me is that they fight for England, for Belgium, for France, yet their own country is oppressed.'

'He's right,' Shay put in.

'Aye, all right, but every man must do as he sees fit.'

'You didn't feel a need to join the British Army yourself?' Sam asked.

'I did not!' Danny said emphatically. 'I might not go around shouting about Home Rule like you two, but I have no great love for England and I wouldn't put my head on the line for it.'

'And would you for Ireland?'

'What sort of question is that?'

'An easy one to answer, I'd say.'

Danny sighed. 'Essentially, I'm a man of peace,' he said. 'I'd fight if anyone belonging to me was threatened, but...'

'And don't you think they will be? When this damned war is over, England will renege on her promises of independence and Home Rule like she's done so often before.'

'Maybe,' Danny said. 'But if it's on the statute book they must debate it sometime and with so many men giving their lives for England, they must feel they owe us something.'

'Oh aye,' Shay put in. 'And will that stop the nonsense with Ulster and make Ireland properly united?'

'Ulster can only opt out for six years.'

'Danny, will you listen to yourself?' Sam almost roared. 'You're as brainwashed as the rest of them. Six thousand years opt out, more like.'

Sam's shout had caused Bernadette to jump on the breast where she was feeding and Rosie took her off and fastened her nightgown up, intending to close the door and help cut the noise out.

'Even so...' Danny put in.

'Even so, even so,' Shay mocked. 'Don't be so mealy-mouthed, Danny. Now, with England's forces and energies directed at Germany and the rest of Europe, now is the time to take up arms and fight for independence.'

No-one noticed Rosie in the doorway, the men were sideways on to her and before them were Phelan and Niall – Shay's young brother. The two lads were looking into Sam's and Shay's faces, hanging on their every word.

'What we want to know, Danny, is are you for us, or against us?' Shay demanded. 'There is no middle way here. When the call comes for Ireland's freedom, will you answer that call?'

Rosie pushed the door to before she heard Danny's reply, but not before she saw the patriotic zeal burning in both of the young boys' eyes. She returned to the bed a worried woman.

Everything settled down after the christening and Rosie told herself, whatever Sarah said, it had been the beer talking with the men that night. Shay had always been a hothead, but it was just talk, surely to God. She mentioned the reactions of Phelan and Niall to Danny, but he told her not to fret. 'They're but boys,' he said, 'not long out of the schoolroom altogether and boys that age love looking up to someone, having someone to admire.'

'So you don't think it's anything to worry about?'

'No,' Danny said. 'But best not say a word to Mammy anyway.'

103

It wasn't long after this that Phelan began arguing with his parents. It was mainly because he wanted to go out at night and didn't always want to say where he went or what time he would be back. Danny told his parents to go easy on him. 'He works hard enough through the day and this is his leisure time,' he told them. 'It's a stab at independence, I mind I was the same at his age.'

'You never went far,' Connie said.

'Well, how far can Phelan get in the two or three hours he's out? He's probably at a neighbour's house. He can't go much further away, I mean, no harm will come to him.'

Danny saw no cause for concern and Rosie, who did, told herself she was making a mountain out of a molehill. The nights were still light enough through August and what could be nicer than walking the hills and dales of Wicklow on a balmy summer's evening?

By the end of August it was the harvest, and that meant all hands to the pump. There was little time to blow one's nose, never mind go out for a wee stroll, and Phelan was as tired as the rest at the day's end and just as anxious to lie in his bed as his elder brother and father.

With the harvest safely in, there was the bog turf to cut and stockpile for the winter. Matt kept his youngest son hard at it beside him, mending fences, whitewashing the cottage and barn, repairing thin areas of the thatch, and any other jobs he could think of.

If Matt was hoping to tire Phelan out by his actions, he was mistaken, for Phelan was toughened by his work on the farm and as the nights

104

drew in he began once more to spend many of his evenings away from the cottage. Connie often wondered where he found to go – if it was just to a neighbour's house, as Danny thought, then why couldn't he say so?

Rosie felt sorry for the lad in many ways. The two had got on well from the first and he was enchanted with Bernadette. It was Rosie he often sought out to talk to. She didn't talk to him about the disagreements he had with his parents, she had no need to, and so he opened up to her. 'They want to own me body and soul,' he complained.

'They're concerned, Phelan.'

'They think I'm a wean.'

'No,' Rosie said. 'They know the age of you. It's a habit you get into as a parent. See, wee Bernadette is just a baby, and I do everything for her, change her, feed her. Later I'll hold her hand as she walks, pick her up if she falls and wipe the tears from her eyes. I'll get her ready for school, buy her copy books and a school bag and fix her dinner.

'And through it all, I'll be there, caring for her, loving her, being the person to lean on. All that care and love cannot be turned off, like water from a tap. As you grow up, parents must adjust and sometimes it's not so easy. Maybe if you talked more about what you're doing, and who you're meeting, it would make it better for them.'

Phelan's reply lent an icy chill to Rosie's spine. 'If Mammy knew the half of what I do some nights, she'd worry herself into an early grave,' he said.

'Phelan, for God's sake, don't do anything silly.'

'A man has to do what he believes in, even our Danny said that,' Phelan told her with a hint of pride.

'But you're just...' Rosie stopped herself in time from calling him a child. He would have really turned against her if she had. But to her he was, the lad was barely shaving yet. 'You're so young yet,' she went on. 'Things often look different as you grow up.'

'I'll never feel any different,' Phelan promised, 'not about this.'

Rosie felt helpless then and Phelan said, 'No-one in the house knows of this but you. Promise me you'll not tell on me?'

'Not even Danny?'

'Especially not Danny.'

That made Rosie uncomfortable, and she wondered later if she should have made that promise. But what had Phelan really told her? Nothing concrete, nothing she could go running to Danny about. What he'd said could mean anything or nothing. Maybe it was just a boy's bravado.

In the end, she sought out Sarah – she thought Sam might know something and maybe talked to Sarah about it. 'I wonder what those two rapscallions Phelan and Niall get up to going out in the black night,' Rosie said casually to her one day. 'Up to mischief, no doubt. Does Sam ever talk about it?'

'No, never,' Sarah said. 'Sam can be as tight as a clam about some things. He reminds me of a wee boy at times. I mind Danny and his friends had secret societies when they were young and sent coded letters to each other and had pass-words to go into what they called the clubhouse. It was nothing more than a dilapidated old shepherd's hut, just off the track up the hillside. It's probably dropped to bits entirely now. The times I crept up there with Elizabeth and tried to listen in. I didn't think it was so grand looking even then, and Danny was furious with us of course.'

'So, Sam is in a secret society then?' Rosie joked. Maybe there was some truth in that – she knew the Irish Republican Brotherhood was a secret organisation. Even the name of it was spoken in whispers and no-one knew exactly who was in it, but its objective was to obtain Home Rule for all of Ireland, Ulster included. It was said in homes about the place, for it was never discussed abroad, that it had grown out of the organisation called the Irish Volunteer Group and they had guns and ammunition.

'I don't know what Sam is involved in, probably nothing,' Sarah said. 'And what's more, I'm not going to worry about it. I think he is just con-cerned about the injured men from the war and feels England were wrong to drag Irish men into a struggle that isn't theirs. To an extent, he has a point, and I can feel as incensed as he can over the loss of life. But sure, Sam's all talk,' Sarah went on. 'Wind and water, Mammy calls him, and she's not far wrong.'

It was hardly reassuring, but Rosie told herself whatever Sam was into, it couldn't affect Phelan and Niall. Dear God, they were barely fourteen. No society, organisation or whatever would use boys, surely to God?

She resolved to put it from her mind. She had plenty to occupy herself and plenty in her life to be happy about, especially Danny and their darling baby.

On Saturdays, Chrissie would come over, and sometimes even Geraldine was allowed to come with her. They usually brought Dermot too, for his temper if Minnie tried to stop him was tremendous, Chrissie told Rosie. 'Course he's never been told no all the days of his life, so it's hard for him to take.'

Rosie knew that, yet Dermot couldn't be faulted in his love for Bernadette and she remembered on her weekly visit home how he galloped from school in an effort to reach the farmhouse before Rosie left. He seldom made it as the nights began to draw in and Geraldine told her he would cry brokenheartedly if she'd left before he arrived.

As the baby grew, so that Rosie wasn't feeding her every few minutes, Connie would insist that Rosie take a trip to town with her sisters as she had before. Someone had to go in once a week anyway to sell their surplus and collect supplies for the house, but after Rosie had the baby, Sarah or Elizabeth would usually do this. Connie seldom left the farm, often saying her gallivanting days were over.

Rosie and her sisters enjoyed the jaunts in on the cart. Even if they bought little, they met friends and exchanged news and gossip. And, as Christmas approached, Rosie was glad of the opportunity to buy some wee presents for the family.

This Christmas would be the first with a baby in the house, and Rosie couldn't help feeling excited about it. Bernadette was a happy and contented child, now struggling to sit up. She had a smile for everyone and would lie for some time in her cradle, babbling to herself rather than crying. Rosie told herself she was truly well blessed.

SIX

By March 1916 it was obvious, and not only to the people in the Walsh household, that something strange was afoot in the country. Women standing around the church doors after Mass talked of their sons and husbands and brothers in whispers. Eventually, Father McNally condemned all secret societies planning subversive activities. He said from the pulpit they were evil and against God. He even read out a letter from the Bishop in the same vein, but personally Rosie felt that it would make little difference.

She was tired. God, they were all tired. The lambing had been difficult that year and a few of the ewes, especially those who'd begun to lamb too early before the snow had cleared in February, had died giving birth. More than once, Rosie had found an orphaned lamb in a box before the fire that she'd have to feed with a bottle.

Bernadette, now crawling, loved the baby lambs and took more interest in them than the rag doll Connie had bought her for Christmas, or the rocking horse Danny had made for her.

Once the lambing was over, the spring planting began, and Danny, Phelan and Matt were out most of the daylight hours and Phelan's evening jaunts were severely curtailed. Yet, Rosie sensed a tension in the air she'd never felt before.

She'd tried a few times to talk to Phelan again,

but he'd always managed to avoid being alone with her. Maybe, she thought, he regretted saying so much to her in the first place. It could have been that, but just as easily it could be the reticence of a boy on the verge of manhood, unsure and a bit nervous of the changes he would be starting to notice in his body. His voice had definitely changed. He'd gone through the embarrassing squeaks and gruffness and the times he'd begun to speak in a high voice and it had dropped an octave, or vice versa, but now it had settled down to a level that marked his childhood as being almost over.

Then, one beautiful mid-April day, there came a pounding on Connie's door. Few people knocked on the door and Rosie, coming from the room where she'd just laid the baby down for a nap, glanced quickly at Connie who was stirring a pot above the fire. She left off and crossed the room.

Dermot almost fell in the door as she opened it. His face was scarlet, his breath coming in short gasps as he struggled for air. It was obvious he'd been running for some time and fear clutched at Rosie. 'What is it? What's happened? Is it Mammy?'

'No. No,' Dermot spluttered between gulps of air. 'It's nobody. Nothing like that.'

'Then what…?'

'You must come, Rosie,' he said, pulling at her skirts. 'You must come and see.' He was jumping from one foot to the other in agitation.

'See what?'

His eyes slithered over to Connie and he

muttered, 'I can't tell you. You must come.'

Connie was amused. 'Go on with the child. See what is so important,' she said. 'Don't worry about the baby, I'll see to her if she should wake.'

Rosie only waited to grab her shawl from the room before taking Dermot's hand. She was grateful for the shawl Connie had given her for Christmas in these chilly spring months. It was of the softest wool, not thick but warm despite that, and it was a deep russet colour. 'Coats are all very well,' Connie had told her on the quiet, 'for Mass and all, and it sets you apart, but a shawl is much easier for carrying a baby or a small wean.'

And how right she was, Rosie thought. Her arms were nearly pulled from their sockets carrying her child to her mother's and she'd thought she would have to leave her behind soon and make her visits briefer until Bernadette was able to walk the distance. But with a shawl she could have her on her back, the shawl around the both of them and tied securely at the front to keep Bernadette safe.

Now she wrapped her shawl around her as she followed Dermot. She had no idea where she was being taken. 'Why aren't you at school, anyway?' she asked her little brother as he led her around the edge of the fields.

'It's holidays,' Dermot told her indignantly. 'For Easter. We broke up yesterday.'

'Oh, right. Well, where are you taking me then?'

'I'm not saying. You have to see it for yourself.'

Phelan, digging over one of the fields, watched the progress of the two with narrowed eyes. He wondered what had brought Dermot pell-mell to the cottage door and where he was taking Rosie, for it was obvious from the direction they were going in he was not making for his own place. Dermot had never come to the farm before without at least acknowledging Phelan and usually tagged along beside him. That morning Dermot had seemed preoccupied with something else and hadn't even seen Phelan's hand lifted in greeting. Something was up and prickles of alarm ran down Phelan's spine.

He lifted his head. His father and Danny were over planting in another field behind the tall hedge and Phelan threw his spade down with such force it sliced into the moist earth, and he set off to follow Rosie and Dermot.

They toiled up the hillside, too breathless to speak much, and suddenly Rosie guessed where they were heading. Somehow, Dermot had found Danny's secret hideaway, the one Danny had told her about, the one Sarah had recently mentioned. She wondered if he'd left treasures behind, things a young boy would value, and that was what had excited Dermot.

And yet, she recalled it hadn't been delight on Dermot's face when he'd hammered on the door. There had been something else there... Trepidation. Even fear.

She turned to ask him but he'd already stopped. 'It's in there,' he said, pointing. Rosie looked at him. Where Dermot was pointing was an impregnable wall of brambles and bushes. 'We can't go through that,' she protested.

'Aye we can,' Dermot assured her. 'Look.'

He held back a bush expertly and exposed a hole that had been hacked between the greenery with the bushes left at the front to hide it, which they did effectively. 'I found this when I was bringing the sheep down with Daddy a few days ago,' Dermot said. 'One of them got stuck in there, its horns caught around the bramble bushes, and Daddy was miles away. Took me ages to free the sheep and pulling at it like that, I saw the hole. I didn't tell Daddy or anyone, but I thought as soon as school finished I would come up here and explore.'

'And what did you find?'

'You'll soon see.'

Rosie looked at the uninviting hole, dim because little light penetrated through the canopy that would be above her head and so low that she would be bent nearly double. She had no desire to go in there. Hadn't this gone far enough? Dermot was too used to grown-ups giving in to him. She'd left in the middle of a busy morning to come traversing the hillside on the mere whim of a child.

'Look, Dermot,' she said. 'I can't do this. I must go back.'

'Oh no!' Dermot cried and Rosie saw actual tears in his eyes. 'You must come. You must see… I can't tell anyone else.'

'Oh, Dermot.'

'Please?' he pleaded. 'I'll hold the bushes for you.'

Rosie gave a sigh and decided she really must find out what had affected her young brother. Bending low, she entered the tunnel. Dermot slipped in behind her and the bushes fell into place with a rustle.

Now it was darker than ever, for the canopy above them successfully hid them from the sun. Unseen branches tugged at Rosie's hair, scratched at her face and snagged at her shawl. Time and again she had to stop to disentangle herself and Dermot would often cannon into the back of her. She was glad of her stout everyday boots that protected her feet from what was underfoot, though she stumbled many a time.

It was impossible to talk and so even when Rosie saw the undergrowth thinning and the dappled light shining between the trees, she made no comment.

Then, suddenly, they were in a clearing. Someone had taken the trouble to cut down the bushes surrounding the cottage. Danny had told her the place had originally been used by shepherds years before, and had been nearly falling down when Danny had used it.

Because of that, Rosie had expected to see a ruin, but this cottage was no ruin. It had new walls built up and was recently whitewashed, the rotting thatch that had obviously been on the roof was lying in a heap to the side of it and had been replaced by new. Even the door seemed new.

'Is this what you had to show me?' Rosie asked.

Dermot shook his head. 'Not the cottage alone,' he said. 'Come on.'

As they approached the place, Rosie noticed the solitary window was so begrimed with dirt that she doubted much light reached the cottage

115

through it, but the door opened without even a creak. Rosie stood in the doorway and surveyed the place. Someone had been here and not long ago either, for peat embers lay in the grate and the place didn't smell of dust or decay or damp, it smelled of cigarettes and paraffin. She saw two lamps either side of the mantelshelf, a box of matches between them.

The floor was packed-down mud, covered over by a large hessian rug. She crossed the room, leaving the door ajar, and lit one of the lamps for extra light. Dermot's eyes were dancing with excitement.

'Now you'll see,' he said as he fell to his knees and rolled the rug back.

Rosie joined him and could plainly see the place where the floor had been cut away in a square and she kneeled beside her brother as he ran his fingers along the edge of the sizeable square and lifted the sod of earth out. Rosie leaned closer, bringing the lamp nearer, and saw that the earth below had been dug away to produce a roomy hole and she gave a sudden shiver of apprehension.

'Look,' Dermot said triumphantly and he pulled two canvas rolls from the hole and began to unwrap them. There were six rifles in each roll and Rosie sat back on her heels and let out a gasp of shock.

She was used to guns, having been brought up on a farm. Her own father as well as Matt and Danny would often shoot rabbits, both to save their crops from being eaten and to supplement the pot, and foxes were also killed. That was nor-

116

mal and natural, but those guns weren't hidden away in what had once been a derelict place.

Dermot, still ferreting about in the hole, brought out tin boxes full of bullets and then some more pistols, again wrapped in cloth. She sat back and surveyed the cache of weapons before them. What on earth should she do?

Suddenly the room darkened and she looked up in alarm. Phelan was standing in the doorway. 'So,' he said. 'Now you know. What d'you intend to do about it?'

Rosie looked at Phelan aghast, her mouth open in shock, her eyes troubled. 'Phelan, I...'

'If you've sense, and you value your life and that of our families, you will put those things back where they came from, go home and say nothing, forget all about it,' Phelan said coldly.

'Are you threatening me?'

'Let's say I'm warning you.' Phelan said. 'These are desperate times and anyone that is not for Ireland is against her and becomes her enemy. What cannot be borne is a spy in the camp.'

'Phelan, I'm not a spy, I'm your sister-in-law,' Rosie said hotly. 'And Dermot is a child.'

'I thought no-one knew of this place,' Phelan said angrily. 'It seemed a perfect place to store ammunition.'

'Danny knew of it.'

'God, aye, but he'd never come up here, not now. He used to meet Shay and the other lads here when they were boys. It was Shay who took me here first. Mind you,' he added, 'he couldn't have used it as it was. The roof leaked like a tap, the mortar was crumbling in the stone walls and the door had rotted away. Left to itself it would be just a pile of rubble by now. We spent ages patching it up. How did you find it?' he suddenly demanded of Dermot.

Dermot loved and admired Phelan, but he was unused to him shouting and being cross – he was unused to anyone being cross with him, come to that – and so he replied angrily. 'I just did, and so what, Phelan? It doesn't belong to you.'

The blow to the side of Dermot's head knocked him sideways. No-one had ever struck him before and he cried out with the pain and shock of it. With an angry look at Phelan, Rosie put her arms around Dermot. 'There was no need for that.'

Phelan ran his fingers through his hair. His eyes looked wild and filled with fear. 'There was every need,' he cried. 'For the love of God will you understand the danger you're both in? Tell me, Dermot, how you found the place and the arms, or I'll beat it out of you and even Rosie won't be able to save you.'

'Phelan, what's got into you?'

'Shut up, Rosie,' Phelan yelled, and he looked at the boy. 'Well, Dermot?'

Dermot was scared of Phelan for the first time in his life. He saw the suppressed fury in him, his fists balled at his sides. He licked his lips nervously and told Phelan the same story he'd told Rosie about the tangled sheep. 'I didn't have time to explore the cottage then, I had to wait till the holidays, and I came up early this morning.'

'Alone?' Phelan demanded.

'Aye, alone.'

'Then what? How did you find the weapons?'

'Well,' Dermot said. 'The place was dark because I shut the door. I knew there were paraffin lamps on the mantelshelf – I'd seen that much when I'd first opened the door – and so I made for there. But the mat must have been ruched up or something because I tripped over it and went flying. Then, when I lit the lamp and lifted the mat to straighten it, I saw the square cut in the mud and I pulled it out to look.'

'Did you tell anyone?'

Dermot shook his head. 'There was no-one to tell. I went for Rosie. I didn't even tell her, I brought her here.'

'You told no-one else?'

'No.'

'You're sure?' Phelan demanded. 'Swear it, Dermot, on your mother's life.'

'Aye, I swear.'

'What about the day you saw a glimpse of the place? Did you mention it to your father?'

'No fear,' Dermot said. 'I didn't know what it was. I meant to explore it on my own. My mother never wants me out of her sight and I wouldn't have told either of them.'

'Where do they think you are now, then?'

'They don't know, I snuck away when they were busy. They'll know I'll make for your place. Mammy will give out to me when I go back.'

'What if your Daddy comes looking for you?' Phelan said. 'What if he goes to the farm and Mammy tells him of you and Rosie going off and making for the hills? He could come looking for you.'

Rosie worriedly saw Phelan had a point. 'So

what do we do?'

'We put all that ammunition back just the way it was and get as far from here as possible. You never come near this place again, Dermot. Do you hear what I say?'

The boy nodded, but Phelan was not satisfied. 'I mean it, Dermot, and you say nothing, not to anyone. This is not a game.'

'Phelan, stop it,' Rosie said angrily, seeing the fear on Dermot's face and feeling the way his whole body shook. 'You're frightening him.'

'He needs frightening,' Phelan said, dropping to his knees and wrapping the pistols up in the canvas cover the way they had been. 'There are desperate men in the IRB and while me and Shay, Sam and Niall would try to protect you, I don't know how much influence we'd have if they found out either you or Dermot had been here.'

'Sweet Jesus, Phelan! What in God's name have you got mixed up in? A fine organisation it must be all right, if it threatens women and weans.'

'I'm fighting for Irish Freedom and the right to rule our own country,' Phelan snapped angrily. 'We've planned and trained for months. Surprise is the key and if that was jeopardised in some way and the British Army were waiting for us, what d'you think they'd do? Shake us by the hand? All I'm saying is neither of you come here again, or mention it to anyone at all, or you might be very sorry.'

'Just two more casualties of war, Phelan?' Rosie asked bitterly, putting the rifles back into the hole gently.

'Aye, if you want to see it that way,' Phelan said

menacingly. 'Come on, we're finished here.'

He roughly pulled Rosie to her feet and kicked the mat into place. 'Let's go.'

He blew out the lamp and replaced it on the mantelshelf and then strode across the room, suddenly plunged into semi-darkness, and opened the door. 'Come on,' he urged Rosie and Dermot in a hissing whisper. 'Every minute we stay is more dangerous. I'll lead the way through the undergrowth, just in case. Not a word now, and go as quietly as possible.'

Easier said than done, Rosie thought a little later as she was pulled to a stop yet again by a thorn snagging her shawl. With the fronds slapping at them and the leaves and mud under their feet, hiding the twigs that broke with a loud snap, it was impossible to move as quietly as Phelan would have liked and he'd keep turning at a particularly loud noise and hiss at Rosie who was directly behind him, 'Quiet, for God's sake.'

Rosie was glad to reach the end of that green tunnel, glad to straighten her back and stand up once more on the path, pulling at the leaves and small twigs caught in her hair and dusting down her clothes as she waited for Dermot. A worry was nagging at her. 'Phelan,' she said. 'Dermot was right in what he said. He told no-one but me what he'd found. Well, he didn't tell me, he showed me. But he was in a state when he came to the farm. Mammy will wonder what it was about. What shall we say?'

Phelan said nothing at first. He led them down the path a little way, where there was a broken tree, and stopped. He knew this was a problem.

Connie would undoubtedly wonder at the behaviour of Dermot. He'd wondered himself, hadn't he?

What else would generate the same excitement for a child? What story could they dream up that would satisfy Connie? 'You could say I found a badgers' sett,' Dermot said suddenly. 'I did once, when I was out with Daddy. It was nearly dark and we saw the mother badger and two babies come out. They hadn't heard us and we stopped and watched them. Would that do it?' he asked Phelan. 'Would your mother believe that?'

'She might,' Phelan said. 'Aye, indeed she might. Say you called for me too on the way,' he told Rosie.

'Why can't you say that yourself?'

'Because I'm going to lead young Dermot home.'

'You needn't,' Dermot said. 'I can go home on my own.'

'I know that fine well,' Phelan said. 'But today I'm coming with you. We need to talk.'

Dermot gave a sigh. Phelan would go on about not telling anyone again. He didn't need to keep on, Dermot wasn't stupid and he was scared enough already to keep his mouth closed.

But he said none of this to Phelan. Phelan, the boy he liked and admired, seemed to have disappeared overnight and had turned into a stern man with a gruff voice and cold eyes, and he was wary of upsetting him.

And so, when, just a few minutes after leaving Rosie, Phelan began to stress again the need for secrecy, he didn't even show the slightest

122

impatience. And then Phelan said, 'I want you to do something for me.'

Dermot was now all ears. He'd do anything to get back in Phelan's good books. 'Aye,' he said.

'I want you to take a letter home to my parents.'

'A letter?'

'Aye,' Phelan said. 'I might have to go away from this place in a wee while and I won't be able to tell my parents till I'm gone.'

'Another secret?'

'Aye, and I won't have them worried more than they will be anyway. If I leave you a letter, will you take it to them?'

'Aye, but how will I know the time to take it?'

'I'll get word to you,' Phelan said. 'After dark. Which room do you sleep in?'

'The end one,' Dermot said. 'You go through Geraldine and Chrissie's room to get to mine. Mammy and Daddy sleep in a corner of the kitchen in a curtained-off bed.'

'Good,' Phelan said. 'So if I throw gravel at your window to wake you up, it shouldn't rouse the house?'

'No,' Dermot said doubtfully. 'But I'm some-times hard to wake up. I'll leave my window a little bit open from now on.'

'I don't know the exact date,' Phelan said. 'None of us have been told that yet, but it will be soon. I'll come as soon as I know. I'll have the letter written and ready. And you'll take it to Mammy on the farm, the day I ask you to.'

'Aye.'

'And you'll not say a word of this conversation,' Phelan said. 'If they ask, say you had your

123

window slightly open and you found the letter on your bedroom floor later that day. All right?'

'Aye.'

'Good man, Dermot,' Phelan said, and Dermot's heart lightened, for it was obvious Phelan had forgiven him for discovering the cottage and finding the stash of arms. He was trusting him now to take an important letter to his parents when he was about business to free Ireland. This Brotherhood thing he was in sounded exciting. Dermot wished he was old enough to join. Maybe Phelan could put a word in for him later, if he delivered the letter and told it exactly as Phelan said.

He waved goodbye at the head of the lane to his farm and went in to face the music. He knew his mother would go for him. She hated the way he was always trailing up to see Rosie and wee Bernadette.

SEVEN

Rosie was very troubled after the discovery of the arms in the disused cottage and Phelan's reaction to it. She didn't know how to treat Phelan after it either, but she was anxious for him and for how his activities would affect the family.

The constant worry gnawing at her made her jumpy and it was noticed by both Connie and Danny. 'What is it, pet?' Danny would ask. 'What are you fretting over?'

How Rosie longed to tell her young husband, who was looking at her in such a concerned way, two deep furrows in his brow. She wanted to tell him everything, but mindful of Phelan's warnings of secrecy, she knew everyone would be safer if she said nothing. She wouldn't be able to bear it if she brought danger to the family that had welcomed her so warmly, and especially to Danny and wee Bernadette. And so she'd try to smile at Danny and say reassuringly, 'Nothing's the matter with me, Danny. I'm grand, so I am.'

But Danny knew she wasn't. 'Has she spoken to you at all?' he demanded of his mother one day as Rosie disappeared with a basket of damp washing to hang in the orchard.

'Not at all,' Connie told him. 'She's not been the same since the day wee Dermot came flying up to the place in a state of great excitement, to show them a badgers' sett of all things. Maybe,' she went on, 'she's worried for the child, for he's not been near the place since. Geraldine told her he's nearly a prisoner on the farm and he's been forbidden to come here as a punishment, because that day he set off without telling anyone where he was going, or asking if he might. Maybe that bothers Rosie, because for all Dermot is a spoiled wee scut, she's powerfully fond of him.'

'I don't know,' Danny said, running his hands through his hair. 'She's different somehow, though.'

Connie knew she was but she'd not been able to get to the bottom of it either. 'Could be just the weather, son. Dear God it could put years on you, the constant rain and the leaden skies. I know it's stopped for now, but not for long by the look of it. Those clothes Rosie is putting out will gain nothing, for the very air is damp and she'll be fetching them in again shortly.'

Danny grimaced and shook his head. He knew it was more than that. Rosie never laughed any more, and the rare smiles she gave never touched her eyes. Then there was the way she behaved with Phelan. She never seemed to have anything to say to him now, yet once the pair of them had been as thick as thieves. It bothered him that she'd tell him nothing and claim everything was fine, when it so obviously wasn't. He was her friend, surely, as well as her husband? There shouldn't be secrets between them.

'Bless me, Father, for I have sinned, it is a fortnight since my last confession,' Rosie mumbled in the small box in the dimly lit, cold church. It

126

was the evening of Good Friday and all the family, indeed most of the church, would, after attending the 'Stations of the Cross', make a good confession that day.

And Rosie had more to confess than most, for she'd decided to unburden herself to the priest about the weapons, safe in the knowledge he could repeat none of it.

So, after the litany of usual sins, Father McNally enquired, 'Is there anything else, my child?'

He knew there was. Years of hearing confessions had sharpened his awareness in listening to people and he knew there was more Rosie Walsh, whose voice he so clearly recognised, wanted to tell him. Rosie, although aware of the rows of people waiting outside the confessional box, knew that if she didn't tell another person about this whole business she'd burst, and so she replied, 'Yes, Father. It's not something I've done wrong, you understand.'

'Go on.'

'I found something, Father. In fact it was my young brother who found it and brought me to see it. It was a cottage, an old disused place. Only it had been done up, made watertight. I wondered at that, for no-one owns it. It's been derelict for years.' Rosie stopped and the priest urged her on.

Rosie swallowed. 'The floor is covered with a rush mat. There is a hidey-hole under it, cut into the floor and covered with a sod of turf that can be lifted out.'

The priest's blood ran suddenly as cold as ice. He knew what kind of thing might be hidden in such a way in an empty, disused house. Hadn't he had mothers weeping in the confessional before today about the menfolk in their lives, who they feared had got mixed up in subversive activities? Indeed, he'd had young men too, who asked for his blessing in their quest to free Ireland from British tyranny. He'd not been able to do that, of course, but he wasn't surprised when Rosie went on in a whisper to tell him what she had found that day and Phelan's reaction to it.

'I think my brother-in-law is mixed up in this Irish Republican Brotherhood, Father,' Rosie told the priest, 'and he said these are desperate times and the organization is run by desperate men and I wasn't to tell a soul what I'd seen.'

Father McNally didn't know how to advise the girl. 'Are you worried about your brother-in-law? What he might do?'

'Aye, Father.'

'Can you not discuss it with your husband?'

'God, no, Father,' Rosie cried. 'The minute I mention a word of this to him, we'd all be in danger.'

'What would you have me do, child?'

'There's nothing you can do, I don't think,' Rosie said. 'I just had to tell someone.'

'All I can do then is pray for you all.'

'Aye, Father,' Rosie said. 'That never comes amiss, at any rate.'

The priest sighed. Ireland seemed poised on the brink of something and in Europe soldiers were being massacred in their thousands, and all the prayers in the world seemed unable to stop any of it. But this was no way for a priest to think, he chided himself. Didn't he preach that prayers

128

could move mountains?

'Try not to worry too much,' the priest told Rosie. 'I know you might think that's easy for me to say but really there is nothing you can do, unless you can talk to your brother-in-law and make him see sense.'

Rosie knew that wasn't an option. Phelan now avoided speaking to her so obviously that even Danny had noticed and had asked if they'd had a fall-out. God, if only it had been just that. She doubted that even if she did manage to talk to him she could make him change course.

'Say a decade of the rosary for your penance,' the priest said, jerking Rosie back to the present. 'And now make a good act of contrition.'

Rosie said the familiar prayer and then, leaving the confessional box, she headed for the side altar where she prayed earnestly for Phelan. She said not one decade of the rosary but three, playing the beads through her fingers. She lit a candle for good measure and left the church feeling she'd done all she could, yet somehow knowing it wasn't going to be enough.

Much later that same night, Dermot heard footsteps outside his bedroom window. Since his talk with Phelan he'd slept lighter than usual and now the sound of boots on the cobbles woke him with a jolt and he was out of bed and across the room in a flash.

Phelan was outside the window, which had been left slightly open just as Dermot had promised it would be. Dermot pushed it wide and Phelan put a warning finger to his lips. He had the letter ready. 'The Brotherhood are off tomorrow evening,' he said.

'Ooh, Phelan,' Dermot said in an awed whisper. 'Where are you making for?'

'Dublin,' Phelan said and bit his lip in annoyance. He hadn't intended to tell anyone. 'I can't tell you any more and it's really best that you don't know, then you can't tell, whatever pressure is applied.'

'I wouldn't tell,' Dermot said, indignation causing his voice to rise.

'Ssh,' Phelan hissed fiercely. 'All we want now is your sisters and parents in here demanding an explanation about who you're talking to through your bedroom window in the dead of night. I thought you had more sense. Are you sure you're up for this?'

'Aye, aye,' the boy assured him, but in a whisper. 'Please? You can trust me.'

'Right then,' Phelan said. 'Now listen. I won't be missed until the milking on Sunday morning and by then, if all goes to plan, I will be installed in Dublin. You take this letter to my family, no earlier than Sunday afternoon. Can you do that?'

'Course I can.'

'You must hide it till then.'

'Aye,' Dermot said. 'I'll make sure no-one sees it. And may good luck go with you, Phelan. I wish I was old enough to join.'

'I should think there will still be work for you when you're my age,' Phelan told Dermot reassuringly. 'By then, though, the Irish tri-coloured flag will be fluttering over the capital and the English driven from our land.'

It sounded stirring stuff and Dermot was captivated. It seemed such a tiny thing to deliver a letter, but then, if that's what Phelan wanted, he would do it and be proud of the part he'd played in the fight for Ireland.

He didn't know yet how he'd get to leave the house by himself on a Sunday afternoon. His mother had not let him go anywhere since that day in the Easter holidays when he'd found the cottage and the guns. But allowed or not, he'd go out to the Walshes' farm that Sunday afternoon, even if he had to sneak away to do so.

'Give Phelan a knock, will you, Rosie,' Connie asked as Rosie came into the room early on Easter Sunday.

'Isn't he up?' Rosie asked, for at this hour he was usually out in the milking sheds with his father and Danny.

'No, he is not,' Connie said. 'He must have been in powerfully late last night. I never heard him and his father will go mad altogether if he isn't in the milking sheds and quickly.'

Connie thought it strange that she hadn't heard Phelan come in. Although she often dozed through sheer weariness, she always heard him. Maybe, though, he'd come in later than usual to avoid his father, for when he'd nearly jumped up from the tea table the previous evening, scraping his chair across the stone flags, Matt had said, 'Where are you off to in such a tear?'

'Out,' Phelan replied tersely.

Matt, usually such a quiet man, slammed his hand onto the table. 'Don't talk to me like that!

131

Out where, boy?'

Phelan looked straight at his father and the look and words were both insolent. 'Let's say I'm going there and back to see how far it is,' he said.

'You cheeky young bugger, you,' Matt cried, leaping to his feet and catching hold of Phelan by the arm. 'You're not too big yet for a good hiding, let me tell you.'

Rosie held Bernadette, who had started to wail, on her knee, and at Matt's outburst her alarmed eyes met those of Danny's. He seemed unconcerned, though, as if he thought Phelan had asked for anything he got. It was Sarah and Elizabeth and especially Connie who were looking upset.

Phelan tugged his arm from his father's grasp and his words had a jeering note to them. 'Like to see you try,' he said and he strode across the room, snatched his jacket and cap from the hook behind the door and was away.

Matt would have followed him, but Connie stopped him. He sat back at the table, shaking his head. It wouldn't be the end of it, no by Christ it wouldn't. Jeered and cheeked by a mere boy and in front of them all. It was not to be borne. He'd have something to say to that young bugger in the morning.

Connie, attempting to change the subject, had said, 'Well, we'd best get cleared away quickly. Sarah will be seeing her young man if I know anything.'

Sarah sniffed. 'If you mean Sam,' she said, 'I'm not seeing him tonight as it happens.'

'Oh,' Connie said, surprised, for Sarah saw Sam every Saturday evening. 'Why's that then?'

'He said he had something on,' Sarah said disparagingly. 'In fact, he said he probably wouldn't be seeing me for a few days.'

'What's he up to?'

'Oh, Mammy, what's he ever up to? More schoolboy nonsense. Him and his secret organisation. The whole thing gets on my nerves.'

Later, when Rosie went through the girls' bedroom to reach Phelan's, Sarah's words came back to mind. Sarah and Elizabeth were still asleep, the two curled together in the double bed. They had no reason to waken yet and she crossed the room softly and tapped lightly on Phelan's door.

There was no answer, nor was there one to her second, louder tap. 'Phelan,' she hissed. But the room beyond stayed silent. There was no option but to open the door. She stood stock-still in the doorway. She'd made up his bed the previous day and it was obvious it had not been slept in since.

She wondered for a brief moment if something had happened to him. Maybe he'd been attacked and was lying in the road somewhere, or had been tipped into a ditch? But she dismissed these fears as quickly as they'd entered her head, for who would do such a thing to Phelan? No, no-one would hurt the lad, but he seemed hell-bent on hurting himself, for she was sure Phelan's disappearance all night had something to do with the Irish Republican Brotherhood. God alone knew what, but for now, Rosie had to go and break the news to Connie that Phelan was missing.

Danny was angry when Rosie told him about his brother. He'd intended to take Phelan to task that morning for the disrespect he'd shown their father the previous night. He honestly didn't know what had got into him the past few days. He'd been as tense as a coiled spring and inclined to snap for no reason.

Now the young hooligan was on a different tack altogether, not coming home at all. Dear God, their father would kill him when he did eventually return. Well if he did, Danny wouldn't blame him one bit. Enough was enough.

The family all went to early Mass that Easter Sunday morning, so they didn't see any of Rosie's family. 'I bet young Dermot will be glad Lent's over?' Connie commented as they made their way home, trying to lighten the atmosphere which had hung over them since Rosie's discovery. 'Didn't he give up sweets *and* chocolates?'

'Aye, he did,' Rosie said, hitching Bernadette higher onto her hip. 'And hard enough it was for him, I'd say. I hardly saw a sweet when I was growing up and Chrissie and Geraldine the same, but God if you'd see the mountain of sweets and goodies Mammy would bring Dermot from town every week, you'd know how hard it must have been for him.'

'Your mammy's a silly woman where young Dermot is concerned,' Connie said.

'Don't I know it,' Rosie said with feeling.

'I wonder if he managed it?'

'Aye, I think so,' Rosie said. 'The child can be determined enough when he sets his mind to it.' She smiled and went on. 'Chrissie told me he had to fight Mammy to give up anything at all for Lent.'

'All weans give something up,' Connie said, aghast.

'That's what Dermot told Mammy,' Rosie said. 'He told her he was the only one at school not doing without something.'

'Aye, weans hate to be different,' Connie said. 'Mind you, both of us gave up sugar in our tea, didn't we, and I can hardly wait to go home now and have a decent cup well sweetened.'

'And me,' Rosie said with a laugh, for no-one had been able to eat or drink yet that day because of them taking communion. Bernadette, tired of being ignored, starting butting at Rosie's face. 'Stop it!' Rosie said firmly. 'Bad girl.'

Bernadette didn't care a fig about being bad and instead squealed with laughter.

'Give her to me,' Connie said, putting out her arms. 'She must be a ton weight now.'

Rosie was about to hand the baby over gratefully, when Danny, catching up with them, snatched her from Rosie's arms and set her up on his shoulders. 'Did I hear your mammy say you were bad?' he said to the baby, laughing at his young wife. 'Not a bit of it. A wee angel so you are.'

Bernadette screamed with delight and beat at her father's head with her podgy infant hands. 'Mind you,' Danny went on, 'your granny's right about you being a ton weight. Nine months old and still being carried about. About time you took up walking.'

Bernadette had no idea what her father was saying, but she knew she was being spoken about and she shouted out her scribble talk in reply as

135

Danny sidled up to his mother and, mindful of the other people streaming past them from Mass, said in an urgent whisper, 'Go on back to Daddy. He's on the look-out for Phelan and if he should come across him ... well, let's say he won't be fully responsible for his actions.'

Connie shot him a startled glance. 'I can't,' she complained. 'The dinner.'

'I'll see to the dinner,' Rosie told her. 'Go on now, smooth down his feathers. We don't want to see murder done on an Easter morning.'

'I can't say I'd blame Daddy, though,' Danny said, as Connie scurried away. 'God, I'd be livid. Christ, who am I kidding? I *am* livid.'

But thoughts of Phelan had brought to Rosie's mind her own family. 'I'll go home after dinner,' she said. 'I have a bar of chocolate for Dermot. It's Easter Sunday, after all, and I should pay them a visit.'

'Will you take the wee one with you?' Danny said, indicating the waving, babbling Bernadette above him.

'Oh, aye,' Rosie said. 'Dermot wouldn't forgive me if I left her behind. In fact, he probably wouldn't let me in the house at all.'

'He is fond of her all right.'

'More than fond,' Rosie said. 'Our baby is well-loved, Danny, and no harm in that, but I won't have her as spoiled as Dermot is.'

'Sure, there'll be no time to spoil her,' Danny said. 'She'll probably have a wee brother or sister before she's much older and when you have a whole squad of them to rear you'll not have a spare minute to ruin any of them.'

Rosie laughed and thought that Phelan could go hang himself. All the worrying she had done about him had achieved nothing at all but upset those around her, particularly Danny who loved her so much. Well, from now on, she decided, she wouldn't lose a wink's sleep over him. She looked up at Danny and smiled broadly. She had the urge to catch up his hand and run with him as if they were weans, the baby bouncing up and down on his shoulders.

Danny was delighted with the smile that lit up her face and hoped whatever had ailed her was now over. He held the baby's feet with one hand and with the other he pulled Rosie close. She felt so loved and cherished it brought tears to her eyes. She took hold of Danny's hand and, united, they walked home together.

Everyone expected Phelan back for dinner. Connie always said his stomach had often brought him home when he was younger. But when the food was served up there was still no sign of him. Matt was raging: it was almost seeping out of him. When he said menacingly that Phelan would have some explaining to do when he did come home, Rosie thought she would not be in Phelan's shoes for all the tea in China.

The meal was an especially delicious one, and with a steamed pudding now Lent was over, which the family lingered over as if determined they wouldn't let Phelan's non-appearance destroy the meal Connie and Rosie had slaved for hours preparing.

It wasn't entirely successful. Phelan's empty

137

chair was a stark reminder of his absence, and Rosie knew Connie's ears were constantly attuned to hearing her son's boots on the gravel path or across the cobbled yard.

They eventually finished the meal and the men settled before the fire for a smoke, Bernadette on Danny's knee, while the women began collecting the pots, Connie taking every opportunity to peer through the window or the door, left open because of the warmth of the day. Rosie's heart ached for her. How could Phelan just not come home like this? He'd know how his mother would worry so.

Matt too was equally worried and also hurt, but he didn't deal with it the same way as Connie and sat before the fire and talked to Danny about everything under the sun as if he didn't have a care in the world. 'Where d'you think he is?' Connie asked Rosie quietly as they folded the tablecloth together.

'He could be anywhere,' Rosie whispered back. 'Maybe he stayed at a friend's house last night and is afraid to come home.'

'You think that's it?' Connie said desperately. Rosie felt her grasping at straws.

What should she say? If she mentioned the Brotherhood and then found Phelan's disappearance had nothing to do with that, she'd endanger the family. 'I'm sure it will be something simple,' she said reassuringly.

By the time the pots and plates were washed and dried, and the room put to rights, Matt had dropped off before the fire and Bernadette had followed suit, cuddled against her father. 'I could put her in the room and we could have a wee walk out if you've a mind to,' Danny suggested to Rosie. 'It's a fine day and you could go on to your mother's after, when Bernadette wakes up.'

'Aye,' Rosie agreed, though in reality her legs ached and she longed to sit and rest. 'Aye, that would be grand. Will you see to Bernadette, Mammy, and I'll get my coat?'

But as Rosie crossed the floor she saw Dermot streak past the window and come to the threshold of the door, bent over, gasping for breath, his brick-red face glistening with sweat.

'What in God's name...?'

'I have a letter,' Dermot gasped. 'It's from Phelan.'

'Phelan,' Matt said, wakened by the boy's name and leaping to his feet. He took the letter from Dermot and tore it open hastily. All eyes were on him as he scanned the words and then he burst out, 'The bloody little fool. He's joined the Irish Republican Brotherhood and he's off to Dublin to answer Ireland's call.'

Danny passed Bernadette to Sarah and came across to his father and took the letter from him, aware that his mother had begun to cry. He too read the letter and then turned to Dermot. 'How did you know this was from Phelan?'

Dermot had been through this many times. He knew not to say he'd had the letter from late on Friday night, and had chosen not to deliver it till now. It would not be a wise thing to do, and to say he'd spoken to Phelan and knew of his plans wouldn't help his case one bit. 'There was a note to me tied around the letter,' he told Danny. And

139

he went on, 'The letter must have been pushed in the window. It was on the floor of my bedroom.'

'When was this?'

Dermot shrugged. 'Don't know, I found it just now and I thought you should see the letter before anyone else.'

'You did right,' Danny said. 'Good boy.' His eyes raked the room. His mother was wiping her eyes with her apron, his father's face set like stone.

'What of Sam?' Sarah asked suddenly.

Dermot shrugged. He knew Sam was involved, but to say so would bring more questions and he might trip himself up and so he said, 'I don't know about Sam.'

Sarah did, though. She knew her man would be fully embroiled in this nonsense, and she too felt tears seep from her eyes and trickle down her cheeks. She held Bernadette tight against her for comfort. The child, unused to being held so firmly, began to wriggle and Danny took her from Sarah and laid her in the cot in the bedroom, where she curled herself into a ball and put her thumb in her mouth and slumbered on, unaware of the turmoil in the next room.

Rosie was standing stock-still, the feelings of alarm and fear coursing through her body so that she tingled with it. She felt raw, as if every nerve-ending was exposed.

'Find him, Danny!' Connie cried suddenly as Danny came back from the bedroom. 'You must go and find him and bring him home.'

Danny encircled his mother's trembling frame. 'I will, Mammy,' he said. 'Don't worry, I'll not come home without him.' And he kissed his mother's cheek in reassurance.

Then Danny went to Rosie who was standing twisting her hands together agitatedly and he looked into her eyes and saw the fear in them. Oh God, he thought, how I love this woman and our child, and yet he knew what he had to do, and he saw by Rosie's face that she knew too. 'I must go, Rosie.'

Rosie wanted to plead with him, remind him he had a wife, a child, responsibilities. He wasn't to do this. She wouldn't let him. By Christ, what was he thinking of, even suggesting it? But she said none of this. She heard the gulping sobs of Connie and the keening of Sarah, who'd sunk to her knees before the mat as if her legs could no longer hold her up.

Her mouth went very dry as Danny pulled her close. 'The boy's not fifteen until July,' he said. 'I'll look for Sam and Shay too and try and make them see sense, but Phelan will come home if I have to drag him every step of the way. By Christ, when I get hold of him I'll knock the bloody head from his shoulders.'

Rosie laid her head against Danny, too distressed to even cry. 'When will you go?' she asked him brokenly.

'As soon as possible. If Dermot has only just found the letter, they might not have gone far and I might catch up with him before he even gets to Dublin.'

Dermot felt guilty at Danny's words. Danny was hoping to find Phelan on the road somewhere. The reality was he'd probably marched with the Brotherhood all the night long, armed

141

with all the rifles and pistols from the cottage, and they were now positioned in Dublin town and up to any manner of things.

He could say none of this. He'd made a promise to Phelan and yet he was sad to see how upset everyone was. They didn't see the glory in the fight that Phelan had seen and suddenly Dermot didn't know who was right. 'I'm sorry,' he spluttered.

'God, child, sure it's not your fault,' Connie said, wiping her eyes again. 'Come up to the table and have a cup of buttermilk and a wee slab of barnbrack. You're a good boy, so you are.'

Dermot felt anything but good, but he did as he was bid.

Struggling to control her voice, willing it not to break, Rosie said to Danny, 'I'll put some of your clothes in a bundle.'

'I'll not need...'

'It might take longer than you think,' Rosie insisted.

She almost stumbled away from him and when she reached the relative privacy of her own room, she leaned her head against the door and let the tears fall at last. She and Dermot knew what no-one else was aware of: the cache of arms. She would bet that hole in the cottage was empty now. This would never do. She wiped the tears from her eyes impatiently and began to sort out fresh clothes for Danny to take with him. She had no illusions about her young brother-in-law, though she knew Danny thought Phelan had just taken off on some half-brained idea of joining some revolutionary group while in actual fact she knew he'd been involved for some time and she had little doubt that whenever he'd left he'd had a rifle in his hands and bullets in his pocket. They intended to kill and maim. She wanted her Danny nowhere near that. But Phelan was just a boy and she knew Danny, as his elder brother, had to try and save him from himself.

EIGHT

'How long d'you think he'll be?' Connie asked Matt.

'How should I know,' Matt answered shortly, anxiety for his younger son's disappearance and his elder son's mission to find him making him tetchy and his voice sharp. 'It's a tidy walk to Dublin, you know, if he doesn't catch up with him on the road somewhere. And that's not the whole of it. Dublin's not like Blessington, a wee small place where everyone knows everyone else's business. Sure, I would say there are numerous places there where a young man not wishing to be found could hide out.'

So that's it, Rosie thought. Could take any time at all. It was like asking how long was a piece of string. She sighed, the burden of what she knew about the hidden arms weighing heavily on her, and she wondered for the umpteenth time if she should tell them. But for what? She doubted that knowledge would make them feel better and she remembered Phelan's warnings well enough. There was no way she would risk bringing further danger or sorrow on this family.

The following day she wrapped Bernadette in her shawl, picked up the chocolates and sweets she had bought as presents, and went across the fields to her parents' house. Bernadette was becoming more beautiful every day. Now her fair

144

hair was beginning to curl as she grew, just like Dermot's, much to his delight. Her eyes, though, were a deep lilac-blue, ringed with dark lashes, while her nose was a cute button. Her mouth was wide and when she smiled you could see her four little teeth at the front. She was going on for ten months old now and could say some words and pull herself up on the furniture. Rosie loved the very bones of her, as did all the Walshes and Rosie's sisters, while Dermot continued to be enchanted by her every word or action.

Rosie's parents took little notice of their only grandchild and Rosie tried not to mind, telling herself it was only what she'd come to expect, but she'd have loved to discuss the baby's progress with her mother, or laugh together at something she did.

But all Minnie was interested in now was Dermot having sneaked away to their house the previous day. 'And with not so much as a by-your-leave,' she cried, indicating the boy standing before her, his face flushed and shuffling his feet on the stone floor of the cottage.

Rosie knew he'd told his parents nothing about the letter, either before he delivered it or after, and she was pleased. Connie had advised Rosie to say nothing of Phelan's disappearing and Danny in pursuit if Dermot hadn't already. 'Sure, we don't want half the county alerted,' she'd said. 'They might be back before we realise they've gone and least said, you know...'

So Rosie didn't enlighten her parents to the reason for Dermot's visit the previous day, but stung by their indifference to her child and by the discoloured bruise on Geraldine's cheek, she cried out, 'Why shouldn't he come and see me, his own sister, and the wee baby he's uncle to? As for not asking permission, if you'd let him come when he wants, he'd not have to sneak away.'

'When I want advice on how to bring up my own son, I'll ask you,' Minnie snapped back.

'Aye,' Rosie commented wryly. 'That'll be the day, but I'm warning you now, tying the boy to your apron strings is not the way to go on. No wonder he deceives you.'

Never had Rosie spoken in such a way to her mother and she looked at Minnie's outraged face after her outburst and wondered if she'd order her from the house. 'Look,' she continued in a conciliatory way. 'Let's not quarrel. Never mind what Dermot did yesterday. Today is a new day. Let's sit down to the fine meal Chrissie and Geraldine have got ready, and after it I'll share the sweets and chocolates I have with me.'

'Well,' Minnie said at last. 'I've never been spoken to in such a way before. I hope you don't think, Rosie, because you're a married woman you can show such lack of respect for your parents. We'll say nothing about it this time, but I'd like you to remember it for the future.'

Rosie bit her lip and took the rebuke without any retort. She heard her sisters' small sighs of relief and saw the look of gratitude Dermot flashed her.

The next day, the Walsh girls, returning to work after the Bank Holiday, came home in a state of great agitation. 'There's been a rebel uprising in Dublin,' Sarah said. 'I hope to God Sam and

Phelan aren't mixed up in it.'

'What did you say?' Matt asked, shocked.

'An uprising, Daddy. It's the talk of the place. We brought you the *Dublin Express* to see for yourself,' Sarah told him, handing her father the paper. The main picture showed Dublin's General Post Office with British soldiers littering the ground before it. From the roof there fluttered two flags and the reporter described them. One was the tricolour flag of Ireland and the other a green flag emblazoned with a harp and the words 'Ireland's Republic'.

'They have taken areas on both sides of the Liffey,' Matt read out to Connie and Rosie, who had stopped their preparations for the meal at the girls' news. 'They also hold the South Dublin Union, The Four Courts and Boland's Mill,' Matt went on, pointing at the pictures in the paper.

'By Christ,' he declared. 'What in God's name are they thinking of?'

'You don't think they have a hope then, Daddy?' Sarah said.

Matt answered gently. He knew she was thinking of Sam, and he was thinking of his sons, one possibly embroiled in the mayhem and the other walking straight into danger because of him. 'How could it succeed, cutie dear? It's like tipping a bucket of water into the Liffey and hoping to make a difference, even ten buckets, a hundred buckets.'

Rosie's mouth was so dry she could barely speak. Fear clutched at her heart. Her Danny, her darling husband, was marching straight into that hell-hole, and all because of bloody Phelan! Surely to God Danny was too sensible to get involved? He was totally against any rebel activity. It wasn't his way. He was a farmer, a pacifist, and although he wanted Home Rule and a united Ireland as well as the next man, he wouldn't think it would be achieved by taking on the might of the British Army.

Connie listened horror-struck to Matt's words and her heart seemed to stop. Phelan wouldn't be involved in any of this. He was but a boy, only fourteen years old. But if he was and she'd charged Danny to bring him home… Oh God, it didn't bear thinking about. Her two boys…

With her heart hammering against her ribs and fear showing in every vestige of her face, she said, 'Phelan wouldn't get mixed up in this, sure he wouldn't?'

It was a plea to Matt, a plea for him to tell her of course Phelan wouldn't. But Matt had worked alongside the boy day after day and knew more of his views than Connie. The look he cast her spoke volumes and she moaned, 'Oh dear Christ, no.'

Rosie could stand no more. She put down the plates she'd been holding since Sarah and Elizabeth had burst through the door and took the cutlery Connie clutched in her hands, putting it on the table and holding Connie tight, two women in distress, taking comfort and giving comfort. Rosie's cheeks were wet when she released Connie. 'Come,' she said, leading her before the fire. 'Sit down, I have something to say to you all.'

She knew then she had to tell them of the cache of weapons she and Dermot had found. The veil of secrecy hardly mattered now, and she knew the place would be cleared. Every gun and bullet would be needed for this uprising and though she doubted her news would help the family, she couldn't let them go on in ignorance.

Rosie crouched before her mother-in-law and told them every last detail.

'Why didn't you tell us sooner?' Matt asked, stunned.

'What difference would it have made, Daddy?' Rosie asked, raising her head to face him.

'I could have kept a weather eye on him,' Matt said. 'Stopped it going this far.'

'Daddy, no-one could have stopped him,' Rosie said. 'He was fully committed to it. I know that much. Anyway, he swore Dermot and I to secrecy. He said if news of where the guns were stored got out, revenge could easily be taken by some of the desperate men of the Brotherhood. I was scared and yes, I admit it, but I wasn't only scared for myself and Dermot, I was frightened for all of you. How could I tell you after Phelan said that, and put you all in danger?'

'That's what made you so jumpy and nervy?' Connie said, remembering back. 'Danny couldn't understand what was the matter.'

'I hated keeping it secret from you, but the alternative seemed worse.'

'Aye,' Connie said with a sigh. 'You could do little else.'

'Well what's to be done?' Sarah cried. 'We can't just sit here and...'

'That's exactly what we must do, all we can do is sit here,' Matt said.

'Maybe Danny will send news to us soon,' Rosie said. 'He told me he'd try to if he couldn't bring Phelan back with him straight away.'

'Let's hang on to that at least,' Matt said. 'And we'll hope and pray for the safety of both our boys and Sam too. I'm away up to the Fergusons after my dinner to see for myself if Willie has any more news of Shay.'

But Willie Ferguson knew nothing further, Matt told his family on his return, though whatever was in the offing, Shay and Niall were fully involved, for both were missing too.

The next day and the one after, Connie expected a letter, a telegram even, to say they were safe, but nothing came and each evening the girls brought home the *Dublin Express*.

It made grim reading and brought only further heartache. There were other minor insurrections in County Meath, Galway and Wexford, the paper reported, but the skirmishes were brought under control quickly, the rebel leaders dealt with and martial law declared.

On Wednesday evening they heard of the ship *Helga* that had sailed unchallenged up the Liffey and begun bombarding Liberty Hall, the headquarters of the Citizens' Army. British guns had been set up in Trinity College and were shelling Sackville Street and the General Post Office buildings, while rebels ambushed a party of ten thousand reinforcement soldiers at Mount Street Bridge, on their way from the harbour at Kingstown. Another gang of rebels had assembled in St Stephen's Green.

There had been heavy British casualties, but eventually the rebels were forced out of the Green and into the Royal College of Surgeons. But by

150

then the whole centre of Dublin was burning.

Food was not getting through to the shops, the paper reported. Normal life for the average Dubliner had stopped. The centre was a no-go area with the army shooting anything or anybody that moved and while Dublin burned, its citizens starved.

Friday's paper told of further reinforcements pouring into the city and the evacuation of the General Post Office. 'This must be it,' Matt commented. 'They can't hold out any longer, surely to God.'

He looked around at the womenfolk, all ashen-faced, and admired their stoicism even though sorrow was deeply etched on their faces. He was coming to realise that he might never see either of his sons again and he wondered if they'd thought that far ahead.

Rosie had. She took Bernadette into bed with her at nights, for the big bed seemed very empty. She was more precious than ever, a wee part of Danny, and, Rosie thought, all she might ever have of him again. She'd never known worry before, she realised, not this gnawing, nagging worry that seemed to occupy every hour of the day. It had lodged like a hard immovable lump in her stomach.

She wished she could do something other than read about what was happening in her capital city a few miles away, but each night she'd see the shattered and shelled buildings in the pages of the newspaper and hear of the Dubliners trapped in their homes and knew she could do nothing but wait and pray.

And then, as suddenly as it had begun, it was over. Matt had gone into Blessington especially to buy the evening paper, as Elizabeth and Sarah finished work at lunchtime on Saturday.

That night they sat around the table and discussed the surrender. 'Maybe I should go and see the situation for myself,' Matt said.

'How could you?' Connie snapped. 'Dear Christ, aren't you run off your feet already and this the busiest time on the farm?'

Rosie glanced at her father-in-law. She knew Connie spoke the truth for the farm work was usually split between Matt and his two sons. Matt was out from dawn till way past dusk each evening and his face was often grey with fatigue.

And yet she understood his need to know, to do something other than sit there and wait. It was killing her too. Someone had to go to Dublin Town and see what had happened to Danny. Phelan could jump into the Liffey for all she cared, yet she knew that Connie would want news of him too. She was also becoming fast aware that she was the only one who could go, for she could hardly expect an older woman like Connie to do it and Elizabeth and Sarah had jobs to go to.

But Rosie had gone nowhere all her life except Blessington village. She was not a seasoned traveller who could nip onto a tram with ease as if she'd done it every day of her life, and now the thought of visiting that war-ravaged city filled her with dread. She remembered the pictures in the paper, the shattered and burned buildings and the ground around littered with the bodies of soldiers and felt a shudder run through her. When she spoke, however, her voice was firm and determined so no-one could guess at her true feelings. 'I'll go,' she said suddenly. 'That is, if you'll mind Bernadette – I can't take her with me.'

'Oh Rosie! Dear God. Don't do this,' Connie said.

'I must, Mammy,' Rosie said firmly. 'Danny means the world to me. If ... if he's dead, I have to know, I'd want him brought home and buried decently.'

'But it's dangerous.'

'No more, Mammy,' Rosie said. 'And don't tell me you don't want to know what has happened to Danny and ... and Phelan?'

She had trouble even saying the young boy's name. She knew if Danny died, she'd not forgive Phelan for as long as she lived. But maybe he lay dead too. She couldn't go on like this. She'd have to go and find out, but for all her brave words to her mother-in-law she was terrified of what she'd see and hear there.

She didn't allow herself to think of it any more though. Instead, she said, 'I shall go on Monday morning if you'll see to Bernadette.'

'Ah cutie dear, do you have to ask?' Connie said. 'I'll look after her and welcome, if you are determined.'

'Aye, Mammy, I am,' Rosie said.

'I wish I could go with you,' Sarah said wistfully. 'But we're rushed off our feet. The supervisor, Mrs Clancy, would take a dim view of it altogether. She's never had any sympathy with the uprising at all. She's called them irresponsible hotheads from the beginning and said that

153

they deserved all they got. She won't even allow us to discuss it at work.'

'I'll find out about Sam for you too,' Rosie said, knowing why Sarah would like to be the one to go.

'Sam!' Sarah cried with a defiant lift of her head that sent her black curls bouncing. 'Don't worry about him, Rosie, he's nothing to me. Did he think of me when he went running off with the other halfwits he'd been playing soldiers with? He did not. Well, he can go hang for I shan't care if he's alive or dead.'

But Rosie knew that feelings for someone could not be turned off like that and saw the deep hurt reflected in Sarah's haunted eyes.

The following day, after a big Sunday dinner which she could barely touch, Rosie went off to her parents' house. She seldom went on Sundays, but wanted to tell them of her decision to go to Dublin the following day. She didn't expect their support, which was as well, for she didn't get it. They were scornful of the rebels' abortive stand and thought her plain mad to go running to Dublin to see for herself. Chrissie and Geraldine, on the other hand, were astounded at her bravery and Dermot gazed at her with pure awe.

It was Geraldine who walked her to the gate as she left and said as soon as they were out of ear-shot of the house, 'I wish I could go with you for I'll worry about you every minute until you're back.'

Going home, Rosie thought she'd be glad of Geraldine's company, anyone's company in fact.

Anyone to help still the panic that rose in her every time she thought of going to Dublin and someone to stand beside her when she found out what exactly had happened to Danny.

But there was no help available. She would have to overcome her fear and panic and so she resolved to set off, resolutely and alone, the next morning.

Just a little later she stopped dead at the farmhouse door and stared at Phelan as he sat on a dining chair beside the table which Connie was piling with food. Rosie didn't take into account Phelan's gaunt state, nor his white, strained face and red-rimmed eyes. He, who'd begun it all, was here, alive, at home in his kitchen, food piled around him like the prodigal son. Anger coursed through her veins. 'Where's Danny?' she demanded.

Phelan looked at her with eyes full of sorrow and shook his head. 'I don't know.'

Rosie put Bernadette down, leaped across the floor and yanked Phelan out of the chair and she shook him violently.

'Here, here,' Matt said, pulling Rosie away from Phelan but holding her tight against him, his arms wrapped around her in support.

But Rosie needed answers and she continued to yell at Phelan. 'What d'you mean you don't know? You must know, you were there, for Christ's sake.'

'Leave the boy now,' Connie said, touching Rosie's arm. 'Let him eat. He'll tell us all in time.'

Rosie sank into a chair and put her head in her hands and wept, for Phelan's presence, without

155

his brother and also without any news of him, seemed to bode only ill.

Phelan didn't tell them all, he couldn't, but he told them enough and as Rosie listened she rocked her daughter on her knee. Bernadette's warm presence tucked against her mother soothed her and helped a little to ease the aching dread in her heart.

'I suppose now you know I was a member of the Brotherhood?' Phelan said with a glance around at them all.

'We know,' Matt said heavily, 'though Rosie didn't tell us all immediately. Apparently you charged her not to.'

'Aye' Phelan said. 'I did, but only because I was feared for her.'

'All right,' Matt said sharply. 'We know now you haven't the brains you were born with to join such a crackpot organisation, so tell us the rest. What use was a young boy like you to them?'

'Well, at first I was just a messenger, and Niall too,' Phelan said. 'I didn't know Danny was looking for me. He'd have had a job tracking me down because I was all over the place. Anyway, Dublin wasn't the safest place in the world to walk about looking for someone.'

Phelan stopped there. How could he tell them, his family, of the exhilaration that had filled him at being part of it all at first? That thought had sustained him in the long march to Dublin and when they'd reached the capital and he'd seen the other rebel groups assembled there, he'd felt his heart almost overflow with pride. He couldn't share this. They wouldn't understand. Unless a person had been there they couldn't. He decided to stick to the bare facts instead and so he went on, 'Even for me and Niall it was scary stuff, going from one rebel stronghold to another with messages. By Tuesday evening it was decided it was too dangerous for us to go on and we'd be more useful with a rifle in our hands.

'We were sent to houses overlooking Mount Street Bridge. More reinforcements from England were expected on Wednesday and they had to cross the bridge from Kingstown Harbour – we were to try and keep them back.'

Again Phelan stopped. He remembered the commander of the few men stationed in the house asking him, 'You handled a rifle before, son?'

'Aye, sir. We have a farm. I've been handling a rifle since I was twelve.' He hadn't added that that was a mere two years before. 'And then I've been a member of the Brotherhood these past months.'

Not, of course, that they fired many shots there; each bullet was too precious to waste. 'Each one is for an English heart,' as Shay would say.

Phelan had remembered standing at the upstairs window early that Wednesday morning. The sun hadn't broken through the mottled clouds and the sky was pink tinged and Phelan had watched in horrified amazement as the *Helga* sailed up the Liffey and began bombarding Liberty Hall. But a shout from below had brought his gaze away from the ship and back to the task in hand.

'A large company of soldiers had unloaded at Kingstown.' Phelan continued. 'We were told to stand ready.'

He remembered his heart hammering against his ribs, and his hands so sticky with sweat he wondered whether he would be able to hold the rifle steady and pull the trigger. He had wondered too what good the handful of them would be against so many soldiers. There was rumoured to be ten thousand of them.

'And then they were upon us. Wave after wave of them,' Phelan said. 'For all we killed, there was another ten to take their place. The commander had a machine gun and the rat-tat-tat of that was continuous as the men went down in rows.'

He didn't tell his listening family how the killings had bothered him. He was a good shot, his rifle usually found its target, but Phelan had found it was one thing to kill a fox to save the poultry and to kill a rabbit for a pie or stew, but quite another to kill another living, breathing human being. Some of the soldiers had looked little older than him and they had jerked and fallen one after the other till the street ran with a scarlet stream of blood. More than once he had felt bile rise in his throat, but feeling sick had been a luxury he couldn't allow himself and he had fought down the nausea as he lifted his rifle again.

'Danny found me there,' Phelan said. 'It had died down by then and the soldiers had routed the lot in the Green and they'd retreated to the Royal College of Surgeons. We knew when they gave a mind to it they'd be back to finish us off, so we were making plans to leave when Danny arrived. He'd met Shay outside and spoken to him.'

'So Shay's alive?'

'He was then,' Phelan said. 'And Danny, and

your Sam, Sarah. Now, I don't know. Danny wiped the floor with the man in charge about Niall and myself. He said he didn't want to belong to a united Ireland won by weans. I was a bit mad hearing us described as weans, but Danny was so angry already with me, I didn't want to give him further cause to go for me, so I kept quiet and so did Niall. He said we were too young to make that sort of commitment.

'But then the man asked him what manner of Irishman Danny was, said that we'd joined the organisation of our own free will, and they needed every man they could get and he wasn't letting anyone go. Danny was angry, raging mad, but so was every other man there and I was afraid Danny would get himself shot. Then Shay suggested Danny took our places.

'I could see Danny wasn't happy about it. I mean we all know what he felt from the beginning about the violence. But he knew that would be the only way that we would be released.

'I begged and pleaded to be allowed to stay, but it was no good. Neither man would listen to me.'

He didn't go on to say he and Niall had watched Danny take the oath of allegiance that the commander had insisted on. He'd sworn the same oath himself, alongside Niall, but theirs was now null and void because of their ages, while Phelan knew Danny's oath would be for life. He knew there was no getting out of the Brotherhood once you were in it.

'Shay smuggled us out,' he went on. 'Everyone was off the streets because the soldiers were taking pot-shots at any movement or sudden

159

noise. Shay said there was a Captain Colthurst I had to watch out for, because he'd shoot the legs from under a person he didn't like the look of. He'd killed four men stone dead just the previous day who weren't even part of the uprising – four innocent men, gunned down for no reason. I told Shay I'd take good care not to come across him.

'We were told to head for home, but neither of us could do that with Danny and Shay and Sam up to their necks in it, so we hung about the streets, taking care not to go too near the centre and be caught in the crossfire.

'By the time we heard of the surrender on Saturday morning we were both light-headed with hunger and tiredness. We hung around for a bit to see if any would be released, but they marched the whole lot off. People said they were to be taken to a place called Kilmainham Jail. It was awful – the crowds pelted them with anything they could lay their hands on.

'I'm so sorry, Rosie,' Phelan said sadly.

'Sorry, huh,' Rosie repeated bitterly. 'That's all right then, if you're sorry,' and then she pressed her face as close to Phelan as she could and said threateningly, *'You'll* be sorrier before you're much older if anything has happened to Danny. I'm off to Dublin to see for myself tomorrow.'

There was a howl of protest from Phelan, but Rosie would take no heed of it. She was determined to find out what had happened to her husband and she intended staying in Dublin until she did.

NINE

Rosie woke the following morning with a pounding headache after her fitful sleep and she wasn't surprised for she was very apprehensive of what lay ahead of her. Of course, she wondered if Dublin would ever recover from the onslaught upon it. According to the papers, many of the fine buildings had been destroyed or damaged in some way. And for what? Damned all, that's what. But what worried Rosie was the news Dublin might hold for her.

Matt Walsh, seeing the consternation on his daughter-in-law's face, was more worried than ever at letting her go to Dublin alone. And he was equally worried about Phelan – seemed to be all at sixes and sevens and burdened down with shame. At least, Matt thought, he might have learned a lesson from it, but at what cost?

Willie Ferguson was all for sending Niall to America where he had relatives to try and keep him out of trouble, but Matt knew Connie would never agree to allow Phelan, at such a young age, to travel so far on his own. But then perhaps there was no need for it at all. When Rosie returned with the news from Dublin, whether it was good or bad, maybe they could learn to cope with it. At least they would know where they stood.

Connie insisted Rosie eat something before she went and she also packed some food in the bag she was taking with a change of clothes in. 'I may not need them at all,' Rosie told Connie, 'for I may be home this evening, but I'll not come home without news of Danny. This is just a precaution.'

'Of course it is, darling child,' Connie said. 'And it's madness to go so far and find out nothing. Anyway, I'd rather you wait till the next morning than try to get home after dark for the trams haven't got lights and God knows, there's been more than enough accidents, even deaths on them.

'But mind,' she went on, 'find the Sisters of Mercy. Like I told you yesterday, I have an aunt in the order, Sister Cuthbert. They're not just Holy Joes, you know, though I'm sure they pray more than enough: but they do great good besides helping the poor and sick and all. My aunt's been in Birmingham, where they have another place, but I had a letter from her at Christmastime to say she's back in Baggot Street in the place they call "The House of Mercy". Anyone will tell you where it is. They'll put you up for the night if you have to stay.'

Rosie was glad to have the name of a safe place if it was necessary and she thanked Connie and helped her pack a basket of provisions for Danny. 'I've hard-boiled the six eggs,' Connie said, 'for Danny would hardly have anything to cook them on. And I've put him in some ham, a circle of soda bread, some slices of barnbrack, a bit of butter and cheese, and his pipe and a twist of baccy.'

'Lovely, Mammy,' Rosie said, wondering if her man would be alive to taste such delights. But she had to keep believing he was. 'I've put him a clean shirt and jumper in too. It will do to cover the basket as well.'

Connie suddenly bit her lip anxiously and cried out, 'Oh God, Rosie, what if…?'

'Mam, stop it!' Rosie said firmly. 'Grieve and cry when you have reason. Let me go and find out before we start speculating. My heart is already as heavy as lead. Don't make things worse.'

She doubted if anything she said would make any difference, but thankfully Matt came in then and she knew Connie would not like to give way before him.

'Are you ready?' Matt asked. 'We must be gone soon if you are to catch that tram.'

'Aye, I'm ready, we can go as soon as I bid Bernadette goodbye,' Rosie said, lifting the child in her arms as she kissed her and told her to be good for her granny and granddaddy.

'She'll be fine with us,' Connie assured her.

'Don't I know that? If I had a minute's doubt, I wouldn't leave her.' She hugged Bernadette tight again and the baby, although surprised to be scooped up in such a way, was only too ready for attention at any time. When Rosie eventually held the child away from her, Bernadette chuckled. She put her podgy baby hands on either side of her mother's cheeks and laughed louder, while Rosie felt tears prick in her eyes to be leaving her behind.

But, she told herself, I owe it to Bernadette to find out whether she has a daddy or not, and so, with a melancholy sigh, she kissed her once more on the cheek and handed her to Connie. She followed Matt out to the cobbled yard where the horse and cart stood waiting, the horse tossing his head and snorting in his impatience to be off.

Phelan stood watching them from the door. Matt noticed Rosie's slight stiffening as she spotted him and he barked at Phelan. 'Don't be standing about, boy, when there's work to be done. Have you weeded the onions?'

'Not yet.'

'Well get to it unless you want to live on fresh air next year,' Matt continued as he climbed into the cart. 'I'll expect it done by the time I'm back.' And with a flick of the reins, the two were off.

They were on the road before Matt said gently, 'He's just a boy, Rosie.'

Rosie was too worried and frightened of what she'd find in Dublin to spare any kind thoughts on Phelan. 'A boy, Daddy. You call him a boy when he was prepared to kill a man for a cause that they were bound to lose, a cause his brother may have sacrificed his life for. Don't try and get me to feel sorry for Phelan. He was old enough to know what he was doing.'

Matt said nothing more. He didn't blame Rosie in the slightest for feeling the way she did about the lad. There was silence between them after that, the only sounds the clop of the horse's hooves and the cart's wheels on the road. Both were too full of their own thoughts to try and make conversation.

Before they came to Blessington they drove along the edge of a large and very beautiful lake that was mainly fed from the River Liffey, running down the side of the Kippure Mountains. Rosie had played by the edge of that lake many a time as a child, then Matt was leaving the lake behind as he turned into the main street of the village itself.

The blacksmith was shoeing a horse as they passed, the doorway open, and Rosie sniffed and caught the smell of hot iron and steam and the blacksmith looked up from his work, the horse's hoof held against his leather apron. 'Hi up there, Matt. Where are you bound for?' Matt gave a wave but didn't slacken the pace of the horse as he shouted, 'Can't stop. Rosie has a tram to catch.'

'A tram is it?' the blacksmith said and both Rosie and Matt knew the man would probably have dropped the horse's hoof and be standing and watching their progress down the street. Many of the shopkeepers, opening for business, came out on hearing the horse's clopping hooves and the wheels rattling over the cobbles, to see who was passing. The little woman from the bakery was one who came out to wave and call out to them and would have stopped for a chat given half a chance.

The plump butcher was already standing in his shop doorway, surveying the day, resplendent in his striped, stained apron. His shirt was pushed up his arms and the bulging forearms beneath looked as pink and succulent as the hams he had hanging from a hook in the shop. 'You're out early Matt?'

'Aye, I'm taking Rosie to the tram.'

'Oh aye,' the butcher said and waited for Matt to explain why, but Matt said, 'Can't stop. See you later.'

Early shoppers hailed them too and Matt knew many would like to know what had brought Rosie and Matt into town together so early. When Matt saw the curtains of the post office twitch as they passed, he knew they wouldn't have long to wait to find out. 'There's three ways of transmitting news quickly,' he remarked wryly to Rosie as the drove into the depot. 'Telegraph, telephone and tell a woman. Some women are better than others, but the postmistress is in a class of her own. Our business will probably have reached America's shores by this afternoon.'

'Does that matter to you?'

'Nay, I don't suppose so,' Matt had to admit. 'Though many will think I'm the worst in the world letting you go all on your own.'

'We've been through this, Daddy.'

'I know, I'm just saying.'

'Let them think what they like, the town's folk,' Rosie said with spirit. 'They don't all know what it's like to wait day after day with no news.'

Matt marvelled at Rosie's courage and she was glad he couldn't hear her heart hammering in her chest at the enormity of what lay ahead.

To distract herself and Matt, she began walking around the depot. She knew it well, not because she'd ridden on the trams but because it was one of Dermot's favourite places. She could understand the fascination it held for a young boy, since it wasn't just a tram stop but had once been the terminus of the tram. Later the tram tracks had been extended as far as Poulaphuca.

There were mending sheds at Blessington where sometimes there would be men working on an engine in overalls, covered in dirt and oil. Dermot would watch them in silence as they worked and wonder if their mammies would give out to them for the state of their clothes and hands and faces, as his mammy surely would if he went home half as bad.

When he had asked Rosie that question one day she'd laughed, even though she really felt sorry for the boy, for her mother always had Dermot dressed up to the nines for a visit to the village. He was always warned to keep his clothes clean and tidy. His sisters never dared let him leap after the other young boys and get up to all kinds of devilment, lest he rip or soil his clothes. If he did that the sisters, not Dermot, would feel the power of their mother's hands and fists for not keeping a better eye on him.

So before she had married Danny and left home, Rosie often took Dermot somewhere that might entertain him. And when he'd finally turn from the engines there was always something to examine in the wagons in the sidings, often waiting to be hitched onto the trams going towards either Terenure or Poulaphuca. Then there was the passing loop too and Rosie would time her visit if she possibly could, so that Dermot would see it in action.

She breathed a sigh of relief when she first saw the steam tram approaching, its horn blowing to clear the track ahead, its funnels puffing out billowing white clouds of smoke that floated into the spring air. Eventually, the tram pulled up at the stop with a hiss of steam.

Matt was delighted to see he knew the conductor. 'Look after my girl, will you?' he asked, indicating Rosie making her way up the tram. 'She's for Dublin and has never been before. Tell her where to get off and all will you?'

'I will and it will be no bother, but Dublin's not a place I'd be making for just now, unless I had to.'

'It's not from choice,' Matt replied sadly. 'The woman is my daughter-in-law and it's her husband, my son, that she's seeking news of.'

'Was he involved in that last little lot?'

'Yes, we think so,' Matt said wearily. 'That's the very devil of it. Danny was against it from the beginning, but his younger brother was caught up in it and him not fifteen until July. When we found out he'd gone, Danny went after him. The boy's home now, him and his friend and both unharmed, but he said Danny took his place and we know nothing more. Rosie said she must go and see for herself.'

'She's a brave lassie.'

'She is that,' Matt said. 'She's fitted into our family as if she's always lived with us and has been a fine wife to Danny and a wonderful mother to their wee baby.'

'Well, please God the news will be good when she gets into the city,' the conductor said. 'Don't you worry, she'll be as safe as houses with me and I'll show her where to catch the electric tram later.'

'Thank you,' Matt said. 'To tell you the truth, I'm worried to death about what she might find out, and on her own too. But I mustn't keep you talking. You have a timetable to abide by. I'll hold

168

you up no longer.'

The conductor nodded and rang the bell for the driver to start and the tram lurched forward. Rosie, settling herself in the seat, had one last brief glimpse of Matt waving to her before they pulled out of sight.

'Hello there,' the conductor said suddenly beside her. 'Return to Terenure, is it?'

'I suppose,' Rosie said. 'Is that where I must change trams for Dublin?'

'Aye,' the conductor said. 'There are no steam trams allowed in Dublin itself. Terenure is just on the outskirts and you have to catch an electric tram from there. But it's fifteen and a half miles away yet, so you can relax a wee while. I'll put you right, never fear. The next stop is Crosschapel.'

The tram rattled on, past Crosschapel village where there was a small delay because there was a siding there and a few passengers to pick up and goods to load in the wagons at the back.

'We'll be at Brittas in a little while,' the conductor said, once again at Rosie's elbow just a little later. 'Busy stop that, and we usually have quite a wait. We bring supplies in for the Kilbride Camp and they all have to be unloaded.'

Rosie didn't mind the stop at all, she had no wish to reach Dublin in any sort of a hurry and she was entertained by the activity at the station, like the unloading of supplies into carts and the people standing in the doorway of the Brittas Inn, looking on and giving advice that was neither asked for nor helpful, and often caused hilarity amongst the onlookers.

The woman sitting beside Rosie was becoming

impatient. 'It should only take one and a half hours to reach Terenure from Blessington,' she told Rosie, clucking her tongue in annoyance. 'At this rate it will be afternoon before we arrive.'

'I don't mind that much,' Rosie said. 'It's all new to me, you see. I've never been on a tram before.'

'Ah,' said the woman, 'well, look to your right as we approach the next station, the mountains of Mourne are visible on a clear day.'

And Rosie did see them soon after, way, way in the distance, dark green with purple swathes here and there. 'You can see for miles,' she said in amazement and the woman smiled.

'We're seven hundred feet above sea level,' she said. 'That's why.'

'Are we?'

'Aye,' the woman said. 'You'll know we are in a minute, for after we're through this station, we'll descend so quickly if you don't hold tight you'll be flung forward, so be warned.'

Rosie was glad she was, for the tram had not long left Crooksling when it seemed to almost tip forward before hurtling down the incline at a terrific speed. Rosie tried not to think about the tales she'd heard of trams jumping off the rails and the number of people killed each year. 'Quite scary, isn't it?' said the woman, seeing Rosie's knuckles whiten where she'd gripped the seat hard.

'Aye, it is,' Rosie replied, sighing with relief that the tracks had finally levelled out and they were now travelling at a more sedate pace.

'My children love it whenever I have them with

170

me,' the woman went on. 'But then children don't see danger, do they? I have three and they have my hair near white at times, the mischief and pranks they get up to.'

'Are they in Dublin, your children?' Rosie asked, thankful to have some distracting conversation.

'No, with their daddy in Terenure, that's where I live,' the woman said. 'I've been up to visit my mother in Poulaphuca. She hasn't been at all well, which is why I didn't want to take any of the children with me this time. In fact, she was so poorly I ended up staying the night. I wouldn't go to Dublin at the moment for a pension.'

'Nor me, by choice,' Rosie said, and then, despite the fact the woman was a stranger, or maybe because of it, she found herself telling her everything. The woman listened without saying a word, but her eyes spoke her sympathy and finally she said, 'it might not be as bad as you fear, my dear.'

'Aye, and it may be far worse,' Rosie said. 'But however bad the news is, it is a hundred times better than knowing nothing day after day.'

The conductor, coming up the tram jiggling his money bag and punching tickets, put an end to anything further the woman would have said, informing them the tram was approaching Embankment Halt.

'This is where we take on water,' the conductor told Rosie, 'and where the mail for Staggart and Rathcoole villages is taken off the tram to be delivered by a fine fellow, by the name of John Kelly, who collects it in his pony and trap.'

'It's fascinating, isn't it?' Rosie said to the woman beside her. 'All the things the tram carries, besides people I mean.'

The woman smiled. 'Maybe the first few times you make the trip,' she said. 'I'm well used to it now. When we come to the next halt, Jobstown, the carters will be waiting to load stone from the De Selby quarries.'

'Tallaght and Killinarden have quarries too,' the conductor commented, 'but we don't get much there. Most of the large boulders are sent to Kilmainham Jail for the prisoners to break into smaller pieces.'

He went silent for a minute, remembering what Matt Walsh had told him about the young woman's husband. According to what he'd heard, all those who'd survived the insurrection had been sent to Kilmainham Jail so her man could well be in that prison. Him and his big mouth!

But Rosie wasn't offended or upset. She knew Danny in jail was the best outcome she could possibly hope for.

As the tram pulled away from Tallagh Halt she had her first sight of the Dublin Hills. She felt her stomach turn over and again doubted the wisdom of what she was doing.

A few minutes later, the woman nudged her and pointed out of the window. 'See that branch line? It goes to the aerodrome, and belongs to the British Government.'

'Aerodrome!' Rosie repeated incredulously.

'Aye, the British and Germans are flying planes now. They're fighting each other in the air as well, or so people tell me.'

'Dear God!' Rosie remarked. 'You'd never get me up in one of those things.'

'Oh I agree,' the woman said. 'If God wanted a man to fly he'd have given him wings, that's what I say.'

Suddenly, there was another sharp dip in the road, and again Rosie had to grip the seats hard to prevent herself falling forward, and then to stop herself being thrown into her fellow passenger as the tram passed so close to the gable end of a set of cottages that she gasped, certain they were going to crash into them.

'It has been known, I believe,' the woman said, when Rosie shared her fears. 'Did you notice the sign?'

'Aye,' Rosie said. '"Beware of the trams."'

'That's because so many people have been knocked down and injured there,' the woman told her. 'One man even said his thatch was set on fire by a spark from the tram's chimney. He couldn't prove it, of course, but still, if I lived there I'd feel in constant danger.'

'And me,' Rosie said with feeling.

Then the tram was running into Templeogue, which the woman told Rosie had been the old depot. She saw it still had the engine and carriage sheds and a smithy further into the village opposite a pub called Floods. But the tram didn't stop and carried on and the woman beside Rosie said, 'Terenure is the next stop and the terminus,' and she began collecting her things together and Rosie did the same.

Rosie said goodbye to the woman as they both left the tram, thanking her for her company and

173

saying she hoped her mother would soon be on the mend.

The woman grasped her hands warmly. 'Best of luck to you,' she said. 'I hope you find news of your man soon, and that the news is good.'

Rosie was unable to speak for the sudden lump that rose in her throat. She was sorry to see the woman go – she had provided comfort as well as distraction – and so was grateful for the conductor coming up at that moment. 'Just make your way down there by that whitewashed wall,' he said, pointing. 'You'll pass the booking office and just after it an iron gate is set into a wall that leads onto Rathfarnham Road. You go through that and to the right you will see Terenure Road East. The halt is there, though there won't be a tram there yet awhile. The tram you'll want has a triangle on it and it's the number fifteen. Have you got that?'

'Aye,' Rosie replied, 'and thank you so much for your kindness.'

'It's my pleasure,' the conductor said and Rosie waved to him. Carrying her bag over her shoulder and Danny's basket in the other hand, she followed the conductor's directions to the tram stop where she would begin the last leg of her journey to Dublin and to whatever the city might hold.

TEN

As the conductor had predicted, Rosie had a little wait for the Dublin tram and when she was settled into it, she realised she had no idea what to ask for when the conductor came abreast of her for her fare. 'Well, where are you going?' the conductor asked. 'We won't be going the whole hog to Nelson's Pillar, that I do know, for Sackville Street is impossible to cross with rubble and fallen masonry.'

'I need to get to Baggot Street,' Rosie replied.

'Oh, then you wouldn't have gone up so far anyway, it would be taking you out of your way,' the conductor told her. 'You need to get off at the corner of St Stephen's Green North and Dawson Road. Baggot Street is only a stone's throw from there, so to speak. Don't you worry about it now, I'll tell you when we get there and point you in the right direction.'

Rosie sank back in her seat and didn't worry about it, not about getting off a tram at the right stop anyway. She had far more pressing worries pounding her brain. She read the signs as they passed through Rathgar and then Rathmines, noting the area became more built up as they drew closer to Dublin.

There were more people on the streets here, more cars and carts and bicycles and the odd omnibus too. She saw whole streets of houses and a few shops here and there. The tram began to fill up and, with all the seats taken, people stood holding onto the straps fastened to the roof as the tram swayed and clanked its way forward.

As the tram suddenly turned sharply, Rosie couldn't prevent herself sliding into a fellow passenger on the hard wooden seats. 'Sorry,' she said, but the woman she'd collided with just smiled.

'It's hard not to crash into one another the way they throw you about in these things,' the woman said. 'Still, not much further now. We're nearly at St Stephen's Green.'

Rosie looked back, but the conductor was talking to someone animatedly and Rosie hoped she didn't go sailing past where she should get off. There was little she could see now through the throng of people. She wished she was on the other side of the tram as they passed the Green, for knowing it had been the scene of action in the rebellion, she would have liked to have studied it, but she could barely see.

Then, the tram suddenly swung right and Rosie saw the conductor making his way through the crush towards her. 'Next stop's yours,' he said.

Rosie picked up her bags and wondered if she should find somewhere to have a hot drink and compose herself before landing on the convent doorstep. But the conductor shook his head regretfully when Rosie asked if there was a café nearby. 'You'd struggle to find a café open,' he said. 'There's been no food in the shops for days, and those restaurants and cafés not looted or burned to the ground will be boarded up.'

Rosie suddenly felt a little frightened and nervous. The tram drew to a halt and Rosie stepped down, as the conductor stood talking to a man passing, the Angelus Bell pealing out telling her it was twelve o'clock, and she knew she had no option but to make straight for the convent.

'Baggot Street you were making for, wasn't it?' the conductor asked, giving a wave to the man as he carried on up the street. 'Have you anyone belonging you? Anyone in this place you know at all?'

'Aye,' Rosie said. 'I have a relative in the convent, at a place called the "House of Mercy"'.

The conductor sighed in relief. 'Angels of Mercy, no less,' he said. 'That's what those nuns are. They help everyone and anyone in need. No-one is ever turned away from their door. You'll get a welcome there all right.' He looked Rosie up and down and then went on, 'You new to Dublin?'

'Aye.'

'Well, you chose a fine time to visit,' the conductor commented. 'If you want to go out and look at the city centre and particularly if you want to cross the Liffey, you'll need a pass. Various barracks and police stations have them, so I hear, or sometimes the sentries guarding the Liffey will be able to issue one.'

'A pass!' Rosie repeated incredulously. 'For going about Dublin?'

'Aye,' the conductor said. 'But remember it's a Dublin that's been at war. People have been killed, houses and shops destroyed. I tell you, if they don't like the look of you, you'll get no pass

177

at all, people say. Only the religious orders can move freely.'

'I see.'

'The nuns will put you right,' the conductor said. 'And you'll have no trouble reaching Baggot Street.' He pointed the way down the road and said, 'Now you go along there now, just straight on and you'll come to Baggot Street in no time at all. Don't look left or right, nor turn down any other road – that man I was just talking to was telling me some of the rebels have occupied a house in Mount Street Crescent. The army have installed a field gun in Merrion Square and are blasting them to Kingdom Come.'

Now that the Angelus bell had died away, Rosie was suddenly all too aware of the sound of rifle fire. There was a sudden loud boom and she shivered. 'I thought there was a surrender?'

'Aye, there is,' the conductor said. 'These are just pockets of resistance. But don't you worry about that. You just get yourself to Baggot Street.'

Rosie nodded and the tram moved away and swung up Dawson Street. She began to walk down the north side of St Stephen's Green, passing people with grim, serious faces. On the corner of the road she came upon the Shelbourne Hotel, now a barricaded and sandbagged structure with not a window in place, its stucco frontage pockmarked with bullet holes. It bore so little resemblance to any hotel she'd ever seen that if it hadn't been for the sign still on the wall above the shuttered entrance, she would never have believed it.

She remembered in the newspaper reports

she'd read about the insurrection that the army had installed field guns in the hotel and on the roof to clear the rebels out of the park. It seemed too awful for words to her to destroy buildings, not to mention lives, for an ideal that burned with a bright flame for only six short days.

Opposite the hotel was a barricade blocking the way into St Stephen's Green and Rosie remembered reading that the rebels had commandeered every vehicle passing to add to it. She saw for herself what the papers had reported – carts, traps, cars and vans, together with the odd bicycle, piled haphazardly one on top of another, pockmarked as the hotel had been and with big holes blasted into the sides of them. Much of the barricade had been dismantled now and she knew it would be easy to climb over and into the park if anyone had the desire to do so.

Despite the conductor's words she decided to have a look for herself. It wasn't as if she was walking into danger: the firing was from the other side and there had been nothing since that volley and the field gun's blast when she'd left the tram. Maybe the mini rebellion was already over and done.

But even though she thought this, she approached the barricade hesitantly, expecting someone to stop her any minute. No-one did, however. Any who passed seemed intent on their own business and there were no soldiers to be seen, so Rosie lifted up her skirts and began to climb, glad of her stout boots as the stack slithered and slid beneath her feet and she heard the sound of glass splintering.

179

Beyond the barricade, huge trenches had been dug, deep swathes cutting through the lush lawns. But worse by far were the limbs she saw sticking up from the trenches she'd thought to be empty, the bodies of rebels killed there: only half-hearted efforts had been made to cover them with earth.

There was a smell about the place, blood and cordite and something more, the putrefying stink of the decaying flesh of limbs exposed to the fine spring weather for days. Rosie felt nausea in her throat and she put her hand to her mouth as she turned away.

The sudden crash of a shell exploding made Rosie almost jump out of her skin, but she refused to allow herself to be frightened and continued to follow the path round until she came upon the fountain. No water gushed out of the metallic structure now nor trickled over the red bulrushes at its base. Rosie saw that once the stone wall around the fountain had been encircled by beautiful beds of flowers but every one had been ground into the earth.

She looked about her and saw that though the trenches might have ruined the lawns, the tops of them and any grass left were sprinkled with blossom of pink and white which had fluttered from the trees. The sight brought tears to her eyes.

She brushed them away impatiently. This was not the time for crying and she forced herself forward across that blackened grass to where she had seen the glint of water in the distance and then suddenly the lake was before her.

It lacked the grandeur of the lake in Blessington but for all that she could see it had once been a pretty place. A bridge spanned its narrowest point and the whole lake was overhung with bushes heavy with blossom and trees with young, bright green leaves and there were a fair few islands cut into the lake, obviously nesting places for the water birds. Not that there were ducks, swans or anything else on the lake that day and little wonder because despite the sun shimmering on the surface of the lake, it was a place of deep sorrow.

It was no place to linger at either, Rosie decided, so she climbed back over the barricade to continue her journey, aware that as she reached Baggot Street the rifle shots and occasional blast from the guns had become louder.

The houses on Baggot Street were large and had been built in the stately Georgian style with steps leading up to them and doors of different colours. Rosie knew they belonged to moneyed people, the professional classes.

Then, as she crossed Fitzwilliam Street, she saw the army field gun and the soldiers around it released a shell just as she passed. There was an earth-shattering boom. Surely no mere house could withstand such a pounding?

She had the urge to run. Her hands felt clammy and her heart thumped in her chest but she told herself to keep calm. She'd come here on a mission to find news of Danny and she couldn't take flight now so she concentrated on putting one foot before the other and looked neither right nor left.

When Rosie eventually came to the 'House of Mercy' she just stood in the road and stared.

The huge building, on the corner of Baggot Street and Herbert Road, was of honey-coloured brick and stood three storeys high. The main entrance had a white stone portico in front of it and a garden before that, which was entered by a small wrought-iron gate. There were two single-storey buildings on either side of the main one, each with doors that opened on to the street, so that the whole structure on the ground floor looked like the letter E. Rosie saw that above the building to her left there was a stained-glass window and she supposed that was the chapel.

She was so awed by the size and splendour, the whole magnificence of it, that it took all her reserves of courage to open that small gate, walk up the path between the well-tended garden, where tulips and daffodils waved in the spring sunshine, go up the wide steps between the pillars and ring the bell set in the wall beside the bright, red door.

She remembered Connie telling her about how the founder of the order, Catherine McAuley, had built the house with money that had been left to her before she'd actually become a nun herself. When it had first opened it had housed a school for the daughters of the gentry. However, it was soon apparent that the needs of the area meant that a school for poorer children should be set up instead. Catherine McAuley's aims, so Connie had said, had been to identify the needs of the people and try to address them in a positive way. Rosie thought they must be considered successful, or they wouldn't be known as the Angels of Mercy.

So, despite the size and grandeur of the convent, she had no doubt that the sisters would welcome her and this was apparent as soon as a nun opened the door. Her face was lined and wrinkled, but her eyes were bright and kindly looking, and she drew Rosie inside before enquiring of her business, saying as she did so, 'Come in, my dear, the streets are not safe just now.'

Rosie found herself in a large, bright hall, the sun shining through the windows, patterning the black and white tiled floor. The walls were half-panelled timber, the top half painted and lined with holy pictures. A blue lamp burned before the statue of the Blessed Virgin at the bottom of the sweeping staircase and the smell of the candles mixed with the smell of food from somewhere. Rosie felt saliva in her mouth at the thought of it.

'My name is Sister Amelia,' the nun said. 'Are you in trouble, my dear?'

Never had Rosie been spoken to so gently by a nun and she began her story of Danny and what had brought her to Dublin. 'My mother-in-law told me to come to you,' she finished. 'Her name is Connie Walsh and she says she has an aunt in the order, a Sister Cuthbert.'

'Oh yes,' Sister Amelia said. 'Not long back from our sister convent in Handsworth. I'll fetch her. She'd want to see you, welcome you.'

As the nun scurried away, Rosie studied the pictures. There was one of Catherine McAuley and, beside that, a picture of 'The Mercy Tree' and a little further along the wall a list of the order's aims behind glass and decorated with holy scrolls. There were fourteen altogether and the first few were as anyone would expect: 'To Feed the Hungry' and 'To Give Drink to the Thirsty', but further down Rosie read, 'To Visit Those in Prison', 'To Comfort the Afflicted', and 'To Forgive Offences'. Rosie was suddenly immeasurably glad she was here with these very special women who she knew would help her find news of Danny and sustain her whatever that news was.

Sister Amelia was soon back accompanied by another nun about the same age, as far as Rosie could ascertain, but her face was not as lined. She had the same warm brown eyes as Connie and Rosie felt herself relaxing as she related her story once again.

'Well,' Sister Cuthbert said as Rosie fell silent. 'First things first. I think a meal is in order. We were about to dish up for lunch when you rang the bell.'

But Rosie knew of the severe food situation in Dublin and protested. 'Oh no. I mean, I know there's little to be had in the shops. I have food with me, my mother-in-law insisted and she packed a similar basket for Danny, if he should be ... if he's...' She couldn't continue, not without breaking down and making a holy show of herself. But Sister Cuthbert saw her distress and interjected. 'Keep your food, Rosie. You may have need of it yet and your husband will be grateful for decent food if you should find him alive and well, please God you will.

'Don't worry about us, for we are well looked after. We had a big bag of vegetables and another

184

of potatoes dropped in only yesterday, enough for a few pans of stew. There is no meat; any to be found is commandeered by the military and yet Sister Miriam, who does most of the cooking, found a couple of dead rabbits outside the kitchen door today.'

She took Rosie's coat, basket and bag and put them in an alcove off the hall and then, with her arm through Rosie's, took her down a corridor into a room where nuns sat on benches either side of a large, dark wood, refectory table. They had steaming bowls of stew before them and a nun stood at a side table with a cauldron before her and a ladle in her hand, doling out generous portions.

Rosie felt light-headed with hunger as the savoury smell rose in the air. All the nuns' eyes were upon her as Sister Cuthbert led Rosie to the head of the table, where the Reverend Mother sat in an upholstered chair. Rosie dropped a curtsey before the older nun as she was introduced and knew instantly that, despite the smile on her face, little would get past this woman.

Her manner, though, was sympathetic towards Rosie as she bade her rise and said, 'Now, Mrs Walsh, my name is Mother Therese and Sister Amelia has told us a little of why you are here in Dublin. Everything else can wait until we've eaten. We are happy to share what we have with you.'

Seldom, Rosie thought afterwards, had food tasted as good as that rabbit stew: the meat succulent and juicy, the vegetables cooked to perfection, the dumplings helped soak up the gravy. They were an unusual colour and had an equally unusual taste, but were more than just edible and Rosie did the meal justice. A few of the nuns asked her questions, but Rosie answered anything she was asked politely although she could barely eat fast enough, such was her hunger.

Her main thoughts, though, even as she ate, was where she would have to go and who she'd have to ask to get news of Danny. After the meal was finished, Mother Therese asked, 'So my dear, I'm sure you are anxious for news of your husband?' and she nodded eagerly.

'The Franciscan Fathers would be the ones to contact,' the nun went on. 'They've been dealing a great deal with the prisoners in Kilmainham Jail. One of them would surely know if your husband is there or not and once that is established, we can go on from there.'

'Oh, thank you Reverend Mother,' Rosie said fervently. 'How do I find them?'

'You don't find them, my dear,' Mother Therese said. 'You can't walk around the streets without a pass: I'm surprised you weren't challenged on the way here. Sister Amelia and Sister Cuthbert will go.'

It was as Rosie was saying goodbye to the two nuns at the door that she heard a shell burst louder than any other had been. It was followed by another and another, whistling through the air and exploding with a thunderous crash. Rosie knew that if the riflemen in the house weren't dead before, they surely would be now. She closed the door sadly.

Only a short while after the nuns had left, they were back and had with them a Franciscan friar who introduced himself as Father Joe. 'I was on an errand of my own,' he said in explanation to Mother Therese and Rosie, who'd come into the hall to see the cause of the commotion. 'And then I was asked to see to the two young fellows who'd barricaded themselves in the house on Mount Street.'

'Are they dead?'

'The one is, the other won't be long following him,' the monk said softly. 'I said a wee prayer, but I had nothing with me to do anything else. I told someone to go for the parish priest and when he came just a few minutes ago I was about to be on my way again, when I came upon your nuns.'

He came across to Rosie and said, 'You must be Mrs Walsh, I've been told your story. You're looking for your husband, I believe?'

'Aye, Father. His name is Daniel Walsh,' Rosie said. Her voice was little more than a whisper. Already she was afraid of the answer the priest might give her. She was suddenly aware of the silence in the room and of Sister Cuthbert edging nearer to her, catching up one of Rosie's tensed fists in her hand.

It seemed an age before the priest said, 'I believe your man is being held in the jail. He was with de Valera's lot in Boland's Mill, after being routed from the house in Mount Street. De Valera was the last to surrender. I was with Father Augustine at the jail when they were brought in and I remember the names being read out – Daniel

187

Walsh was on the list.'

Rosie felt the breath she hadn't even been aware she was holding leave her body in such a rush that she felt light-headed and would have faltered had it not been for Sister Cuthbert. Her Danny had not been blown into a million pieces, or riddled with bullets and thrown into a makeshift grave in St Stephen's Green. He was alive!

But despite the monk's words, his face was grave, and Rosie asked, panicking. 'What is it, Father? Is Danny injured, or sick?'

'To my knowledge, he isn't,' the priest said. 'He isn't, at any rate, in the prison infirmary.'

'Can I see him? Are they allowed visitors?'

'They are indeed allowed visitors,' the priest said. 'In fact, I was on the way to Kilmainham Jail myself today. I have a wedding to arrange.'

'A wedding?'

'Aye,' Father Joe replied. 'One of the leaders of it all, Joseph Plunkett, is still determined to marry his sweetheart, Grace Gifford. It will have to be done speedily I'm thinking. Joseph is one of the ones to be put before a court martial tomorrow.'

'What will happen to them, Father?'

The monk lifted his hands in a gesture of helplessness. 'Mrs Walsh, I am a simple friar. I have no crystal ball.'

'Have you no idea?'

'My idea might be totally wrong,' Father Joe said.

'Even so. Please, Father?'

The friar regarded Rosie and her anxious face and knew it would be no kindness to buoy her up

188

with false hopes.

'Mrs Walsh, I think they will be executed – shot.'

'The leaders, you mean? Just the leaders?' Rosie cried desperately as Sister Cuthbert, hearing the distress in Rosie's voice, put her arms around her.

'Mrs Walsh, if you'd seen how many British soldiers have been killed, you'd know the government will not be prone to leniency.'

So, Danny might be alive now, might have survived the carnage, but for how long? She felt hatred for Phelan rise up inside her and fill her with white-hot anger, so she felt as if she was on fire, even while her body shook with fear for Danny.

Suddenly, Rosie was overcome with a blackness descending around and about her like a cloak, and she slithered from the nun's enfolding arms to the floor.

The pungent stench of smelling salts brought her around some time later and she lay on the floor where she'd been placed, a pillow under her head. 'Sorry,' she mumbled, embarrassed.

'No need to be sorry, my dear,' Sister Cuthbert said. 'It was of no matter at all. If I help you, can you sit up in the chair that Father Joe has brought in?'

Rosie gave a brief nod of her head. Sister Cuthbert helped her up and she waited for a moment for her head to stop spinning, swaying slightly on her feet so that Father Joe came to her other side and both helped her into the chair. But, once settled, she lifted her eyes and said,

189

'Can you take me to the jail, Father? Can I get to see Danny?'

'Do you think you'll be able for it?' Father Joe asked. 'I will take you with me and gladly, but it's a tidy step.'

Rosie looked up at the monk, his kindly face full of understanding and sympathy and she said, 'That was a momentary weakness only. I must see Danny, Father. I won't rest till I do.'

'Well then, we'll go along together as soon as you feel fully recovered,' the monk assured her. 'You will be all right in the streets when you are with me. We'll need no passes.'

Sister Cuthbert went away and came back through with a glass of water. When Rosie had drunk it she felt much better, stronger altogether, and more able to face whatever lay ahead of her. 'I'm ready, Father Joe,' she said.

'Are you sure now?'

'Aye. The fresh air will probably do me good,' Rosie said with conviction. She put on her coat, glad of it because though the day was fine, it always gave her confidence to wear a proper coat and she thought she might have need of confidence before the day was out.

It was when she lifted the basket that Father Joe asked, 'What's in there?'

'Food for Danny. My mother-in-law packed it for him, just in case, you know... We didn't know whether he was alive or dead, but we hoped and prayed. I washed and ironed a good white shirt, I'm sure he'll have need of one now and a jumper in case it's cold. I shouldn't think prisons are renowned for their good turf fires, not, of course,

190

that I've had any personal experience.'

'No indeed,' Father Joe said, peeling back the clothes at the top and looking at the produce in the basket.

The monk knew there was little chance of Danny having any of that food, or the shirt and jumper. He wondered whether he should tell Rosie that, but decided not to. Let her keep her illusions for a little longer. He did, however, relieve her of the basket, for it was a weight and they had a distance to go. Just minutes later they were scurrying down Baggot Street towards the bridge over the Grand Canal.

'I have great respect for these men in the jail,' the monk said as they walked. 'They've even impressed some of the soldiers, for every man jack of them is brave, and all I've spoken to were, and are, prepared to sacrifice their lives for Ireland's freedom.'

'Foolhardy though surely, Father?' Rosie said. 'Many people think that.'

'Aye, it may have been foolhardy,' the, monk went on. 'But a noble act for all that. It brought the eyes of the world upon us. If these men are shot, they will at least have died with honour and will be buried respectfully. Masses will be said for them and their relatives will have a grave to visit.'

The priest's words were of little comfort to Rosie for she'd heard the same sentiment expressed often and it didn't help.

They left the city centre as they passed the bridge that Rosie had travelled over in a tram just a wee while before. One of the soldiers at Portobello Barracks raised his hand in salute as the priest passed and there was a chorused greeting when they passed Richmond Barracks on the other side of the road a short time later. No-one challenged the two, or asked where they were bound for, or demanded to see passes. Rosie was grateful and knew it would have been a different story had she been on her own.

In fact, the soldiers seemed quite relaxed. 'I suppose the threat's over now,' Rosie said. 'All involved in it are either dead or behind bars. They have no reason to be alarmed.'

'No, indeed,' the friar said. 'Nor the ordinary Dublin people either, thank God, and for all my admiration for the rebels there was much hardship and poverty during the uprising and it led to lawlessness. I've seen children searching the mounds of burned and bombed rubbish for anything useful, and the sweet shops and toy shops have been cleared of stock.

'There was also great loss and tragedy amongst the ordinary people not involved at all. Men and women were taken prisoner by the army at Ballbridge and thirty-six people, men, women and children, were killed in a house in Haddington Road. A wee twelve-year-old boy was killed stone dead himself as he was giving a drink to a dying soldier.

'I wonder if it will ever be the same,' Father Joe continued pensively. 'Some buildings are surely lost forever. The Hibernian Academy was burned and it had all the spring collection of paintings and other works of art, many of them just loaned. Only the good Lord knows what can be done about that. I imagine they'll be insured. The worst of it is, they believe the curator, Mr Kavanagh, was burned to death in the building too. Then there were twenty horses belonging to Clery's, the department store, burned to death. Only one escaped alive.'

Rosie could imagine the terror of those horses. All animals were afraid of fire. She imagined their screams would rent the air and felt her stomach turn over with the horror of it all. Afterwards, the stink of burning horse flesh would have hung in the air. She wondered why the loss of those horses had affected her more than the deaths of human beings.

There was silence as they walked along, each busy with their own thoughts. Father Joe branched away from the canal not long after they passed Richmond Barracks in to Cork Street, which led to Marrowbone Lane where he was able to point out the docks of the Grand Canal to Rosie before turning right into James Street. 'It's not far now,' he said. 'It's in Inchicore Road just a little way along here.'

Rosie nodded her head for she was too nervous to talk much and was having enough trouble putting one foot before the other when really she wanted to run the other way and pretend all this was a bad dream. But then they turned the corner and there it was, the massive structure, built of blue-grey brick. There were high walls surrounding it with coils of barbed wire on top of them.

Rosie turned anguished eyes to the friar and her knees began to tremble. She felt weak with longing to see with her own eyes that Danny was alive, yet she was filled with fear at the thought of entering that forbidding place.

Father Joe understood much of the thoughts stumbling through Rosie's troubled mind and said gently, 'Take heart, my dear. I am sure that Danny will be gladdened at the sight of you.'

It was that thought which spurred her on, and so she took a deep breath yet she doubted she'd ever have plucked up the courage to go into that building alone.

ELEVEN

The door to the jail was arched and had a decoration of coiled sea serpents on the top of it but the entrance itself was fitted with a thick black grille. Father Joe pulled the bell pull and smiled encouragingly at Rosie.

The man who came to open the door was fat and sloppily dressed, despite the uniform he wore which was stained and crumpled. A sizeable bunch of keys was attached to his belt and he used some of these to release the grille gates, opening them with a grating sound. 'Good afternoon, Father,' he said, ushering them into a small passage. 'The Governor has been expecting you this long time.'

'Yes, I'm sorry. I was unavoidably delayed,' Father Joe replied. 'I hope the Governor will have time now for a few words.'

The man didn't answer immediately, intent on securing the door. Rosie noticed that he first dragged the grille closed with a clang of metal and the steel door was slammed shut after it before it was also locked and barred.

She was aware of the disturbing way the man was ogling her and she raised her chin and met his look steadily, determined not to show any reaction. Yet the whole place depressed and frightened her. She had the urge to beat on the gates and beg to be let out again into the fresh air, for there seemed little here and what there was was fetid and unsavoury.

Before Rosie gave way to this impulse, she heard Father Joe say, 'This young woman is looking for her husband, a Daniel Walsh. I believe you have him here.'

The man looked at Rosie contemptuously and shrugged. 'Might have. We have lots of prisoners here. Anyway,' he added as his eyes slid over Rosie with scorn. 'If she wants to visit, she'll have to have a word with the Governor.'

'Then maybe you could tell him that we're here?' Father Joe retorted crisply. 'And we will ask him.'

There was the merest of pauses before the man, sighing heavily said, 'You'd better follow me.'

The door the prison warder opened from the passage led to a steep flight of stairs and the two went up after the man. The power of the cloth, Rosie thought, and guessed that without the monk, she'd not have got half so far. As it was, Governor Greene said he would be pleased to see them and they were ushered into his office.

A large wooden desk piled high with files dominated the room, with a bookshelf in one corner and a filing cabinet in the other. The governor greeted them at the door and bade them sit down in the chairs on the other side of the desk. He then sat down opposite them and asked Father Joe, 'Have you come to talk to the groom?'

Rosie remembered the monk saying that one of the prisoners wished to marry and he was going to officiate at the Nuptial Mass in the prison chapel.

'Aye,' Father Joe said. 'I am doing that, all right, but I'm here for another reason too. This young woman,' and he indicated Rosie as he spoke, 'is looking for her husband, name of Daniel Walsh. I have reason to believe he is here?'

'Let's see, then,' the Governor said. 'I had a fair few in over the weekend. I haven't the names of them all yet. Was your husband one of the rebels, madam?' he demanded sternly.

It was useless to deny it, to tell of his love of peace, of the charge his mother made on him to find Phelan and his own filial duty as the eldest in the family. She merely nodded. 'Aye.'

'One of those who killed and maimed and near burned the whole city to the ground, Mrs Walsh?' the governor went on. 'A place where decent people couldn't go about their lives, get to their job of work, or buy food in the shops?'

'Come, come,' Father Joe chided. 'None of this is Mrs Walsh's fault. The family need news of him. Is he here or is he not?'

Governor Greene looked down a list in the front of one of the files. 'Aye,' he said. 'We have a Daniel Walsh here. He says his home is in Blessington, County Wicklow.'

'Aye, that's him.' The cry burst from Rosie's lips. 'I've travelled from there today. Can I see him?'

The governor seemed to give the matter some thought, leaning back in his chair and drumming his fingers together. It seemed an age before he said, 'I should think that could be arranged. We have a room set aside. Come, I'll show you the way and have your husband sent for.'

Rosie stood up and bent to lift the basket Father Joe had placed on the floor beside his chair. The Governor had assumed it belonged to Father Joe, as he'd carried it in, but now he said to Rosie, 'What's this?'

'It's ... it's for Danny,' Rosie said. 'Some food his mother has packed from the farm and a clean shirt and jumper. I'm sure he has need of them.'

The Governor took the basket from her and, placing it on the desk between them, peeled back the clothes laid on top. He couldn't see all the food, but what he did see was good enough. His eyes widened with greed, his face taking on an almost lascivious look as he ran his tongue over his lips before saying, 'You can leave this here. Visitors are not allowed to bring anything in that is not vetted. I'm sure you understand. I'll see your husband gets the things later.'

Rosie, looking at the man's face, knew Danny would never even get a sniff of what was in that basket but she also knew she could do nothing about it. 'Very well,' she said. 'Can I see him now?'

She was eventually shown into a stark bare room, cut in half with a metal grid ending at a solid wooden counter that reached to the floor. On either side of the grid were set hard wooden chairs and Rosie sat down on one as the Governor indicated. She heard the click of the door as he left the room and she waited.

Afterwards, she wasn't sure how she prevented the cry from escaping from her lips when she saw Danny come in. He'd not shaved for a week and she'd half expected to see a beard and moustache forming. What she didn't expect was the red-rimmed ravaged eyes, nor the split lip and vicious bruise scarring one side of his face. Nor did she expect his shambling gait, his hands manacled together, his arms folded across his stomach. His clothes were in tatters and stained with blood, sweat and dirt and a rancid smell emanated from him.

Rosie hadn't seen her husband for eight days, that was all. It might have been eight years, eighteen years, the change was so great. His voice when he spoke was husky. 'Rosie, you shouldn't have come here.'

Rosie looked at the warder who'd followed Danny and stood by the door, his face implacable with eyes staring straight ahead, but able to listen to every word spoken. Well, she thought angrily, let him bloody well listen. 'I had to come, Danny. We knew nothing and I was going mad with worry.'

'Did Phelan make it back all right?'

'Oh aye,' Rosie said with bitterness. 'He and Niall came home without a scratch. And your mother is killing the proverbial fatted calf as if he was some sort of favoured prodigal son.'

'It's her way.'

'Aye, I know,' Rosie said with a sigh. 'He could tell us nothing of you. Nothing of any value for all he hung about in Dublin till the surrender. I wanted to kill him.'

'I told him to go straight home. I knew you would be worried.'

'Well the news he would have brought would

hardly have made us worry less,' Rosie said. 'Oh, Danny, you've no idea what it was like. I love you so much and I couldn't rest, none of us could, till we found out what had happened to you. And now to see you here like this... Oh, God, Danny. What happened to your face?'

Danny was glad Rosie couldn't see his bruised and battered body which was damaged far worse than his face. His eyes slid over the guard and he said with a shrug, 'We lost.'

Rosie didn't pursue it. She'd seen the sideways look Danny had given and understood: she had no desire to make things worse, but she longed to put her arms around him, to put soothing salve on his bruised and grazed cheek, to look after him. It was breaking her heart to see him in such a place and in such a condition. 'Oh, Danny,' she said in a whisper. 'I miss you.'

'And I you. More than I can say,' Danny replied, tears glittering in his eyes.

Their hands on the counter moved towards the wire and their fingers touched softly beneath the tiny gap. 'No contact,' rapped out the warder. They sprang apart as if they'd been stung. Rosie valiantly swallowed the lump in her throat that was threatening to choke her and said, 'Your mammy packed some things for you in a basket, and I put you in a clean shirt and jumper, but I had to leave it with the Governor.'

'And that's where it will stay,' Danny said in a low voice. 'But don't worry about it. That's the least of my problems.'

'What will happen to you?'

Danny shrugged. 'Some of the leaders go for

court martial tomorrow. They said they'll be shot, but no-one knows for sure. When they've got rid of them, maybe they'll start on us.'

'Oh, God, Danny, no,' Rosie cried brokenly for she couldn't prevent the tears seeping from her eyes then and trickling over her cheeks. But hadn't she faced this fact already? Even as the priest had given her hope that her husband was alive, his grave face and voice had spoken of further heartache to come. But now, to hear Danny speak of it so calmly…

'Ssh, Rosie,' Danny pleaded. 'Don't cry, please. I knew what I had to do and knew too that there could only be one outcome. I said that from the beginning.'

'Phelan was a bloody little fool,' Rosie said through her tears. 'If I had him in front of me this minute, I would choke the life out of him and take pleasure in it.'

'Ssh, Rosie, Rosie, don't cry, please. This doesn't help,' Danny said. 'We have to take the situation as it is. It's you I worry about, you and wee Bernadette, and Daddy working the farm with only Phelan to help him, and Mammy fretting about me all the days of her life. These are the things that drive sleep from my mind at night.'

'I can't bear it, Danny.'

'You must, because I can do nothing to change it,' Danny said softly. He remembered telling Rosie once that she should fear nothing while he was with her. He'd promised her he'd never do anything to hurt her but now he found it hard to bear the helplessness reflected in her eyes. He shut his own eyes for a moment and then opened

201

them and said, 'Tell Sarah that Sam is in with me in this hell-hole, and Shay too.'

'Time's up!'

There was so much Rosie still wanted to say. She wanted to tear down the grille and enfold her husband in her arms and tell him how much she loved him and would continue to love him till the very breath left her body.

'Goodbye, Rosie.'

'Can I not come again?' Rosie asked bleakly.

'It would serve no purpose,' Danny said. 'Go home and raise my daughter to be good and honest and upright and tell her of her father.'

Danny was almost pulled from the room and Rosie's last vision of him was through a mist of tears. She leaned her head on the counter and cried broken-heartedly.

All the way back to the convent, Father Joe talked. He'd seen the sorrow etched on Rosie's face and he knew it went too deep for her to make small talk for politeness's sake. But he chatted away anyway as they walked back, that lovely, spring-time evening.

They were almost back in Baggot Street when Father Joe said, 'Are you returning to Wicklow tonight?'

'No,' Rosie said. 'Connie was certain the nuns would be able to find a room for me somewhere.'

'They will, surely. You won't be the first person they've sheltered,' Father Joe said. 'So you'll go home tomorrow?' he ventured, anxious that she spend no longer than she had to in Dublin.

'Aye. Danny ... well he doesn't want me to visit

any more. He ... he says there's no point.'

'Write to him,' Father Joe advised. 'I'm sure he'd be glad of that.'

'Aye, I will do that, Father,' Rosie said. 'And thank you for your kindness to me. I don't think I'd have got so far without you.'

The priest smiled. 'Aye, God gives us some privileges,' he said. 'Now, go in and rest yourself – I'm sure you're worn out with the emotion of today.'

Rosie was bone-weary, but tired as she was, she didn't want to go back to the convent just yet. She wanted to walk through the streets and see for herself the damage to the city, see what Danny had had to endure. It made her feel closer to him, somehow.

She knew she'd probably never be allowed to wander free in this way without the priest as her escort and so she said, 'I am tired, Father, you're right, and low in spirits, but I have a yen to see the damage to the place and it will be what they'll ask me about at home. Have you time to come with me?'

Father Joe had a million and one things to attend to and had been wondering, as he'd walked back, how he'd fit them all in. But he felt sorry for Rosie and so he pushed his own concerns to the back of his mind and said, 'I have nothing to do that won't keep. I'm at your disposal, Mrs Walsh, and I'll be happy to accompany you.'

Rosie followed Father Joe as he turned away from the 'House of Mercy', back up Baggot Street, past the square where the army's field gun still stood. It was silent now and guarded by soldiers who looked at them dispassionately as they passed, but didn't challenge them.

'We go up here,' Father Joe said, turning left at the top of Merrion Street.

As they walked on, the streets became more crowded and Rosie realised many were doing what she herself was: assessing the damage to their city. They continued up between Trinity College and the Bank of England and over the bridge spanning the grey, torrid River Liffey.

Once over the bridge, Sackville Street was before them and Rosie was appalled at what she saw. The remains of a barricade stretched across the front of it, parts burned to cinders, so it was easy for them to clamber over. The street itself was full of rubble and charred beams, smashed roof tiles, cardboard boxes and glass that splintered under their feet. Over everything was the stench of smoke and cordite that swirled in the air and caught in Rosie's throat when she breathed in.

So much was destroyed and so many buildings reduced to piles of scorched and blackened masonry. And those not burned completely to the ground were locked up and barricaded to guard against looting.

'See, that used to be Hopkins, a silversmiths,' Father Joe said, pointing to a pile of masonry debris littering the pavement. 'And that,' he said, pointing, 'was once the Hibernian Hotel.' Rosie noted the buckled iron girders were the only things left of it, sticking up through the mounds of rubble.

The Post Office was a burned-out shell. Some

walls were still standing but looked as if a sudden push would send them toppling over, and many had giant holes in them. Inside were piles of debris and the acrid stink of burning lodged in Rosie's nostrils as she looked about in amazement. 'At one time, Dublin was burning from Talbot Street down to the Quays,' said Father Joe, waving his hand to the right. 'Once these used to be buildings, shops, houses; now there's precious little left.'

It was just a sea of rubble. Here and there a building had escaped and still stood, Nelson's Pillar being one, but Rosie couldn't help wondering how safe those buildings were.

'There were barricades everywhere,' Father Joe went on. 'That's what helped the fire take hold so quickly. Every road they held they barricaded the corners of with bed mattresses and pillows and they had barbed wire strung across with rebels on guard.'

'I know they commandeered cars and lorries and carts and all sorts for the barricade at St Stephen's Green,' Rosie said. 'I went in on my way to Baggot Street to see for myself.'

The priest was talking again and pointing to the right of the post office. 'Henry Street is impossible to go down due to falling masonry, and Moore Street is the same. Moore Street was where one of the rebel leaders Michael O'Rahilly was shot and killed along with nineteen others early on Saturday morning. Padraic Pearce, one of the leaders of the uprising, told that to a fellow brother of mine, Father Augustine, who'd been visiting the rebels in prison.

'He said Michael was trying to draw fire away from them, Padraic and his brother Willie and the others. They knew they had to leave the General Post Office before being roasted alive, but they had James Connolly with them and he was badly injured. So Michael O'Rahilly led an assault on the street to cover their retreat, as they crept into houses in Moore Street carrying Connolly on a litter.

'It was all to no avail, though, and they were forced to surrender eventually that same day. Later, two dead rebels were found in Moore Street, lying side by side and holding hands people say.'

Rosie sighed. 'That is the tragedy. So many dead. Grieving families throughout Ireland. England too, of course, for even the soldiers belonged to someone and for all that we're no further forward in our struggle for Home Rule. In fact, this might have put it back.'

Father Joe knew Rosie was right. She'd spoken the thoughts of his heart. Her whole body spoke of dejection and she stood staring all around her at the carnage and destruction, her eyes full of pain. 'Come,' he said gently. 'We can do no good here. Let me take you back to the Sisters where you may eat a little something and rest yourself.'

Rosie had seen more than enough and so she allowed herself to be led away and they made their way back through the people thronging in the streets.

The nuns fussed over the state of Rosie when Father Joe delivered her back. 'Come and eat something at least,' Sister Amelia said to the monk. 'It will help you so.' But Father Joe wouldn't stay. He said he had too much to do, but Rosie thought he probably wouldn't stay for a meal because he knew the nuns had little enough to eat themselves.

When Rosie was led into the refectory and saw the meal before them was just potatoes in their jackets and a dish of salt, she bitterly regretted handing over the basket with all the food in it to the governor at the prison. She knew it would fill his fat, smug face, while these good and holy women were reduced to eating scraps and nothing else. Well, at least they could share what Connie had given her, she thought.

'Wait,' she cried as they pressed her to sit, and she ran from the room for her bag, tipping its contents on the table before them. Ham, cheese, hard-boiled eggs, barnbrack and soda bread all spilled out. It didn't go far amongst so many, but Rosie tried to divide it as equally as possible.

As they ate, Rosie told them about Danny, although she didn't stress how badly he looked, or tell them about his battered face.

'So, what do you intend to do now?' Reverend Mother asked.

'I must go home tomorrow,' Rosie said. 'I have a baby to see to and a family waiting for news. As for Danny...' She gave a resigned shrug. 'He doesn't want me to see him in that place. Father Joe said to write to him and he's right, I suppose – I can do no good hanging about Dublin.'

'We must be out early tomorrow,' Sister Cuthbert said. 'To see if we can find any food for you, for you have shared every morsel you had with us.'

'I was glad to do it,' Rosie said. 'I just wish it had been more.'

'I know that, Rosie,' Sister Cuthbert said. 'But you cannot go back without a bite to eat. We need food ourselves too. We have a surfeit of vegetables and a few potatoes, but nothing else in the convent at all.'

Rosie guessed as much. 'I'll go out and help you find anything there is about and gladly,' she said, 'and don't worry, the trams go back fairly regularly.'

So the next morning very early she set off for the city, a basket over her arm. Sister Cuthbert went with her.

'Johnstone Morney Bakery are the only people still baking in the city as far as I know,' the nun said. 'We'll get bread if we can, and if not bread then flour. Sister Amelia and Sister Miriam are going up to Findlaters, that's where they got the pea flour she made the dumplings with yesterday, and maybe they'll have some hard biscuits too.'

Pea flour, Rosie thought: it explained the strange colour and even stranger taste of the dumplings she'd tried.

The queue outside Morney's, even at that early hour, was enormous. Everyone was rationed to two large loaves each and two pounds of bread flour, but Rosie and Sister Cuthbert came away well satisfied with their share. When the two other nuns came back with more pea flour and sweet biscuits, everyone was heartened.

Later, Rosie bade farewell to the nuns and left them with genuine regret, wishing she could help them in some way. She had immense respect for them, for despite their straitened circumstances they hadn't hesitated to welcome her warmly and share everything they had with her.

TWELVE

When Rosie alighted from the Dublin tram at Blessington it was nearly two o'clock and she felt more wearied by the news she had to impart than the journey itself. She had not notified Connie and Matt of her return and so didn't expect to be met, but she didn't mind the walk out to the farmhouse. She'd done it often enough.

However, she had just left the depot when she was hailed, and she turned to see Willie Ferguson approaching her in his pony and trap. 'Were you sent to meet me?' she asked.

'Not exactly,' Willie said, helping her into the seat beside him. 'But I knew where you'd gone. God, half the county knew and as I was going into Blessington anyway, I told Matt I'd wait on a bit to meet a few trams. They thought you might be back today.' Seeing Rosie's white, drawn face and fearing what she would tell him, he asked gently, 'Did you find Danny?'

'Aye,' Rosie said with a sigh. 'He's in Kilmainham Jail. Shay's with him too and Sarah's Sam. I didn't see them, I was just allowed to see Danny, but he told me.'

'Thank God!'

'Don't be so quick to thank the Almighty,' Rosie said sharply. 'Some of the leaders are to be court-martialled today. The rumour is they'll be shot first and the ordinary men will follow after.'

'Does Danny feel that?'

'Aye, and he's not the only one. I'm not telling Connie and Matt, and I'd be obliged if you'll say nothing. They have enough to worry about as it is, without my telling them that too.'

Willie nodded. He understood that and then he asked, 'Was he injured at all?'

'Not in the uprising,' Rosie said. 'But now his face is black and blue, and he shambled into the room like a man three times his age, bent over and his manacled arms wrapped across his stomach.'

'Beaten up?'

'Could be nothing else. He could tell me little with the guard in the room the whole time.'

'You do well not to tell Connie about any of this,' Willie said. 'I'll say nothing, never fear, nor will I give the whole story to my own wife.'

Most people in the village now knew where Rosie had been heading the day before and shopkeepers and shoppers alike stood in the street to watch and wave. Some called out a greeting, but Willie didn't stop and Rosie was grateful. She had too much on her mind to answer inquisitive villagers and anyway, apart from Willie Ferguson, she really thought Matt and Connie should hear first.

'I don't know how I'm going to tell them,' she confided as the road stretched out before them. 'Although essentially, of course, it isn't the worst news. It's the best we could hope for in the circumstances. It's just with this court martial and all...'

'Who told you they were to be executed?' Willie asked.

'There's Franciscan monks that visit the prisoners,' Rosie explained. 'Good job they do with the Catholic Church speaking out against the uprising, even from the pulpit. The prisoners would get scant help or sympathy from that source and God knows when you are set to meet your maker, then you need all the spiritual help you can get. Sister Cuthbert said these Capuchin monks are sort of an independent order and I say Thank God for them. But even Father Joe, who went with me to Kilmainham Jail, thought they would all be executed in time. He didn't come straight out with it, I had to press him, but that's what he thought.'

'I'll take myself up there and see my boy myself,' Willie said after a moment's reflection. 'I'm ashamed that I let you go up and see first.'

'I was the only person that could go. Daddy is already rushed off his feet as it is,' Rosie said.

'Well, I am rushed right enough and Niall is as good as useless at the moment. This business has hit him and Phelan harder than they're letting on, I think.'

'Don't ask me to feel sorry for them,' Rosie said through tight lips.

'Aye, I know, lass, you don't have to say it,' Willie said. 'And I've a debt to your man that it may take a lifetime to repay, for I know if it hadn't been for him offering to take Niall's place, I might have two sons in jail now, or one in jail and one blown to Kingdom Come.'

Rosie said nothing. Willie was right – her Danny had sacrificed freedom and maybe his life for Willie's son and his own brother but suddenly she felt resentful at him doing that. Did she and Bernadette count for nothing? But then how could he have come home and left two mere boys to their fate? How could he have faced his mother, held his head up, if he'd saved his own skin while his brother was blown to pieces or was incarcerated in a jail, awaiting his turn to be shot? She knew he could never have done that. She knew the manner of man she married yet she knew she would suffer all the days of her life because of his values.

But she didn't berate Willie, or blame him in any way. No-one could have turned Phelan or Niall from a cause they believed in, however misguided, and no one could have talked Danny out of trying to save Phelan from himself. She imagined it would have been much the same way in the Ferguson household, the man, Shay, and the boy, Niall, would go their own way.

The sigh she gave, though, spoke volumes and made Willie feel immensely sorry for her. He had no words to express how he felt and so, when he dropped her at the head of the lane there had been an uneasy silence between them for some time, and Rosie was glad to reach the farmhouse gate, despite the news she had to impart.

She thanked Willie warmly and stood for a moment watching him pull away before turning to walk towards the cottage. Rosie spied Matt working in the field alongside Phelan, shading his eyes from the sun as he scanned the road. The minute he saw Rosie alighting from the cart he gave a cry to Phelan and both left their work and came scurrying to meet her.

Connie too had spotted Rosie through the window as she crossed to the fire, and catching

213

Bernadette up in her arms she ran up the lane as Matt and Phelan raced across the fields.

Connie's mind was awash with questions, but she saw the exhaustion Rosie tried so valiantly to hide and she told Matt to wait till Rosie was in and resting herself before pestering the life out of her.

Anyway, the moment belonged to Bernadette who was holding out her arms to the mammy she'd so surely missed. 'Mammy, Mammy!'

Rosie took the child from Connie, passing Connie her bag, and she cuddled Bernadette close, burying her face for a moment in her soft, sweet smelling, golden curls. She took comfort in her small daughter, as yet unaware that she might have no father to take joy in her growing up, and she hugged her all the tighter.

And so Rosie was soon divested of her coat and sat before the fire, her child on her knee and a cup of tea beside her. And then she told them all straight what had happened to Danny, that he was alive but in jail.

'Oh, thank God,' Connie said. Rosie didn't check her as she had done with Willie. She had a mental picture in her head of Danny, beaten and bruised and half-starved, and tears sprang to her eyes but she bent her head towards Bernadette to hide her face while she swallowed back the lump in her throat.

'Did you see him just the once?' Connie asked.

Rosie nodded. 'He didn't want me to visit further,' she said. 'It's a godawful place, Kilmainham. Father Joe advised me to write.'

That, at least, was something Connie could do

for him. 'Well, if that's what he wants, we'll all send him a letter, so we will.'

'I'm sure he'll be grateful,' Rosie said, and then she decided to change the subject because the sadness of remembering how Danny had been and what might yet happen to him, a sadness she was unable to share, was dragging her down.

Instead, she said, 'Dublin was a sight, you'd never believe it, the damage was colossal when you think the insurrection was all over in six days.'

'You told us none of this, Phelan,' Connie said, almost accusingly.

Phelan shrugged. 'I was more worried about Danny. But, Rosie's right, the whole centre of Dublin seemed to be on fire at one point.'

'Dear God,' Connie said. 'For this to happen, just a few miles from us.'

'The food situation was worse,' Rosie said. 'Dublin was being starved to death.'

'Aye,' Phelan said. 'Me and Niall could get barely anything at all to eat. A lot of roads you couldn't go into either, even to search for food, for the army was taking potshots at anything, or anyone that moved.'

Rosie shot around to look at the boy and fixed him with a glare, her eyes sparking with anger. 'You deserved all that and more,' she snapped. 'You chose to go and put your life in danger and take the lives of others. I'm talking here of innocent people, people who had no hand in any uprising of any kind and had no wish, other than to go about their daily business and feed their families.

'Open my bag, Mam,' she demanded swinging around to Connie. 'See what the nuns gave me

215

for the journey and what they will have to eat today as well.'

'Dry bread?' Connie said, opening the linen cloth bundles. 'Aye,' Rosie said. 'Yesterday evening, they only had potatoes and salt until I shared with them the food you packed for me. Dinner was only better because some kind person had given them a sack of vegetables. That bread you have in your hands we had to travel nearly the length of Dublin and then queue for hours to get. Some people with families, small children and the like, must be worse off. The nuns are liked and respected and looked after by the Dublin people, but I tell you times are hard just now for everyone there. You would scarcely believe it. And for what?'

It was a challenge she threw open to Phelan and one he wasn't able to answer. He'd been eaten up with shame since Danny had ordered him home and with some of the shame came the realisation once he was out of the house, away from the noise and the shooting and the killing, that he'd wanted to go. He was relieved there was a 'get out' clause for him. But he'd shared these thoughts with no-one, for he wasn't stupid.

When he'd reached home and saw how distressed Rosie and his mother were, he felt guilt dragging him down. Now Rosie was back, had seen for herself the horror and had found Danny and the others alive, but for how long God alone knew. Sometimes, when he realised what he'd done, he could scarcely live with himself.

Rosie, who he'd once thought so much of, now looked at him as if he were a slug, something she'd found under a stone. Well he deserved nothing more than her scorn and he lowered his head, hiding his face, which had flushed crimson with embarrassment at her scrutiny.

Connie felt sorry for Rosie, sorry for them all, but Phelan, she was sure, had just been caught up in the glory of it: he'd not thought deeply of the consequences. Why would he, he was just a boy, fourteen years old? But Rosie blamed him, and who could wonder at that either. She hated the feeling between them, when they had been so friendly in the past.

Matt, trying to be peacemaker, turned the attention from Phelan and the ruination of Dublin and remarked, 'Dermot will be here as soon as dinner is over. He'll be like a dog with two tails to have you back.'

'How d'you know?'

'How do I know what? That he'll be up here, or that he'll be happy to see you?'

'Both,' Rosie said with a thin smile.

'Well, the child wasn't far away from the house from dinnertime yesterday,' Matt said. 'We told him it would likely be at least today before you got back, but nothing would do him but wait until it got dark to see if you were coming home. Mark my words, he'll be here.'

'Maybe you should pop and see your mother when you've had a bite?' Connie said.

'She wouldn't be a whit interested, Mam.'

'Even so, she is your mother after all.'

Rosie would make no promises. 'I'll see how I feel when I've eaten. At the moment I'm jiggered, not just tired, bone-weary, but I might perk up if I eat. I'll just pop Bernadette into the bedroom,' she said, lifting the child who'd fallen fast asleep against her shoulder.

'Aye, there's another glad to have you back,' Connie remarked, stroking the child's curls gently. 'Mind you, she's not been a bit of bother, but there's no-one like their mammy at that age.'

Pity she may have no daddy soon, Rosie wanted to fling at Phelan, but she wouldn't go down that road again. Some things were best left unsaid and she didn't want to upset Connie further so she smiled at her and carried Bernadette across the room, saying, 'I'll help you get a meal together when I've settled her.'

'You'll do no such thing,' Connie said. 'There's just the four of us, and I can knock up a bite for us in no time at all. You sit and rest yourself.'

But Rosie, though tired, was unused to sitting still, and she had no desire to do so now because she wanted no more time to sit and think. God knows she'd done enough of that when she'd been in the tram coming home.

She stood in the room for a moment looking at her child sleeping in the cradle, her thumb in her mouth, and felt her heart turn over with the fierce love she had for her. She was such a delight and joy to bring up, and one day, she promised herself, she'd tell her about her daddy and the great man he'd been. She bent and kissed Bernadette gently on the cheek and then went back into the kitchen, closing the door behind her gently.

Matt was right: Rosie had barely finished her dinner when she saw Dermot run past the window. He didn't even make a cursory knock on the door, but opened the latch and walked straight in. He flew across the room when he caught sight of Rosie and threw himself against her. 'Oh, Rosie, I'm so glad you're back.'

Rosie couldn't help but be deeply touched by the child's arms tight around her and the relief in his voice. 'I'm glad to be back too, Dermot.'

'Did you find Danny?'

'Aye, I found him,' Rosie said.

'Where was he?'

'In jail, and Shay Ferguson and Sarah's boyfriend Sam Flaherty with him.'

'And... Is he all right?'

Rosie felt she could tell Dermot even less than Connie – he was only a young boy – and so she forced a light note into her voice and said, 'He's grand.'

'Oh, I'm glad,' Dermot said fervently. 'Will he be in prison long?'

It was hard to remain positive so Rosie said, 'I don't know, Dermot. I imagine he'll have to go to trial.'

'Oh.'

'Well, they did do wrong, pet. They'll have to be punished.'

Dermot shot a look at Phelan. 'Did you know it was wrong?'

Phelan shrugged. 'I didn't think that when I marched off with the Brotherhood. I know now all right.'

Dermot digested this. He remembered Phelan telling him how he was fighting for Home Rule and independence for Ireland and it had sounded a fine thing to do. Dermot had wished fervently

219

he could be part of it. And now, here was Phelan looking downhearted and defeated, saying he knew the whole uprising had been wrong. And Danny was in jail.

It was confusing, but then a lot of things confused him, and he remembered the promise he'd made Geraldine. 'Will you come down to the house? Geraldine wanted to come with me to see if you were back, but Mammy wouldn't let her.'

'Did she let you out?'

Dermot shook his head. 'No, but I got away. She keeps Geraldine hard at it.'

Rosie could guess that. She knew exactly what Geraldine's life was like under her mother's thumb, but she was surprised Dermot not only saw that but was ready to give voice to it. She shook her head. 'I can't just up and come like that, Dermot,' she said. 'There's dishes to be washed and Bernadette is asleep in the bedroom and...'

'Go with the child and see your parents and your sister,' Connie urged. 'I'll soon see to these few things and I'm here if Bernadette should wake.'

'Ah, Mam, I hate to ask you after you've been seeing to her while I was in Dublin.'

'It's a pleasure to me, Rosie. Go on now.'

'Aye, Connie's right,' Matt said. 'They'll be concerned for you. It's only right you should see them, let them know you're all right.'

So Rosie allowed herself to be persuaded and later, as she sat in her parents' house with a cup of tea and a slice of cake Geraldine pressed upon her, she knew if it hadn't been for her brother and sisters, she'd never have gone over the threshold of the place.

Minnie and Seamus had been scathing and scornful about the rebellion from the start, but they were worse now. They wouldn't stop going on about it and had no sympathy about Danny going off to Dublin in search of his young brother. 'The boy shouldn't have been allowed to get involved in the first place,' Minnie said. 'I'd soon put a stop to Dermot doing such a thing.'

Rosie said nothing. She'd have valued a measure of sympathy, a comforting arm around her shoulders, but knew she'd get nothing like that from the cold pair before her. But even as she thought this, she knew from the lift of Dermot's chin and the look in his eyes at Minnie's words that Dermot would go his own way when the time came.

She didn't stay long. She couldn't, even for her sisters' sake, and using Bernadette as an excuse was soon on her way back home, glad to leave the depressing house where she had been born and reared for seventeen years, but which had never ever felt like home.

Later that same day, as Connie laid the table for dinner and Rosie attempted to feed egg yolk and bread and butter to Bernadette, Sarah and Elizabeth came in waving the *Dublin Express*. Pleased though they were to see Rosie back safe and sound, they had news of their own. The fifteen leaders of the Easter Uprising had been condemned to death. The leader of the rebels, Padraic Pearce, was one of the ones to be executed the following day, while his brother Willie and Joseph

221

Plunkett were amongst those to be killed later that week.

Rosie, remembering the name, wondered if Joseph Plunkett had married his sweetheart and if he had what earthly good it had done either him or her.

'The two Pearce men,' Matt said. 'They only have the two. God, wouldn't that just tear the heart out of you, losing two sons?'

'Listen to yourself,' Connie said scornfully, as she tipped a pan of potatoes into a dish on the table. 'Sure, just one son killed would tear the heart out of you. But at least they'll have the benefit of the last rites and will have died cleanly and respectably.'

But privately she wondered to herself whether it would matter that much how and where a mother lost her son. True, a person might have a grave to tend to show him that he would never be forgotten but, if Danny were to be shot because of his part in the uprising, the sadness and horror of it would stay with her for ever and so would the guilt that she had sent him to his death by charging him to find Phelan and bring him home. God Almighty! No wonder Rosie could barely look at the lad, never mind speak to him. It was a wonder that she didn't lay some of the blame on her shoulders as well, for Rosie's loss and Bernadette's were as great as Connie's own.

Rosie thought the same way as Connie, but she was even more sorrow-laden, for she was positive that Danny would suffer the same fate as the leaders in time and she also faced the terrible realisation that they might never know. The rebel leaders had made history so their names would be published in the press. They were newsworthy. If they reported on the execution of the others at all, they'd hardly bother printing the names and so her husband could be shot at any time and tipped into a pauper's grave, along with other prison inmates, and she might never even find out where he'd been buried.

The pain of these thoughts never left her as the executions in the stone-breaker's yard of the jail went on and it was a pain she could share with no one, for she hadn't told Connie what Father Joe and Danny thought would happen and couldn't load it on her now.

Only one of the leaders had been pardoned and that was Eamon de Valera. Matt read the news out of the *Express* one evening after the meal. 'It's been reduced to a life sentence,' he said.

'How come?' Phelan asked. 'He was as involved as any other.'

'He has an American passport – he was born in New York, it says here,' Matt said.

Rosie shivered. The thought of spending her life in a tiny cell and only being let out to break big stones into smaller ones every day of her natural life didn't bear thinking about. She thought she'd rather be dead.

Rosie knew Danny wouldn't be able to stand being shut up for life like de Valera, and she also knew he would have no choice in the matter, and neither would she.

THIRTEEN

Rosie mourned the loss of Danny as if he were dead, as indeed he might well be. Every week she wrote to him as Connie did, but he didn't write back and this upset both women. 'Sure, what would he have to say?' Matt said when they mentioned it to him. 'In there, I should imagine one day slides into the next, each day the same.'

'I ask him questions,' Rosie protested. 'Surely he could answer those? And I tell him about Bernadette. You'd think he'd make some comment.'

But Matt could understand why Danny didn't write. As for telling him about the child he was likely never to see, it must have been like a knife in his heart to read those words.

After a month of silence, Connie was all for making the journey to Dublin with clothes and food for Danny, but Rosie stopped her. 'I think he has to wear prison uniform now,' she said. She hesitated over the next bit, for she'd never told Connie what had really happened to the basket of food she'd given her, but she did so now, unwilling to give the governor another good feed at their expense.

'You mean he got none of it?' Connie exclaimed. 'But the shirt and jumper, what happened to them?'

Rosie shrugged. 'I had to leave the whole thing with the Governor. I doubt Danny ever got a sniff of the food in the basket and the clothes would certainly have graced someone else's back. You must remember the meagre fare to be had in Dublin at that time, but even now, with things possibly different, I think good farm food would not get past first post and that's the Governor's office.

'Added to that, Danny will not want to see you there. Write to your aunt, Sister Cuthbert. Maybe the Franciscan friars are still visiting the prison. You might get news that way.'

It wasn't what Connie wanted to hear but she knew Rosie spoke the truth and so she did as she suggested. Sister Cuthbert wrote a lovely letter back, saying Father Joe, who'd accompanied Rosie to the prison, was just one of the friars visiting. But because he knew Danny was related to her and he remembered Rosie, he popped in now and then to see how he was.

Here, Sister Cuthbert hesitated. She hadn't known Danny before, but Father Joe had told her of the silent, morose man, his prison clothes hanging off his sparse frame. His face had lost its ruddy glow he said, and his pale cheeks were sunken in his face, for the paltry prison fare was barely enough to keep a man alive, especially as they worked from dawn to dusk at back-breaking work like smashing large stones day after day.

In Danny's eyes, the friar read the sorrow, exhaustion and sheer hopelessness that was lodged in his heart, but the man himself never spoke of it. Not that he was alone in these feelings, he told Sister Cuthbert, for most men incarcerated there were the same. So Sister Cuthbert told Connie that Danny was as well as could be expected in the circumstances and to keep writing even though he didn't answer. Let him know he's not been forgotten, she advised.

He hadn't, and the loss of him was like a leaden weight Rosie carried constantly with her, but in the end she had to push it to the back of her mind for life had to go on. There was still a dairy to see to, a house to clean, food to be cooked, clothes to wash and a baby to rear. It saddened her that Bernadette might know nothing of the father who had walked away that day but, surrounded by Danny's family and visited plenty by Rosie's sisters and Dermot, she barely missed him either.

In England, conscription had been introduced in January 1916 for, as the casualty lists rose, there were, perhaps understandably, fewer volunteers. In May of that year, this was extended to married men if conscription fell below fifty thousand a month. It was never introduced in Ireland, though it was proposed, for the authorities were fearful of the reaction, especially as such a move had been slammed by the Catholic Church.

This caused some resentment in England where men were given no such choice and when Ireland announced that German ships could dock there without fear of attack, this resentment was increased, causing riots and demonstrations against the Irish Catholics in many English towns and cities.

In Ireland, Catholic fervour was at its height and

the papers going on about all the Irish boys killed on some foreign field, fighting in some other country's war, were intensifying people's anti-war feelings.

They recounted tragic tales like that of the five Furey brothers from Wexford, who'd all been killed in the first ten months of the war, or the death of John Conlon, the young drummer boy, who was only fourteen. Could a boy have done much damage to the German armies armed with just drumsticks, the papers asked.

That was just the tip of the iceberg and there were many, many more instances. Most Catholics had read the poignant pleas for prayer and stories in the *The Messenger of the Sacred Heart,* the magazine sold in the churches. Each issue was similar since the war had begun. An officer might thank the Sacred Heart for his escape during bombardment, while a mother might thank the Sacred Heart for her son's recovery from severe wounds or an infantryman would thank the Sacred Heart for protection during his twenty-two months at the front.

These were typical of many requests. And then they were the obituaries for those who had died or who were missing.

There were also reports on the courage and bravery of the Catholic priests of the front who refused to stay behind lines and shared the trenches and conditions with the men they ministered to.

Many were killed alongside the soldiers they served, and mothers and wives commented to *The Messenger* the things their surviving menfolk wrote of the priests and how comforted they were to have them there. Many said even the non-Catholics had nothing but praise for them.

Each Mass now had a full congregation and when Dermot, along with other boys and girls his age at the National School, made their First Holy Communion on 19th June, the church was so full that there were people standing three-deep at the back.

Dermot, with his mop of golden curls that no macasser oil could tame, clutching his white missal and playing the ivory rosary beads through his fingers, looked angelic.

Like all the boys, his shirt was pristine white and so was the satin sash he had draped over one shoulder, but Chrissie told Rosie their mother had been all for going to Dublin to get him a silk shirt for the occasion. 'Daddy said she wasn't to go. Dublin was a place of unrest still and he could have a cotton shirt like any other boy,' Geraldine put in.

'Thank God!' Rosie said fervently. 'Why does she always want to make Dermot different? I'm sure he must hate it.'

'There's more than Dermot has to do things they hate,' Geraldine said with feeling. 'And they have to put up with it. He gets his way in most things, as you well know. Maybe it's a small price to pay.'

Rosie knew what Geraldine was talking about and she knew she had a point, for Dermot was thwarted in so very little, and so she said nothing more.

The Battle of the Somme began on 1st July 1916, almost a fortnight after the First Communions. So confident were the British of victory, they let the newsreels onto the battlefield for the first time.

There was no way the army could lie about the casualties now, or whitewash anything because the cameras continued to record it and it was shown on *Pathé News* at the cinemas. For the first time, British and Irish people saw what was happening to their menfolk. Blessington had no cinema, but the outrage of those who'd seen the films was reported by the papers, which carried many pictures of the dead and injured.

There had been so much bad feeling against Britain as the lists of the Irish boys and men killed in action rose. Requiem Masses were said throughout the land, though there were precious few bodies to bury. Many thought if their men were to die at all, let them at least die for their own country and serve under the flag of green, white and gold, struggling for Home Rule and Irish independence.

Conscious of this feeling in Ireland, and the open disapproval from America over the handling of the uprising and speed of the executions, the Government released many of the men from Kilmainham Jail before Christmas 1916.

After the execution of the leaders, Danny and the other men waited to be summoned to a court where the verdict would be decided before they had a chance to open their mouths. This would be followed fairly speedily by a trip to the stone-breaking yard to stand before a firing squad.

As day followed day and slid into weeks and months, the fear didn't lessen, it intensified. Danny thought they were playing cat and mouse games with them all, and he, like many more, became increasingly jittery and nervous.

None of the rebel prisoners were told they were to be released. After their sparse breakfast one mid-December morning, Danny was led back to his cell instead of into the yard. He didn't ask why, knowing that in that place it was better to ask few questions and keep one's head down.

They'd been led back to their cells once before when the rebel leaders were taken out to be executed, and Danny wondered if it was now their turn. There had been no trial, but when did that matter? The Franciscan friar, Father Joe, continued to visit and told him the wave of public opinion had swung in their favour – people were now more sympathetic to the reason they'd been fighting – but Danny had thought, so what? People's sympathy, however sincere and heartfelt, could not breach the walls of a prison, and so he'd taken little heed of Father Joe's words.

He lay on his bed and waited. He wasn't sure how long he stayed there, but it seemed an age. He closed his eyes, but didn't sleep, couldn't sleep. You had to be alert in these places.

He heard the tramp of boots on the stone corridors, opening some of the doors, and was on his feet and beside his bed before the key had turned in his lock. If this was it and he was to be led out to die, then he'd go with his head held high.

'You're for out, Walsh,' the guard snapped.

'Out?'

'Out. Home. Are you deaf?'

'Home?'

'Here,' the guard said, putting his hand into the big bag beside him that a colleague was holding and flinging clothes at him. 'Get changed.'

When the door clanked shut behind them, Danny stared at it for a moment or two. Was this some sort of sick joke? He fingered the civilian clothes thoughtfully, wondering who they'd first belonged to. They weren't his, certainly, but then his had been so tattered and worn he doubted they'd have been good for anything but the incinerator.

Suddenly he was seized with a desire to be free of the coarse prison garb and he tugged the stained, soiled clothes off in haste and pulled the shirt over his head. The trousers he'd been given hung loose on him and he wished he had a belt or braces to hold them up. There were no underclothes of any kind, nor a jumper over the shirt that might have kept him warm on that raw December day. But that was it, and he knew he should be grateful he had at least been given a coat, and he put that on and then sat on the bed again and waited.

He couldn't totally believe he was to be allowed to go free until he was in the road outside the prison with the door firmly slammed shut behind him. There were other men with him, chatting and laughing with one another, slapping each other on the back, light-headed with relief, filled with exhilaration. 'God, how I could sink a good few pints of Guinness now, Walsh,' said a man beside him. 'That's if I had a penny-piece on me,

231

of course. How about you?'

'Oh aye,' Danny said. 'That would be grand.'

In fact, Danny hadn't a thought of Guinness or anything else either. His one desire was to go home, to hold his dear wife in his arms and cuddle his baby daughter and give his mother a kiss.

He had a sudden, urgent desire to be away from Dublin, knowing if he ever came back to it again it would be too soon. He knew he should go and see Father Joe and tell him about his release, but almost as soon as the thought was in his head, he rejected it and turned for home.

He had no idea of the time, and the thick steel-grey clouds in the sky gave him little clue, but he knew the winter days were short and all too soon it would be dark. At first he strode out briskly, anxious to reach home as quickly as possible. However, he'd walked for little more than an hour when he was forced to rest, shocked he'd tired so easily. He was hungry too, but that mattered little: he'd not been full since before he'd entered the prison and the feeling of yawning emptiness was a familiar one.

He sat for a moment at the side of a stream, after taking a long drink of it, knowing if he was to get to the farmhouse before black night descended on him he had to get on. He couldn't rest every hour. In his inadequate clothes he didn't give himself much of a chance of survival if he had to spend a night in the open. He knew he'd be found stiff in a ditch, nicely gilded with frost, and the months of waiting would have been a cruel waste.

The ringing tramp of boots on the road made him suddenly alert, wondering even now if he

232

was to be hauled back to jail. There was nowhere to hide and it would be of little use anyway. If they wanted you back, they'd hunt you down without a doubt.

But, unbelievably, Shay and Sam came into view. 'Dan,' Shay cried when he saw Danny. 'Why didn't you wait for us?'

Why hadn't he? The thought of freedom and going home had driven everything else from his head.

'I didn't know if you were getting out too,' he said. 'And I couldn't bear to hang around Dublin to find out.'

'I can understand that well enough,' Shay said. 'But we knew you were out, we asked people, but no-one knew where you'd gone.'

'Why have they let us lot go?' Danny asked,

'I don't know and nor do I care,' Sam said. 'We're out, we're free, and that's what matters. I'm glad you decided to take a rest or we'd never have caught up with you.'

'Aye, maybe,' Danny said. 'But I was just thinking, I can't keep resting every hour if I want to reach home today. The cold eats into you when you sit for any time.'

'Aye. That wouldn't be hard either,' Sam said in agreement. 'For it's a bleak and icy day, right enough.'

'Shall we go on, then?' Danny asked, and the three set off together.

Many times that long trek back, Danny was glad of Shay and Sam. All three men were weakened and ill-nourished from their stay in prison, but they helped one another both by encouragement and physically.

In the beginning they sang all the rebel songs they could remember to keep up their spirits. But they did this only when they were out in the open, for they were far quieter when they were passing any houses on the roadside. Danny was glad the day was cold enough to keep those who didn't have to go out beside their own fireside and there were few to enquire where they were bound for. They knew their release would not be public knowledge yet, and so when asked they just said they were on their way up from Dublin and left it there.

They never went through the villages, either, but skirted them. Whatever Father Joe had said about the change in public opinion since the executions, they didn't intend to put it to the test. This inevitably made their progress slower and when darkness eventually descended, the going got tougher and they were still nowhere near home.

Finally they had to rest again. Full darkness had descended and within minutes of stopping, Danny's feet began to throb with cold, and icy fingers trailing through his body caused his teeth to chatter. 'Jaysus, but I'm cold,' Shay said, leaping to his feet and slapping at his body with his arms. 'How much longer d'you think?'

'It's hard to tell,' Danny said, so weary now his voice had begun to slur. 'An hour. Maybe two.'

'Christ. D'you think we'll make it?' Sam asked quite seriously, but Danny answered encouragingly.

'Of course. Come on, we'll set off now. Are you ready, Sam?'

'Not really,' Sam said. 'My legs are shaking. They feel like rubber.'

'If you sit much longer you won't be able to feel them at all,' Danny said, hauling Sam to his feet.

'And by Christ, I'm so hungry I could get started on a table leg.'

'We're all hungry,' Danny snapped. 'Talking of it does no good.'

'Oh, I don't know,' Shay said. 'It will encourage us, surely. Think of a plate thick with rashers, a couple of eggs and as many potatoes and bread and butter slices as you could eat.'

Danny felt saliva fill his mouth at the very thought of it. He saw it before him, could even smell it. Oh God, what he'd give for that this minute.

By the time Danny bade his friends farewell and made for the lane to the farmhouse, he was having trouble focusing, and even putting one foot before the other seemed almost too much of an effort. Twice he'd fallen on the road and had to be helped up and Shay and Sam were in no better shape – the last few miles they'd helped hold each other up.

Now he was at his own farm gate, alone, and wasn't sure if he'd make the last few yards. His head swam as he left the support of the gate he was hanging on to. He felt himself falling after a few stumbling steps forward and saw the ground coming up to meet him as he fell heavily.

Groaning and cursing, he got to his knees and then to his feet slowly with the help of the hedges on one side of the lane. Hanging on to them, he made his way, crablike, towards the farmhouse. The light from the Tilley lamp set in the window shone out like a welcoming beacon. Eventually he stood swaying outside the farmhouse door.

Rosie had had no notification of the Government's decision, and there had been nothing in the paper, and so the family were totally unprepared for Danny's appearance. They were sitting down to their evening meal and each of them had a basin of thick stew served from the large pot, now put back on the hook above the hearth to keep hot. Two dishes piled high with potatoes in their skins were there for people to help themselves. Even Bernadette was at the table in the special chair with long legs that Matt had fashioned for her and Rosie was bending over her plate, removing the skin from the potato and mashing it with a bit of gravy from the stew to moisten it.

This was the scene that Danny saw as he lifted the latch and pushed open the door. The smell and warmth made him feel light-headed and he stood gripping the door jamb to prevent himself sinking to the stone-slabbed floor.

Rosie stared at Danny aghast. Her thoughts were racing. What in God's name was Danny doing here?

But before she was able to voice these thoughts, Danny, who knew he couldn't take another step without falling on his face, cried, 'Help me.'

Rosie caught Danny before he fell and Matt got to the other side of him and together they helped him into a chair before the fire. He sank into it with a sigh of sheer relief and closed his eyes.

Around the table there was stunned silence. No-one but Rosie had seen Danny since he strode away that Easter morning, but even the shambling, battered, bruised figure she'd seen just once eight months ago bore no resemblance to this man, her husband. His face was grey, what could be seen of it above the thick stubble. His cheeks were sunken, his lips cracked and chapped, his red-rimmed eyes like pools of sadness. Even Danny's hair was now liberally streaked with white. Rosie was shocked by his thinness – even through his coat she'd felt the bones of him.

'Mother of God, what have they done to him?' Connie breathed, as Rosie gently unbuttoned his coat.

But Rosie didn't answer, for at that minute Danny opened his eyes and held Rosie's, and her heart turned over in pity for this man who'd suffered so much. 'Food, please, Rosie,' he said. 'I need food.'

'There's plenty in the stew pot,' Connie said, crossing to the hearth.

'I'll give him mine,' Rosie said. 'That on the stove will be too hot yet awhile.'

Danny sat, his arms by his sides, while Rosie spooned him the stew with the potatoes she'd dropped into it, as he was unable to lift his arm to feed himself. He tasted the deliciousness and warmth of it as it trickled down his throat. Bernadette, who was bewildered seeing her mother feed a big grown-up person, began shouting to be let down. 'Hush, Bernadette,' Sarah admonished.

'Let her be,' Connie said from the hearth where she still stood staring at her son. 'She can come over to me.'

Danny's eyes widened as the child came into view and he stared at her. He'd barely noticed her at the table, but now... He'd left behind a wee crawling baby, but eight months was a long time in the life of a child and Bernadette was now a walking, babbling toddler who stared at him with her bright eyes curious as to who this strange man was. He tried valiantly to smile at her reassuringly.

Rosie spooned the last of the stew into Danny's mouth, and asked, 'Do you want some more?'

'Aye,' Danny said shortly, and Rosie said, 'I'll take it from the pot, but it will be hot. You'll have to wait while it cools.'

While Rosie busied herself, Connie, wanting to take the hopeless look from her son's face, said to Bernadette, 'Look, child, here's your daddy come home again.'

Bernadette looked interested in the name she'd heard now and then, though she had no idea what a daddy was. 'Will you sit up on his knee a wee while?' Connie said. 'While your Mammy is getting him something to eat.'

Bernadette would have none of it and as her grandmother tried to release her onto the man's knee she began to writhe and struggle and scream, loud enough to lift the thatch. 'Leave it, Mam,' Rosie said sharply, for she'd seen the look of pain cross Danny's face. 'Take her back to the table. She's barely eaten anything.' To Danny she said, 'Don't mind her, pet, she's just a baby and doesn't know you yet.'

'I know that,' Danny said. 'Don't worry.'

But despite Danny's words, he was deeply hurt

by Bernadette's reaction. He'd accepted the fact she'd hardly know him on his return and had even discussed it with Sam and Shay on the way back. If he'd thought further about it, he would have known the child would have grown, but he carried in his head the picture of how she'd been when he'd left. This child was like a stranger. If she'd been a little quiet or shy with him he would have accepted it, but he'd never imagined she'd struggle and scream the way she did at the thought of sitting on his knee.

Rosie, though, thought Bernadette's attitude understandable, but there was another more pressing concern in her head. 'Danny,' she said tentatively, 'What are you doing here?'

'I haven't escaped, if that's what you mean,' Danny snapped back, annoyed. 'I was released along with a few others this morning. I've been walking ever since.'

Rosie let her breath out in relief. Since he'd appeared in the door she feared the sound of army boots down the lane, kicking open the door and dragging Danny away again, this time to shoot him dead.

The stew and warmth were beginning to slowly revive Danny and this time he was able to hold the basin of stew himself. Rosie handed him a slice of bread too and he tore into it like a wild animal, revelling at being able to do so. He and his fellow inmates had tried to make the one slice of bread, given with very thin soup, last by taking small nibbles of it and chewing it to nothing in an attempt to make them feel fuller. It hadn't worked, but now with two bowls of stew and potatoes and

239

bread inside him, he began to feel almost human, and as he drained the second bowl he leaned back again in his chair. 'God that was good.'

Around the table, the family still sat in shock at Danny's sudden appearance and at the state of him, and any conversation was stilted and strained. Phelan was so affected, Rosie saw, he was unable to eat, and when he pushed his basin away and got to his feet it was almost half-full.

After the meal, as the women began clearing away, Matt crossed to the hearth to sit next to his son and saw he was fast asleep in the chair. 'Best thing for him, I'd say,' he commented to Connie and she nodded and fetched a blanket from their bed to tuck around him.

Rosie made tea for them all and they talked in whispers so as not to disturb the slumbering Danny. Connie said in a fierce whisper, 'What have they done to my son? I can't believe it, Sister Cuthbert said he was fine.'

'She wouldn't have seen him, remember,' Rosie said. 'She'd go on what the Franciscan friars told her. Anyway, if she'd known the true state of things, what was to be gained by telling you? You couldn't help the situation.'

'No, but...'

'Don't torture yourself, Mam,' Rosie said, laying her hand over her mother-in-law's kindly. 'Whatever has happened to Danny is in the past. He's home now, released and without charge. We'll soon have him back hale and hearty, the way he used to be.'

'God, you're a wonderful girl, Rosie,' Connie said. 'God smiled on us the day Danny brought

240

you in the door.'

Rosie was glad she'd reassured her mother-in-law, but she wasn't sure Danny would ever be the way he was. That vibrant young man who'd strode out so confidently on Easter Sunday eight months before had gone forever, she feared.

FOURTEEN

Rosie was thrilled and overwhelmed that Danny had been released from jail. She didn't know why nor did she care, all she knew was that he was free, a thing she thought she never would see, and she hoped and prayed that with good food and plenty of rest a glimpse of the old Danny would return.

Danny seemed to worry over his physical strength. 'I'm as weak as a kitten,' he complained to Rosie one day. 'I used to break rocks six days a week, twelve hours a day, on a starvation diet but now the slightest thing tires me.'

But Rosie wasn't worried about that aspect at all, certain in time Danny would regain his physical strength. 'That's reaction only,' she told him reassuringly. 'You must give it time. And at least there is no danger of your starving here. Your mother is determined to fatten you up.'

Rosie spoke the truth, for Connie, desperately worried for her son, was constantly pushing food before him and urging him to eat up. At first, he could do so only sparingly and even then he was often sick, the food being too rich to the person who'd lived on a plain and meagre diet for so long.

It was the kind, loving Danny Rosie missed and missed so much she often cried in bed after he had fallen asleep. She missed the closeness between them, the way they could talk for hours, their hugs and cuddles, the times Danny told Rosie how much he loved her, what she meant to him, the sex they had enjoyed so much and she often wondered bleakly if it was all lost for good.

When he'd first come home, she had tried to hug him but he had shrugged her off and when she'd tried to tell him how much she loved him and how glad she was that he was home again, he answered her with a grunt. She wished he would talk about his ordeal, convinced that it would help him, but when she asked about it he snapped at her. But then he shouted at her for very little nowadays and would often reduce her to tears she tried desperately to hide from the family.

Matt tried to make allowances for his son. 'Such a thing is bound to change a man,' he told Rosie when he came upon her weeping in the barn one day. 'Prison, I would say, has brutalised Danny, and that's a fact.'

Phelan was with his father and said, 'All well and good, Daddy, but none of that is Rosie's fault. I never get a civil word out of him, but by God, I don't deserve one. But Rosie has done no harm to anyone.'

'I know that, son, but...'

'And Sam went through it too and he's falling over himself to be nice to Sarah.'

Sam was determined to win Sarah over. Though he looked as bad as Danny, he'd delivered a wrapped present to the Walshes' house on Christmas Eve. Sarah, who'd refused to see or have anything to do with Sam since his return, was intrigued enough to open this box in her room.

The gasp she gave brought the other three women in to see what had caused it, and Sarah held up the shawl. It was the loveliest thing Rosie thought she'd ever seen, rose-pink and shot through with threads of silver and knitted in the finest and softest wool. God alone knew where Sam had got such a thing.

'Of course, I can't accept it.'

Elizabeth couldn't believe she was hearing right. 'Course you can.'

'No, I can't,' Sarah said, with a regretful sigh. 'To accept such a thing would be in the nature of a promise.'

'You wrote to him in prison,' Elizabeth pointed out. 'Wasn't that a promise?'

'No,' Sarah declared. 'That was just to cheer him up. Don't forget, we never thought they'd be released, then, did we? What do you think, Mammy?'

Connie smiled and said grimly, 'I think, cutie dear, you must do what your heart tells you, even if your head tells you different. But don't accept the shawl if the man means nothing to you.'

'He doesn't mean anything to me,' Sarah declared, packing the shawl away decidedly. 'I shall return it to him tomorrow after Mass.'

She tried, Rosie knew, for she'd seen Sarah remonstrating with Sam outside the chapel. She had no time to watch the outcome, the day was too cold to linger and she had to hurry home to look after Bernadette and see to the dinner so that Connie could go up to the later Mass with the men, but she did, however, see Sarah sneaking in

244

the door later, still holding the box.

That evening, friends and neighbours called around for the usual Christmas jollification and Sam was amongst them. When, later, Sarah and Sam went for a walk, Rosie noticed the shawl around Sarah's shoulders. 'She's kept it then,' Elizabeth remarked beside Rosie. 'If she didn't want it, she could have given it to me. It wouldn't have offended my sensitivities one jot.'

Rosie gave her a push and they laughed together but then Rosie caught Danny's eyes on her, morose and brooding. She tried to repress the sigh of impatience as she made her way towards him.

He'd snapped at her already quite a few times that evening, Rosie recalled, and many times had brought the eyes of the company upon them both. He contrasted badly with Sam, doing his level best to woo Sarah. Rosie felt saddened and frustrated by Danny's behaviour.

She didn't know what could be done about it. She'd married him and that was that, she had to make the best of it. Crying and complaining would hardly rectify matters. And that is what she had told Phelan that day in the barn. 'It's of no matter,' she said, brushing the tears from her eyes with her hands. 'I'm silly to let Danny upset me. Sure, don't I know he means nothing half the time?'

Phelan said nothing more, but he felt sorry for Rosie and he knew his parents did too. He was glad they were more or less back on their earlier footing for when Rosie had returned from Dublin after seeing Danny that one time, she'd

245

seemed to hate him, and with reason, he thought, but for some time he'd felt the difference in her.

Rosie could have told him, eight months was a long time to keep hold of a hatred of someone she shared a house with.

No-one could have been unaware either how sorry and filled with shame the boy was. He did everything he could to make amends and Matt often praised the amount of work he did for one so young. Nothing seemed too much trouble for him and he did everything he could to lift the heavy work of the farm from his father's shoulders.

But his saving grace, as far as Rosie was concerned, was the way he was with Bernadette and just as importantly how the child loved him. She knew Connie would be happy if they at least drew some sort of truce and as time went on, Rosie was able to view the whole thing differently and see that Phelan had made a mistake and had only seen the glory of war. He'd been unprepared for the blood and the carnage and the swift and overwhelming British response. He'd also been unprepared for Danny's intervention and he'd told Rosie this. By then, even he'd thought the mini rebellion was doomed but there had been nothing he could have done to stop Danny taking the place of him and Niall for he'd been determined to get them released. Rosie knew what manner of man Danny was and that Phelan spoke the truth and gradually the animosity between them lessened.

Sam became a regular visitor at the farmhouse as

the year progressed. Sarah was now officially walking out with him and he was full of charm and good manners when he appeared at the house. In contrast, Danny was often silent and miserable looking and seldom had a good word for anyone except Bernadette, though sometimes his attitude unnerved her too. When he shouted, she was often frightened and her eyes would grow large with alarm, and sometimes she'd shake for she'd seldom heard a raised voice in the whole of her young life. But when he wasn't cross, she'd often seek his company and he always made time for her. One February evening, Rosie was returning home from her mother's house. Bad weather had kept her from visiting since the week after Christmas and she'd left Bernadette with Connie for she had a streaming cold. She came around the corner of the barn she was surprised to hear muted voices inside there and the sheen of a light beneath the door.

She recognised Shay's and Danny's voices as she approached and felt filled with apprehension. Why would Shay be skulking about the barn, talking secretly to Danny, instead of sitting up in the room like any other body? She crept nearer the door to listen.

'I don't care about the bloody meeting,' she heard Danny say. 'I want no more part in it.'

'You signed the allegiance, Danny.'

'Aye, fool that I was,' Danny said. 'You know why I was forced to do that, Shay.'

'Danny, for Christ's sake will you listen to me?' Shay cried. 'It doesn't matter a tinker's cuss why you signed, the fact was you did. It's for your own

247

good I'm saying this, Danny. It's just a meeting, that's all, and if you're not there a very dim view will be taken of it altogether.'

The blood in Rosie's veins seemed to run like ice. Dear God! Was it starting up again? She'd not stand it. She had the urge to burst into the barn and demand an explanation, order Shay from the farm and forbid Danny to listen to him. But this Danny, returned to her from Kilmainham Jail, was like an unexploded bomb, and she wasn't at all sure how he would react if she did any of those things.

She turned away regretfully and made her way to the house, and once there was glad of Connie's chatter for it covered her worried silence. When Danny eventually came in, he refused to even look at Rosie.

Why didn't she ask what manner of meeting it was that Shay was so insistent he attend? But this Danny could not be asked questions like that.

She thought maybe he'd tell her when they were alone in bed, but Danny said not a word. But then, she told herself, he hadn't been aware that she had overheard anything, and Rosie almost wished she hadn't.

The following night, after the evening meal, Danny, instead of following his father to the other side of the fire for a smoke, made instead for the door. He took his jacket from the hook behind it and said, 'I'm away out.'

'Out!' Connie repeated in surprise, while Matt asked, 'Out where?'

Rosie said not a word. She wasn't able to speak,

248

the roof of her mouth had gone uncommonly dry and her limbs had begun to tremble. Danny glanced from his parents to her, but it was to his father he spoke. 'Just out,' he said. 'I'm a grown man, not a wean to be questioned.'

'It was a civil question.'

'Aye, and you got a civil answer,' Danny replied, as he opened the door and let the winter air in. He looked across at Rosie and said, 'Don't wait up, I don't know what time I'll be in, but I'll likely be late.'

Rosie couldn't even nod her head. She stood as if frozen to the spot and not until the door closed behind Danny did she feel she could move. 'Do you know where he's bound for, lass?' Connie asked, and Rosie shook her head.

'No, but I think he's going to a meeting. I heard him talking to Shay out in the barn,' she said, and turning to Phelan asked, 'Do you know anything about it?'

'How would I?' Phelan asked. 'Danny barely bids me the time of day.'

But Phelan did know. At least, he knew that the meeting was in O'Connor's in Blessington, for Niall had overheard his brother say so and had told Phelan that it was called by a man nicknamed Red McCullough, because of his shock of ginger hair. He remembered Red from his own time in the Brotherhood and knew him to be a dynamic and persuasive man with a pure hatred for the English. Phelan was deeply worried for his brother. But to tell his family any of it would not help and might cause them further worry and he didn't know how any of it was to be resolved.

Danny strode along the road with a determined step. He wondered why Rosie had not said a word to him about where he intended to go that night. She couldn't know anything, surely? And yet she acted so strangely. Anyway, he thought determinedly, she needn't fret, none of them needed to, for this was the finish of it – he was going to tell them this night that he'd done his share and was going to do no more.

'I was forced into it, in order to release two young boys who should never have been allowed to join in the first place,' Danny tried to explain to Red McCullough later that evening.

Red looked at him dispassionately and replied, 'That's neither here nor there.'

'I think it is.'

'What you think doesn't count,' Red said ominously. 'Once you join up, it's for life. You can't pick and choose.' He glanced at Danny contemptuously and went on, 'What manner of man are you at all, to fall at the first post?'

Danny grabbed Red McCullough by the neck, but two other men pulled him away and held him by the arms as he yelled, 'First post? That foolhardy plan for a few ill-trained and badly equipped men to take on the might of the British Army was doomed from the start. I knew that. And yet I gave it my best shot and brought down as many soldiers as the next man, so don't you try and say now I lacked courage.

'And then, for this ill-fated exercise, I lost eight months in jail, as you did I know,' he added as Red held up his hand as if to interrupt. 'Now my wife is nervous of the man I've become, my child terrified of the stranger in her house, and my brother does the lion's share of the work on the farm that will one day be mine because I've not regained the health and strength I once took for granted.

'So,' he finished. 'Don't talk to me about first posts. That was the last post as far as I am concerned and I want nothing more to do with all this again.'

'Sit down, man.'

'I'll not,' Danny said. 'I'm not staying.'

Immediately the grip the two men had on his arms tightened. A chair was brought and Danny manhandled into it. He would have sprung up from it again, but he took a look around the room and knew if he tried he would be forced back down, for every man in the room was ringed against him, even Shay and Sam. Added to that, the outburst had taken it out of him and so he sat in the chair and wished he was anywhere but in that room listening to Red McCullough's plans for the regrouping of the Brotherhood to plan their next strategy.

Rosie was woken in the early hours of the morning and lay for a short while wondering what had roused her while Bernadette slumbered on. Then she heard the noise again. Looking across, she saw that the space beside her was empty and with a sick feeling consuming her, she slipped from her bed, grabbing a shawl for her shoulders.

Danny, always a moderate drinker, was as drunk as she had ever seen anybody and stumbling about the kitchen. She didn't know what that meant at all, but now wasn't the time to discuss it. She had to get him into the bedroom and his bed before he roused the house. 'Come away in, Danny,' she pleaded, catching his arm. 'Come on, the morning will be on top of us before we know it.'

Danny gazed at Rosie, bleary-eyed. This was his wife, the woman he had promised to love above all others, whom he did love above all others. He had no wish to be separated from her again, not for any reason.

He allowed himself to be led into the room, and sat on the bed. 'I told them, Rosie, I wanted no part of it.'

'Hush,' Rosie cautioned as she bent to unfasten Danny's boots, 'the wean's sleeping.'

'Aye,' Danny said, 'the wean. I told them she was terrified of me. They wouldn't listen. They don't care.'

Rosie barely heard Danny's words. He continued to mutter as she fought to remove as many of his clothes as she could. Suddenly he said, 'They're mad, the lot of them.'

He began to cry then, the great gulping sobs of the maudlin drunk, and Rosie pushed him down onto the bed and put her arms around him. Anxious only to keep him quiet, she soothed him, 'Hush, Danny pet, hush.'

Danny felt a stirring inside himself with the nearness of his wife that he had worried he'd lost forever. The old Danny would have taken time to arouse her too, but this Danny hadn't time for such niceties and so when he entered her she was far from ready and bit her lip to prevent a cry of pain escaping. Danny, however, was well-satisfied and quickly, and as he lay spent on top of her he said softly, 'Rosie, my lovely Rosie.'

It was the first gentle thing he'd said, Rosie thought, but he had needed to get drunk to say it. Suddenly compassion for this confused and unhappy man rose in her and as she eased herself away from him with difficulty as he was now a dead weight, she said softly, 'Hush now, and go to sleep.' But she was talking to herself for Danny was already dead to the world.

The next morning Danny was slow to rise, and Rosie left him in bed, thinking a cup of tea might help him wake up. She was sluggish with lack of sleep herself, for she'd lain awake long after Danny had fallen into his stupor. She had been wondering if this was to be the pattern of her life now, and hoped to God it wasn't.

She'd just wet the tea when Danny entered the kitchen and at the look in his red-rimmed eyes, she felt sympathy for him. Not so Matt, who crashed in through the cottage door minutes later and surveyed his son across the kitchen, an angry scowl on his face. 'So, you're up at last.'

Danny took the cup of tea Rosie handed him and had a scalding gulp of it before he answered his father. 'Aye, I'm up.'

'Well, let me tell you,' Matt said scathingly. 'Your free time is your own, while it stays your free time. When it eats into your work time, it begins to be my business. I suggest you sluice your thick head under the pump and get away to the byre where your brother has been working alone this last hour.'

Matt waited for no reply, but went out through the door again. Rosie didn't know how to break the uneasy silence. The only sounds in the room were the ticking clock, the peat settling in the hearth and the gulps of tea that must have been scalding the mouth off Danny.

When he eventually left, Rosie sighed in relief. 'We know the state he was in last night,' Connie said, having entered the kitchen. 'We heard him and we heard you trying to quieten him. I've never seen Danny that way. Did he give you any reason for it?'

Rosie thought there was no point in worrying Connie by repeating the ramblings of Danny the previous night. 'What drunk man says anything sensible at all?' she said. 'He said a lot of blathering nonsense that I paid no heed to.'

'I'm heart sore for you, girl.' Connie said. 'And I hope this isn't going to be the way of it from now on. His father will never stand for it.'

Nor I, Rosie thought, but she knew she'd have to stand it, for she was married to Danny and had promised to obey him for better or worse, in sickness and in health.

Rosie hoped Danny would talk to her about where he'd gone the previous night and what had caused him to drink so much, but he'd said nothing, so later that night in bed she asked tentatively, 'Where did you go last night?'

Danny, having no memory of his ramblings the night before, thought briefly about not telling her. Why worry her? But maybe it would be best if she knew. 'O'Connor's,' he said briefly. 'We had a back room there.'

'We?'

'It's what's left of the Brotherhood that Phelan got mixed up in. Most of them I shared the jail with. Red McCullough runs the whole show. He was a good friend of Michael Collins.'

Rosie had heard of Michael Collins from the *Dublin Express.* 'Was he there too?'

'No, he's still in jail,' Danny said. 'He wasn't in Kilmainham Jail. He was sent to Richmond Barracks and then to some place in Wales and is still there apparently.'

'Danny, I don't want you mixed up in anything like this again,' Rosie said.

'Nor I. I told them that.'

'And what did they say?'

Danny sighed. 'They reminded me I signed the allegiance and that it's for life. I can't get out of it.'

'But you must be able to,' Rosie cried, alarmed. 'If you want to have nothing more to do with them, surely to God you can say so?'

'I tried saying so,' Danny said. 'I tried till I was blue in the face.'

'So what does it mean? What stupid thing are they planning now?'

'I couldn't tell you even if I knew,' Danny said. 'It wouldn't be safe for you to know. But last night was just a pep talk – nothing was decided.'

But something had been decided, Danny knew, and it was that he realised he had no idea how he was going to get out of this organization before he was dragged into it again. That was the reason he'd drunk himself stupid.

All through the remaining weeks of February and into March, Danny went to meetings every week, sometimes twice, and always returned the worse for wear. He could tell Rosie little of what went on, and so she ceased to ask, but worry ate at her every time.

Connie and Matt had a good idea what Danny was up to and Connie urged Rosie to give him a talking to, but Rosie knew Danny was haunted himself by the whole thing and said nothing.

Danny didn't need to tell her how interest had been rekindled in the Brotherhood since the executions in Kilmainham Jail. She knew the rebels had become martyrs and the Catholic Church itself had had an upswing because of the monks' descriptions of the pious way each man had met his death. This had swung the Church's sympathy a little to the fight for Home Rule, so now the numbers attending the meetings had risen dramatically in that little room behind O'Connor's pub, and Red McCullough began talking of guerrilla warfare, just as Danny remembered Michael Collins had. 'First we need weapons,' he said at a meeting in early April, and none could argue with that. The few weapons they'd once had had been seized.

Danny's was the one voice which spoke of the political solution and putting their trust, initially at least, in the convention planned for later that year when delegates from Dublin, Belfast and London were to meet to discuss the 'Irish Problem'.

'Oh God, will you listen to the man,' one shouted as Danny voiced his proposal. 'Whenever have the English played fair with us? Aren't Irish bodies littering France and Belgium now? And have we achieved anything through their sacrifice?'

'Maybe this will be different.'

'And maybe pigs might fly if they had a mind,' another said.

'We need weapons. We can't do anything without weapons,' Red said again. 'Are you with us, Walsh, or against us?'

'You know my views.'

At the same meeting, two raids were planned, one on the arsenals at Kilbride Camp on Thursday evening, just two days away, and another at Richmond Barracks the following Saturday. Volunteers were asked for. It was noted that Danny put himself forward for neither of these. 'What about you, Walsh?'

'What about me?'

'What will you do?'

'Nothing,' Danny said. Shay was beside him as he spoke and Danny heard his sharp intake of breath.

'You're in this the same as all of us and don't forget it.'

'No, I'm in this because you forced me to be,' Danny said.

'I think you're a rotten coward,' a man shouted from the back. 'An English arse-licker.'

'I'm neither,' Danny said firmly, though his fists were balled by his side and he longed to send the man's teeth down his throat. 'I'm just an

Irishman trying to get on as best I can and one who feels we should wait for the results of the Convention before we make any sort of move.'

He was shouted down and booed at, and later, outside, with the meeting over, Shay said quietly, 'Christ, man, will you ever learn to keep your mouth shut?'

'How can I?'

'You best learn, for there are some amongst these men who would shut it for you and permanently,' Shay warned.

Rosie knew there was something serious afoot. She couldn't say how, she just knew, and the tension in Danny on Thursday evening was almost tangible. 'Can you tell me?' she said that night as they lay in bed.

'You know I can't.'

'Right. I will ask just one thing. Are you involved?'

'No.' Danny could at least say that definitely. 'It's nothing whatsoever to do with me.'

That should have made Rosie feel better, but it didn't and she slept badly. Later, she was roused by a rapping at the window and she awoke with a jerk. Danny too was awake instantly, and he jumped out of bed and ran to the window. 'Shay?'

'Let me in, Danny, for Christ's sake,' Shay said, and Danny opened the window wide. Rosie sat up in the bed, pulling a shawl around her as Danny lit a lamp. 'What is it?' he said; even in his agitation he spoke in a low voice lest he woke his sleeping child and indeed rouse the whole house.

'They were waiting for them at the Kilbride Camp,' Shay said. 'Three were shot dead, two captured and the rest of us got away.'

'Ah Christ!'

'That's not all,' Shay said. 'They're blaming you, Danny.'

'Me?'

'They think you tipped the soldiers the wink.'

'Jesus Christ, I'd never do such a thing. Speak against my own countrymen?'

'I know you wouldn't, Danny,' Shay said. 'That's why I'm here and I'm risking my life to do it. You must leave here this night and go into hiding, they'll be coming for you.'

'What are you talking about?'

'The Brotherhood. They think you've betrayed them.'

'Well, I'll put them right.'

'D'you think you'll be believed?'

'God, Shay, this is Ireland, not New York or Chicago.'

'Aye, it may be Ireland, but I'll tell you it's just as dangerous. They hold you responsible for the reception committee awaiting them at the camp.'

'What will they do?' Rosie asked, frightened.

Shay didn't answer but his eyes said it all and Rosie knew they would kill Danny if he stayed. Danny knew it too, but he refused to accept it. 'Come on, Shay, I'm not afraid of them.'

'Then you're a fool,' Shay said. 'You must leave, Danny, and quickly.'

'Don't be silly,' Danny said. 'Where would I run to?'

'The safest place would be England,' Shay said.

'There are cells of resistance like this all over Ireland.'

'I have no intention of fleeing my native land for anyone.'

Shay shrugged and said angrily, 'I've risked my life to try and save yours and fine thanks I've got for it. I thought you might have given a thought to your parents, or Rosie and your little daughter, but there, I've done my best. Just don't say I didn't warn you.'

Shay had turned away towards the window and Rosie, after a beseeching look at Danny, called him back. 'Wait, Shay, for God's sake.'

'I can't wait,' Shay said, 'Jesus, how can I make you see sense? Do you think I would be here in the middle of the night if it was some sort of joke? I'm a dead man if they ever hear of this.'

Rosie shook her head, confused. 'I understand what you say, Shay. But why are they blaming Danny?'

'Because he wouldn't take part and spoke against them on more than one occasion. He knew all about the raids, the times, the arrangements, everything. You can see why they think that way. But every minute you delay is more dangerous and not only for yourselves alone.'

'It's madness, Rosie, you must see it,' Danny said. 'I know no-one in England.'

But what Rosie saw was her husband before her, and the thought of him dying, blasted through the head or heart, caused her physical pain. 'You must go away, Danny,' she urged him. 'It may only be for a short time.'

'Where, for Christ's sake?'

Rosie desperately thought for a moment and remembered where she went once before for help and advice when she'd been in dire straits. 'The Sisters of Mercy, they'll help you, I'm sure. You know, where your mother's aunt was?'

'She's in Dublin now, not England.'

'Aye, but there's another convent in Handsworth in Birmingham. Maybe you could go there for a little while?'

'I hate this whole idea.'

'It might only be for a time,' Rosie said. 'Think of it that way.'

'I'll think of it this way,' Danny said. 'I go nowhere without you.'

'Danny, talk sense.'

'If Shay's right and I'm in danger, then so are you,' Danny said. 'If I'm not to be found, maybe they'll start on you.'

'Surely to God they'll not hurt women or weans.'

'Who knows what they'll do,' Danny continued. 'But I'd never have a minute's peace away from you, I know that. If you won't come for yourself alone, come for Bernadette's sake. Could you live with yourself if anything happened to her?'

Rosie went cold at the very thought. She'd once thought she'd follow Danny to Siberia if he asked her and she knew that was now being put to the test. She shivered in apprehension although her voice stayed firm enough. 'If you think it is that serious, then of course we must go.'

Danny went up to wake his parents and tell them of events. 'My father knows of this,' Shay said, as Rosie began. 'He'll drive you to Dublin tonight.'

'Surely we can wait till morning?'

'Jesus, Rosie, did you not listen to a word I said. The men are raging and could descend on us at any time,' Shay said, visibly nervous. 'Dear God, Rosie, I'm terrified myself, so I am.'

It was Shay's reaction that finally convinced Rosie that they had to leave and right away. She hoped it wouldn't be forever – God knows she'd miss the place. Connie came into the room, then, as Rosie was packing, and said in a horrified whisper, 'God, child, this is terrible. You can't go just like this.'

'I can't not go,' Rosie said. 'It's too dangerous for us to stay here.'

'But like this ... skulking away in the dead of night as if you have done something to be ashamed of.'

'Mammy, I dislike it as much as you.'

'Would you think of leaving the child?'

'No, Mammy,' Rosie said horrified. 'I'd never rest away from her and I don't know how long we'll have to hide.'

Connie heard the catch in Rosie's voice and took her in her arms as she cried out her fear and helplessness. 'The happiest time of my life has been here,' Rosie told Connie faithfully. 'I love you all dearly and I'll miss you sorely. But Shay believes they will come for Danny, and soon, and if Danny was to be killed, life for me would lose all meaning,' and she remembered the time she thought she would never see him again. Now she knew how Danny had stood against the IRA's demands, the dilemma of which had caused him to behave so oddly, she loved him more than ever and knew for his sake and his safety she would follow him to the ends of the earth.

'I know what he means to you, Rosie,' Connie said, 'and if you must go away then you must. I'll put some food together for you.'

'Thank you, Mammy,' Rosie said, glad that Connie understood, but it was with a heavy heart that she began to pack up their clothes and other items she'd hate to leave behind, although she knew they had to travel as lightly as possible.

She'd almost finished when Connie came in with parcels of food and another large, linen-wrapped bundle. 'The clock,' she said. 'Have you space for it?'

'Mammy, I can't take that,' Rosie protested. 'It's the family clock.'

'And aren't you still family even though you will be so far away?'

'Aye, but...'

'Child, I have nothing else I can give you.'

'I want nothing.'

'Take it to please me. It will be your link with home.'

Rosie was touched and she knew it was important to Connie that she take the clock and so she didn't protest further.

'God, girl, for this to happen?' Connie said. 'My heart is broken, so it is.'

'Ah, Mammy,' Rosie said, and she put her arms around Connie and they cried together.

'Come on,' said Matt suddenly at the door. 'You must away quickly. There's no time for tears now.'

Rosie knew he was right and yet she understood

Connie's distress, She picked the still-sleeping Bernadette up, wrapped her in a warm shawl for the night air was treacherous and hurried out into the kitchen where Danny stood ready.

'Have you enough money, Danny?' Matt asked as they stood at the door with a very impatient and obviously nervous Shay beside them. 'Aye, Daddy,' Danny replied, 'and I mean to get a job as soon as I'm able.'

'Just in case it's not as easy as you think,' Matt said, pushing two ten pound notes into his hand.

'Ah, Daddy no...'

'Yes,' Matt insisted, and went on, 'It's all right to be stiff-necked when you only have yourself to think about, but if you won't take money for your-self then take it for Rosie and wee Bernadette.'

Danny gave a brief nod and pocketed the money.

'Will you not at least bid the girls farewell and Phelan too?' Connie asked.

'No,' Danny said. 'There's no time, and anyway, the fewer that know the better.'

Matt at least understood that. 'How are you going?' he asked.

'Across the fields, it's quicker.'

'Then take a lantern or you'll break your neck,' Matt said, giving them the one lit in the kitchen. With another tearful hug the four were on their way.

It was much shorter to Shay's father's farm across the fields, but it was a cold and miserable journey and Rosie was afraid she'd stumble and fall, and drop the child. She knew she would be glad when she reached the farmhouse.

'Why is your father putting himself out like this?' Danny asked. 'I mean, it's a fair hike for anyone, and in the dead of night too.'

'He owes you a favour,' Shay said. 'He's always felt it since you stood in for Niall last Easter. This is his way of paying back the debt. Anyway, it wouldn't do for your own father to be seen to be away from the farm the night you disappeared. I'll not be suspected because I was with them tonight, and my family too will be semi-protected by that. This is the most sensible way.'

Maybe, thought Rosie. But she could list a whole lot of things she would put under the label of sensible before this trek they were to undertake through this coal-black night. But she didn't share her thoughts.

Danny grasped Shay's hand suddenly. 'I'll never forget this, Shay,' he said. 'I know we've been mates for always, though we've different opinions about how to obtain Home Rule, but I know what you have risked coming here this night.'

There was a lump in Shay's throat as he put his arms around Danny. How he wished things could be different but he'd done what he could to protect him, because he knew he was no traitor. 'Go on now,' he urged, 'and Godspeed.'

And they turned the corner at the bottom of the lane to see Willie, having heard them approach, leading the horse before the cottage.

FIFTEEN

'Now are you comfortable enough, for it's a fine step of a journey we have before us?' Willie Ferguson asked, tucking a blanket around Rosie and her child as they lay in the cart.

'Aye. Yes, I'm grand,' Rosie said. 'Are you coming in too, Danny?'

Danny still wondered if they were over-reacting, whether this headlong dash was really necessary, but if Shay and Willie were right then he didn't think he could hide away in the back of the cart. He should be up at the front beside Willie where he could watch out for danger for any one of them, but he wasn't going to tell Rosie this. 'No,' he said, 'I have no sleep on me to tell you the truth. I'll stay up here with Willie for a while.'

Rosie had her hands too full with Bernadette to argue the point. The night air had eventually roused the child and Rosie held her tight against her and fervently hoped the cart's movements would send her off again. She was bone-weary and in no fit state to deal with an active and wide-awake toddler.

Rosie did eventually doze off, but as the cart went over stony ground or the sides of fields in an attempt to avoid the roads, she was thrown from side to side and jerked awake often, so that any sleep she snatched was fitful.

As the cart pulled into the outskirts of Dublin, she awoke with a pounding headache and saw Danny slumbering beside her. She eased the sleeping child from her stiff arms and lay her gently beside her father. She watched her settle against Danny with a sigh and smiled. She thanked God she'd got over any strangeness she had had with her father. Danny had tried hard with her, she had to admit, for even when he ranged against the whole world, it had never included Bernadette whom he loved with a passion. She clambered up to see where they were, but it was too dark to see anything much.

It was still cold, and as soon as Rosie left the relative shelter of the cart she felt the chill dampness in the air and it hardly helped her feel more optimistic about what fate lay before them.

'Is it awake you are there?' Willie said. 'We'll be coming to the canal before too long. Baggot Street's not far away then at all.' He glanced over at Rosie as he spoke. 'You all right?'

'No, Willie, I'm not,' Rosie heard herself saying, too dispirited and nervous to pretend. 'I feel sick with fear every time I remember what Shay said, and I'm heart sore to be leaving all that I hold dear behind, not to mention my native land too, for some strange and alien place.'

'I'd feel the same,' Willie said. 'God, sure Ireland is where I'd want to bide till my time is up, but it's not a safe place for you all to linger in just now. Please God you'll be able to come back soon.'

Rosie felt the pressure of two hands on her shoulders, and turning she saw Danny had wakened and was behind her.

'I'll make it up to you, Rosie, I promise,' he said and he kissed her cheek.

Rosie's stomach gave a lurch and she knew she loved and adored this man, and life without him was unthinkable. Whatever sort of place Birmingham was, she could cope if she had Danny beside her. 'I know, Danny,' she said, smiling, and set her face resolutely towards Dublin and the future, whatever it held.

The nuns welcomed Rosie back warmly, even at that early hour, and were courteous with Danny, enchanted by Bernadette, laughing when she said she was freezing cold and hungry.

Willie hadn't gone into the convent with them, though they'd pressed him to at least have a warm drink. He'd refused, too anxious to get back home before he was missed.

After they'd all eaten, Danny spoke to the Reverend Mother about the reason for their intrusion in the convent and she said he'd done the right thing; the only thing. 'Dublin, though, is not a place you can bide for long safely,' she said. 'Handsworth will be safer and that is where you must go. As soon as the day is properly begun we will send the Reverend Mother there a telegram and ask them to put you up for a wee while. Until we receive their answer it would be better for you to stay in the convent and not go outside for anything. You don't know who might be on the streets at all.'

As Sister Cuthbert had spent some years in Handsworth, the Reverend Mother asked her to send the telegram and stress the urgency of getting the family away from Ireland as speedily as possible. The answer came that very afternoon. The Walsh family would be welcome.

'Now, you need to get to Kingstown to the mail boat,' Sister Cuthbert told them. 'There is a train going from Westmoreland Station and there is a mail boat which leaves on the evening tide – you might just make it.'

'If it's all the same to you,' Rosie said. 'I think I need a good night's sleep in a proper bed and so does Bernadette. I'd rather stay here the night and leave in the morning.'

Danny would rather have left as soon as possible, but agreed to abide by Rosie's decision for he'd seen the strain lines on her face and knew, however inadvertently, he was the one who had put them there. 'It will be all right, Rosie,' he assured her that night as he held her tightly in bed. 'It might be a wee bit strange at first, but we'll cope if we're together.'

'Of course we will,' Rosie said, glad of the dark that hid her expression from Danny. When his even breathing told her he was finally asleep, she cried the tears she'd held back all day, taking care to muffle them in a pillow.

Bernadette woke full of beans the next morning, ready for whatever the day might throw at her, while her parents were full of trepidation. After a hurriedly eaten breakfast, the family were ready for the off and Sister Cuthbert said she would lead them as far as the station. 'Wouldn't do to draw attention to yourselves asking directions of a passer-by,' she said. 'It's a sad fact, but you can be sure of no-one in Dublin today.'

And will it ever be safe again? Rosie thought as she lifted Bernadette into her arms, tied her securely inside the shawl and picked up her large bag. 'Wait,' cried Sister Miriam, hurrying from the kitchen just as Danny and Rosie were preparing to leave. 'We're not as badly off as we were last time you came to visit,' she said to Rosie and put some small packages into Rosie's hands. 'A little something for the journey.'

'Ah, sure you've done enough,' Rosie protested.

'We've done very little,' Sister Miriam said, 'and I'll not have you arriving at our sister convent faint from hunger. Think at least of the child.'

Rosie didn't argue further and tucked the packages well down into the bag. Soon the small group was walking through the dark morning. The sun wouldn't rise for some time yet, but at least there was little wind, Rosie thought, praying that would mean the journey across the Channel might be a smooth one.

It was probably as well she didn't know how turbulent the Irish Sea could be, but first there was the station to contend with and that was unnerving enough. The steam trains already in panted black smoke into the stale air like some wild beasts. Water dribbled onto the rails beneath them with a hiss and spit of steam and occasionally one of these untamed beasts would let out a screeching whistle. The first time this happened, Bernadette let out a scream to match the train in decibels, and wriggled in Rosie's arms as if she wanted to bury herself deeper. Rosie held on to her, taking comfort from the child's warm body because the noise had unnerved her just as much.

Danny came back with the tickets he'd bought. He didn't seem fazed by any of it and began loading their luggage onto the train. Rosie was anxious to get them all aboard, away from any curious eyes, and she hitched Bernadette around onto one hip while she embraced Sister Cuthbert.

'Write to me when you're settled,' the nun urged. 'Tell me how things are?'

'I will,' Rosie promised, and Sister Cuthbert's lips brushed Bernadette's forehead and she ran her hands over her golden curls.

'Look after her,' she said. 'You have a treasure there.'

Danny said emotionally, 'That's what I'm trying to do, care for them both. D'you think I'd be trailing them to England if there was any other way?'

'No, Danny,' Sister Cuthbert replied. 'You're doing the only thing possible and I wish you Godspeed.'

If Rosie hadn't been so apprehensive she might have enjoyed that train ride through the dark morning, finding the rhythm of the wheels on the tracks and the slight sway quite soothing. Bernadette eventually relaxed enough to let go of her mother's neck.

They saw nothing of the town, even though the day had lightened a little, for they were ushered speedily from the train to the harbour where a mail boat awaited, rocking slightly in the water. *The Hibernian,* Danny read out from the side.

'Now we'll see if we have sea legs or not.'

Rosie thought she'd not die dissatisfied if she never had to put that to the test, but she chided herself that that was no way to go on. There would be tougher times ahead, she was sure. And yet she hesitated at the gangplank, looking down at the sudsy grey water lapping around the sides of the boat. 'God, wouldn't you hate to end up in that?'

'Aye,' Danny agreed, 'and we'll take care not to.'

Rosie followed Danny, who carried Bernadette up the gangplank, past the sailor checking the tickets and boarding passes and up to the deck where Danny pointed out the two piers almost enclosing the harbour. 'That gap doesn't look big enough for this boat, does it?' Rosie said fearfully.

'I know what you mean,' Danny said. 'But it must be, for they travel this route twice every day. Mind, I'd say you'd have to be a good pilot to steer it so well.'

Bernadette was shouting to be let down, but the deck, with the water slapping and swirling to the sides of them, was no place for a toddler, and though the early morning was cold, Rosie didn't want to go inside yet. She wanted to wait until the boat was moving and so Danny put down the bags and case and lifted Bernadette onto his shoulders.

It wasn't a long wait they had. Soon the gangplank was raised and the thick hawsers unwound from the bollards on the dockside. Then the ship gave a shrill shriek that caused Bernadette to put her hands over her ears, the engines throbbed

272

into life, black smoke billowed from the two funnels and the boat moved slowly through the swirling frothy water.

Rosie waited until the boat had successfully negotiated the gap between the East Pier and the West and was in the open sea before she turned again and looked at the shores of Ireland disappearing into the murky gloom of the morning. Guessing some of her thoughts, Danny put a hand on her shoulder. 'We'll be back one day,' he said. 'This won't be forever.'

Rosie sighed. She wasn't at all sure of that, but she wasn't going to share her fears. 'Aye, I know,' she told Danny instead and gave his shoulder a squeeze.

'Come on, let's go in,' he said, 'Bernadette must be cold for I surely am.'

Inside, the noise and the smell of cigarettes and Guinness hit them. 'Do you want a drink?' Danny asked. 'Shall I see if I can get us a cup of tea each and some milk for Bernadette here?'

'Aye,' Rosie said. 'A cup of something might settle my stomach.'

'I'm feeling that way myself,' Danny said, putting Bernadette down.

Bernadette took some watching. Everything was new and exciting and she wanted to explore so Rosie was constantly running after her and bringing her back, which didn't help her churning stomach.

The tea Danny eventually brought back was welcome, but it didn't make Rosie feel less sick and she had barely finished it when she had to run out to the deck and deposit most of her early

273

breakfast into the sea.

Half an hour later, Rosie thought she'd never felt so ill in the whole of her life. Danny was little better. 'It's not sea legs we want,' she told Danny. 'It's sea stomachs!'

'Aye,' Danny said. 'Thank God Bernadette seems to be all right.'

'Aye,' Rosie agreed with feeling, not at all sure she could have coped with the child being sick as well.

But Bernadette was being happily entertained by the antics of a family near to them. The woman looked from Bernadette's smiling face to the green-tinged ones of her parents and asked sympathetically, 'First time over?'

'Aye.'

'I was sick as a dog the first time too,' the woman said. 'I'm well used to it now.'

Rosie wasn't sure she could ever become used to it, for the bile continued to cause her to run to the rail, along with other passengers, even when her stomach was empty.

She was so glad to see the shoreline of Wales in the distance, for she knew her ordeal would soon be at an end.

On the train she felt slightly better and pointed out the landscape to Bernadette. As they left Holyhead behind, the fields with the mountains in the distance was so reminiscent of Ireland that Rosie felt a sharp pang of homesickness.

They passed over a girdered metal bridge and noted the sea on either side of it and Rosie said to Danny, 'Where the boat came in, at that place,

Holyhead, must be on an island.'

Before Danny could answer, another passenger in the compartment said in an accent Rosie found hard to place, 'You're right, it's the Island of Anglesey and this bridge goes over the Menai Straits.'

'Thank you,' Rosie said. 'It's our first time over here.'

'Well, I know from your accent where you're from. Where are you bound for?'

'Birmingham,' Danny said.

'Birmingham, is it,' the man said. 'You have work there?'

Danny thought it better not to tell the man too much. He said, 'Aye, my uncle's getting me set on with him in one of the factories.' He shot Rosie a warning glance as he spoke, but she knew what he was doing.

'Plenty of work around now, I'd say,' the man went on. 'Making stuff for the war.'

Beside her, Rosie felt Danny stiffen. She knew he'd be against making anything for a war that had nothing to do with Ireland, but while that was all well and good, a job was still a job. Even if they were staying in England for a short time, they couldn't live on fresh air.

She said none of this. When they got to Birmingham and saw what was what, Danny would surely see the sense of that himself.

The train was travelling along by the sea, steel-grey waves fringed white on the dull April day, but Rosie could imagine the beauty of it in the sunshine, shimmering blue like Blessington Lake and surrounded by mountains.

She noted the place names as the train pulled in to all the small stations, some with such funny names she could hardly pronounce them: Llanfairfechan, Penmaenmawr, Conwy. 'Welsh names, I suppose,' Danny said. 'Some of the Irish names would be the same if we were allowed to use them.'

'Aye, I suppose so.'

Bernadette dropped off to sleep again against Rosie as they passed by Colwyn Bay. 'You'll be changing at Crewe, no doubt,' the man asked Danny.

'Aye, the man in the ticket office told me that,' Danny said.

'It's the next station after Chester, where I get off, so you'll know it,' the man said. 'Anyway, it's a big enough place,' and he gave a nod in Bernadette's direction. 'She looks worn out from travelling already.'

And she's not the only one, Rosie thought, but she said nothing and smiled at the man over the child's head.

But Danny had seen the tiredness in Rosie's eyes and said, 'Pass the child to me, Rosie, you look all in.'

Rosie was glad to hand Bernadette over, for her eyes felt incredibly heavy and she closed them thankfully. Within minutes she was asleep and didn't wake again until the train was pulling into Chester. Their fellow passenger bade them goodbye and as he left the train, Rosie was amazed to see so many soldiers milling on the platform. She realised the events in Ireland had slightly overshadowed the war raging on foreign fields not that far away.

Crewe Station was busy, noisy and very cold. As there was a delay for the connecting train, Danny led the way to a small café on the platform. Rosie was glad of the reviving tea and the girl behind the counter readily agreed to heat up some milk for Bernadette. They opened the food packages that Sister Miriam had given them. It put new heart into Rosie and she was glad she was able to change Bernadette too and make her more comfortable. But she saw the little one's eyes were puzzled and Rosie knew she'd be wondering what was happening. Until that point, her short life had been familiar and safe, and now she was being taken away from the only home she'd ever known, over land and sea, away from her doting grandparents and loving aunts and uncles; and she was too young for Rosie to explain any of it.

They'd been on the go since five o'clock that morning. Now it was half past two and they were on the last leg of their journey, but Birmingham was another hour away and it would be nearly dark then, for the thick, dense clouds had turned the afternoon as dusky as evening.

Danny and Rosie spent the time on the train from Crewe to Birmingham amusing Bernadette. They drew on their stock of songs, nursery rhymes and finger games to amuse her. As well as this, Danny could do wonderful things with a length of string that he always carried in his pocket.

When all that paled, Danny took his small daughter on a tour of the train. They went up and down the corridors, from the guard's van at the rear of the train to the start of the First Class carriages at the front and back again. Bernadette plodding along in front of her father on her sturdy little legs.

The train pulled in at New Street with a squeal of brakes and hiss of steam and in minutes the Walsh family were out on another dusty, windy platform. Rosie looked with trepidation at the press of people, hearing the raucous shouts of them and the sudden gales of laughter, seeing the porters pushing their way past and the man at the newspaper kiosk advertising his wares. Bernadette had begun to grizzle at the chaos of it all, but Danny, on the other hand, gave a heartfelt sigh of relief. Thank God, he thought, now they were all safe. He'd never have thought he'd be here, standing on a station platform in the middle of England and being thankful for it; but he was and he vowed he'd do all in his power to make a good life for his family here for as long as it took.

He swooped his weeping daughter into his arms and set her on his shoulders, and she was so surprised she stopped crying and began hitting the top of his head with her hands, laughing. 'Will you stop beating the head off your poor father,' Danny said in mock anger. 'Fine show of respect that is.'

Bernadette laughed louder and wriggled on his shoulders, and Rosie smiled at the pair of them. Danny was further relieved to see that smile. 'That's it, Rosie,' he said, buoyed up. 'Let's make the best of it, if only for the sake of the wee one.'

'I'm trying to, Danny,' Rosie said. 'I'm coping

278

the best way I can.'

'Let's go then,' Danny said, and lifting up one of the bags and with Bernadette carried high, he led the way.

Outside the station, the roads seemed packed. There were new petrol-driven taxis and horse-drawn hackney cabs waiting in a line. Behind them were horse-drawn omnibuses and petrol cars and lorries, and swaying trams weaving in and out between the rest of the traffic, and Rosie thought she'd be feared to even cross a road in this place.

'We'd best take a cab,' Danny said. 'We'd never find this place else.'

Rosie was scared to go in a petrol-driven taxi and so they opted for one of the horse-drawn ones and Rosie was staggered when the driver alighted to let them in. 'You're a woman!'

'Yeah, that's right,' the woman driver replied with a laugh. 'Where've you been the last three years?'

'In Ireland,' Rosie told her.

'Oh that explains it,' the woman went on. 'Here in England, at war, there are few big strapping men about like your old man; just the old, the young and the useless. It's left to the women. I had to take over when my old man was called up, or my kids would have starved and there wouldn't have been a business when he came back, that's assuming he does of course, and in one piece. I ain't the only one, it's women drives the omnibuses and makes the weapons and all sorts.'

'I'd never have thought...' Danny began.

'Wouldn't yer,' the woman said, almost contemptuously. 'Who d'you think runs a country when all the men are in the trenches, or maimed, blinded or killed. D'you think we just fold up and die?'

'Like I said, I never thought of it at all,' Danny said. 'Maybe I should have, but when you're not involved, when it doesn't affect you, you don't think.'

'No,' the woman said, suddenly tired of the conversation and impatient to get on. 'And right now I have a business to run. Where you making for?'

'Hunter's Road, Handsworth,' Danny said, lifting Bernadette from his shoulders as he spoke and placing her into the hackney cab. 'St Mary's Convent.'

'Oh yeah, I know that all right,' said the woman. 'In you go then, and I'll have you there in the swish of a pony's tail.'

Rosie had never travelled in such splendour and told herself to enjoy it, for she probably wouldn't do so again in a hurry. As the cab moved into the swell of traffic she saw the driver was right, it was mainly women driving the horse-drawn carts and working on the omnibuses, and most of the conductors were women too.

They drove through streets full of traffic, lined with houses all squashed together and whole parades of shops, like the entire street of Blessington around every other street corner. Hunter's Road was a far more prosperous area. The houses were larger and more imposing, set back from the road and encased with privet hedges or brick walls.

The convent was by far the biggest building in the road. Built of red brick and with a red-brick wall in front of it, it was an L-shape, with small leaded windows to the ground and first floor and arched attic windows facing the road. The cab driver turned into the cobbled yard before the convent and Rosie noted the presbytery, a smaller and less imposing building alongside the convent.

Rosie gazed at it, nervous of entering such a place, but Danny wasn't. They had come this far, been assured of a welcome, and he had to find somewhere for his wife and child to lay their heads that night. He helped Rosie from the cab and paid the fare, wincing at the price and was glad Rosie hadn't heard it. With a wave of her hand the cab driver expertly turned and began to move off and he went up the steps to a door with 'House of Mercy' printed above it, and rang on the large bell there without the slightest hesitation.

At the convent they were all welcomed warmly. Danny and Rosie were summoned into Reverend Mother's office while the nuns cared for Bernadette, and Danny explained his position and the reasons for them landing at her door. She listened without a word and then said, 'What d'you intend to do now, Danny?'

'Find a job and a place to live for my wife and child,' Danny said. 'I'll live in England as long as I have to.'

The Reverend Mother known as Mother Magdalene, was impressed with Danny's resilience and spirit, but she continued, 'How d'you feel about violence now?'

'I am essentially a man of peace, Reverend Mother,' Danny said. 'I seek dialogue and discussion and political change being undertaken to give Ireland Home Rule. Others have less patience and that led to the ill-timed insurrection. I had a hand in that, though as I explained to you not through choice. I want no part in further violence, but there is also no way in which I would betray the Brotherhood.'

'They don't believe that?'

'No, Reverend Mother,' Danny said, 'because someone did betray them. I spoke openly against their policies; someone obviously kept their comments to themselves and worked against them. They'll never believe that the traitor wasn't me, and now that I've disappeared it will prove their theory; and yet to stay would put my wife's and child's lives in jeopardy as well as my own.'

Reverend Mother nodded and smiled and Rosie felt her whole body relax when she said, 'I think you had good reason to flee your homeland, Danny, and you and your family are welcome to stay here until you are back on your feet.' Rosie's breath escaped in a sigh of relief and she felt safe and secure for the first time since she'd left Wicklow.

SIXTEEN

Rosie woke to a cacophony of sound. The strident noise of the hooter, which had wakened her in the beginning, still lingered in the air. Danny slumbered on and so too did Bernadette, in a cot at the foot of the bed, while Rosie got up and stood looking out the window.

It was still early and dark outside, but in the light from the gas lamps she saw the delivery vans and carts beginning their rounds and she heard the clop of the horses' hooves and the clatter of cartwheels over the cobblestones. Over this was the splutter and rumble of the petrol-driven vehicles, the noise of the trams from the nearby Lozells Road.

'This is the city awakening,' she said to herself, and then she felt Danny's hands on her shoulders.

'How long have you been standing here?' he chided gently. 'You're frozen.'

Rosie hadn't realised how cold she was until that moment and she snuggled against Danny, grateful for his arms around her. 'What are you thinking?' Danny said.

'Nothing terribly deep,' Rosie replied. 'Just how different it all is. Bound to be, I suppose.'

'Will you hate living here so much?'

Oh yes, with all my being, Rosie might have said, but instead she told Danny, 'I'll get used to it. It's all strange to me at the moment. You must give me time.'

'All the time in the world,' Danny said. 'I'll make it up to you, see if I don't.'

He wished he could turn the clock back, but if he could, what in all honesty could he have done differently? But he'd had no idea that once the insurrection was over he was still bound to the Brotherhood, nor that they'd want to start it all up again. Because he'd refused he was exiled to this Godforsaken place, his farm, his inheritance given to the boy who'd started the whole thing. Had he stayed and carried out the ambushes and assassinations they wanted eventually he would have been captured and shot, or imprisoned for life. Some bloody choice!

He felt sorry for Rosie, but he didn't say this. Rosie didn't need pity, and as she said, she'd get used to it. The first thing he must do was find a job.

Danny had no idea that finding work would be so hard, especially as he didn't care what job he did, and he set out that first day full of confidence. However, he was to find the Irish people, because of their stand against conscription and their friendly relations with Germany, were not popular. There were plenty of factories, most of them war related, and he realised that although he'd not wanted to make anything for the war, it was all right to feel that way when you didn't need the money.

As soon as Danny spoke it was obvious where he came from and that alone put many employers' backs up. They all asked him why he wasn't in uniform and when he explained he'd just arrived from Ireland where there was no conscription, he'd see many of them curl their lips in contempt.

'Tell me,' said one potential employer, 'why I should set on someone like yourself to make things for a war you don't agree with? Why shouldn't I employ a woman instead, at half the pay, mind, who needs the job to provide for her family because her man is away fighting or she is widowed?'

Danny, remembering the woman cab driver, had no satisfactory answer. But he tried. 'I need a job too, sir. I too have a wife and child to provide for.'

'That's your problem,' the man said, totally unmoved. 'You should have stayed in Ireland. You'll get no work in my factory.'

As one day followed another, the answer seemed to be the same everywhere he tried. He became very despondent.

Rosie could sympathise for she'd had a taste of it herself. The day after they'd first arrived at the convent she'd gone to the Mass at seven o'clock and met a few other parishioners. But the following week she went to nine o'clock Mass, leaving Bernadette with her daddy who'd gone to the earlier one at seven. Mother Magdalene had recommended the parish priest, Father Barry, be told the real reason for the family fleeing Ireland, and everyone else told that Rosie was a niece belonging to the Reverend Mother, over for a wee rest.

There were few men in the congregation that Sunday, Rosie noticed, and nearly all that were there were in uniform. She couldn't help feeling uncomfortable. Afterwards, leaving the church, one of the women said to Rosie, 'Where's your man then? Over for a wee rest, the Sister said. Is he on leave, like?'

'No, he's not in the army,' Rosie explained. 'We didn't have conscription in Ireland.'

'My husband didn't wait to be conscripted,' the first woman said sharply. 'Volunteered, he did, and proud to do so.'

'And my sons,' another said. 'Had one killed on the Somme and one at Gallipoli. Heroes, both of them.'

'Oh the Irish would rather side with a Hun,' an older man said. 'Colluded with them they did. Probably been doing it for years.'

The faces around Rosie looked angry and hostile and Rosie thought back to the friendly people she'd seen every Sunday after Mass in Blessington. 'I don't know anything about all this,' she told them helplessly. 'We're just trying to get by, like everyone else.'

'Aye, well some of us have to get by without our menfolk and some don't have anyone belonging to them to come back either.'

'Yeah, and some like me have to work their fingers to the bone to put food on the table,' another put in.

Rosie had had enough. 'Excuse me,' she said, pushing past and through the crowds, and they'd all stood and watched her leave. She didn't tell Danny, there was no point, but she knew what he was going through in his search for work. Two days after the encounter after Mass, a letter came for Danny one morning after he'd left, and when he returned and opened it a white feather fluttered to the floor. Both knew what it meant, the sign of cowardice, and Danny felt sick as he picked it up and ran his fingers along it.

'Who would do this?' he asked Rosie in puzzlement. She remembered the antagonistic people after Mass and knew it could have been any one of them.

She told Connie none of this when she wrote to her later that day. She'd put off the letter, hoping that Danny would have got a job and she'd have good news to tell them, but she knew she could delay no longer. She didn't mention Danny's lack of success in seeking employment or that their little store of money was disappearing at an alarming rate.

She concentrated instead on the positive aspects of where she was living:

It is well served by shops, so many around us you wouldn't believe it. I go out every morning to do the shopping for the convent and I take Bernadette in the large and commodious pram one of the Sisters got for me. Bernadette loves it and she gets what fresh air there is here and I can pack so much around her.

Milk is delivered to the door and so is bread, and the convent uses a lot because of the school they have for the poor children of the area behind the convent who often come with no dinner. They run a nursery for mothers working in war-related jobs too, and so when the milk cart brings the churn to the door it's not uncommon to have three or four large jugs for him to ladle into each day.

287

It's odd to have shop bread all the time. I mind the time I could knock up a loaf of soda bread in minutes and now there are perhaps four or five loaves delivered here. Most of the other food stuff needed I am able to fetch for them. They are grateful to me for doing that, for what with the school, nursery, and visiting the sick and needy, they haven't much time at all.

The convent itself is in a pleasant position, for it is opposite a small grassed area called Spring Garden and I often take Bernadette there in the afternoon. It's nice for us both to feel grass beneath our feet and the flowers are pretty, and though Handsworth Park is beautiful it's a tidy walk.

I hope everything is fine with you and everyone is well. I'd value a letter. I miss you all so much. For safety's sake, can you address your letter to the Reverend Mother, Mother Magdalene, and though I'm including a letter for my parents, the girls and Dermot, please don't tell them where we are, it's best that as few as possible know.

Please God, Rosie thought, next time I write I'll be able to tell them Danny has a job.

Rosie only went once to the Bull Ring, the massive open market that the nuns had told her about and insisted she visit, and they minded Bernadette for her one day while she spent precious money on a tram to the city centre. Once alighted from it, she had stood by a enormous store called Lewis's that seemed to be on both sides of a very small road.

She was quite mesmerised by the amount of traffic, and more people than she'd ever seen in her life, and far more shops. The nuns had written down explicit directions as to how she would get to the Bull Ring and she followed them until she stood at the top of the High Street, looking down the hill to the market below, bustling with people and alive with noise.

On one side of the hill there were shops and Rosie noted them as she passed. Shops selling sweets, shoes and newspapers were side by side, and next to them a tailor's advertising suits for thirty bob. Then there was a café, and a pet shop with kittens in the window and a large parrot in the doorway, and another tailor's where, with their thirty-bob suits, a free waistcoat was included.

Rosie was quite dazzled by it all. And then she was at the bottom of the hill and the noise and press of bodies was almost indescribable. Either side of a large statue on a podium with a wall around it were barrows, many with canvas awnings, piled high with produce or articles of every kind. Around the statue were women selling flowers and the different fragrances wafted before her nose as she was pressed to buy. The statue, she noted as she passed it, was of Lord Nelson. She recalled the pillar in Dublin, dedicated to the same man, that she'd seen in her quest to find news of Danny. It had been one of the buildings in that area left undamaged and she remembered it had stood straight and tall amongst the sea of rubble, like a beacon of defiance.

As she continued walking through the Bull Ring, she caught a whiff of fish as she passed one road leading off to the right and then she was amongst the barrows. She was astounded to see that those with bread, cakes, sweets, fruit and veg, poultry, rabbits and fish were side by side with those selling crockery, material or junk, and the amalgamated smells filled the air.

Her attention was taken by a man selling spinning tops. 'On the table, on the chair, little devils go everywhere,' he chorused, seeing Rosie's interest. 'You want one, lady? Only a tanner.' Rosie would have loved to buy one of those brightly coloured tops and she knew Bernadette would be delighted with it. But sixpence was sixpence and she shook her head regretfully and turned away.

At the next barrow a hawker was plying his trade to a crowd of women in front of him. 'Come on, ladies, who'd like a pound of tomatoes for just fourpence. Now I can't say fairer than that, can I?' and then leaning closer to one woman he went on, 'And for Gawd's sake don't tell your old man. I'm only letting them go dirt cheap because I like the look of you. Any of you lovely beauties want the same?'

The woman surged forward and Rosie walked on, smiling at the man's banter. It was all so different from Ireland, she thought.

Amongst all the noise and laughter and the hawkers and costers advertising their wares, there was one strident voice calling out incessantly, but Rosie couldn't catch the words. But then as she came out nearer the church she had seen in the distance, she saw the caller was a lady standing outside a shop called Woolworths and she was selling carrier bags. And that was what she was shouting about: 'Carriers, handy carriers,' over and over.

Before the church, Rosie saw, was a fringe of trees all in blossom in front of which trams and dray horses were pulling their heavy loads before disappearing down a side street.

The nuns were right, she thought, it was the most fascinating place. And then she saw the Market Hall. It was an imposing building. Arched windows were either side of the stone steps supported by Gothic pillars, but Rosie didn't only see the grandeur of the place, she saw the men there selling razor blades and bootlaces and even wind-up toys from trays around their necks. One had just one leg, another only one arm, and another had a placard around his neck saying he was blind. Rosie knew without being told who these men were. They were the flotsam of a war that the Government had led them into and then cast aside once they'd served their purpose.

The joy of the day had gone for Rosie after that. She visited Woolworths and Peacocks and looked in the windows of the Hobbies shop; she even passed the men on the steps to go into the Market Hall, but neither the wonderful array of goods there, nor the fabulous clock the nuns had told her about, nor even the playful animals in Pimms pet store, could totally shake off the despondency the sight of those poor, maimed men had evoked in her.

She bought the vegetables and the rabbit meat the nuns had asked her to fetch back and was glad to leave the Bull Ring behind and make her way home again.

There was no need anyway to visit the Bull Ring, for the area where they were was, as she'd told Connie, well served for shops and she liked her little jaunt out every day, especially now the weather was a little warmer. It was nice to see the shopkeepers' pleasant faces and hear the polite way they spoke to her. They knew nothing of Danny here and only knew what she'd told them; that she was a niece belonging to the Reverend Mother over from Ireland for a wee rest because she'd been ill.

No one doubted her, why should they, and the consensus was she was a pleasant little body and doing the right thing by coming to the Sisters, for by God they'd put her right if anyone could. And that baby of hers! God, she'd melt many a heart, that one, with her blonde curls and brilliant and unusual violet eyes and beautiful smile. She looked like an angel so she did.

It made a sharp contrast to the people who went to the convent chapel where her and Danny were now virtually shunned by those attending Mass. Mother Magdalene was aware of it, but she hadn't a clue how to help the situation. She had a great regard and respect for the women of Birmingham anyway who'd set to with a will to run the country in the absence of their men and endeavoured to bring their children up decently.

There were many now, both in the Catholic church and out of it, wearing the black bonnets denoting widowhood. Small wonder they had little patience with a fit and healthy man like Danny, living off the nuns and seemingly too scared to fight. Even had she told them the truth she doubted they'd feel differently, and she could hardly blame them. Not, of course, that she could tell anyone why Danny and Rosie were there. It would be far too dangerous.

Rosie particularly liked shopping on Saturdays, for then the children would often be out with their mothers. As the weather warmed up a little she saw little girls in smart lacy pinafores over their dresses that reached almost to the top of their little button boots. Their long hair would often be loose and held off their face with a bonnet or straw hat. The boys always had caps on their heads and stiff white collars at their necks, their knickerbockers fastened just below their knees and grey socks leading to good strong boots on their feet.

These, however, were the more well-to-do children and some of them came with a nursemaid. Often other girls in service would be queuing at the shops too, many in black dresses with white aprons over them and white mob caps on their heads. They'd usually have a smart basket over their arm as they gave in their orders at the butchers for what Cook wanted and picked over the vegetables at the greengrocer's and only bought the best.

There were, of course, other poorer mothers whose children were not half so well dressed, and Rosie often felt a pang when she saw their pinched faces and stick-thin arms and legs, and especially if their mother wore a widows' bonnet.

When they received Connie's reply to Rosie's letter, they knew whatever their circumstances now, and however difficult things were, they were right to leave Ireland when they did.

Dear Rosie,

I'm so glad you arrived safe and well, and though I miss you dreadfully you did the right thing in disappearing. The IRA came for Danny. They came in the night brandishing rifles and I was feared of my life. I told them Danny had taken you all to New York, America where I had an uncle. I don't know if they believed me. They said it was a quick decision and I said it had been planned some time, Danny was just waiting for an opening, a job offer. He wasn't interested in farming. You'd have been proud of the tale I spun.

Anyway, they finally left and before they went, one of them said to me, 'Wherever your traitorous, lily-livered son is, tell him to stay there if he knows what's good for him.' You needn't worry for a minute that I would tell a soul where you are. Your parents have asked and your sisters and Dermot have hardly stopped begging for your address or some clue where you've gone, but I never said a word, nor won't I either for it wouldn't be safe...

'We can't go home until this madness is over,' Danny said.

'That's like saying when the war's over,' Rosie said. 'And that's limped along for three years and shows no sign of stopping.'

'America will be in soon, you'll see, then there'll be a turning point.'

'How can you be so sure?'

'Well, no country can stand its ships being sunk and its people drowned when they haven't even begun hostilities,' Danny said.

Rosie hoped Danny was right and that America's intervention would bring a speedy end to the war, that had and still was claiming so many young lives. She was beginning to dread the sight of the telegraph boy, knowing soon another family would be in mourning for a husband, brother, son, favoured uncle, for every soldier belonged to someone.

But another worry was pressing on Rosie, and that was the lack of money if they had to stay in Birmingham for any length of time. They could pay for their keep for just one more week when she asked to speak to the Reverend Mother.

'What is it, my dear?' Mother Magdalene asked gently, knowing there had been something on Rosie's mind for a day or two.

'It's money, Mother Magdalene.' The words burst from Rosie's lips. 'We haven't savings enough to keep us longer than next week.'

The Reverend Mother bit her lip. She longed to tell Rosie she could stay and was welcome for as long as she liked, but she had many demands on her purse and anyway she knew a little of Rosie now and knew she wouldn't accept what she considered charity. 'What do you intend to do, Rosie?' she asked.

'One of us must work, Mother Magdalene,' she said. 'Danny is unable to gain employment, so I think it's down to me.'

'He won't like that.'

'He'll like going hungry even less,' Rosie replied sharply. 'And I'll not do that to our child. I've seen enough of them half-starved around here to last me a lifetime. The favour I must ask of you concerns Bernadette,' Rosie said. 'Could she have a place in your nursery?'

'Well, it is essentially for mothers working for the war effort,' Mother Magdalene said. 'What line of work would you be looking for?'

'That's just it,' Rosie said. 'I don't mind what I do as long as it pays enough for us to live decently. I wondered if you knew anything of wages?'

'I know a little,' Reverend Mother said. 'But Sister Ambrose would know more as she's in charge of the nursery.'

'War-related work pays the most,' Sister Ambrose said later when Rosie asked her what she could expect to earn. 'Dunlop's pays well. The factory is almost all moved up the Tyburn Road now, right out in the countryside, but they keep a factory in Rocky Lane, Aston.'

She didn't tell Rosie the smell of carbon and rubber constantly emanating from the two women working at the factory who had children at the nursery would nearly choke you when they came to pick them up. Nor did she tell her of the carbon dust engrained in their hands and faces and even their hair; that it was little better in the mornings they'd told her they would go each Sunday to the baths in Victoria Road to have a good soak: it was the only time they could get really clean.

'Then there's the ammunitions works at Kynoch's in Witton that pays well,' Sister Ambrose said. 'There's quite a few go there and there's a tram. I could ask someone to speak for you.'

Rosie thought about the women she'd seen

about with yellow faces, who were called the Canary Girls as one of the shopkeepers told her. The discolouring was caused by the sulphur in munitions work. 'Is there nothing else?'

'Aye,' Sister Ambrose said. 'There's shop work and work at HP and Ansells and numerous other factories, not to mention work in the Jewellery Quarter, but they won't pay nearly as much.'

'Right,' Rosie said, her decision made. 'As I don't fancy Dunlop's, Kynoch's it will have to be. That's where Rita Shaw works, isn't it?'

'Yes,' Sister Ambrose said, 'she does, and a decent and respectable woman she is. Her husband Harry is overseas and she has little Georgie to provide for. We've looked after the child for well over a year now, and she has a house in Aston, which isn't so far away. How well do you know her?'

'Not that well,' Rosie said. 'We've just exchanged a few words now and then. But I'm sure she'd put a word in if I asked her.'

'No doubt of it.'

'Well I shan't say anything just yet,' Rosie said. 'I must talk Danny round first.'

'Rosie.' Sister Ambrose said. 'I know it's none of my business, but most of the married women have men overseas. Have you thought what you'd do if you found you were expecting?'

Rosie shook her head. Whether it was depression through not having a job, or the proximity of the nuns, Danny had not once touched her intimately, never mind going further than that, since they arrived in Birmingham and this was another reason why she was anxious for them to get their own place.

'I wouldn't find myself expecting at the moment,' she told Sister Ambrose. 'There is no question of it just now.'

Their eyes held for a moment and Sister Ambrose understood how it was. 'Right,' she said. 'You best talk to your man.'

The man in question shouted and roared. He forbade Rosie to go to such a place. He said she was deliberately shaming him.

Rosie let Danny's anger and scorn wash over her. She refused to be upset, whatever he said, for she knew that her taking a job could be the straw that broke the camel's back for Danny. His rage was against the unfairness of life.

For two days he was out from dawn to dusk, tramping the streets, asking every factory he passed if they had work. The answer was always the same. His despondency turned to despair and the second day he faced Rosie across their room. 'How much money have we left?'

'Five shillings,' Rosie said. 'And I must give that to the nuns this week for our keep. After that, there isn't a penny.'

Danny sighed and Rosie felt sorry for him. He gazed down at Bernadette asleep in her cot, her thumb in her mouth, and said dejectedly, 'I'm a failure to you, Rosie. The promises that I'd make it all up to you, I have broken.'

'You're no failure in my eyes, Danny.'

'I know what I know,' Danny said bitterly. 'But, for Bernadette's sake, I can sit on my pride no longer. Do whatever the hell you like.'

The next morning Rosie collared Rita. She'd liked her from the first, sensing in the no-nonsense Rita a person like herself. Rita's face was yellow and there was a coppery tinge to the long brown hair she wore coiled up but her dark brown eyes were full of life and determination, despite the fact they were often red-rimmed. Rita knew little of Danny and Rosie didn't mention him now. She just said she needed a job and did she think there would be a vacancy at the place she worked.

'I'll ask for you,' Rita said. 'But I'd say you have a good chance of being set on, they're always wanting people. I'll ask them today and when I come to fetch Georgie tonight, I'll give you the answer. All right?'

It was more than all right and when Rita came that night and told Rosie that she was to go up the next day and see a Mr Witchell, who was boss of the place, Rosie could hardly contain her delight.

Next morning, Rosie went through what she had to say to the boss of the munitions works in the short tram journey, for she'd decided a modicum of the truth was needed. So she told him that they'd left Ireland, for it wasn't a safe place to be at the moment, and that she'd been ill so they'd come to the convent as one of the nuns was an aunt of hers. 'Danny, my husband, had hoped to get work of some sort,' she said, 'but so far he's been unsuccessful.'

'So you decided to take up a job instead,' Mr Witchell said. 'How did he take to that?'

Rosie, remembering Danny's rage at her suggestion, said, 'Not very well at first, but he came round in the end.'

299

'So he's not likely to come storming up here lambasting everyone and drag you home by the hair?' Mr Witchell asked with a twinkle in his eye, and the mental picture was so alien to anything Danny would do that Rosie smiled properly and felt her nerves flutter away. 'No,' she answered, 'I don't think so.'

'And have you done any work like this before?' Mr Witchell said and shook his head. 'I'm supposed to ask that question, but, to be honest, few people have experience making guns and bullets.'

'I haven't either, sir,' Rosie said. 'But I'm willing to learn.'

'I'm sure you are, and I'm willing to try you out,' Mr Witchell said. 'You can start next Monday morning at seven-thirty sharp. Wages start at two pounds and ten shillings. So how does that suit?'

'It suits very well, sir,' Rosie said, and she ran her right hand surreptitiously down the side of her dress before she shook hands for it was clammy with sweat. Two pounds and ten shillings was a good wage for anyone and a fortune for a woman. It would secure their future for the time being at least. As she left the office she had the urge to skip along the road like a lunatic, but somehow managed to control it.

She was up bright and early the following Monday morning and waiting for Rita at the door of the nursery. 'Your wee daughter is gorgeous,' Rita said as the pair scurried up Hunter's Road. 'She's like an angel and her smile would melt a heart of stone.'

'And she knows it,' Rosie said. 'The nuns would have her ruined altogether if I allowed it.'

Rita laughed. 'I can well believe it. She's the sort of child you'd love to spoil.'

Before Rosie was able to reply they'd turned from Hunter's Road into Lozells Road and saw the tram lumbering towards the stop and had to put a spurt on in order to catch it.

Once on the tram, Rosie was anxious to talk about the job, because her stomach had being doing somersaults all night at the thought of it.

'The supervisor on our section is Miss Morris,' Rita told Rosie. 'She's a decent sort on the whole, as long as you don't take advantage like. She can't abide that. You have to wear these bloody awful, dark green overalls, nearly down to the floor they are, and a hat that every vestige of hair has to be tucked under. Mind, you'll be glad of them, for the yellow dust swirls about in the air and gets everywhere.'

'Don't you mind about your face turning a yellow colour?'

'I care more about paying the rent, putting food on the table so me and Georgie can eat decently and I can dress him in respectable clothes and put a bit of money in the Post Office for when my Harry comes back,' Rita stated emphatically. 'That's all I care about.'

'Aye,' Rosie said. 'I agree with you. That's all most of us want.'

'Come on,' Rita said suddenly, 'the next stop's ours. I'll take you in to Miss Morris and she'll sort you out.'

They went in through the huge metal gates and

down a side alley to a squat brick building, and once inside, Rita pointed out the clock where a queue of girls waited. 'You'll be given a card today,' she said, 'and the first thing you do is punch it in there. If you're late they dock your pay, and if you're persistently late they take off an hour for every minute or sack you altogether, so be careful.'

Suddenly Miss Morris was in front of them and she shepherded Rosie along with the others to don the uniform, which was just as hideous as Rita had described.

She hadn't been exaggerating about the dust either, for it did seem to get everywhere, and the stink of it went up Rosie's nose and to the back of her throat as soon as she entered the factory floor, making her cough. 'You'll get used to it,' Miss Morris said. 'I was the same at first – sometimes my eyes would itch and burn, but they're all right now.'

Rosie wiped her own streaming eyes and looked around and thought it must be the most unwelcoming place in the world. She was suddenly very nervous. What did she know about making things for a war? What if she made a mess of it? She might last no longer than a day. And then what would you live on, she told herself sharply – fresh air? – and surely all the women had to start somewhere.

She mentally straightened her shoulders and told herself firmly to stop being so stupid. She gazed around the long room. It was very dimly lit except at the tables where the girls sat, where a naked bulb sent a pool of light over everything.

'You'll be making detonators,' Miss Morris said. 'I'm setting you up beside Betty, who'll soon put you right over this and that.'

'I will too,' Betty said, moving her chair over to make more space and smiling at Rosie. 'Come on up beside me and I'll show you what's what.'

Betty was much older than her and Rita and her yellow face was so lined that Rosie could see the dust settling in the folds of her skin by the end of each day. Her grey eyes were kindly, though, and the little tufts of hair that Rosie could see at the sides were grey. Altogether, Betty was plump and comfortable looking and Rosie was glad she was the one to show her what to do. She knew if she didn't pick it up straight away, Betty wasn't the sort to lose patience with her. Some of her nervousness melted away and she smiled back at the older woman.

She found out all about Betty Martins that day. 'I've been a widow more years than I care to remember,' she told Rosie, 'I'm a Brummie, though, through and through, and proud of it. I live in the same courtyard as Rita in Aston.'

'My two sons had itchy feet and both sailed to America years ago when my Alf was still alive. They've lived there ever since and send money home regular. They've been on at me for years to go over there, but Brum is where I'll live until I go out in a box and I've told them straight. This is home to me.'

Betty's steady chatter and store of jokes helped the day pass more quickly, though by the time the last hooter sounded and Rita and Rosie were walking to the tram stop, Rosie confessed to

303

feeling very tired. She told Rita about Danny and his fruitless search for work. 'So I'll not mention being tired to him,' she went on, 'or he might nag at me to give it up. One of us must work and if he can't find employment and I can, then I must be the one. He doesn't see it quite that way, of course.'

'Pride, see,' Rita said. 'Terrible thing, a man's pride. Still, at least you got yours to go home to. My hubby's "somewhere in France".'

Rosie sighed. 'I know. Danny has been having a hard time because he's not in khaki.' She lowered her voice and went on, 'Someone even sent him a white feather.'

'No!'

'Aye, it's a fact.' Rosie said. 'If you've lost some-one, then… Oh, I don't know. Maybe I'd feel the same.'

'I wouldn't,' Rita stated firmly. 'I mean, I worry about my old man every minute of the bleeding day, but I don't think I'd feel any better if some other bugger was dragged into it as well.'

Rosie was glad Rita felt that way, but Rita didn't ask why Danny wasn't in uniform and Rosie didn't enlighten her, for Rita had presumed that he'd been proved unfit at the medical.

Danny saw the tiredness etched on Rosie's face when she got in that night. He saw she tried to hide it and it hurt him down to the pit of his stomach that Rosie was forced to go out to work. But he said nothing about it. What was there to say?

Bernadette at least had enjoyed her day at the nursery. Her shining eyes said it all, though she was tired when Rosie picked her up and had no qualms that night at least about going to bed. Danny asked Rosie little about her day and the job she did, but the nuns were full of questions.

Rosie answered them all despite her weariness and then said, 'We can start looking around now for a place of our own. You've been more than kind, but I know you didn't intend to put us up for so long.'

'There was no time limit specified,' one of the nuns pointed out, and Rosie knew that, but also knew the convent hadn't facilities to put people up for long periods of time. She would also feel better with her own place, her own front door to shut. It might make it better for Danny too. She was well aware how he hated his jobless state paraded before the nuns daily, and the attitude of the people at the chapel hardly raised his self-esteem in any shape or form.

She felt emotionally and physically drained, and soon after the meal she made her excuses and went to bed. She stirred when Danny slid in beside her some hours later, but made no sign of being awake.

Perversely, as Danny's even breathing filled the room, she lay beside him wide awake. Tears of tiredness and disappointment smarted behind her eyes and she brushed them away angrily, for she knew the time for tears was well past.

SEVENTEEN

The Walshes were to discover that finding a place to live was not easy, and four weeks after Rosie began at Kynock's, by the end of June, they were still at the convent.

Rosie was finding the work tedious and unpleasant, the conditions bad and some of the women coarse, both in language and behaviour, but she liked the money. She was able to put some of it away in the Post Office as Rita advised and she knew she'd need every penny when they did eventually get a place of their own.

She got on well with Rita, whom she travelled to and from the convent with each day, and Betty too. It was Betty who told her of the old woman called Gertie who lived down her yard. 'Poor old sod,' Betty said. 'Won't be with us long, I'm thinking. She has no family, so the neighbours see to her in the day, like, but it's the night-time. She could do with someone with her, but with an old codger like that you got to be careful, ain't you. I mean, anyone that moves in has got to be honest and respectable, so I thought of you. It will be a start, like, and then, when Gertie does pop her clogs, the house will be yours. Possession is nine-tenths of the law, or so folks say.'

Sharing a house was not the start Rosie had in mind, but it would be better than living at the convent till the end of her days. But there was her

306

job and the problem of getting Bernadette to the nursery.

'We could do it, I suppose,' Rosie mused. 'After all, Rita manages to get Georgie to the nursery every day?'

'I'll say she does. Has to get up early, though, and then she takes a tram from Victoria Road. It nearly passes the factory in Witton Road, which is probably maddening, but she says she knows Georgie is well-looked-after at the nursery and he's happy, and of course it's free to all women doing war work.'

'I don't mind getting up early,' Rosie said. 'I'm well used to it.'

'Why don't you and your man go along and see the place first?' Betty said. 'It's six the back of forty-two Upper Thomas Street.'

'That's a funny address,' Rosie remarked.

'Well, you are down the yard, you see, number six, but that house is at the back of forty-two, which is on the street itself. Helps you find the places, see?'

She went into the convent, Bernadette in her arms, bursting with the news. But she thought Danny had to hear first, and when she couldn't see him she asked where he was.

'In his room, I should think,' one of the nuns told her. 'It's where he spends most of his time.'

Rosie didn't like the sound of that and so she left Bernadette with the nuns and went up the stairs.

Danny lay full stretch on the bed on his back, the picture of misery, and Rosie felt her heart sink. 'What is it, Danny?' she said, curbing her impatience and hoping he didn't hear it in the tone of her voice.

But Danny wasn't listening to tones. He looked up at her and said, 'You mind de Valera was released just a few days ago?'

Rosie did remember. His picture was in the paper. All the remaining rebels had been released, Michael Collins amongst them, and the paper maintained it was because of pressure from America, but whatever it was they had made much of de Valera's release because he'd been in Dartmoor Prison.

'Aye,' she said. 'What of it?'

Danny sat up suddenly. 'I'll tell you what of it,' he said. 'He's gone straight to East Clare and stood for Sinn Fein, young Redmond's seat, him who was killed in France, and he's won a resounding victory. D'you see what it means, Rosie? Sinn Fein is the political wing of the IRA and it may be years, if ever, before we can go back to Ireland.'

That gave Rosie a jolt too, but she knew to sympathise with Danny was not the way to deal with this. 'Well if that's the case, and our life is here for the time being, isn't it good I've got some news about a house?' and she told him the tale.

Danny showed little enthusiasm and Rosie had the urge to shake him hard, but she controlled herself and said instead, 'We could go up for a look after tea if you like, the nights are light till almost ten o'clock at the moment.'

'If you want, we'll go.'

'Oh, Danny, snap out of this,' Rosie cried, exasperated. 'All right, you haven't a job yet, but for heaven's sake, you're not the only one, and while I'm working it's not a disaster. Surely to God you want us to get our own place?'

'Aye, and look at the job you have to do to afford it,' Danny said. 'I don't want you there. It's dangerous and it will poison you in the end.'

'Don't exaggerate, Danny,' Rosie said. 'All right, the dust gets into my nose and throat and sometimes makes my eyes itch, but I'm not the only one. The women who've been there longer say it happened to them at first. I'll get used to it.'

'I still say…'

'Then you'll have to say it later,' Rosie said leaping to her feet. 'The dinner will be ready and getting spoiled.' And with that she went out of the room, leaving the door open, and Danny had no option but to follow her.

Aston wasn't far from Birmingham city centre: there were plenty of factories around and a fair selection of shops clustered around Aston Cross where the big green clock stood. It had four faces to it and stood in a little island of its own and people used to say that each clock face showed a different time. Back-to-back houses, and the entries leading off the street to further houses down the courtyards, abounded in Aston, streets of them, squashed against their neighbours on grey pavements before grey roads. Rosie found it depressing that first evening. The sun didn't seem to penetrate these grim places and yet Rosie knew she had to be grateful to even be considered for any sort of dwelling, the housing shortage being so acute.

Betty was looking out for her, as she'd said she would be, and as soon as Rosie and Danny emerged from the dark entry she left her house and came to meet them. Rosie was so appalled, looking around the yard, she nearly failed to introduce Betty to Danny. Fortunately she remembered her manners and Betty shook hands with the man, glad he had a firm grip.

Betty saw he was good-looking, well-muscled without being fat, and fine and healthy looking. She knew idleness would not sit easily on his shoulders. Rosie had told Betty as she had Rita that Danny couldn't find work, and, like Rita, Betty presumed he'd been deemed unfit for the army. Not that he looked unfit, but, well, it all went to show, she thought, and though she could do nothing about getting the man a job, maybe she could find them a place to live.

Directly in front of Rosie was a lamppost and beside it a tap that she presumed was for the whole yard's use, and Betty told her later that that was the case. 'That there is the brew house,' she said, jerking her finger in the direction of a building to the side of her. It was squat and looked as if it seen better days for some of the small windows had been smashed and the door stood half-open, the hinges at the top rusted away.

'There's the miskins for the ashes and that,' Betty went on, 'and the dustbins beside them and the lavvies are at the bottom of the yard. And this,' she said, turning Rosie around, 'is the house.'

Eight houses opened onto the court and all were three storeys high and built of blue-grey bricks, with windows so small Rosie guessed little light would get in there. She noticed that before each door pavement slabs were laid, but the rest of the yard was covered in grey ash.

Betty pushed the washing aside that was spread out on the lines criss-crossing the yard and held up on tall props. 'We all used to wash on Mondays, before this damned war,' Betty said. 'Now, with a lot of women working, we wash when we can.'

'Where does Rita live?' Rosie asked as they walked across the yard.

'Just two doors down,' Betty told her. 'Said she'd be over as soon as she gets the young one to sleep. And Ida Roberts lives next door. She's a good sort is Ida, do anything for anyone.' She lowered her voice and went on, 'Lost her man Herbie at the Somme. God knows how she manages, for she has three nippers and young Jack, the eldest, is only ten. She said she'd find it hard to get a job of any sort and look after the kids proper like. I'm inclined to agree with her, 'cos it's not as if she is burdened down with relatives offering to help like, even though her husband's people don't live so far away. Still, nowt so queer as folk, as my old mother used to say.'

Then they were over the dirty greasy step and in through the door, and Rosie was almost knocked back by the smell. It was the smell of poverty and neglect, mixed with damp and the stink of stale food. But over it was the stench emanating from Gertie, who lay staring at them with wide open eyes, her white hair straggled about her as she lay in an iron-framed bed jammed up against the

311

window. 'It's all right, Gert,' Betty told the old woman gently. 'These are friends of mine.'

Rosie forced herself to move closer to Gertie, taking in the reek from her unwashed body and the unmistakable smell of urine. Whatever care the neighbours gave Gertie, they hadn't the time to keep her clean as well. Yet the alternative was the workhouse and that very word struck terror into the hearts of old and young alike, and from the tales Rosie had heard of such places she wasn't surprised. 'Hello, Gertie,' she said. 'I'm very pleased to meet you.'

Gertie didn't speak, but nodded and smiled, displaying a mouthful of rotting teeth just as Rita bounced in the door. 'What d'you think?' she said.

'Give them a chance,' Betty said. 'They're only just over the doorstep.'

And then to Rosie and Danny she said, 'There's a table and chairs in her bedroom, not much cop by all accounts, but they had to move summat out to get the bed in. She was getting too doddery to make the stairs. Weren't you, Gertie?'

Gertie didn't answer, but smiled and seemed to relax a little as Rosie's eyes slid over the room to the greasy black range. Two armchairs and a cupboard set into the wall was all there was in the room.

Rita saw it through Rosie's eyes. 'It ain't so bad,' she said. 'You'll be able to spruce it up fine, Rosie. A nice rug before the fire will cover up the scuffed lino and some cushions on the chairs will make it look a bit more cheerful, and a good clean of course. It would benefit from that.'

Rosie knew she spoke the truth, and despite all its drawbacks she knew they would take it. It wasn't what she wanted, none of it was what she wanted, but that was the way her life had seemed to go lately.

'The whole place needs a thorough clean,' Rosie told the nuns that evening, 'and Betty and Rita said they'll give me a hand on Saturday. I need to buy a few things too. There is a double bed in the bedroom above, but I'll need a new mattress for it and new sheets and blankets and stuff, and some crockery too, for Gertie has little and I'd not like to cook much in her pans. I'll go to the Bull Ring after work tonight.'

'You'll have plenty of time,' Reverend Mother told her. 'They're open till about ten in the summer.'

Rosie knew the Bull Ring was where bargains were to be had and she knew she'd have to close her eyes to the suffering around her and concentrate on buying things for her new home.

'You won't mind sharing the house with the old lady?' one of the nuns asked.

'Not at all,' Rosie said. 'She is a frail old thing and mostly bedridden now. She is wandering a bit in her mind, you know, but God knows but that might come to us all when we get to her age. I'll mind her fine once I'm home from work and the neighbours have been marvellous with her, so they have, and Betty says they'll still see to her in the day while I'm away.'

'And you, Danny, what do you think?' Sister Ambrose asked.

'Me?' Danny said. 'Me? I don't think. This will be Rosie's house and her hard-earned money paying for it.'

'Don't be stupid, Danny,' Rosie yelled, furious at his attitude. 'Would you say it was just your house if your money was paying for it? When people are married, they share things like money. It's the way it is.'

'No,' Danny cried. 'It isn't the way of it. The man should earn the money and the woman bide at home, minding the house and the children and her man. Admit it, Rosie, even if just to yourself, you married a useless bugger.' Danny slammed out of the room, banging the door loudly behind him, so hard it juddered in the hinges.

Rosie was ashamed and angry at the way Danny had behaved and she saw the nuns had lowered their heads and knew they were embarrassed too. For a while no one spoke and then Rosie said, 'Well, I don't really care how Danny feels about this house. It's no palace and I don't pretend it is, but in time it will be ours, not mine, ours, and if he can't see that he must be blind.'

'He feels guilty that he can't provide for you,' one of the nuns said.

'I know that, but it doesn't really help,' Rosie said. 'I can't help the fact that I have a job of work to do and he hasn't and we'd be in a right pickle if I wasn't earning. I could do with support when I get home, not doom and gloom and bad humour.'

The nuns said nothing and Rosie knew she'd embarrassed them further and really it wasn't fair to load her problems onto their shoulders, for they couldn't help. She excused herself and left the room, and then stood outside it unsure of where to go. She hadn't any desire to sleep, but there was nowhere else and so she mounted the stairs resignedly.

Danny was sat on the bed, still fully clothed and he had his head in his hands. He looked up as the door opened and said, 'I'm sorry, Rosie. I don't know what came over me.'

Rosie had wanted to scream and shout at him, but she found she couldn't, the man was upset enough. She shrugged. 'It's all right.'

'No,' Danny said, getting up and walking towards her. 'It isn't all right at all. I shouldn't take my resentment out on you. I'll try to be better, and again I say, I'm sorry.'

'Danny, I love you,' Rosie said, sitting down on the bed and taking his hand. 'Everything I do is for you and Bernadette. Surely you know that?'

'Aye, I do,' Danny said. 'Deep inside I know, but sometimes, oh God, Rosie, the need for a job, it sort of overpowers you.'

'Eventually you will get a job,' Rosie said firmly. 'You're not the only one to be unemployed in this city and you know it as well as I do. Let me work while I am able to and when you do get a job, I'll be more than willing to stay at home and rear Bernadette and any brothers and sisters she might have.'

'Ah, Rosie, why do you put up with me?'

'Because I love you,' Rosie said. 'How many times must I say it, Danny? You are my life.' She took Danny's face in her hands and kissed his lips softly and he put his arms around her and they

315

fell back on the bed together and Danny knew he wanted to make love to his beautiful and loving wife. When Rosie felt Danny's penis harden against her as he held her close, she felt a longing to match his. Danny's fingers fumbled to loosen her garments. They dropped to the floor one by one until she was naked and then Danny took off his clothes quickly and turned out the gaslight before sliding into bed beside her.

His lips sought hers and his hands slid over her body, stroking and caressing until she felt her nipples harden into peaks of desire and she groaned in an agony of lust. When Danny eventually entered her she was more than ready, but she tried to muffle her moans of ecstasy and bit her lip to stop a cry of triumph escaping from her, lest the sounds reach the ears of the nuns or rouse the sleeping Bernadette.

At last, inside, she was warmed by the feelings of being loved and cherished. She thought any intimacy was gone forever and she rejoiced that it hadn't, and tucked against Danny, she went to sleep.

Danny readily agreed to look after Bernadette the following Saturday for he concurred with Rosie that the house more than needed a thorough clean. In fact, he had been appalled by the place but he had said nothing. He was in no position to but he would have liked something better to rear a family in. However, he was a realist and he knew they were lucky to get a house, even one they shared with Gertie. He'd spoken to many men in the dole queues who lived with their family in one room or, if they were lucky, a couple of rooms, and he tried hard to be grateful for what they were moving in to.

Rosie was grateful that Danny had been more amenable and staggered that so many women in the court had turned out to help her clean the house.

Ida in particular was interested in who would live next door to her and Rosie took to the woman straight away. Despite her problems, startling blue eyes danced in her round open face and gentleness seemed to seep out of her. Rosie couldn't help thinking that though the house she lived in left a lot to be desired, she could put up with that for the friends she'd be living amongst.

'I do want to clean Gertie up too and try and do something with the bed she's in,' Rosie told them all. 'But not straight away. I think she might be frightened by us all descending on her like this, so I'd like her to get used to us being here first.'

'Good idea,' Ida said. 'Perhaps one of us should sit by the bed, reassure her like, and maybe hold her hand a bit.'

'That should be you then, Ida, cos I've never seen such a patient soul,' another woman said.

'I'd do it to start with,' Ida said. 'But I'm not sitting there all day like Lady Muck, and watching the rest of you graft. That would hardly be fair. We'll take turns.'

While Rosie took her turn, she talked to Gertie. She told her they were coming to live with her so she could be looked after better. 'You're not to worry about a thing,' she said. 'I'll never let you go away from here, so don't you be fretting about it.'

'D'you think she understands you?' Ida said, hearing the promise.

Rosie shrugged. 'I don't know, but I have to say something. I feel bad enough muscling in on her today and then moving into her house, and all without her having a say in any of it.'

'Don't feel bad about that, for Christ's sake,' Ida said. 'What was the alternative? The work-house for the poor sod, or having a bad fall in the night and lying in pain and alone. Believe me, you're doing Gertie and us one big favour. It's hard enough seeing to her in the day, especially for those at work and with families too, but at night... We couldn't do that, so we're all glad you've come.'

Ida's words made Rosie feel better. 'She's asleep,' Ida said. 'Let her rest awhile. I tell you, Rosie, this getting old lark is a bugger, and I wish there was some way round it.'

'Aye, and me,' Rosie said, tucking the blankets around Gertie's chin gently. Gertie woke again while the women were having a break and a bit of dinner, and Rosie was glad of it because she needed to change Gertie and her bed too. 'I got a bolt of cheap towelling down the Bull Ring the other night,' she told the women. 'It had a fault or something. I thought it would make nappies for Gertie and then I picked up one of those rubberised sheets at the Rag Market. It should protect the bed at least.'

'I'm afraid we didn't always get round to washing her and that,' Ida said.

'You did your best,' Rosie said firmly. 'Now I'm here it will be easier for you all, and for Gertie too hopefully. We'll have to lift her gently onto a chair because she's just skin and bone.'

She was no weight, but still they used four women to lift her into the chair before the range. Her sheets were sodden and Rita had a bucket of water ready to steep them in. Betty helped Rosie strip the bed, turn the mattress, and remake it with the protective sheet.

Gertie's nightdress too was wringing wet and Rosie lifted it off her and washed her all over with water she'd had heating on the range. Then she put on one of the nappies she'd cut from the bolt, and secured it with nappy pins before slipping a clean nightdress over her head.

'We'll change her during the day,' one of the women promised and they moved her back to the bed. 'Try and keep her a little drier at least, the poor old sod.'

'Do what you can,' Rosie said. 'I just want her to be a little more comfy.'

As Ida spooned bread soaked in gravy into Gertie's mouth – which was all that the old woman seemed able to take – Rosie surveyed the room. Everywhere was clean at least, and the smell of neglect had left the place. The other things Rita had suggested, the bright cushions and rag rug, would have to wait until she moved in.

Rosie could hardly believe how kind the women in the court had been, although they were naturally curious about her. She told them what Rita and Betty had already been told: that she'd been ill and had come to spend a few weeks with her aunt who was a nun at the convent. She wondered what they'd make of Danny and whether they'd react the same way as their fellow parishioners at the chapel, or the employers of the factories where Danny had tried to find work. She hoped not, but gave a sigh. It didn't do to worry overmuch about something she couldn't do anything about.

Rosie really didn't see how she was going to be able to get Bernadette dressed and ready so early in the morning and also try to see to Gertie, but Danny took the situation in hand after the first two fraught mornings. 'Look, Rosie, why do you have to run yourself ragged? I might be a man, but I'm not totally useless.'

'I know that, Danny, but...'

'But nothing, Rosie,' Danny said. 'I can help Gertie after you've left for work. If I can feed Bernadette, I can help an old lady just as easy, and I'm sure I could take Bernadette to the nursery and fetch her home in the evenings too? I won't stop looking for a job, mind, but while I'm unemployed I may as well make life easier for you. I mean, I bet you nearly pass the factory in the tram on the way to the nursery?'

'Aye, near enough,' Rosie said. 'If we're upstairs you can see the gates on Witton Road. But ... well, there's Rita's Georgie as well.'

'No doubt I could cope with him too,' Danny said. 'He's not a bad little chap.'

'Oh Danny, it would be marvellous so it would,' Rosie said. 'You wouldn't mind?'

'I'd mind far less than I mind you supporting the entire house. In fact it would make me feel better to be doing something and might raise my standing with the neighbours who must see me as a lazy bugger.'

Danny had a point; there were so few fit young men out of uniform that he did stand out a bit. Unbeknownst to the Walshes there was much speculation amongst the women in the courts and streets about Danny, almost as soon as they moved in, and the women had drawn their own conclusions.

'Why d'you think he ain't in the army then?' one asked Ida one day. 'I mean, you live next door to them.'

'Don't mean I know all their business,' Ida retorted. 'Maybe he has flat feet.'

'Flat feet don't keep you out the army!'

'It does,' someone else put in, 'My uncle has them and they turned him down.'

'Why?'

'I dunno. They just do.'

'All feet are bleeding flat, ain't they?' another said. 'I mean, I don't know anyone what's got round feet.'

'It's summat to do with the instep,' another offered.

'Well that Danny Walsh don't look like he has flat feet to me.'

'How would you know with his bloody boots on?' Ida said. 'And it must be flat feet, cos there ain't another reason that I can think of that the army would pass up such a strong, well-set-up man.'

'Who cares why he ain't in the bleeding army, any road,' another said. 'It's nice to have a man about the place, maybe he can fix the brewhouse door before winter because the wind slices through there like a knife.'

'Yeah and the maiding tub leaks like a sieve.'

'Yeah, and I'm sure he'll stop that dripping tap in the yard if we ask him, cos if that drip ain't fixed it will freeze solid in the winter.'

Danny did all that was asked of him, glad to be able to fill his days with something useful. Eventually, the news filtered through that Danny Walsh had never been for an army medical to find out if he had flat feet, for he was Irish, and though there had been volunteers from Ireland there was no conscription. Gradually, the women's attitude to Danny changed to resentment.

They still approved of Rosie, who kept her place clean and tidy and her child respectably dressed, despite being at work all day, and was kind to Gertie too and so relieved them of some of the burden, but what was wrong with Danny that he was in none of the Forces?

Danny was more aware of the women's feelings than Rosie, who was too busy to really see, but he said nothing to her for she could do little to change the situation, and anyway she had to work alongside and live amongst these people.

EIGHTEEN

Eventually life established a pattern. Rosie would get Bernadette and herself up and dressed before Rita and Betty came up the entry and then Georgie was left in Rosie's house. The three women would be joined by others from doors and entries along the street until there would be a fair few of them waiting for the tram.

Danny would get Bernadette's breakfast, and while she ate it he'd pour Gertie a cup of tea and spoon porridge into her mouth. Like Rosie, Danny always spoke to the old lady when he came in and out or when he was doing something for her. He didn't know if she understood, but Rosie always said their voices seemed to soothe her. Gertie rarely answered, but she nodded and smiled and Danny thought that she liked being acknowledged.

After he delivered the children to nursery he seldom went straight back to the house, knowing it would be full of women doing personal things for Gertie, things it would be unseemly for him to watch, never mind do, and instead, every fine day he would often find himself going down to the clock tower at Aston Cross and along Rocky Lane, past the Dunlop's works to the canal. The sludgy grey-brown water was as far from the babbling streams and rivers in Wicklow as it was possible to be and yet he liked the place.

Danny often felt that if he hadn't the canal to visit each day, and the boaties to pass the time of day with, he'd have gone mad, for there were few other men about. The narrowboats and barges, many decorated with roses and castles in bright colours and of all different shapes and sizes, travelled up and down the canal carrying goods and sometimes people from one place to another. They held a fascination for him, as did the large shire horses that pulled many of them.

Danny was grateful for the friendship of the men on the canal, for while many ordinary people and employers saw Danny as a Catholic Irishman, therefore one of the rebels, a trouble-maker and a friend of the Hun, the boaties were different. They were a law unto themselves. He particularly liked a boatie called Ted Mason, and one day Ted said to him, 'No-one's got a good word for us, either. Calls us river gypsies. We ain't gypsies and they ain't got any right to say so.'

Danny sympathised with Ted, for his narrow-boat was always spotless and gleaming. Danny was asked aboard for a meal one day after he'd helped Ted's youngest son Syd leg the narrow-boat through a tunnel after Ted had hurt his back. As the narrowboats had no engines, when a tunnel was reached, a child or woman would lead the horse around the tunnel to meet up on the other side while the rest of the family would have to haul the narrowboat through the water. The usual way to do this was to lie out on boards long enough for your feet to reach the sides of the tunnel and leg the narrowboat through.

Danny was surprised how much effort it had

taken and how his legs had shook after it, and when Ted's wife Mabel asked him in for a bite and a drink he accepted gratefully. However, when Danny went through the double doors to the cabin below, although the space was small he was amazed at what he saw.

To the left of him was the cooking stove, raised up on a plinth, and gleaming pots and pans hung on hooks around the stove while the chimney disappeared through a hole in the roof. Opposite the stove was a bench that Ted explained was turned into a bed at night. 'Syd sleeps there,' he said. 'Len used to too before he was called up. Syd, thank God, is too young yet. He's only sixteen.'

Syd looked anything but pleased by this news and Danny thought it was amazing how Ted and Mabel had reared such a surly son. Ted had explained before that the boy didn't like the life on the canals. 'He was born and bred to it. I can't understand him at all,' Ted said. 'Our bed folds up against the far wall and that's the bed he was born in, same as his brother. Now Len, he's a proper boatie. Got a feel for it somehow, and I tell you I'll be glad when this little lot is over and he's back home again.'

Danny could plainly see the discontent in the younger boy's face and thought it a pity he couldn't see how fortunate he was. But then, whenever could a wise head be put on young shoulders?

'Sit down, sit down,' Mabel urged as Syd handed Danny a bottle of stout. 'We were glad of your help today. Syd could never have got the boat through that tunnel on his own. Mind, Ted is his own worst enemy. He won't see he's getting older and has to take a bit more care.'

'I'm not in my dotage yet, woman.'

'I didn't say you was.'

'Stop the blether, woman,' Ted said. 'Me stomach thinks me throat's been cut.'

'I'll cut you in a minute, Ted, you're that aggravating,' Mabel said, but Danny saw the twinkling in her eyes as she lifted the casserole dish from the oven and began to serve it onto the thick brown plates that Danny saw were stored in a cupboard hidden by the table, which would be folded up against it when not in use. As he ate he looked about the small cabin. Every piece of wood visible was stained and varnished and on the side panels were the rose and castle designs, and there were also shining brasses and plates of lace on the walls.

After the meal was washed down with the stout, Mabel got up to make the tea and Danny had never seen such a teapot. It was large and the same brown as the plates, but the knob on the top of it was in the shape of another miniature teapot, and the matching sugar bowl and milk jug had little crocheted circles covering them.

Ted, seeing Danny's interest, was amused, and handing him a cigarette after the meal, he said, 'What d'you think of it, then?'

'I think it's grand,' Danny said. 'I never imagined it to look anything like this. Were you always a boatman?'

'Yeah, always, like my father before me and his father before him and so on. My grandfather didn't live on a narrowboat, though, he had a cottage on the land but he was driven off by the railway in 1843 and had no alternative than to do what others before had done and live on the narrowboat. My dad was the first one of us to be born on a narrowboat, then there was me, and then our Len in 1887.'

'What about school for the children?'

'We teach them to write their name and reckon up and as much reading as they need to understand the toll tickets,' Ted said. 'That's as much education as a boatie needs. It's more important to understand the locks, be able to steer the boat and be strong enough to leg it through the tunnel. Book learning don't teach them those things.'

'I see that,' Danny said. 'And you have it lovely and cosy.'

'Oh, Mabel keeps it like a new pin,' Ted said. 'We're always proud of our boats.'

'I'm not,' Syd said. 'I'm sick of it, piddling up and down a little ribbon of water and at a snail's pace.'

'We know your views only too well, young man,' Ted growled. 'And they needn't be shared with visitors. When you're a man you can decide for yourself, but for now you'll do as you're damn well told.'

Syd glowered but said nothing more, and as he burst through the swing doors, Danny heard Mabel give a sigh and he felt sorry for her. He wondered if father and son rowed often. It certainly seemed an ongoing argument and he remembered the rows his father used to have with Phelan and the little good it had done in the end. Still, this wasn't his fight, and he felt guilty even having been witness to it. 'Can you stick around for the next day or so,' Ted asked suddenly, handing Danny a half-crown. 'Just till me back is properly healed, to help with the heavy stuff and legging and that.'

'As long as I can take and fetch the children from the nursery I can give you all the help you want,' Danny said.

'Good,' Ted said. 'Take half a crown today and more tomorrow depending on how long you work.'

'Seems fair,' Danny said, delighted to be earning, however little it was.

Rosie was pleased for Danny's couple of days' work and the odd jobs he picked up sometimes on other boats because of it. But she knew those odd shillings he brought home would be of little use to keep them all and when she became aware that she'd missed a period in August she was thrown into a panic. 'What am I to do?' she asked Rita and Betty at work the next day, biting her lip in agitation. 'We can't manage without my money.'

'There are places...' Rita began. 'If you don't want it like.'

'What d'you mean?' Rosie said appalled. 'Get rid of it? Rita, what do you take me for? I'm a Catholic and couldn't do such a thing.'

'Glad to hear it,' Betty said. 'Too bloody dangerous for one thing. Look,' she said to Rosie, 'It ain't the end of the world, is it? I mean you can work for months yet, and I should have a word with them nuns and ask if they'll take on a babby and...'

'What about feeding the child?'

'You ain't the only one to work with a baby you know,' Betty said. 'They can have bottles of milk these days.'

'That's right,' Rita put in. 'Sadie Miller went back nearly straight after the baby was born. 'Course, her mother lives just around the corner and she was showing me the bottle. It's shaped like a boat and with a rubber titty on both ends. Anyroad, whatever you decide, you'd best tell your old man before he tumbles to it himself and realises half of the Kynoch's workforce and all the neighbourhood have been aware of it before he was.'

'Aye, Rita's right,' Betty said in support.

Rosie knew that Rita was right too, and yet she hesitated, not certain how Danny would react.

And when she told Danny in bed a few days later, he didn't know how to react either. He should be delighted, for lovely as Bernadette was, she needed a playmate, and, deep down, he wanted a son. He kept this fact hidden from Rosie, knowing how she'd felt after Dermot's birth. Had he been able to provide for his family properly he would have welcomed Rosie's news, but as it was he was quiet.

'Say something, Danny, for God's sake,' Rosie pleaded.

'What?' Danny snapped. 'What can I say? I'm over the moon so I am, another child I can't provide for.'

'Don't!' Rosie cried, hurt and angry at Danny's

329

reaction. 'You said that just as if you're blaming me all the time, for having a baby and for having a job. Well, I might have got the job on my own, but you had something to do with this baby and don't you forget it. A fine future the child will have with this sort of welcome from its own father.'

'I'm sorry, Rosie,' Danny said, chastened. 'Don't fret, I will love the baby well enough when it arrives, and I'll try harder not to feel sorry for myself and secure some sort of job, any job, and as soon as possible.'

'I'll go back to work after I have the baby,' Rosie said.

'Oh no you won't. I've told you, I'll get a job.'

'Fine!' Rosie said. 'But if you don't, I can go back.'

'Don't be stupid, Rosie. How can you do that?'

'As long as the nuns can take such a young baby on, I can manage it,' Rosie said. 'Other mothers have gone back.'

'A baby needs its mother.'

'Maybe, but they also need to eat and be kept warm,' Rosie said. 'Come on, Danny,' she went on, conciliatory now. 'Be reasonable. I know you'll do your best, but if in the end it's not enough, then there is this alternative.'

Danny shook his head. He didn't like it. Didn't like any of it, but what could he do about it – damned all, that's what, and all the talk in the world wouldn't change the situation. He sighed and put his arms around Rosie. He didn't need to speak. She understood and kissed his cheek.

'So de Valera is president of the Irish Volunteers as well as head of Sinn Fein,' Danny said after reading the letter his mother had written. 'He has the political and revolutionary movement all sewn up.'

'Aye,' Rosie said. She'd read the letter but she hadn't time to worry over it much. Her pregnancy, now in its fifth month, was dragging her down. She'd been violently sick since September and not just in the morning either, and by November she was more than feeling the effects of it. It was harder each bleak, cold morning to push herself from her bed and out into the inky blackness with only tea to sustain her, for her stomach would accept nothing else.

She'd also developed a cough and wasn't sure whether it was from the munitions or the cold, but the spasms often doubled her over and made her chest and back ache, and, together with the pregnancy, she often felt wretched.

Added to that, Gertie was failing fast and Rosie thought that the coming winter was going to be her last. She slept most of the time now, and had lost so much weight, for her appetite had dropped. Her wrinkled cheeks had sunk in and Rosie could see her ribs when she washed her gently. 'Eat a wee bit more, Gertie?' she would urge, holding the spoon out, but Gertie would keep her lips tight shut and shake her head. 'Come on, to please me?'

'She's wasting away,' she complained to Danny once. 'It's as if she's given up.'

'Wouldn't you?' Danny said. 'I mean, what the hell has she got to live for?'

Little enough, Rosie had to acknowledge, for Gertie's mind had gone a long time ago, and all she and her neighbours were doing was keeping her body ticking over. Obviously she had decided enough was enough, and after all, wasn't that her decision?

She didn't know what the Catholic position would be on that, though, and yet hesitated to ask Father Chattaway, for all she liked the priest at St Joseph's, which was their nearest Catholic Church now. She didn't want to be made to feel guilty about possibly not trying harder with Gertie, or be forced to send her to some institution or hospital, where they could sustain her some other way.

Danny agreed with her. 'What could they do but force-feed her?' he said. 'Since I've been here I've been hearing what they did to the suffragettes before the war. It was an inhumane and barbaric way to treat women and many never fully recovered from it. You could never subject that frail old lady to such treatment. Don't fret, Rosie. You do your best and so do the neighbours. They might have little time for me, but even I have to admit they are kindness itself to Gertie.'

Danny's comments eased Rosie's conscience for she knew however ill Gertie became, she could send her nowhere. A promise had been made to her that she'd never be put in the workhouse. Rosie could not renege on that and betray her in such a way.

None of her neighbours could recall the old lady going to any church that they knew of, and Rosie knew she would have to stir herself, for

Gertie had no relatives to see to her funeral when she did pass away. She found the Reverend Gilbert at St Paul's in nearby Park Road to be a very kind man, who seemed more worried about her than Gertie. And he was, for he saw a young woman who was obviously pregnant and yet far too thin, and one with an almost continuous rasping cough. When she said she worked at the munitions works he was thoroughly alarmed.

'I must work,' she said firmly when he expressed concern. 'My husband is unable to find employment and we have a wee girl. Now there is the funeral to pay for. We will inherit Gertie's house when she passes away and so I couldn't live easy if I let her lie in a pauper's grave.'

Reverend Gilbert admired the young woman's plucky stance. The lilting voice told him where she'd come from and he guessed she was a Catholic. They always seemed to make much of death, often having a party after the funeral that some might think unseemly. They seemed to celebrate the life of the deceased and yet openly mourned their passing, and the vicar had a sneaking regard for that philosophy. To be able to grieve as well as remember with a certain amount of joy and pleasure the years the deceased had had on earth, was surely more healthy than the stiff upper lip many of his parishioners portrayed.

So he understood Rosie's need to have the old lady buried decently when her time did come. 'Shall I come and have a wee chat with her?' he said.

'You can come and welcome, Reverend, but Gertie is not up to chatting. She doesn't know

333

where she is half the time, her mind is wandering d'you see?' Rosie told him.

But for all that, he did come, Danny told her one evening just a few days later. He sat by Gertie's bed and talked to her and held her hand and Danny seemed impressed with him. 'I'm glad he held her hand,' Rosie said. 'She likes that. When I hold her hand she is aware of it and her grip tightens. I think it comforts her. We don't really know what goes through her mind. She may be afraid of dying. We'd never know, would we?'

'No,' Danny said. 'And we can only do so much. And for now, you've done enough. You've coughed non-stop since you've come in and you're puffing like an old steam train. Bed is the best place for you.'

Rosie didn't need persuading. She tried valiantly and for quite a few days to hide the severity of her cough from her employer, fearing losing her job. She also tried hiding it from Danny and muffled her coughs in a pillow at night. The cold and damp didn't help, nor did the cloying, acrid green-grey fog that often lingered through the day, seeping through anything a person held over their mouths. Gertie's house too, like most houses in the court, was so damp the walls were often wet and none of this helped Rosie. Small wonder she didn't seem to be getting better, but worse.

She looked down on Bernadette sleeping in the cot, tracing her face lightly and gently with one finger. The child stirred slightly and sucked more intently on her thumb and Rosie's stomach contracted with such love for this child. She wondered if she'd ever love another baby as she loved her darling daughter. She was such a delight and a pleasure to rear, and so sunny and usually happy that she was a bit of a favourite in the court. Rosie prayed she would stay fit and healthy and catch nothing, including her mother's cough, for the houses were breeding grounds for disease which often ran rampant through the entire place.

She shook herself mentally as she undressed and climbed into bed. What was the matter with her, worrying about things that hadn't happened yet? Hadn't she enough cares that she had to search for more? She closed her eyes and when Danny came up with a cup of tea, he found her fast asleep.

Gertie died on Monday 6th December and Rosie couldn't be truly sorry, for she felt sure Gertie had wanted to go. The women collected from door to door for flowers and Rosie knew it was their way, but she'd have been glad of the money put towards the cost of the funeral; for even the price of the plainest of coffins alarmed her and it made a large hole in the money she had saved.

She wasn't able to attend the funeral service the following Friday, for Catholics were not allowed to go to any service in another church, but she followed the hearse to Witton Cemetery to see her laid to rest. 'You don't need to do this,' Danny had said. 'Let me go. I could go along to the cemetery after I've taken the children to nursery.'

'No,' Rosie said firmly. 'I must do this last thing and say goodbye to Gertie. Really, considering the age of her and the years she's lived here, there will be few enough to show respect.'

Danny shook his head but didn't argue further. He knew how obstinate Rosie could be at times, but later, after she'd gone, he watched the large raindrops slapping on the black ash, which he knew would in time turn it into dirty slurry, and heard the wind gusting against the windows, and worried about his wife. For now he could do nothing about Rosie, but he made sure he wrapped Bernadette and Georgie up well for their tram ride to Hunter's Road.

The Reverend Gilbert would have told Danny he had reason to worry about Rosie. She stood surrounded by her friends, Ida and Rita and Betty, who'd each taken a day off work, more for Rosie's sake than Gertie's. The vicar was glad the woman had some support. She stood in the rain-sodden cemetery with the wind whistling around them and coughed the entire time he was intoning the few prayers over the coffin being lowered into the earth.

When Rita moved away from Rosie she staggered and would have fallen if Betty hadn't held her. 'Come on, girl,' she said. 'Home for you. You should never have come.'

'I had to, for Gertie…'

'Gertie wouldn't have wanted you to put yourself at risk, would she now?' Betty said. 'Not if she was in her right mind she wouldn't.'

'We must put the clods of earth on top of the coffin,' Rosie protested as Betty steered her away.

'D'you think for one minute the poor old sod will worry about that?' Betty said firmly.

336

'Betty's right,' Ida said, worried at her friend's pallor. 'Gertie is at rest now and worrying about nowt.'

The Reverend Gilbert had watched them go and he knew that unless great care was taken of Rosie, she could easily be the next candidate for the undertaker's service. He called Rita to one side and advised her to call the doctor.

However, a doctor wasn't called in lightly, for they cost money, and so Rita said nothing to Danny of the vicar's advice. He could see for himself that Rosie had overtaxed herself and when he said she should get into bed without delay they supported him, despite Rosie's protests that she was fine.

'You're not fine. Don't be a bloody fool altogether,' Betty said sharply. 'You'll have to have a few days from work I'm thinking, get yourself properly right.'

'Oh no... I...'

Rosie made to rise from the chair she'd almost fallen into, but Rita pushed her back. 'Stop it, Rosie, and show a bit of sense for God's sake,' she snapped. 'You have a wee child to think about and another you're carrying. Think of them if you won't think of yourself.'

Rita's words did make Rosie think, and she eventually agreed to go to bed, but didn't admit how glad she was to undress for she felt far from well. Her whole body ached and her chest burned. The coughing shook her whole frame, making her head swim, while the pain went in a band from her chest round to her back and then everywhere else, even to her fingers and toes.

'Is this flannelette petticoat you took off the only one you have?' Rita asked suddenly, for the women had followed her upstairs.

'No,' Rosie said. 'I have another in the drawer in the chest. I bought two with the winter coming on.'

'Do you mind if I cut the hem from this one?' Rita said, holding it up. 'Flannel soaked in warmed camphorated oil and placed on your chest helps. It brought our Georgie round when he had the whooping cough last year and I have some camphorated oil in the house.'

Rosie nodded her head, knowing she'd agree to anything that might help, and Rita began tearing the petticoat hem into strips.

Despite the women's loving care, Rosie worsened as the day wore on. The women stayed with Rosie while Danny went to fetch the children home, and shortly after he returned Rita went home with Georgie and took Bernadette too. Eventually there was only Betty left, for Ida had gone home too to see to her family. 'Should I fetch the doctor, Betty?' Danny asked her. 'I'm worried sick about her.'

'I would,' Betty said. 'You should catch him at evening surgery if you go now.'

'Will you stay with her?'

''Course I will. I ain't got the same calls on my time as Rita and Ida.'

'I'm grateful, Betty.'

'Get away with you,' Betty said. 'What are neighbours for if it ain't for helping each other? Go and fetch the bloody doctor and see what he can do to put our Rosie right.'

Danny was glad to go, glad to get away from having to watch his wife struggling to breathe. She was semi-delirious and sweating so much the sheets were damp, and she threshed on the bed and was too weak to lift herself when the coughing fits shook her whole body.

He hated to see her suffering so and he castigated himself for ever bringing Rosie to this disease-ridden place of squalor.

She might not have been safe at the farmhouse, though. Desperate things were happening in Ireland, although perhaps she could have been left in Dublin. Maybe the nuns or Father Joe could have found her and Bernadette a safe place to live.

Instead of giving that any thought at all, he'd fled to Birmingham, where they lived in a damp slum, and he hadn't even the wherewithal to pay the rent or put food on the table. So he'd allowed his wife to work in a dangerous factory and couldn't even insist she stopped when she became pregnant, or when she first developed that hacking cough. He felt he could insist on little while he had no job himself. And now he had the doctor's bill to look forward to, from savings depleted already by the cost of Gertie's funeral. However, none of this mattered. That was just money, for God's sake. What mattered was getting Rosie fit and healthy again.

'Bronchitis,' Doctor Anthony Patterson said after examining Rosie. 'And a bad dose of it. I should have been called much sooner. Keep a sharp eye on her, for if she's not careful she'll develop pneumonia and then we're really in trouble.'

'I've been putting hot camphorated oil on flannels and laying them on her chest,' Danny said. 'A neighbour told me it helped her son.'

'Probably did,' the doctor commented. 'And it can't do any harm, but your young wife is in a bad way. I'll make up a lotion for you to put on her back as well as her chest and something to ease that cough. That's all I can do.'

'Thank you, Doctor,' Danny said. 'Is ... is Rosie very infectious? You see we have a little girl.'

'Keep her well away if you want her to survive,' the doctor said. 'Children often haven't the strength to fight diseases such as these. As for the child she's carrying ... well, we'll just have to wait and see. Call me in again if you need me.'

All through Saturday and Sunday Bernadette stayed at Rita's, for after the doctor's warning, Danny couldn't risk having her in the house. Rosie, meanwhile, coughed and spluttered and fought for each gasping breath and tried to ignore the griping pains encircling her stomach from her back. Occasionally she couldn't prevent a groan escaping her, but if one of the women attending her asked if she had pains, she always shook her head.

She told herself she'd be fine. Bed was the best place. That's all she needed, a wee rest and she'd be grand again in time, and the baby would be born in just over three months' time, fine and healthy. She tried to curb her coughing and when she couldn't help herself she put her arms around her stomach protectively.

She knew Danny was worried about her and

340

she told him not to be, she'd be better in time and he was the one lying on a tick mattress beside the bed, which Betty had loaned them. It could be neither comfortable nor warm enough with just the one blanket, but whenever Rosie said anything, Danny told her not to waste her concern on him but to concentrate all her energies on getting better.

Then, on 14th December, Ida was staying with Rosie while Danny took the children to nursery and she'd popped down to make a drink for them both when she heard Rosie give a cry. She galloped up the stairs to see Rosie in bed, her eyes wide with alarm. 'Oh help me, Ida. Please, please do something.'

Ida threw back the covers and saw the water soaking the bedding and knew, early or not, Rosie's waters had gone and she doubted the baby could be saved.

'Oh God, I'm sorry, duck,' she said, giving Rosie's arm a squeeze.

'Do something, Ida,' Rosie cried desperately. 'God, I'm not even six months gone.'

Ida shook her head slowly, although her own eyes glistened with tears.

And then Rosie gave an agonised moan and drew her legs up to her chin, just as Danny came in the front door. He heard the sound and came bounding up the stairs.

'Oh Jesus Christ, what is it?' he cried, seeing his wife in so much distress.

'She's miscarrying,' Ida told him quietly. 'Her waters have gone.'

'Shall I fetch the doctor?'

341

'No, I'll ask one of the nippers to go,' Ida said and Danny nodded his head.

'Please, I'd be grateful,' Danny replied and then with another look at his wife said, 'and the priest. Ask Father Chattaway to come too.'

'It's too soon,' Rosie gasped. 'Much too soon.'

The doctor knew that too, but also doubted that Rosie could have carried the child full-term, for even as he examined her, her coughing racked her body and she groaned with the pains encircling her stomach.

Instinctively, Rosie tried to keep hold of the child, trying not to push when the contractions came. But then she'd be overcome by a spasm of coughing, and through each one the child seemed to slip further away from her, nearer to the world it would never grow up in.

Father Chattaway sat before the fire, keeping Danny company and fearing for the emotional turmoil of the woman above them, seriously ill and in the throes of a childbirth that was months too early.

'Hush, easy,' the doctor said to Rosie. 'Gently now.'

But tears of helplessness ran down Rosie's face. 'Dear God,' she cried. 'Help me, please.'

However, she knew in her heart it was no good. God wasn't listening to her. She knew she would eventually give birth to a child she wouldn't rear and she wanted to scream and hurl things, but she hadn't the energy to do either.

'Come on now,' the doctor chided, but gently for he was smote with pity for the young woman.

'It's got to come out, you know that. You must push.'

'I can't.'

'You can and it will be for the best in the end. When the next one comes, you must push.'

Rosie gave a sigh and yet she knew that the doctor was right and though she gave a howl of dismay she was ready with the next contraction and pushed until she could push no more. And she continued to push and Ida encouraged her and held her hand while the doctor's hands worked to help the child into the world.

It was a little boy, tiny and quite dead, but perfect, and even the doctor's heart constricted. Tears seeped from Ida's eyes at the pity of it. 'I want him baptised,' Rosie said. She knew unbaptised children could not enter heaven, but existed forever in limbo, and she wanted none of that for her son.

'I can't baptise him, you know that, Rosie,' the priest told her. 'The child didn't live.'

'You can, you must,' Rosie cried and when the priest again shook his head sadly Rosie began to scream and the sounds seemed to bounce off the walls and went on and on, and brought the doctor running up the stairs to see Rosie threshing on the bed. He knew she would have to be sedated and he took the ether out of his bag, and with the priest holding her as still as he could the pad was placed over her mouth and held tight.

'What brought this on?' the doctor asked when Rosie had succumbed to the anaesthetic.

'She wanted the child christened, but I couldn't do it.'

343

'No, of course,' the doctor said. 'She wasn't in her right mind.'

'I know that,' the priest said. 'Can you deal with the body? I think all trace of it should be removed before she wakes.'

'I'll see to it. Don't fret.'

Rosie went rapidly downhill for a few days after the baby's birth. When she awoke from her drugged sleep and found the child's body gone, she wept scalding tears of grief. It was as if she'd not given birth at all, as if it had all been some terrible, awful dream. There was no name, no Requiem Mass, no funeral, no grave, and Rosie didn't really care if she recovered or not.

'How is she?' Rita asked as she popped in on her way home from work one day.

Ida, who had taken on the main bulk of the nursing through the week with Betty and Rita at work, shrugged. 'As you'd expect,' she said. 'The death of the baby hasn't helped and she'll need to take care for she is quite poorly.'

Betty and Rita knew Ida spoke the truth and knew too it would be the network of women who would care for Rosie.

Danny was often overwhelmed by Rosie's grief, but the women seemed to take it in their stride and share in it, putting their arms around Rosie and crying alongside her just as easily as they raised her from the bed when the coughing spasms threatened to choke her.

Danny, without much hope of finding employment, especially this close to Christmas, was often drawn to the canal where he'd stay until the cold drove him home. There he would find the house cleaned and tidied and often there might be a nourishing meal left cooking in the range, for he was a man, and therefore not considered capable of cooking much and especially not food for a sick person.

He had no need to worry about washing and ironing clothes either, for the women took it in turns to do the Walshes' wash with their own. Danny couldn't help but be grateful for this, but it made him feel totally useless. He didn't know what to do about money either, for they had so little left now. The worry was pressing upon him and causing his head to pound with it. He couldn't share this with Rosie. How could he load her with a problem she had no way of solving and one which might worsen her already precarious state of health?

Betty, however, knew things must be bad. Gertie's funeral was enough to pay for without doctor's bills for Rosie. Danny was going around as if he had the weight of the world on his shoulders and so she popped in after work one evening when there was the chance of catching him alone.

Danny wasn't surprised to see her, thinking she had come to see Rosie, but she shook her head when he walked across to the door to the stairs. 'No, not yet, Danny,' she said. 'I'll go up and see Rosie in a minute. I want to ask you about money.'

Danny eyed her cautiously. 'Ask away,' he said and added an attempt at levity, 'but don't ask for a loan for I haven't the funds just at the moment.'

'Be serious, Danny.'

'I'll be serious if that's what you want,' Danny burst out. 'I'm worried to bloody death about money and that's the truth. I have just about two shillings and that is all we have in the world, and we're nearly out of coal. The rent is due tomorrow and the cupboards are bare. Is that serious enough for you?'

'And there's no work about at all?'

'Would I be sitting on my behind all day like this if there was?' Danny asked, and added, 'One thing I'm not is work shy.'

'All right, lad. Don't bite me bleeding head off.'

'I'm sorry, Betty. I know it isn't your fault, but I'm at my wits' end and don't know what to do.'

'Well, lad, I can see that,' Betty said. 'And all I can suggest is that you go down the Town Hall and see about this here poor relief.'

'Poor relief?'

'It's given to families what's fell on hard times like. Don't know much about it and thank God I've never had need of it, so far at least, but I know of many that has. That's your best bet.'

Danny hated the thought of accepting money like that. It was like charity, but he couldn't afford the luxury of pride while he had a sick wife and wee child. He said nothing to Rosie for it might distress her to find out how very nearly destitute they were, but as soon as he'd delivered the children to the nursery the following morning, he went off to the city centre.

NINETEEN

The Town Hall was such an imposing building that Danny felt nervous even standing in front of it. It had carved stone pillars at the front and a canopy of stone above those pillars supporting the first and subsequent floors. Solid wooden double doors were at the top of four white steps that looked as if they were made of marble, and Danny had to force himself to go up those steps and open the door. His feet sank into the deep red carpet strip, which masked the sound of his boots as he approached the desk at the end.

He looked at the young woman behind the counter and wished he didn't have to discuss his business with her, but he had no idea where to go. 'Poor Relief!' she repeated after him, her nose tilted as if he'd suddenly developed a noxious smell. 'Through the door to your right, third door on the left.'

'Thank you, miss.'

She didn't answer and Danny didn't wonder at it. He felt totally humiliated, but he followed the girl's instructions and the third door on the left opened onto a grim waiting room with three occupants already there. One was a man who looked as depressed as Danny, but was far shabbier, and the other two were dishevelled women. Both had babies and one had a toddler besides. Her baby was crying, a thin, plaintive cry that

347

struck at Danny's soul for it was a cry of hunger, evident by its sunken-in cheeks and chapped lips.

Danny hoped that Bernadette would never have to suffer hunger or cold and thought for the first time that it was probably a blessing in one way that the baby hadn't survived. What use was his pride now, he asked himself? He would stand on his head or walk across hot coals to secure money to provide food and shelter for his family.

'Name?'

He hadn't heard the woman approach the desk, but he heard the snap in her voice all right. The other people had obviously already been dealt with, for they didn't move but just looked at him with deadened eyes.

'I haven't got all day.'

'I'm … I'm sorry,' Danny said, getting to his feet and approaching the frosty-looking woman. She had her hair scraped back in a bun, wire-rimmed spectacles perched on a long narrow nose above a drooping discontented-looking mouth and high-neck black blouse fastened beneath an inde-terminate chin with a cameo brooch.

All this Danny took in, in one glance, but what held him fast were the eyes, brown-grey and as cold as steel and now those thin lips opened just enough to rap out again. 'I asked your name?'

'Danny Walsh,' Danny said and she entered it on the form before her. He was fine with the address, but when her pen hovered over another box and she said, 'Occupation?' he just stared at her. He hadn't any occupation. That was the problem surely? 'Unemployed?' the woman said and Danny nodded. 'What was your previous employment?'

'I was a farmer.'

'A farm hand?'

'No, a farmer. I mean, my family owned the farm. It was in Ireland.'

Immediately, the receptionist's manner changed. 'Please take a seat, Mr Walsh,' she said, glaring at him icily.

Danny sat down, wondering at the receptionist's manner. Was it to be the same story here, as soon as he mentioned Ireland? He couldn't risk that. He needed these people. It was his last port of call and he didn't know what he'd do if they refused to help him.

He didn't know how long he sat there. The shabbily dressed man and the two women had been called through and he hadn't seen them again. More bedraggled people had joined Danny in the room, shuffling through the door almost apologetically. The city's poor, he thought, reeking of neglect and all needy, and Danny felt more depressed than ever.

Eventually it was his turn, and by then hunger had begun to gnaw at him, but that hardly mattered, and the sooner this was over the better. He got to his feet and followed the man who'd called him through.

He bade him sit on the other side of the table and asked him questions about Rosie and Bernadette, which he filled in on the form before him, and then Danny said, 'We've been here since April, staying with the Sisters of Mercy in Handsworth because one of the Sisters was a friend of my wife's.' He considered the lie a necessary one.

'And why did you come to Britain? To a country at war?'

'Well, Ireland isn't exactly a safe place at the moment either,' Danny said.

'Did you register when you arrived?'

'Register?'

'I take it you did not,' the man barked. 'This country has been at war for three years, and not helped greatly by Ireland, I must say – quite the opposite in fact. We cannot have Irish citizens just waltzing into the country unchecked. Some are reputed to be a friend of the Hun.'

'I swear to you, sir, I am not,' said Danny.

'Well, you would hardly admit to it,' the man said. 'And I think I know why you didn't register: it was to make sure you weren't sent to the front.'

Such a thing had never crossed Danny's mind and he said, 'No, really, that wasn't it at all. There is no conscription in Ireland.'

'Ah yes, but there is here,' the man said. 'And the fact that you are on British soil means you are eligible for conscription.'

The roof of Danny's mouth had suddenly gone very dry. What was the man saying? 'What d'you mean, sir?'

'I mean that you can and will be conscripted for the army.'

This wasn't what Danny had in mind at all. 'I can't,' he said. 'I have a sick wife and small daughter to take care of.'

'Many of the men in our front lines have families, and if their wives go sick they cannot go running home. There are hospitals if your wife is sick enough and orphanages for your daughter.'

Danny's mind recoiled from that, but the man

was implacable. 'There is no choice in the matter,' he barked out. 'You can't expect to arrive in this country and have money handed out to you when you've put nothing in and are balking at the idea of fighting to keep England safe.'

Danny tried again. 'I knew nothing about registration,' he said, 'and it wasn't a thing the nuns would know. Anyway, I was unable to find employment – my wife worked at the Kynoch works making explosives until she became ill. She developed a cough, which turned to bronchitis and she has just miscarried our baby.'

'Distressing though that must have been,' the man said coldly, 'it could be considered expedient, for it would be one more mouth to feed.'

Danny didn't answer at first. He was too angry at the man's callousness, but he knew to show anger would be madness. In the end he was able to control himself enough to say, 'Are you saying if I enlist, my family can be helped, and if I don't we can all starve as far as you're concerned?'

'You don't seem to understand the position you are in,' the man said, a cold smile playing around his mouth. 'If you fail to register, you can be imprisoned, and if I were to call the authorities now, that's what would happen.'

Danny, remembering his time in Kilmainham Jail, gave an involuntary shiver. 'However,' the man went on, 'I feel you will be of more benefit to England by joining the army. Have you any problem with this?'

Danny had any number of problems. He remembered months before saying spiritedly that he'd never fight for England and that he wouldn't

351

even work in a war-related industry. However, the reality was he would have worked anywhere that would have given him a wage.

Now, if they wanted to continue to eat, he had to agree to join the army. 'I have no problem,' he said. 'But this is going to take time, surely? We have no money, the last has gone on doctor's bills. The rent is due and there's little food in the house.'

The man shrugged. 'You do not qualify for unemployment or poor relief, since you are not of this parish, but there are funds available called Distress Funds, and the Distress Board will find out if you are eligible as soon as I receive confirmation that you have enlisted.'

'We really need money now, however little it is.'

'Then you are one of many, Mr Walsh,' the man said. 'I've told you of the decision.'

'But when will this Distress Board meet?'

'Well not before Christmas now,' the man said, 'and certainly not before the 28th of December. By then you should be in the army. I suggest you take yourself off to Thorpe Street Barracks now and enlist. If I don't hear from you or them by tomorrow, when we close the doors for the holidays, I will not hesitate to inform the authorities about you.'

'There is no way I can have some money now?' Danny asked desperately, and the man shook his head.

'No way at all,' he said.

Later, Danny stood nervously outside Thorpe Street Barracks. He estimated it to be about lunchtime, or just after, and hoped all this would not take long for he had the children to pick up before six.

As he stood before the Recruitment Board he realised if he admitted to already being months in the country it might go against him and so he told them he'd just arrived in England with his wife and child, Ireland having become a violent and turbulent country, and wanted to enlist in the army. Shay and Sam wouldn't recognise him, he told himself, but patriotism was all right on a full belly.

The recruiting officers took in what Danny told them and saw before them a healthy young man, ready and willing to fight. 'D'you have any preference as to which regiment you'd wish to serve in?'

'No.' Why would he? One was the same as another to him.

'Well, here we recruit for the Royal Warwickshires, but we could make enquiries about the Royal Dublin Fusiliers.'

Danny didn't want that. Dublin was too close to Blessington for comfort. What if any of the men recognised him and carried tales home. 'The Warwickshires will suit me fine, sir.'

'Good man,' the recruiting officer said, rubbing his hands together as if with glee. 'Now, as the time is pressing, Christmas only around the corner as it were, what if you have the medical now and your uniform sorted out. Then you'll be ready to join your new unit after Christmas, some of whom are already at the training camp in Sutton Park.'

Danny hadn't expected to be dealt with so speedily. But he was soon before a doctor to be prodded and poked and examined, his chest and back sounded and in the end pronounced A1 fit and well able to go overseas after training. Shortly after this he was measured for the uniform that they said would be waiting for him when he joined his unit on the 27th December.

'What is the pay, sir,' Danny said, thinking of Rosie and Bernadette.

'You've heard of the King's shilling?' the recruiting officer said, and at Danny's nod, said, 'Well, think yourself lucky for until 1915 you would have had just one of them a day, seven shillings a week, but after 1915 it was increased to two shillings a day.' He looked at the form before him and said, 'Oh you have a wife and child, so sixpence will be taken off you for your wife and a penny for your child.'

Danny, appalled at the meagre amount, cried, 'But my wife, what will she live on?'

'She will have a separation allowance,' the recruiting officer said. 'It amounts to a shilling and a penny a day, sixpence from you, plus the allowance of twopence for the child from the government and a penny from you. Altogether this brings your wife's weekly income to be in the region of, let's see, eight shillings and four pence.'

It was too little. It was a pittance. The rent was half a crown a week. But what could he do? 'Can I give her something from my pay,' Danny asked.

'You can certainly make an allotment for your family,' the recruiting officer said. 'Many men do that.'

Danny breathed a sigh of relief. He would allot at least seven shillings to Rosie, more if he could, but as yet he didn't know what expenses he might have. 'What does she do to get this money?'

'She needs to take your marriage lines and the child's birth certificate to the Town Hall,' the man said. 'She must go herself, no-one can go in her stead, and she must also take any children she is claiming for. Stress upon her there must be no delay. She must present herself there as soon as they open their offices after Christmas.'

And this is the news Danny had to go home and hit Rosie with. He knew she would be terribly upset. He'd gone out to beg for funds and had come back with no money and the news he was a soldier in a war that had killed thousands and thousands of men so far. He hadn't even anything to sweeten the bitter pill. Dear God, he thought, life is a bugger right enough.

Rosie wasn't upset, she was distraught. She heard words spilling from Danny's mouth, words like registration and prison and Poor Relief and Distress Boards, as if it was a foreign language. She felt far from well, her chest was burning and incredibly tight and her ribs and stomach and back ached from her coughing, and now this news was making her suddenly terribly short of breath.

Danny, aware of the rapid change in her countenance and her lack of breath, was worried. 'Sit down, Rosie, for God's sake, and try and calm yourself.'

'How can I calm myself?' Rosie demanded. 'We have two paltry shillings to bless ourselves with and little food, and only a few nuggets of coal and rent to pay.'

'I know that, Rosie,' Danny said wearily. 'And let me tell you I begged and pleaded with the man. As for hunger, not a bit has passed my lips since I had a slice of bread spread with dripping for my breakfast.'

'I know,' Rosie said. 'And I'm sorry, but Danny, what are we to do?' Danny looked at her and she began to tremble at the look in his eyes, for she knew in that moment what Danny had done. She didn't even need to hear the words but they came anyway.

'I've enlisted.'

'Dear God. No! Say it isn't true. Oh Danny, Danny.'

Rosie had risen to her feet and was grasping his lapels with her hands, her voice high, almost hysterical, and her breath coming in short pants. Her mind was rejecting his words. He couldn't do this. He mustn't. She wouldn't let him.

But Danny's words cut through the rambling thoughts running wild in Rosie's brain while his hands had detached her own agitated ones and his strong arms had encircled her as he told her in his strong but gentle voice how it was, how it had to be, how there had been no other path open to him but the one that led to prison.

When Rosie realised and knew she could do nothing to change or even delay this decision Danny had been forced into, the tears poured from her in a paroxysm of grief and Danny's arms tightened around her, for she'd sagged against him and he was afraid of her sinking to the floor.

Eventually he lowered her tenderly back into the chair. 'I must go back and see the man and tell him what has transpired, for if I don't do this he will inform the authorities. I'm going to ask Ida to sit in with you while I'm gone. All right?'

Rosie nodded, though she knew nothing would ever be truly all right again, and Danny left a very anxious man.

Christmas was a fraught time. Rosie was too ill to enjoy the festivities and well aware that this might be Danny's last Christmas. She would have liked to have made it a special time, but even if she'd had the money she wasn't able to.

But lack of money was a pressing problem. Danny had toured all the greengrocers in the area, begging for the boxes the goods arrived in, which he broke up in the cellar to eke the coal out, but both knew if it hadn't been for the odd shovel of coal from the neighbours they would have all perished. He was desperately worried that he was leaving Rosie with just pennies to survive. 'You must go up straight away tomorrow to see the unemployment people with your marriage lines and Bernadette's birth certificate to qualify for separation allowance,' he told her the morning he was leaving. 'You're far from well enough to go out in this perishing weather, but they won't let anyone else go instead, and you must take Bernadette, they told me that.'

Rosie was frantically concerned too. 'How long will it take to come through, this separation allowance?' she asked.

'I don't know, pet,' Danny said. 'One thing I do

know is that the sooner you see about it, the sooner you get it, and remember, tomorrow's Friday, so if you don't go then you'll have to wait till Monday. Ask about the Distress Boards while you're there,' he said. 'They were meeting again tomorrow as well. Maybe you'll get something from that.' Suddenly, Danny pulled Rosie close and said, 'I'm so sorry, I haven't even enough time to see to all this for you.'

'It isn't your fault.'

'Not my fault!' Danny echoed. 'I feel it is. In fact I feel I've made a balls-up of the last few years of my life. And that might be all right, if you hadn't had to bear the brunt of it too.'

'Hush, Danny,' Rosie said, kissing him. 'Don't go like this. I know you had no choice in what you did and you've suffered as much or more than I have. Anyway, isn't that what marriage is all about, for richer or poorer, in sickness and health? Go, Danny, and try and keep yourself safe, and when it's over and you come home I'll be here waiting for you.'

Danny ground his teeth. 'I can't help worrying, Rosie,' he said. 'As soon as I can I will arrange to send you more money.'

'You will not,' Rosie said firmly. 'You'll be fighting in a war and the times you're not in the trenches you'll be entitled to spend the wee bit of money you'll have left. I won't be the only woman to be managing on so little, so don't fret about me.'

'No, Rosie, I couldn't rest. You couldn't feed yourself or wee Bernadette on so little. Other men do, the man told me.'

358

'All right,' Rosie said. 'But you are not to leave yourself short and if you stay any longer you'll be late reporting in and I don't think the army takes kindly to being kept waiting.'

Danny knew Rosie spoke the truth and Bernadette too was looking worried, catching the tension in the air. He lifted her into his arms and said, 'You'll be a good girl for Mammy, sure you will.'

Bernadette nodded her head briskly and wound her podgy arms around her father's neck and he felt his heart contract for love for her. But then he set her down and took Rosie in his arms and kissed her, hungrily, longingly. When he'd left them, after striding across the courtyard, Rosie lifted her daughter into her arms for comfort and sank into the chair in floods of tears. Bernadette patted her mother's face, not understanding her grief, but her actions made Rosie cry more.

The following day, Betty and Rita insisted Rosie take a shilling each from them, and a penny for the tram that they insisted she take both ways. Rosie had too little to protest much. She was grateful for the money because the day was too raw and cold for her to want to walk and even the exertion of getting to the tram stop caused her to cough so badly she often had to stand on the road, turning her face from Bernadette and covering her mouth to try to protect her. She sank onto the seat of the tram thankfully, glad she had to trek no further.

She was glad too that the Town Hall wasn't far from the terminus in the city centre, and went in and stated her business there to the receptionist who rose to greet her. Her reception was different from Danny's, now that she had a husband who'd enlisted in the army, and she was shown into a cubicle and a woman sat the other side of it to check her credentials and fill out forms.

'How ... how long will it take before I get the money?' Rosie asked, and added, 'You see, we have none. I was working and had to leave when I had bronchitis and went on to lose my baby and am not yet able to look for any other type of employment. My husband came for help and was told something about a Distress Board.'

'Your husband was here before?'

'Aye. Yes, before Christmas.'

'Then there will be a file on him,' the woman said. 'Wait here please.'

Just a few seconds later she came into the room reading the notes inside a folder. 'It says here you've been in the country eight months,' the woman said, tight-lipped. 'Your husband was unemployed and he'd not registered.'

'He knew nothing about registration,' Rosie said hotly, angry with the unfairness of it. 'Neither of us knew we were doing wrong. We lived with the Sisters of Mercy at St Mary's Convent and because my husband was unable to find work I worked in Kynoch's works at Witton. We didn't apply for anything until I became too sick to work.'

'Your husband had to be coerced into enlisting.'

'He wasn't coerced, he was forced,' Rosie declared. 'There was no option left open to him,

360

but you got your way, he's away training now and before the New Year is very old I imagine he will be in the thick of it and he may die just as easily as those who went more willingly. Bullets and shells do not discriminate.'

A voice inside Rosie was telling her to be quiet, to stop berating the woman before her, stop trying to be clever, that this woman could make trouble for her, that she must try and ingratiate herself. But she wasn't able to do it. For the first time in her life she wanted to smack the face of the woman who was looking at her as if she was some sort of slug that had the audacity to crawl out from under a stone.

'You have an unfortunate manner,' the woman said haughtily.

'It's an unfortunate chance that's brought me here,' Rosie bit back. 'I am forced to beg money from you so I don't have to hide from the rent man again this week and can put food in front of myself and my child until the separation order comes through,' she said. 'Now can you tell me anything about Distress Boards?'

'They meet today. If your case is put before them they will write to you with their decision. They will probably visit your home.'

'That will all take time. How will I live until then?'

The woman shrugged. 'That's not my problem.'

Rosie got to her feet. She would not beg further. She lifted Bernadette up, her legs straddled either side of her hips, and strode from the room, willing herself not to cough, not to show any weakness before any of these people who considered them-

361

selves better than the poor because they were fortunate enough to pick up a wage at the end of the week. She had two shillings to last her till God alone knew when and that had been a gift from her good friends. She knew she had to spend it with great care and hoped the landlord was imbibed with true Christian charity and would be patient for his rent.

The following Monday was New Year's Eve and that morning she had a letter from the Board and took it around and showed it to Ida. 'You might get summat then if they're coming for a look tomorrow,' Ida said. 'Let's have a dekko at the house like.'

'Why?'

'Cos I know that's what they'll do. If there's summat, anything that they consider you don't need, they'll say you got to sell it before they give you owt.'

'Oh God, Ida, they must give me something,' Rosie cried. 'With the nursery closed until the seventh of January, Bernadette has lived on bread and scrape for two days with the prospect of more of the same tomorrow, because that is all the money would buy, for I had to have a couple of bucketfuls of coal or we'd have frozen to death. I'm on my beam-ends, Ida. If they give me nothing, Sweet Jesus, I might go clean mad altogether.'

And she really thought she might, for worry and constant hunger was driving her insane. She might fall upon them, clawing their self-satisfied faces or putting her hands around their scrawny necks and squeezing tight.

'Listen to me,' Ida said. 'Get rid of two of them hard-back chairs. They'll probably say you have no need of four, and pull up the rag rug and hide the cushions as well, and that clock, I'd get rid of that straight off.'

'I'd never sell that,' Rosie said. 'No matter how hard up I was. Connie gave it to me the night we left. It's my link with home.'

'Rosie, they won't give a tinker's cuss about that,' Ida said firmly. 'You'll have to get rid of that picture above the fireplace too, I'd say.'

'I can't do that,' Rosie said, appalled. 'That's the Sacred Heart of Jesus, the nuns gave it to me when I left the convent. Most Catholic homes have a similar one.'

'I'm telling it how it is, bab,' Ida said. 'I've seen them buggers in action. Christ! You'd think it was money out of their own bleeding pockets they was giving you. You can store the stuff in my place and have it back later, but honest, it's best to be careful.'

Betty and Rita weren't at work as Kynoch's hadn't started back yet after Christmas and they both agreed with Ida. Betty went further and suggested she lift the eiderdown and a couple of blankets from her bed and the rug from the bedroom floor and advised her to get rid of some of her dinner plates and cups.

'It seems a shabby way to go on,' Rosie said doubtfully.

'It's the only way,' Betty said firmly.

Later, seeing the disparaging way the people from the Distress Board peered and poked around her house, Rosie knew Betty and Ida were right. She blessed her friends for putting her wise, for the man and woman did scrutinise her crockery and bedding as well as everything else and eventually agreed to give her five shillings.

'Five shillings,' she complained to Ida. 'It's not that I'm not grateful, but the rent's due again this Friday. That will be three weeks owing.'

'Pay summat off,' Ida advised. 'Some landlords give you six weeks, some only four, so pay summat off it you can.'

'Out of five shillings, Ida, talk sense,' Rosie said, and yet she trembled at the thought of being thrown out of her home. She'd end up in the workhouse and so would her child. They'd be separated, she might never see Bernadette again. She'd not stand that, she'd go mad. With Danny gone and the baby dead, Bernadette was all she had. Her knees trembled so violently she had to sit down. 'What shall I do, Ida? What can I do?'

'There is one place,' Ida said thoughtfully. 'I applied to it once when my old man joined in 1914 with thousands of others and they took weeks to work out my separation pay, but this SSAFA place gave me money like, till it was sorted. I suppose they still do that.'

'Weeks to sort out,' Rosie repeated horrified. 'How many weeks?'

'It won't be like that for you, duck, don't worry,' Ida said reassuringly. 'They ain't joining up in droves like they was then, but on the other hand,' she added, 'they don't rush themselves, the army.'

'Where is this place? Have they an office or what?'

'An office, a sizeable one on Colmore Row. You can't miss it, just up from Snow Hill Station and on the same side.'

'What was the place called again?'

'SSAFA,' Ida said. 'Stands for "Soldiers', Sailors', and Airmen Families Association". I think they might help you. They d'ain't make me feel I had no right to live on earth either, like some do.'

Rosie gave a shudder. She knew exactly what Ida meant. If only she didn't feel so weak, if she could lie down and let someone else deal with it. But she knew if she was to live day to day, feed herself and her child, keep the house passably warm and pay the rent, she needed help, and the only place she knew she might get it was the organisation Ida had used and benefited from.

She took her marriage lines, Bernadette's birth certificate and Bernadette herself, as she'd done before, and the next day set off for the SSAFA office on Colmore Row.

Here she found people in sympathy with her, people who knew what she was going through, who professed concern for her and Bernadette, and after taking all the details and particulars, the fund awarded her an interim payment of ten shillings and Rosie felt the worries slide from her back as she held the note in her hand.

It wasn't a fortune, but it was enough to pay some of the back rent and leave something over, together with the five shillings. If only she knew how long it had to last her. Still, she was able to answer Danny's first letter cheerfully enough. She sidestepped questions about her health because there had been little change there. The slightest thing still made her breathless, but the neighbours were all willing to help. Ida in particular would fetch her shopping in and help her with the wash in the brewhouse and eventually, slowly but surely, as January slid into February, she began to feel stronger and her cough eased a little. She'd had to appeal twice more to the SSAFA office and as her rent was up to date she'd received seven shillings and six pence, but by the third week in January her separation allowance had been sorted out and she received eight shillings and four pence a week, plus the allotment of a further seven shillings that Danny had promised her. Life suddenly looked more hopeful, especially with Ida on hand.

She was very fond of Ida and the woman was a dab hand at making a shilling do the work of two. Though being a widow meant she got more each week than those with living husbands, ten shillings a week, a widow's pension, another five shillings for her eldest son Jack, and three shillings and sixpence for his younger brother and little sister, she still had to be careful with every penny.

Rosie wouldn't have changed places with Ida, though, or any of the women wearing the widow's bonnet. 'Don't you miss your husband,' she asked Ida one day. 'You seem to have got over it quickly.'

Ida thought about it for a bit and then said, 'Yeah, I miss him, and I shed bitter tears at the time when I first heard. We all cried, me and the nippers. Jack was cut up about it bad cos he was real close to his dad. I mean, the other two loved him and he loved them and all in all he was a good man, a good provider and a great father, but between him and Jack there was a certain something. Anyroad, I couldn't just give way, could I? I mean, I had to be here for the nippers.

'It ain't the same, anyroad, as if he'd been killed in the normal way. A lot of families haven't got a dad coming home every night. Look at Rita, she ain't seen Harry since he went off. Twice she's been over the moon as he's supposed to be coming home and it's been cancelled.

'I suppose although I know Herbie's dead and everything, I can kid myself he's somewhere in France. Maybe I'll feel it a bit more when the whole shindig is eventually over and those who have survived at the end of it come home.'

'I think you're ever so brave,' Rosie said admiringly.

'No, I ain't brave, Rosie,' Ida said. 'Thing is, I'm no different to anyone else. It's summat you've got to get over. You got over losing the babby, d'ain't you?'

'I still think about it. It comes over me sometimes in a wave,' Rosie said. 'And when I least expect it. The letters from Ireland from the nuns at Baggot Street and from Connie and my sisters were a comfort. Even Dermot wrote and said how sorry he was.'

'Well, you're lucky they're there, then,' Ida said. 'For at least you had support. Herbie's family live here in Birmingham, but from the day he died, well, it's as if we ceased to exist too. And I do still think of him, and for me it's odd things start me off, a snatch of a song someone's whistling in the street, or a sudden whiff of the Woodbines he smoked.

'Just the other day,' she confided, 'I dropped half a crown and it went under the cushion of the chair Herbie always sat on and when I shoved my hand in to get it out, fishing about like, I found summat else along with the money, and when I pulled it out it was one of his socks. I was always telling him off for taking his socks off downstairs and just leaving them there, but, you know, the sight of that sock, well, it proper upset me.'

Rosie heard the catch in Ida's voice and gripped her arm. 'I understand that perfectly.'

'But we cope,' Ida said positively. 'We have to. I will, and you will, and when your Danny comes back home there'll be more babbies for you, mark my words.'

But her eyes met Rosie and Rosie knew it was *if* Danny came back, not *when*, but neither woman spoke of it.

TWENTY

As February began drawing to a close, Rosie could feel herself improving and getting stronger, and though the cough still lingered the intensity of it had gone. Now it was more of an irritant than a worry.

And then, one morning at the very end of the month, she got a letter from Danny that set her heart singing. 'He's coming home,' she cried to Rita as she called to collect Bernadette. She bent to tuck the scarf inside her daughter's coat and missed the look on Rita's face for she knew if Danny was coming home it was probably embarkation leave. But she didn't want to dim the dancing light in Rosie's eyes and neither did Ida when Rosie went in waving the letter later. Poor cow, she thought, but what she said was, 'You fit to come up the Lozells Road with me Saturday evening. The butcher there, Rowbotham and White's, nearly gives the stuff away. I go up most weeks while Jack gives an eye to the little ones for us.'

'I'd like to go,' Rosie said. 'It would be nice to get something decent in for once and the money doesn't go that far.'

Ida knew it didn't, and she also knew Rosie was inexperienced in making it stretch. She'd told Ida how her mouth would water sometimes when she thought of the succulent ham they often enjoyed at Connie's, with as many eggs as you wanted

369

and thick creamy butter spread as lavishly as you liked on soda bread still warm from the oven.

'Them days is gone, bab,' Ida said, 'for now anyroad. But where's your patriotic duty? D'ain't the government say we should have two meat-free days a week?'

'God, I often have a week of meat-free days like every other body,' Rosie said. 'Mind, I've done better since you took me in hand.'

Ida had showed Rosie how to boil a pig's head, which cost just thrupence, till the meat fell off the bones. With the meat and jelly transferred to a china dish, seasoned and pressed down with a saucer weighted with a flat iron, it was made into tasty potted meat that could be spread on bread as an alternative to dripping.

Rosie had also cooked and eaten tripe for the first time and found cooked pigs' trotters surprisingly satisfying to gnaw on. Cows' heel too was dirt cheap, and though it took a lot of cooking, mixed with vegetables it made a good solid stew.

But with Danny expected home on the following Monday, it would be nice to get something a bit tasty with which to welcome him.

In the end, Rita went with them the following Saturday evening too, when Betty offered to mind Georgie as well as Bernadette, and the three women hurried off up Upper Thomas Street towards Victoria Road. It was bitterly cold and mist swirled about them, muffling the sounds of both people and vehicles. The streetlamps and lights from the shops shone through the haze, lighting up for a brief second the people filling the pavements; the shoppers with serious faces out for a bargain and those more relaxed off for a stroll, and couples entwined and at ease, bent on an evening's entertainment.

Rosie, not usually out at night, sniffed and realised even from the top of Upper Thomas Street the tangy whiff from the HP Sauce factory and the thick sultry smell of malt from the Ansell's factory was still in the air, mixed in with the general odour of dampness and petrol fumes.

More pleasant was the delicious aroma of coffee, which wafted outside the many coffee shops they passed every time a door was opened. They were mainly small places with windows so steamed up that the prices, which were usually printed on the window with a bar of soap, could barely be seen. 'I could murder a cup of coffee right now, couldn't you?' Rita said suddenly. 'This cold eats right into you.' Rosie could have too, but she had no money for such things.

But at least a café would be a respectable place for a woman to go into, while only loose women would enter one of the many pubs. They were the prerogative of the men.

Rosie had never been inside one, but as the group passed a pub called the King's Arms the swing doors opened and there was a sudden burst of sound and the smell of beer and tobacco assailed her nostrils. She had a tantalising glimpse of the firelight from the coals dancing in the hearth, lighting up the horse brasses behind the gleaming bar and the brass rail in front where a bank of men stood. 'D'you know,' she remarked as they moved on, 'they look inviting places, those pubs, friendly like.'

'They're not so friendly to the poor souls trying to entice their men out of them before they've spent all their wages,' Ida said. 'You see enough of them outside the pubs sometimes, huddling near the door, often with children in tow as well. Poor sods, I feel sorry for them. I mean, my Herbie used to like a drink as well as the next, but he never saw me or the kids go short.'

'Nor mine,' said Rita. 'Me and Georgie would always come first with Harry. Your Danny's the same, ain't he, Rosie? I mean he's lived here months now and I ain't never seen him truly bottled.'

'No,' Rosie said. 'He'd never be like that. He's a moderate drinker and not even that if the money's tight.' She too felt sorry for the bedraggled, often barefoot women, or the shivering ill-clad children outside some of the pubs they passed in the damp and the cold. She remembered when Danny had taken to drinking more heavily than was usual, before they had left Ireland, and how upset she'd become at times and how Matt and Connie had disapproved. Danny had done that for a few weeks only, all told. Many of the women they passed that night looked resigned, as if they'd had years of this way of life already and had more years of it yet to come.

All that was forgotten as they reached Six Ways. Lozells Road was before them, but wafting to the right of them was the overpowering stench of decay from the Dixon and Rider Company at the back of New Street that crushed animal bones.

'Gawd blimey, let's go out of this before we're gassed to death,' Ida said, dragging a rag from her pocket to cover her nose as she spoke. Neither of the women argued with her and they quickened their pace. Rosie tried to hold her breath until the stink was behind them.

Many of the shops were pulling down their blinds as they passed, shutting up shop, but the Picture Houses seemed to be doing a roaring trade, Rosie noticed, as they passed first the Aston Picture Palace and then the Lozells Picture House as they made their way to the butcher's. She had a great longing to see inside one of these cinemas for she'd heard them spoken of often. She'd never thought of going while they lived with the nuns, feeling certain they wouldn't approve, and since living in the court she'd never seemed to have the time or money, but the thought of seeing moving pictures ... it was magical somehow.

But then she brought her mind back to the present for Rowbotham and White's butcher's shop was before them, and judging by the crowds outside the shop, many women had had the same idea as themselves.

Despite the press of people, the butcher was fair and Rosie came away with a piece of pork, half a pound of liver, half a dozen pigs' trotters and a large pot of dripping. She was well-pleased. 'I should cook that pork tonight if I were you,' Ida said. 'For it don't smell too fresh and has probably been in his window all day.'

Rosie had already decided that herself and on Monday she was able to put before Danny a meal fit for a king, the slices of cold pork warmed with onion gravy, and served with potatoes, cabbage and carrots. 'That was a wonderful meal, Rosie,' Danny said as he mopped up the last of the gravy with a slice of bread. He was glad to see Rosie so much better. The cough was almost gone, colour had begun to return to her cheeks and a spring was once more in her step.

He blessed the women in the courts for caring for Rosie and Bernadette till Rosie was able to take up the reins again, for he knew he had news to tell her that would probably knock her for six. He didn't know for certain that this was embarkation leave, they weren't told that as such; it was just a feeling he had, and what the older ones in the unit had told him.

He didn't intend to share that with Rosie yet. Time enough at the end of his leave. And Rosie did enjoy their few days together. The money was no more plentiful, but that didn't matter. Rosie was glad she wasn't at work and Bernadette didn't go to nursery either, with her daddy home. The weather was kind to them and they took a walk together most days, Bernadette between them till her legs tired and then Danny would throw her up on his shoulders effortlessly and she'd squeal with delight.

Rosie had never been down to the canal till that time. The sludgy brown oil-slicked water didn't impress her, but she was enchanted by the brightly painted narrowboats pulled along by the shaggy-hoofed horses that reminded her of the work-horses they had on the farm. She noticed how often Danny was hailed; only now the boaties took in Danny's army greatcoat and the army-issue boots beneath and their eyes were sympathetic.

But Danny had no time for sympathy. He lifted Bernadette from his shoulders and holding her hand tight, he led her to the edge of the canal and then took her down to the lock gates and explained their function. Rosie, following behind, and watching her small daughter, wondered if she'd understood a word of what her father said, for it was confusing to her at first. But, understanding it or not, she'd stood as good as gold, basking in the attention he was showing her, and when Danny had explained it all again to Rosie and she grasped what he was trying to say, she had to own it was an ingenious way to move water up or down.

Danny was sorry Ted wasn't around for Rosie to meet, and Rosie too would have liked to have met the family. She'd have liked to have taken a peep in the cabin too, for when Danny described it, about ten-foot long and six-and-a-half-foot wide, it sounded so small, even to someone in a cramped back-to-back house, and she would have liked to meet Ted's wife and shaken her by the hand.

'That was a family narrowboat,' Danny told Rosie that day as they wandered along the bank holding Bernadette firmly. 'There's lots of other types. It was an education for me, those few days I worked alongside Ted.'

'Other boats people live on?'

'Not always,' Danny said. 'There's an Ampton boat that no-one lives on. It's eighty-seven-feet long, Ted said, too big to even go through the locks, so it operates on a stretch of water that has no locks, carrying coal from Cannock Chase and Wolverhampton collieries. Then there are the day boats, or Joey boats, just doing short daytrips out. And you should just see the Shroppie Fly move.'

'Shroppie Fly?'

'Aye, and fly is what it does, near enough. It's six-foot wide and two-foot deep and carries perishable goods from the Mersey Docks to Birmingham and to other midland towns served by the canals. There's two men run these boats and they are pulled by two galloping horses working in tandem and can reach speeds of ten miles an hour.'

'Goodness,' Rosie said, and saw the excitement in Danny as he spoke of these different boats. She knew he was probably happier here than anywhere and she was glad he'd shared it with her and Bernadette.

Another day, the family went down to the Bull Ring and wandered between the stalls, many calling out their wares, and Bernadette, watching and listening, was fascinated by it all.

She too noticed the wounded ex-servicemen and at first asked in her high-pitched voice why those men had just one arm, or that one had no legs. Rosie was embarrassed, but Danny wasn't. 'They're servicemen from the war,' he'd say. 'And they were wounded there.'

Rosie gave a sudden shiver at the mention of it, but she hid it well and followed Danny and Bernadette who'd wandered off to look at the cluster of flower sellers around Nelson's Column. Bernadette wanted to know who the statue was and again Danny explained. 'He was Nelson, a famous and very brave sailor, and he was so fearless people want him remembered. There's another statue to him in Dublin, but that one is at the top of a high tower and there's steps inside that you can go up.

'One day I will take you back to Dublin,' Danny promised, 'and we'll climb that tower together.'

Bernadette clapped her hands with delight, but Rosie wished Danny hadn't made that promise. Bernadette had no concept of time and would think Danny meant next week. She couldn't see them going back home for years for the British efforts to introduce conscription in Ireland had caused people to flock to join Sinn Fein, who were against it. Even the Church, while opposed, at least on the surface, to violence, said no Irishman should be forced to fight for the English and called on the Irish people to resist this violation of their freedom.

But, she decided, she wouldn't spoil this day by thinking sad thoughts, and she followed Danny and Bernadette up the steps to the Market Hall.

Bernadette seemed interested in everything she saw. The chirruping budgies and canaries and the endearing kittens and boisterous puppies at Pimm's Pet Store enchanted her. 'I wish we could buy her a wee dog or cat,' Danny said, seeing his daughter's pleasure. 'But we can't do such a thing to an animal where we live. They need space to run.'

'Aye,' Rosie agreed, 'and food to eat, when we have little enough money to feed ourselves.' She knew she wouldn't have minded a cat to curl on her knee when Danny wasn't home and Bernadette in bed, an animal to hug and love. But she could not bring any animal into that tiny house, that teeming courtyard, where it would only have the streets to roam and every likelihood of it being killed on the road before it developed the cautiousness that would come with maturity.

And then the clock began to strike and even Bernadette forgot the animals. She'd not noticed the clock before but her attention was fastened on it now all right. So, it seemed, was everyone else's too, for many people seemed to stop what they were doing and watch as the lady and three knights banged the bell with their hammers.

'It's a magnificent piece of workmanship, that,' Danny said, and Rosie agreed with him. It was of solid wood, carved so elaborately that Rosie could have studied it for hours, but Bernadette was tugging on her parents' hands and they smiled at each other over her head and made their way outside.

'I think that was another hit,' Danny said to Rosie later that night after a sleepy Bernadette had been tucked in bed.

'Aye,' Rosie said. 'And Bernadette took the wounded servicemen in her stride far more than I did, for I still felt sick as I looked at them.'

'She doesn't understand like you do, that's why,' Danny said. 'She accepts what she's told and doesn't have any inkling of what those men, and possibly their families too, go through. Anyway, my darling girl,' he went on, 'neither of you will be upset by tomorrow's planned outing, for if the weather remains fine I'd like to take you to Aston Park.'

'That will be nice for Bernadette,' Rosie said. 'And for me too. I miss the feel of grass beneath my feet sometimes.'

It was no distance either and the day was dry, though cold and grey, but it didn't seem to bother Bernadette as she danced between her parents. However, she barely noticed the gravel path between the lawns either side, or the high wall with the bare trees stretching their gnarled tentacles in the air at the entrance to the park, because her attention was taken by the hurdy-gurdy man they met as they crossed Albert Road.

The man's bright brown eyes shone out of a wizened, creased face. He wore a coat like an army greatcoat that reached the top of his cobbled boots, and a greasy cap was pulled down on his head, and he didn't interest Bernadette in the slightest. What enchanted her was the monkey he had with him, which was tethered to the organ by a long chain. Rosie, sharing her daughter's amusement at the monkey's capers, was at least pleased to see he was dressed, for she'd seen others shivering, their teeth chattering with cold. This monkey looked fairly happy, his darting movements were almost like dancing to the music and threatened to dislodge the red fez he had at a jaunty angle on his head.

Bernadette clapped her hands and her little feet danced to the tunes the organ produced through the perforated paper rolls, and when the music eventually drew to a close the monkey lifted the fez from his head and waved it before Bernadette with a flourish. Even Rosie and Danny had to laugh.

There was little money to give to the hurdy-gurdy man in the Walsh household at that time, but even so, Rosie extracted two farthings from her purse and let Bernadette drop them in the proffered fez. 'Thank you, Mam,' the hurdy-gurdy man said.

'I'm sorry it wasn't more. You entertained my girl so well,' Rosie said.

'Ah no,' the organ-grinder said. 'She's good for business,' and Rosie noticed for the first time the women drawn out from their warm firesides to their doorsteps by the sound, smiling at the child's pleasure, and their own children edging closer.

Bernadette had not wanted to leave, but Danny, watching the sky, said it was coming to rain and knew the outing to the park would have to be a short one anyway. Bernadette went with them willingly enough, but her head was turned back to watch the man and the monkey and they heard the strains of other tunes as they went between the ornate iron gates and into the park itself.

The beautiful flowerbeds were almost bare due to the time of year and only snowdrops and crocuses had pushed their way up through the frozen earth. The trees were leafless and sad-looking. 'What's that?' Bernadette said, pointing.

'A bandstand,' Danny told her. 'Do you want to see?' Rosie watched them approach it and remembered the bandstand in St Stephen's Green, that beautiful park the rebels had tried their best to ruin.

However, even she was intrigued by the stocks they came upon as they walked towards the lake,

380

with the majestic spire of Aston Church in the distance. She'd heard about stocks but had never seen them. This one had six holes, enough for three people's hands, with a wooden bench for the unfortunate ones imprisoned there to kneel or sit on. Rosie stood at the iron fence in front and said, 'Wouldn't it be awful to be put in that thing?'

'Aye and pelted with soft tomatoes and rotten eggs,' Danny agreed. 'Of course, though, Rosie, we don't know what the people did to deserve that sort of punishment.'

'No,' Rosie said, but she shivered and hoped Bernadette didn't ask too many searching questions about the stocks. Bernadette, though, was happily swinging on the railings and was, for once, paying no heed to her parents' chatter.

Danny swung Bernadette up on his shoulders as they came to the lake, gun-metal grey in the dull daylight and lapping gently at the edges. 'Do they have boats out on here in the summer?' Danny asked, but Rosie shook her head. She didn't know.

'If they do I'll take you out,' Danny told Bernadette. 'I rowed across Blessington Lake many times as a lad. Would you like to go out on a boat, Bernadette?'

'I don't know,' Bernadette said uncertainly, not knowing what a boat was.

'The only boat she may remember is the mail boat we travelled on,' Rosie reminded Danny. 'No wonder she's confused.'

'She'd hardly remember that,' Danny said dismissively. 'But no matter, darling. Now, I'm going to show you a fine house.'

And it was fine. Aston Hall. Huge and full of splendour and Rosie could just stand and stare. A large carpet of winter flowers and evergreen shrubs decorated the circular flowerbed before the sweep of gravel drive that went up to the wide front door, and to either side of the building there were protuberances with gabled windows and domed roofs, and chimneys everywhere. 'Oh, isn't it wonderful?'

'Aye, it is,' Danny agreed. 'But, you see, what you must remember is that all this park, the lake, and even the church I would imagine, belong to one man, one family. It's hardly decent for one family to own so much. It isn't only Ireland where oppression occurred. The ordinary Englishman is no freer than we are.'

Rosie knew Danny was right and she looked at the house again and wondered how just the one family could live there and fill these rooms. What an army of servants it would command to clean and service such a place and how many little boys had been pushed up into those many wide chimneys where they would scorch their arms and legs and fill their lungs with soot.

'Come on,' Danny commanded, guessing her thoughts. 'No sadness today. It's time to take a rather special young lady to the playground.'

That night, snuggled up together in bed, Danny tried to prepare Rosie.

'Do you know for certain you are for overseas when you report back to your unit?' she asked, her voice high and upset.

'No-one knows anything for sure in the army,'

Danny said. 'But that is the rumour.'

'But it's so soon,' Rosie complained. 'You have just a few bare weeks' training.'

'I have had as much as the next man.'

'Oh dear God, I can't stand it.'

'You must,' Danny said, holding her hands tight. 'You're all Bernadette has. And I want you to promise, if anything happens to me...'

'No,' Rosie broke in. 'I'll promise you nothing, for nothing will happen to you. I'll pray for you morning, noon and night.'

'If it does,' Danny insisted, then as Rosie continued to shake her head he said sharply, 'For Christ's sake, listen, Rosie. I want to know that you'll be all right, I want you and Bernadette to go back home to Wicklow, to Mammy.'

'I don't want to think of it.'

'You must,' Danny said. 'For I'll not rest until I have that promise.'

Rosie had to promise. However distasteful she found everything, she couldn't allow her husband to face the enemy with anything else preying on his mind. Just the thought of him going at all filled her with panic and fear, and she wished she had the power to stop this war that seemed to serve no purpose but that of stripping countries of all their fit, young men.

The next day, after Danny had gone, Betty and Rita came in as Rosie was sobbing helplessly and were at first sympathetic and then irritated. 'Stop being such a bloody stupid cow,' Betty said at last. 'No good blarting. So your man's gone. He ain't the first, and he won't be the last. Stop feeling sorry for yourself. You got a babby to see to. Think of her, can't you? She's upset too. Where would Ida's have been if she'd let go like this?'

'I can't help it.'

'You can and you bloody well will.'

'You don't understand,' Rosie said. 'I love Danny so much and ... I can't go on without him.'

'Do you think I don't love my husband,' Rita said angrily. 'He's never even seen Georgie and the child's going on for three. Twice he was due leave and it was cancelled. How d'you think I feel sometimes?'

The terrifying pain didn't abate in Rosie. It still pounded through her veins and thumped in her heart, but she saw her fear reflected in Rita's eyes. She'd never even seen Rita look particularly upset and realised she'd been repressing her emotion before friends, neighbours and Georgie, and she realised that life for everyone else would go on and she had to go on too, however hard it was.

TWENTY-ONE

Rosie lived for the letters she wrote to Danny and waited anxiously for his replies, though he could tell her little. She scoured the papers now to find out what was happening in this raging, never-ending war and while she'd always been saddened by the sight of the telegraph boy, now it would set her limbs shaking and she'd break out in a sweat.

Everything mattered more to her now, the black-bonneted widows and those wearing black armbands and the maimed and lame, who begged on the streets or clustered about the Bull Ring. She thanked God daily for the good friends she had made who helped sustain her.

Bernadette had returned to nursery when Danny rejoined his unit and now Rosie took the two children, but she felt time hanging heavy on her hands. However, though she was coping with the money well enough with Ida's help and advice, as March was drawing to a close and the bitter snap had gone out of the early morning and evening air, Rosie's cough eventually ceased and she told Ida she was going to try and return to work in the munitions.

'D'you think you should?' Ida said. 'It might have been that that made you sick in the first place.'

'And it might not have had anything to do with it,' Rosie retorted. 'I'm feeling stronger altogether and I'd like to put some money by.'

But it wasn't to be, for there were no vacancies at Kynoch's now. More women feeling the pinch had joined and there was no job for Rosie, and she had little desire to try anywhere else.

'I'll look out for you, like,' Betty said.

'Yeah, if there is anything you'll be the first to know,' Rita promised.

Rosie was disappointed and the news from the front didn't help. She knew the Government had been worried too when more formal meat rationing had begun in February. It barely bothered the poor, who in the main could only just afford to eat enough to keep themselves alive, and generally meat didn't figure highly on their grocery bill, but it showed the level of the Government's concern that such measures should have to be introduced.

'But I'm more worried about the fuel rationing,' Betty said. 'Bloody good job the days are a tad warmer, that's all I can say. These bloody houses are damp and draughty enough. If you couldn't have a good coal fire in the chill evenings, life wouldn't be worth living.'

'Yeah, they say theatres and restaurants are going to have to close early and all,' Rita said.

'Well we won't lose sleep over that, eh?' Betty said. 'Like to see us having a weekly date in a theatre or dining in a restaurant all lah-di-dah.'

'I've been to a theatre,' Rita protested.

'Yeah, up in the Gods I bet?'

'Well, yeah.'

'Well they don't heat that anyroad, do they?' Betty said. 'They're worrying about the ones in the plush seats down the front. They're afraid of them getting their tootsies cold.'

'You're right,' Rosie said with a smile. 'It will affect us little.'

And fuel rationing didn't affect her much, as long as she could get enough coal to heat the range to cook an odd meal here and there. She'd done as Ida recommended and used the heat to cook more than one thing at a time to eke out the coal, and so she managed, like most of the other women.

She wrote often to Danny, telling him each time how much she loved him, and as promised she prayed for him each night and morning. Then, after Mass on Sundays, when the soldiers were often prayed for, she'd sometimes spend some of her precious resources on a candle and say another wee prayer.

But soon all three woman had plenty to think about, for a large battle involving British and Australian forces began at a place called Amiens just a few days later. Allied losses were massive, so the paper said, and Rosie bought one every day and each evening the women pored over them.

Rosie wrote a long letter to Danny and at the end of it she wrote:

…*Please remember not to try and be a hero. Remember your family – it's breaking our hearts that we have no news of you. I love you with all my being, Danny, and I don't think I could go on without you.*

Please, please, as soon as you are able, write and let

me know that you are safe.
All my love
Rosie

But no letters came and the battle raged on and all the women could do was wait. Rosie took comfort in her religion. She'd found Father Chattaway from St Joseph's a nice, approachable priest and she'd wished she had the money to have a Mass said for Danny, but she couldn't afford that. However, she did pop in to say prayers often, pleading with the Almighty to keep Danny safe.

Father Chattaway found her there in mid-May, kneeling down in one of the pews, her eyes tight shut, her lips moving, her face full of misery, and he felt heart sore for the woman, for he knew full well who she was praying for. The sound of his feet on the stone aisle gave Rosie a start and her eyes jerked open. 'I'm sorry to disturb you,' Father Chattaway said. 'Please go on.'

'It's all right, Father, I'm done anyway,' Rosie said dejectedly. She was going to add she didn't know whether it did any good when she realised who she was speaking to. She couldn't take the priest giving out to her as well. She was feeling too depressed for that, so she said nothing.

But Father Chattaway heard the woman's hopelessness in the tone of her voice. 'Would you like a Mass said for Danny?' he asked.

'Oh aye, Father,' Rosie said. 'But I can't spare the money you see.'

'There will be no cost,' the priest said. 'It'll be my gift to you, to help you over this traumatic time.'

'Oh, Father,' Rosie said, overwhelmed, and the priest smiled.

'I take it you approve of that.'

'Oh, thank you, Father.' Surely God would listen if a whole Mass was offered for Danny's safety? Rosie thought, and she blessed the priest for his understanding. 'Thursday,' the priest went on. 'The early morning Mass will be dedicated to Danny.'

Rosie's heart was a little lighter as she left the church and she knew she would be back at seven o'clock on Thursday morning and she would ask Ida to mind Bernadette and Georgie till she came home again.

A week after the Mass, a letter dropped through Rosie's letterbox. She recognised neither the postmark nor handwriting and so ripped it open anxiously.

> *Dear Rosie,*
> *I've not been able to write to you for a time because I've broken my right arm. But now I am in a military hospital and well on the mend and a kind nurse has offered to write to you on my behalf. I don't want you to worry at all and hope to be transferred to a hospital near home soon.*
> *Look after yourself. Big hug to Bernadette.*
> *All my love,*
> *Danny*

Rosie dropped the letter on the table where she'd sat to read it and put her head in her hands. Danny, her Danny was injured. He'd broken his arm, but he would heal.

The man was alive when so many others were dead, and he was safe until he was fully recovered at least. 'It's from Daddy,' she told Bernadette, who was sitting beside her, shovelling porridge at a rate of knots. 'He's alive!'

Bernadette had been unimpressed by the letter, but now she was pleased to see her mother smiling where for so long there had been a frown between her eyes. She was glad her daddy was alive, but she hadn't considered him any other way. She was too young to understand death, but she did understand when her mammy said, 'Daddy's been injured, and he may be coming home for a wee while until he is better.'

'When?'

'Soon, I hope,' Rosie said. 'Now you sit there like a good girl and drink up your milk while I make the beds.'

And Bernadette sat and swung her legs and drank her milk and thought about her daddy and the fun things they'd done together and excitement began to build inside her at the thought of it.

She knew any minute Georgie would be coming in, for since her mammy had recovered she'd taken Georgie and her to the nursery to make life easier for Rita, she said, and Bernadette couldn't wait to tell him. So Georgie and Rita were barely over the threshold when Bernadette burst out, 'Mammy's had a letter from Daddy. He's been injured and he's coming home soon.'

Rosie was coming into the room as Bernadette spoke and she saw the blood drain from Rita as she held on to the door for support, and Rosie crossed the room in two strides. 'God, Rita! What is it? Are you all right?'

She blatantly wasn't. What stupid things we say, Rosie thought as she led Rita to a chair and pushed her into it. 'Bernadette said...' Rita began. 'Bernadette said you ... you had a letter from Danny?'

Rosie could see the pain reflected in Rita's eyes. 'Aye,' she said. 'It came this morning. He's been wounded.'

'Did he write himself?'

'Yes, well, no, one of the nurses wrote. He's broken his arm, you see.'

'But you weren't informed by the military?'

'No.'

'Then it can't be serious.'

'No, well, not life-threatening anyway,' Rosie said.

'You must be relieved?' Rita said in a deadened voice and then her anguished eyes met those of Rosie and she said in a low moan, 'Oh Rosie, what am I to do?'

Rosie felt her heart lurch. For weeks the two women had grown closer in their common worry over their husbands. They'd comforted one another, cheered each other up. But before saying anything to Rita she removed Georgie's coat and said, 'Go away up to the attic to play, the pair of you. I'll not be taking you to nursery for a wee while yet.'

The children were glad to go and Rosie had seen that they'd both been unnerved by the atmosphere. As their scampering boots could be

391

heard on the stairs, Rosie enfolded Rita in her arms. 'Don't give in now,' she pleaded. 'God, you've kept me on track more than once. Just because I had a letter today doesn't mean anything has happened to your man.'

Betty came in as she spoke and caught the last sentence. 'That's right, girl,' she said to Rita. 'Tell you what, bad news travels fast. If owt had happened to your man, you'd have been told by now.'

'How can you be so sure?' Rita demanded.

'I ain't sure,' Betty said. 'Life ain't like that. I ain't sure I won't be killed on the horse road on me way to work, but one thing I is sure of is the fact that unless we get our arses up the road pronto, we'll miss our tram and lose money.'

'Do you want to call in sick today, Rita?' Rosie asked.

'What? And have some other bugger take my job,' Rita said with a spark of spirit. 'Not likely. Anyroad, I don't want too much time to think and work is the solution to that.'

'Come on, girl,' Betty urged. 'We really will be late if we ain't careful.'

'I'm coming,' Rita said. She pressed Rosie's hand. 'Thank you,' she said and added, 'Say goodbye to Georgie for me.'

Rosie was glad to see them go. Glad to be able to hug herself with delight at the news of Danny she was just coming to terms with. She wasn't aware of the smile plastered all over her face that cheered many on the tram as she took the children to nursery. Sister Ambrose, whom she shared the news with as she left the children at the door, was truly delighted for her. She'd known of her anxious weeks waiting for news.

She wrote to Danny's family and her sisters that night, knowing they'd been worried too about the absence of letters, and included a special word to Dermot, who Connie said had plagued the life out of her for information since Danny had enlisted. She also sent a more stilted missive to her own parents, because she thought she ought to, though she was sure neither of them cared that much.

When Rosie got the go-ahead to visit Danny after he was transferred to the General Hospital in the city centre, she was stunned by the state of him. He was as white as the pillow he lay against, his head bandaged and a cage over his plastered leg. His arm too was plastered and when he saw Rosie's worried face he gave a grin. 'Cheer up, I'm nearly fully fit now and by God you should see the other fellow.'

'Oh, Danny,' Rosie said, half-laughing, half-crying.

'Now,' Danny admonished. 'No crying over me. It will dampen my plaster, and anyway, you're here to cheer me up.'

'I know, I'm sorry,' Rosie said. 'It's the shock. You said nothing about any other injuries and yet I should have known they don't use a valuable hospital bed up just because a person has broken their arm.'

'It was the shrapnel that was the main problem,' Danny told Rosie. 'I was peppered with it. I was blasted into a shell hole you see. Cut my head, but that wasn't that deep, it just needed a few stitches. My leg was in a bit of a mess but they've operated on that, and my arm was broken but the shrapnel went everywhere and they had to poke about a bit to root it out.'

'When will you be home?'

'Soon, I hope. I get the plaster off my arm tomorrow and then we'll see how the leg heals, but they do say I have good healing skin.'

'Will your leg ever be really right again?' Rosie said. She wanted him to say no, to say he'd never be truly fit, because that way he wouldn't have to go back to the war. He could go home and stay safe.

Danny knew what was in her mind and shook his head. 'Sorry old girl. In another two or three weeks they say I'll be as good as new.'

'Oh.'

'I'll have a spot of convalescence at home first,' Danny said. 'That's something to look forward to, surely?'

Danny's leave *was* something to look forward to, however brief it was, and Rosie decided to concentrate on that. There was also the fact that she could now visit Danny twice a week, and while he was here being patched up he was safe.

The weather was bright and sunny each day as June drew to a close and July began, and Rosie was contented as long as she didn't think long and hard of her old home alongside the Wicklow Hills. In the dusty courtyard the air often seemed oppressive and anything but fresh, and in the house, dust motes danced in the sun that slanted in through the windows.

Betty and Rita said the heat in Kynoch's works was unbelievable. 'The sweat drips off you,' Rita said. 'Me and Betty take our sandwiches outside at lunchtime. It's still warm, but there's sometimes a bit of a breeze and the air, bad as it is, is bound to be better than the munitions, where the smell would knock you back at times.'

Rosie was glad Betty and Rita had taken to doing that when she heard the news of the explosion on the 5th July, for it saved their lives. Eighteen others, mainly women, died in the blast. Rosie was stunned by the news. She went to see Rita and Betty, who'd been caught in the blast and cut with flying glass and injured by debris. They'd been taken to the same hospital that Danny was in, to be patched up. They were in shock, all the women there were in shock. Most of them had known it was dangerous work, but no-one had thought of accidents happening to them. Accidents happened to other people, surely?

Rosie sat and suffered for her dear friends, holding their hands, scared of their stillness and their deadened eyes. Suddenly, Rita looked Rosie full in the face and said in a horrified whisper, 'Miss Morris is dead too you know, and Mr Witchell.'

'Ah, no,' Rosie said. She thought of the fair supervisor and the kindly man that had interviewed her and made her laugh and she felt tears prickle the back of her eyes at the tragedy of it.

She tried to control herself. She'd come there to see her injured friends, to be strong for them, not to wallow in tears and upset them totally. Suddenly she felt a splash on her hand and realised Rita was crying the first tears she'd shed, and then Betty's shoulders began to heave and the three women clung to each other and cried out their sadness.

There were so many funerals and Rosie could go to few of them because of her religion, but she went to the graves at Witton Cemetery later, for every girl that died had been there when she was and so had been known to her. It had been a depressing time. She'd watched heartbroken parents mourning their daughters, even the rather elderly parents of Miss Morris, and motherless children crying, and stunned, grief-stricken husbands trying to cope.

They'd all gone back to Rosie's after yet another funeral one day, all down-hearted and shaken. 'I didn't realise Mr Witchell had six children, did you?'

'No,' Rosie said. 'And every one of them crying.'

'Except the widow and she was so white and shaking so much I thought she was going to pass out,' Betty said.

'Well, I've lost confidence in the place and that's the truth,' Rita said and Rosie could hardly blame her. 'There's no lines up yet, anyroad, but I don't know whether I'll go back. I mean, I have Georgie to think about.'

Just at that moment, a shadow went past Rosie's window and her heart almost stopped when she realised that it was a telegraph boy and in his hand was a buff-coloured telegram and he was making for Rita's door. She didn't know what to do. It was as if she was frozen to the spot.

She forced herself to move and she turned, but when she opened her mouth no words came out.

The look on her face was enough, however, and both Rita and Betty were on their feet. 'What is it?' Betty cried, but Rita had no need to ask for through Rosie's window she could see a telegraph boy knocking on her door and Rosie could scarcely bear the pain she saw reflected in Rita's eyes.

'Dear Sweet Jesus,' she cried in anguish and she sank to the floor with an animal-like howl. Rosie too was on the floor, beside Rita, and Betty, who now knew what the commotion was about, went out and took the telegram from the boy. She hoped against hope it would say Harry was missing in action, to give Rita some vestige of hope, but when she tore it open it said 'killed' and her first thought was, *Poor sod. He ain't never going to see his son now.*

Rita's grief was profound and deep and for the first few days Rosie barely left her side, afraid she might do something silly for she'd said more that once that life without Harry wasn't worth living. Left to herself she doubted Rita would ever have left her bed, let alone made a meal or washed her face, and the women, many in similar circumstances, rallied to support her.

Even Danny was affected when Rosie told him, for even though he'd never met the man, he liked and respected Rita and was sorry about her husband and also shocked at the accident at Kynoch's. 'You see why I didn't want you in a place like that?'

'I do,' Rosie said, 'and I have to say it fair shook

me up. Anyway, it's decided Rita won't go back to work. As she says, if anything happens to her, Georgie will be an orphan. Poor child, he doesn't understand and I hope Rita isn't too over-protective now. She won't let him go to nursery at the moment. She says he's all she's got and we couldn't argue with that.'

Ida was better than anyone with Rita, having gone through the experience of losing her own husband not that long ago. Rosie felt almost guilty that her man would be home soon, but Betty told her not to be silly, she wasn't to blame for Harry's death. Danny could give no indication of when he'd be home; he said it depended on how the leg responded to the schedule of exercises they were doing, but Rosie was content to wait.

She'd taken to going to Rowbotham and White's most Saturday nights as it made her money go further, and that Saturday, 13th July, was no different. That evening, though, Bernadette was tired and a little crotchety and Rosie asked Betty if she'd babysit at her house so that she could put the child to bed. 'She's like a weasel and that's the truth,' she said to Betty, coming back into the room after tucking Bernadette into her cot.

'That's not like her,' Betty said. 'She's always so sunny.'

'It makes me worry she's sickening for something,' Rosie said.

Betty knew what Rosie was worried about for Spanish flu was sweeping Europe. People said it was caught from the fleas that lived on the rats that shared the trenches with the soldiers, and unbeknownst to themselves, the soldiers had taken the infection back to their homes. There was no cure for this flu. You either had the constitution to fight it or you didn't, and the young and elderly fell prey soonest.

But worrying about it did no good either, and Betty said, 'For God's sake, Rosie, will you stop fretting till you have something to fret over. The child's probably just worn out. God, if I bounced about like she does at times, I'd be worn out.'

Rosie still had the frown between her eyes but she said, 'You're probably right, but anyway, bed's the best place for her. D'you want me to bring you anything?'

'I'd love a nice bit of liver. That bit you shared with me last week has given me a real taste for it. I could cook it up in a casserole tomorrow and take a bit round to Rita. I don't think she's had much but endless cups of tea since the telegram came, and that was five days ago. She can't go on like this. She's got Georgie to think about.'

'I'll see what the butcher has, but if he's got some liver I'll get some for you,' Rosie promised as she fastened her coat.

'Ida going with you?'

'Aye, one of the other neighbours is sitting in with Rita.'

'Poor sod,' Betty said. 'She's that cut up, and of course she hadn't really got over that business at Kynoch's either.'

'It's early days yet,' Rosie said. 'She'll get through, everyone has to I suppose.' But she shivered as she said it and hoped she'd never have to experience it herself.

About an hour later, both women were back home. Rosie, pleased with her purchases, was smiling and she shouted as she opened the door. 'Got you a lovely piece of lamb's liver, Betty.'

She stopped dead in the doorway for a second, for Betty wasn't sat in the chair before the range, Danny was. With a yelp of delight she dropped her bag on the floor and was across the room on his knee, her arms around his neck in seconds. 'Oh God! Oh Danny! What are you doing here?'

'I was going to be discharged on Monday,' Danny said. 'And I got the chance of a lift this evening and I asked if I could come early and surprise you. The doctor examined me and said I could, especially as I have to go back every day for exercises for the next week, and here I am. I told Betty she could go home if she liked. I'd listen out for the child.'

'Danny, I don't know what to say.'

'Don't say anything,' Danny commanded. 'Kiss me.'

Rosie wound her arms about his neck again and kissed Danny, and it was as if her touch lit a furnace inside both of them. 'Oh God, Rosie, how I want you.'

Rosie wanted Danny tonight too, and badly, but she had liver for Betty. 'Take it then and quickly,' Danny said. 'And hurry back, for Christ's sake. I'll be in bed waiting for you.'

In a way, Danny was glad Rosie wouldn't see him bumping his way up the stairs on his bottom. It might upset her and she would start fussing and it would make him feel stupid. Once on level ground, he could use sticks quite adequately, but he wanted to be in bed when she came in.

Rosie had never been in and out of Betty's house so quickly, but Betty saw the light of excitement and longing in her eyes and had no wish to hold her up. She knew as well as any that once Danny returned to the battlefield a buff telegram might be handed to Rosie any day. They had to snatch each moment they could together and hope for the best, there really was nothing else to be done.

TWENTY-TWO

Two days after Danny came home it was Bernadette's third birthday. There was little in the way
of presents and not even any fancy food, but they
tried to make the day a little special for her and
Rosie was touched by the tissue-wrapped rag doll
Betty had given Rosie on her way to work. She
was working on a different line, she said. 'I could
have got Rita set on, but she said no. She can't
risk it.'

'I don't blame her,' Rosie said. 'I didn't realise
how dangerous it was.'

'Why d'you think they pay us so much?' Betty
said. 'You must have tumbled to it. You ain't
stupid and you were more than glad of the
money.'

'I was,' Rosie agreed. 'And I probably knew deep
down but shut my eyes to it. Danny was always on
at me. But anyway Betty, thanks for Bernadette's
present. She'll be delighted with it, I know.'

'Where is she? I thought she'd be up with the
larks.'

'She's playing with her daddy,' Rosie said, and
added with a smile, 'I don't know which one is
the worst. He has her ruined. She's quite happy
to stay in the cot till I fetch her when Danny's
away. Now Danny's here she shouts to be let out
and he gives in to her. She clambers all over him
and I was worried at first she'd hurt him, but he

402

says no. But then, he would say that. He won't hear a word said against her.'

'And why would he, girl?' Betty said, and Rosie said with a sigh.

'Aye. How could it be any other way?'

And would she want Danny different? No, dear God she wouldn't, and her heart went out to Ida and Rita.

'Go on down and see Rita today, will you?' Betty said, interrupting her thoughts.

'I surely will, Betty, there's no need to ask,' Rosie said. 'She's bringing Georgie to a little tea party here this afternoon.'

'Maybe that will cheer her a wee bit, for she's still in a bad way,' Betty said, and Rosie promised to do her best.

As prophesied, Bernadette was enchanted with the doll and she called her Belinda. It had two scarlet blobs on the cheeks to match the rosebud mouth and there were two brilliant blue eyes below a mop of hair made of brown wool. 'Where did she get the stuff from?' Danny asked.

'She told me from scraps left over from her rag rug,' Rosie said.

'Some of those pieces wouldn't be put in a rag rug,' Danny said scornfully. 'And who painted the face on?'

'Betty must have.'

'The woman's a genius if she did,' Danny said. 'She should go into business and get out of the bloody munitions.'

'Danny, few people around these doors could buy a rag doll, however cheap it was.'

'You wouldn't sell them around the doors,

would you,' Danny said. 'I bet one of the stalls down the Bull Ring would snap them up. Look at the clothes it's wearing as well.'

Betty had sewn a dress of light blue taffeta with a bit of lace at the collar and cuffs, and covered that with a knitted coat of navy blue that reached the knitted boots in black that covered her stubby feet.

'Talk to her about it then,' Rosie said.

'I will,' said Danny and added, 'And she'll take as much notice of me as you did and that was bugger all.'

'Ssh,' Rosie admonished, her finger to her lips, for Bernadette was playing with her doll by the range just a few feet from them.

'She's not taking a whit of notice,' Danny said.

'Don't you believe it,' Rosie hissed in a whisper. 'Her ears are cocked all right. Sister Ambrose told me she called someone a bloody basket yesterday.'

'I bet that raised a few eyebrows.'

'It's not funny,' Rosie said, though she was smiling herself. 'I was really embarrassed. I didn't know what to say.'

'Oh that's simple,' Danny said airily. 'Tell her if she says it again I'll skelp the skin from her bottom.'

'And of course she'll believe it,' Rosie said sarcastically, for Danny never even raised his voice to the child, let alone his hand. 'And then she'll behave perfectly.'

'She's not badly behaved,' Danny protested, 'and God knows, when I've seen and taken part in the violent massacre that's going on across the channel I can't be that concerned over a wean saying a few bad words she doesn't know the meaning of.'

'I'm not asking you to be concerned, but be careful around Big Ears.'

'Who's Big Ears?' Bernadette demanded.

'See,' Rosie said with a triumphant laugh. 'I'll leave you to explain who Big Ears is, Daddy. I'm away to see Ida.'

Danny had decided to go without his cigarettes and had used the money to buy wee cakes and sweets for the children at Bernadette's party. That alone would have guaranteed success for the little ones and not even Rita's heavy, sorrow-laden eyes could stop Georgie's cries of delight.

'Harry was my life,' Rita told Rosie, watching Danny playing with the children. 'I don't want to go on without him.'

Rosie sympathised. Wasn't that what she always said about Danny? But Rita couldn't give in this way, not in front of Georgie, and she told her so. 'He doesn't know he has no father,' she said. 'He's just a wee boy and not able to understand the word never. Sure, a week is a lifetime when you're three, but he'll know something is wrong and for his sake you've got to go on.'

'What d'you know about it?'

'Nothing,' Rosie admitted. 'But Ida knows.'

'Oh yeah, Ida,' Rita spat. 'Told me time is the great healer. Fat lot of use. Maybe she couldn't stick her old man, was glad he was dead, but Harry...'

'Rita! That's a wicked thing to say. She's found a way to cope, that's all.'

'Well I haven't and I don't want to cope. Without Harry I'm just half a person and you keep your nose out of it. When I want your opinion, I'll ask for it.'

Rosie knew Rita was not angry, more bitterly hurt and in despair, for she'd seen it in her eyes and heard the catch in her voice and would have liked to have talked more with her, but the children were claiming her attention.

Danny had one ear on the conversation between his Rosie and Rita, even as he kept the children amused, and he knew Rita was near the end of her tether. He'd seen men in the trenches with the same desperation in their eyes. Women were luckier than men, though, he thought, for they can weep, while a man who did the same would be dubbed a nancy-boy. He could see that Rita needed to cry before she could even begin to look forward.

Rita didn't stay so long and Rosie was glad, and guilty because she felt glad, but Rita's behaviour and countenance had put somewhat of a damper on the proceedings, although Rosie doubted the children were aware of it, especially as Danny had kept them entertained.

Later in bed with Danny she tried to imagine life without him if he was to wind up dead on a foreign battlefield somewhere. But it hurt too much to think that and she shut her eyes against the pain of it and felt the weight of Rita's sorrow on her heart.

'You can't fret for the whole world,' Danny whispered, knowing Rosie was still awake.

'I know. It's just...'

'Loving someone hurts like hell at times,'

Danny said. 'How d'you think I felt when you were so ill with bronchitis? I was out of my mind with the worry that I'd lose you. It's what people take onboard when they love someone, but someone said once it's better to have loved and lost than never to have loved at all, and whoever they were, they were right.

'In time, after Rita has truly grieved for Harry, she will remember the times they shared, however brief, and no-one can take those memories away from her. Maybe she'll share them with Georgie so he'll know the manner of the man his father was and it will be a comfort to them both.'

Would it comfort me? Rosie thought, and prayed that she need never know. 'Oh hold me tight, Danny,' she pleaded, and Danny held her in the circle of his arms until she fell asleep.

'Don't send Bernadette to the nursery,' Danny pleaded the day after her birthday. 'God, I see little enough of her. The doctors have encouraged me to walk now and I could take her with me. Come on, Rosie, I'll be back in that infernal bloodbath soon enough.'

Put like that, Rosie could hardly refuse, and with her at home each day there was no reason to send Bernadette anywhere.

'I think I'll keep her at home now all the time,' Rosie said. 'She'll have Georgie to play with. They get on really well.'

'Aye, don't I know it, and I have no problems taking Georgie with me too when I go out with Bernadette, and she won't mind.'

That was undeniable. Georgie was Bernadette's best friend and she thought it sad that he had no daddy, for she thought her own wonderful. She always felt safe with him. He was strong and brave and yet gentle and kind. He was always ready for a game and would read to her for hours or better still tell her his own stories that he said he'd learned from his parents. She didn't mind sharing her daddy with Georgie.

Danny treasured all those days. His home seemed like an oasis of calmness and peace in a world gone mad.

In the fields of war he'd seen man's inhumanity to man displayed in horrific and barbarous ways. It was a place where to survive at all, you hadn't to allow yourself to be touched by anything, or to care about anyone, for feelings were better kept securely under lock and key.

So when you heard the screams and saw the men with limbs blown off or half a head, or those bullet-riddled and still jerking, and those dead and dying, floundering in their own blood and guts, you could view it all dispassionately. It was war and they were casualties of it, not human at all, just a statistic.

Over the top and on and on into the hail of bullets and whining shells was the only thing that mattered. Mates you'd shared a smoke with minutes before would shudder and jerk before you, crumpling to the floor, and you could barely spare them a glance.

Just before he came back to England, Danny, his rifle poised, bayonet fixed, was attacked by a German in a dugout past No Man's Land. He'd practised attacking with a bayonet into bales of straw but he never thought he could use it on a human being. However, he found he could.

He saw the man's eyes widen for a split second and his mouth opened in a scream as the blade impaled him. He sank to the slurried ground and when Danny pulled his blade out it had blood and mangled body organs attached to it, and Danny vomited onto the mud.

He'd killed men before, both in the insurrection in Ireland and in the war, but he'd shot them with a rifle and though he'd seen that his bullets had reached their target, and seen them fall, somehow he was removed from it. It was nothing like impaling someone who stood next to you and he found he was shaking with shock at the abhorrence of what he'd been forced to do.

'Good man, Walsh,' said his commanding officer, coming upon him at that moment. 'Wipe your bayonet, lad.'

Danny bent to run his blade over the mud and when he heard the shell he instinctively curled up. The officer's body was split into pieces and distributed over the dead German and Danny's vomit, and the blast of it threw Danny into a pit. That had ensured him a Blighty, which is what a pass home through injury was called by the British.

Bernadette and Rosie were not part of that life. They were so clean and pure, innocent of what he had to do. Thank God! But any time he spent with them was so important to him.

When he'd been forced to enlist he told himself it was those two he was fighting for, and all through his training he'd thought often of his beautiful wife that he loved so much he ached, and Bernadette, whom he adored.

The thoughts and memories of his family he took with him to the battlefield, and he would hold them in his head and his heart like a talisman against evil. Amongst all the carnage and terrible suffering, the vile things it had forced him to do, it had given him some purpose.

Danny had been home ten days when he was deemed fit to rejoin his unit. Rosie had known he would be, for she'd seen his leg become stronger each day with dread.

The day he left she looked deep into his eyes and traced his cheeks and chin with fingers that trembled, and then she lifted up his hands and kissed his palms.

'Ah, Rosie,' Danny said, and pressed her close so she'd not see the tears glistening in his eyes, but she felt the emotion pounding through his body and told herself she mustn't cry. She mustn't make it harder for this man she loved, or Bernadette, biting her lip with anxiety. 'And me, Daddy,' she said in a tentative voice.

'And you, certainly, Princess,' Danny said, scooping her up with one arm, and they stayed like that for a moment. Danny and Rosie, full of their own thoughts, and Bernadette, content for a moment to have her mother and father to herself, and she cuddled tight against them both. After a while, though, Bernadette pulled away a little so that she could see her father's eyes and asked, 'Are you going away like Mammy said?'

'I'm afraid so.'

'When will you be back?'

'I honestly don't know, Bernadette.'

'Will it be soon?'

Danny shook his head helplessly. 'I can't tell you that, pet, for I don't know myself. The army doesn't tell you.'

'Georgie's daddy was in the army,' Bernadette said and Danny saw the pucker on his daughter's forehead and he answered gently,

'That's right.'

'Georgie's daddy ... Georgie's daddy. That won't happen to you, will it?'

Danny felt Rosie give a start and saw the stricken look on Bernadette's face. But he knew he could give no bold assurances that he would be fine. Instead, he said, 'I hope not, Bernadette, for my place is here looking after you and Mammy.'

'That's all right then,' Bernadette said satisfied, and Danny let her down to the floor where she returned to her doll, Belinda.

Rosie, seeing her daughter's attention taken elsewhere, said quietly to Danny, 'There may be more than myself and Bernadette to see to by the time you come home.'

'You mean...'

'It's early days, but I'm a week late,' Rosie said. 'I wouldn't have said until I was sure, but I wanted you to know.'

'Oh God, Rosie,' Danny said, hugging her tighter. 'You are happy about it?'

'Of course I am, if I'm right,' Rosie said.

'It's not too soon?'

'Not at all. And I'm fine and healthy, and if I

411

am expecting I don't care how difficult it will be, I'll want this baby; your baby.'

'I wish I was here to take care of you.'

'I'll be taken care of, don't you worry. It may help Rita, give her something else to think about, or it may make things harder for her. I don't know, but either way I can do nothing about it and I want a son for you, Danny.'

'Now, you know I said...'

'Aye, and I saw your face when the last child died.'

'I would have felt the same if the child had been a girl.'

'No,' Rosie said, 'there was more than grief, there was disappointment. Promise me, though, that if I am carrying a child and it turns out to be a boy, you'll still love Bernadette as you do now.'

'How could I not? I adore her, you know that.'

But Rosie had seen it time and again and not in her own home alone that a man could seem quite satisfied with a wee daughter until a son should be born, and then the daughter would often be considered of no account. She didn't want that treatment being handed out to Bernadette. She gave a sigh, for she knew she had to be satisfied with what God sent, and anyway, she trusted her good, kind husband.

'Mammy will be delighted at the news, all of them will,' Danny said.

Rosie knew they would be. They'd all sent lovely messages of sympathy and condolence last time, when the child was stillborn. And yet, she cautioned Danny, 'Don't let's say anything yet. It would only disappoint them if I'm wrong.'

'All right,' Danny said. 'I see that that's sensible and I'll say nothing until you give me word.'

'I only told you this early because ... well, with your going away and everything...'

'You thought it might encourage me to take greater care?'

Was that the real reason that I told him? Rosie thought. Maybe subconsciously she had, but could anyone take any more care in a war of such magnitude?

'Don't worry,' Danny told her. 'Bullets bounce off me. I'll come back hale and hearty and in one piece.'

'Don't, Danny,' Rosie said with a shudder. 'It's like tempting fate.'

'Fate be damned,' Danny said. 'That's what I intend, but if I don't go now and sharpish I'll be up on a charge before I get to the Front.'

Rosie's smile was watery, but it was a smile, for she'd promised herself no tears. 'Take care of yourself if you can at all,' she said.

'And you take care,' Danny said, holding Rosie in his arms. 'I'll worry about you every minute that I am away.'

'I'll be grand,' Rosie said. 'And I'll be here waiting for you.'

Danny kissed Rosie and knew in quiet moments, after an assault, or as they were waiting to go over the top, the image of his brave wife standing there with a tremulous smile just touching her lips would sustain him. And yet his stomach turned over at the thought that he could be killed in an instant. Every evening he marvelled he was still alive. Well, long may it continue, he thought, and

413

swung his kitbag up on his shoulder.

He stopped before he went up the entry and looked back at the two women in his life, framed in the doorway. 'Bye Daddy,' Bernadette said with a wave of her little hand.

'Bye pet,' Danny said, and though he spoke to his daughter his eyes sought Rosie's and at the look in them he felt the prickling behind his own. But he was careful to wipe his eyes with his handkerchief before he stepped into the street. It would never do for people to think him a sissy.

After Danny left, Rosie contacted the nursery. It had been playing on her mind for some time that Bernadette was taking up a nursery place under false pretences, for the nursery was set up primarily to release mothers for important war work. Now that she had no intention of working, Bernadette really had no right to a place, and Rosie had written to the Sisters at the convent explaining this and went on to thank them all sincerely for the help and support they had given them since they'd arrived in Birmingham.

She also wanted to see something of her daughter, knowing she would be at school before she knew it, and she hadn't just the streets to play in. They were but yards from the park and Rosie intended to make full use of it.

Then there was the flu, which was still sweeping, seemingly unchecked, throughout the whole of Europe. She knew she couldn't protect Bernadette totally from every disease that there was, but she felt the risk would be enhanced if she was to mix with so many children and their mothers.

'What about Rita?' Ida said when Rosie told her Bernadette wouldn't be returning to nursery.

'She must make up her own mind,' Rosie said. 'But she's not sent Georgie since his father died, so I don't think she'll mind.'

Rita still grieved for Harry and maybe always would, and while her swollen eyes still often had blue smudges beneath them she'd begun at last to make an effort for Georgie's sake, and was beginning to take control of her life again.

'Lifesavers, kids is,' Ida said. 'Christ, I don't know what I would have done if I hadn't had my kids when Herbie copped it. Topped myself too, most likely. But when you has kids you can't go about weeping and wailing and thinking of yourself all the bleeding time. You see to the nippers and any crying you do, you do at night in bed.'

Rosie found she was enjoying Bernadette's company at home, and with the schools closed for the holidays, Rosie, Rita, Ida and the children, including Ida's three, Jack, Billy and Gillian, spent many happy days in Aston Park. Jack was a lovely boy, who took his duties as man of the house and elder brother seriously. He was used to minding his own little brother and sister and had no problem with keeping an eye on Georgie and Bernadette too, and didn't even seem to mind pushing them on the swing or on the roundabout. Rosie always felt she could relax more when Jack was there.

By the time the schools opened again after the holidays in September Rosie was fairly certain of her pregnancy. 'My period was due just three days after Danny came home on the thirteenth of July, but there's been nothing.'

There were other signs too. Rosie's breasts were tender and when she stood before the mirror she could see her veins standing out on them. She felt exhilaration flow through her at the thought of another baby in her arms, tugging at her breasts, a part of her and Danny.

She was hesitant telling Rita, but whatever Rita might have felt inside she seemed delighted for Rosie, though there was a wistful tone in her voice as she said, 'You must make sure of this one. You mustn't do anything to jeopardise this child.'

Rosie had no intention of doing anything that might harm this baby, this child she longed for so much. She wrote joyful letters to Danny, the two families in Ireland and the two convents in Dublin and Handsworth. She basked in their congratulations and took heart at the prayers to be said and novenas begun, and thought few children had been as longed for as this one. With the power of the Roman Catholic Church behind it, how could anything go wrong?

October was a cold and blustery month and Rosie was often glad she could lie in bed in the morning and listen to the wind hurling itself around the court, rattling the ill-fitting windows and seeping under doors to chill the very legs off a body. The news from the Front was cheering for a change, because it was said the Germans were in retreat. Austria had offered a peace settlement in August but it had been rejected. 'Going for the kill,' Betty had remarked 'and why not?'

'Too right,' another said. 'The bloody Hun started it and I don't see why we should stop now till we have them by the balls.'

'Serve them right,' said a woman who'd lost two sons. 'I hope they gets them by the short and curlies and shakes the bleeding life out of them.' There was a murmur of agreement, but for all that there was a more optimistic air around than there had been for four long years.

When Austria signed a revised peace plan on 3rd November, everyone knew it was the beginning of the end, and only eight days later, on a grey and dismal Monday morning, when Rosie heard the church bells pealing and the factory hooters blowing she hardly dared to hope that it meant something. She shot to the door and realised that most of the neighbours were doing the same and looking at each other in stupefaction.

Then Ida, who'd run up the entry to see if anyone knew anything, came back, her face aglow. 'It's over,' she said. 'The war's bloody well over!' There was a whoop of joy from the women and Rosie laughed as she was caught around the waist and hugged and kissed and swung around like a wean by one person after another. 'There's a bloody great party going on at Aston Cross,' Ida said. 'Get Rita and we'll go and see.'

'Oh I don't know.'

'Come on,' Ida urged. 'It's bloody history, ain't it? War to end all wars this is, and there won't never be a carnival like this again.' Then, as Rosie still hesitated, she added, 'Ain't I got more reason to be bloody miserable than you have? Peace come too late for me and my old man, d'ain't it?'

What answer could Rosie make to that, and maybe to let her hair down was just what Rita needed and Ida too. Not far down Upper Thomas Street the noise of the crowds could be plainly heard. 'Keep a weather eye on them kids,' Ida warned. 'I heard it's a madhouse down there.'

And it was a madhouse, and Rosie and Rita tightened their hold on their children's hands as they plunged into the melee. Wonderful, tremendous excitement and relief had gripped the people and they laughed and shouted and hugged and sang, and over it all the bells pealed a chorus from all the churches around and the beat was given by the factory hooters and the lids of the miskins some were banging together. People thronged the streets, some still in their work overalls, and children, seemingly released early from school, weaved in and out between the rapturous crowds.

People shook hands or clapped each other's backs, or kissed and hugged perfect strangers, and no-one seemed to take offence. Someone would start the line of a song – 'Rule Britannia' was popular, or 'There'll always be an England'. But these stirring tunes gave way to, 'Keep the Home Fires Burning' or 'It's a Long Way to Tipperary' and the tumultuous noise rose higher and higher.

'God, look,' Rita suddenly cried, pointing. 'They've stopped the trams now.'

It was true. The crowds were so great, nothing could move. Carts and the odd car were already gridlocked, but now trams couldn't get through either. The passengers didn't seem to care and in a mass they abandoned the tram and joined in the party, and the driver and conductor scratched their heads for a moment or two before obviously thinking their passengers had the right idea, for they then left the tram too.

They'd reached the big green clock at Aston Cross when Rosie's hand was grasped suddenly by a neighbour. 'You're Irish, ain't you?' he demanded. 'Can you dance?' And before Rosie could form a reply she was pushed into a circle, ringed by onlookers, where one man with a fiddle and another with an accordion had begun an impromptu concert.

Rosie felt a stirring of excitement for she'd not danced since the Christmas before she left Ireland and what better excuse to dance than today? Danny had survived the war and he'd be coming home when thousands wouldn't and she gave Bernadette into Rita's care, lifted her skirts and danced a jig.

Bernadette gazed at her mother, speechless, but from the first the crowd had clapped and cheered. Then Rosie began another jig and some people linked arms with those near them and leaped around merrily until the pavement and streets were one seething mass of dancing people.

'God, but you're a dark horse,' Ida said, when ages later they'd let Rosie stop dancing and the women had eventually broken through the crowd.

It was so marvellous to be part of it, Rosie thought, and she had great respect for the numbers celebrating along with the rest wearing the widow's bonnet like Ida and Rita, or sporting the black armband. Everyone was applauding the fact that this terrifying war was over. And her Danny was one of the lucky ones and soon he would be home again. She didn't know what the future held, no-one did, but at least Danny now had a future and she thanked God from the bottom of her heart.

The carousing was going on in their own courtyard and it continued until the early hours of the next morning, and as it was no good going to bed, however tired you were, because you wouldn't be able to sleep, Ida, Rita, Rosie and Betty joined in the merrymaking with the rest.

Women made up sandwiches and other savouries, clearing out their cupboards. Pubs not only stayed open well after they should, with the police turning a blind eye on this very special day, but many also donated drinks to the parties to help them go with a swing.

No one attempted to put children to bed and they continued to run the streets. Rosie felt light-headed both with relief and unaccustomed alcohol and she saw Ida was in a worse state and so was Rita. 'Good luck to them,' she said to Betty. 'They have little reason to celebrate, but every reason in the world to drown their sorrows.'

'Yeah, and it might do them a power of good,' Betty said in agreement and she linked hands with the two women, and with Rosie hanging on to Ida the four women swayed together while they sang all the old favourites with everyone else. Then Betty led a column of people up the entry and into Upper Thomas Street where people joined them from the various parties going on, until one long snake wound down the street and back up again.

As the sound of revelry eventually died down a little, Rosie tried to coax Bernadette to bed, though it wasn't easy. Bernadette was well into her second wind and looked set to stay up all night, but Rosie ached everywhere with weariness and she also knew that Bernadette would be the very devil in the morning. 'But I'm not tired,' she protested. 'Not a bit, Mammy.'

'Well I am,' Rosie said. 'And it's late, very late. Later than you've ever stayed up. Anyway, the party's over now. Everyone is going home.'

There was no denying that, although there was the occasional shout heard, or the snatch of a song begun by a group of intrepid revellers, but most had returned to their homes and the streets were almost quiet again.

'I'm still not tired,' Bernadette said.

'Then you must lie on your bed and stay awake,' Rosie said. 'While I will stay in mine and sleep the sleep of the just.'

'But Mammy...'

'Bernadette, there are no buts. I'm not discussing it, I'm telling you how it will be.'

Bernadette wasn't stupid. She knew there were times it was much healthier to give in, especially when her mammy spoke in a certain way, for to argue on then might merit a ringing slap on the back of her legs. So she sighed dramatically and said, 'Oh, all right then,' and Rosie suppressed a smile.

She was almost too tired to make the stairs and yet she longed to lie between the sheets and think of that wonderful, stupendous day as she drifted off to sleep.

She didn't know what time she woke up, but she immediately felt a strange stickiness between her legs. She eased herself up in the bed and lit the lamp and saw the blood on the sheet and it still running from her. 'Ah, dear Christ, no,' she cried. 'Sweet Jesus, please, oh please have pity on me?'

The answer was a drawing pain that began in her back and went in a ring around to her front and caused her to lift her knees almost to her chin.

Rosie was out of bed in an instant. She packed herself with cotton pads, pushed her feet into her boots, and pulling a coat around her she went into the freezing night to knock on Ida's door.

Ida had been more drunk when she reached her bed than she'd ever been before and so was slow to wake. Once roused, she stared at Rosie, bleary-eyed and swaying slightly on her feet.

Rosie was too panicky and fearful to see that and she blurted out, 'Ida help me. I think I'm losing this sodding baby as well. I'm bleeding, for God's sake!'

The words, Rosie's anguished face, and the night air sobered Ida somewhat and she cried, 'You poor bugger! Ah Christ, it ain't bloody well fair. Get back to bed. Give me a minute to throw some clothes on and I'll be in.'

'Fetch the doctor, Ida.'

Ida knew if Rosie was losing blood there was little the doctor could do. 'Rosie,' she said gently.

'It will cost an arm and a leg to get him out at this time of night and Christ knows what state he will be in if he's been partying like the rest of us.'

'Please, Ida,' Rosie begged. 'It doesn't matter what it costs. I'll gather it together somehow.'

'All right, calm yourself,' Ida said, because Rosie's over-bright eyes and high, hysterical voice alarmed her. 'I'll get our Jack up. He can go like the wind and you know he'll have to go away past Salford Bridge to the doctor's house up on the Birmingham Road there. Go in out of the cold. I'll be in directly.'

Ida shook Jack awake and told him of the urgency of the message before struggling into her own things. She thanked the Lord that one of their neighbours cleaned at the doctor's private house, for people like them wouldn't usually be told where a doctor lived, and while Ida didn't think the doctor could do much to save the baby, maybe he could help Rosie and save her going to pieces altogether.

When Rosie got home the linen pads were soaked through and the blood was trickling down her legs. Heedless of this, she kneeled on the bedroom floor, put her head on the bed, and cried out her despair while the blood pooled around her knees.

TWENTY-THREE

Anthony Patterson had no wish to leave the warm bed he'd fallen into just a couple of hours before. He had even less inclination to speed through the night to one of the teeming back-to-back houses. His wife, who hated that aspect of his work and was always urging him to leave the working classes to their own devices and concentrate on his richer clientele, was incensed. 'What is it?' she said irritably when her husband came into the room and began to dress after answering the persistent banging on the door.

'I've got to go out, Susie. It's one of the women from Aston Cross. She's losing her baby.'

'One of the lower classes?'

'Yes.'

'Then why make it your concern? Let her lose it. What odds will it be to them? You won't be able to do anything.'

'Yes, but...'

'Come on back to bed,' Susie said seductively. 'I know there is something you'd rather do.'

Anthony stared at his wife. For years now she'd denied him, saying she found that side of marriage distasteful, and at times, to his great humiliation, he had been forced to seek satisfaction elsewhere, though he'd always burned with guilt afterwards. Now, Susie, who'd been quite tipsy going to bed, a very unusual state for her, was opening her arms to him. She was still a very beautiful and sensuous woman and her luscious lips were parted slightly, invitingly, and he felt himself harden.

But he'd left the child standing in the hall, feeling it was too cold a night to let him stand outside, and he shook his head from side to side. 'I can't, Susie,' he said. 'I'll probably not be long. Wait for me.'

'I'll wait for no man,' Susie Patterson said icily. 'I'm ready now, and if you spurn me it will be a long time before I let you near me again.'

'I'm not spurning you. It's just...'

'Oh, go. Go on, run to your working classes if you care for them before me.'

'It's not that.' But Anthony knew he was wasting his time. Susie was turned on her side, her back to him. Dear Lord, life was a bloody bitch, he thought as he pulled on his trousers.

He was glad of the blast of night air as he stepped into the road. He was taking the car. He never usually took it into the maze of back-to-back housing, knowing the children would be over it like flies, but tonight there would be no-one about and they'd certainly get there quicker.

Never had Jack been so excited and yet a little frightened at the same time as the car picked up speed as it hit the main road, the headlights slicing through the dark and gloom, and he sat on his hands so that the doctor wouldn't see them shaking and felt tremors running all through his body.

Doctor Patterson was amused at the child's so

obvious delight, but hid his smile. He could easily bet that it was the first ride he'd ever had in a car and it would raise his standing amongst his peers considerably. He didn't ask him any questions about Rosie Walsh, for he knew the boy had told him all he knew, and so the silence stretched between them, and Jack was glad of it, for he doubted he could have spoken sensibly to the doctor if he'd asked anything.

However, when the car drew to a halt at the top of the entry, Jack said, 'D'you want me to mind it for you?'

'No, there's no one about,' Doctor Patterson said, scanning the dark and empty street. 'All partied out and asleep,' he said. 'And I bet you could do with your bed?' he added as they walked down the entry.

'Yeah, I'm whacked.'

'Go on in,' the doctor said as they stepped into the yard. 'Is your mam in with Mrs Walsh?'

'Yeah, she went in when I came for you.'

The doctor was glad. Ida had riddled the range into life and had the kettle just coming to the boil as he gave a tap on the door and walked in. She gave a sigh of relief as she saw the man standing there. 'Thanks for coming out, Doctor. I don't think you can do much. She's losing blood. She's above in the bedroom. I've padded the bed with towels, but it's still coming.'

'I'll go straight up,' the doctor said. 'But first I'll wash my hands if that water is hot.'

'It's boiling, Doctor.'

'Then will you do me a favour and make me a cup of tea,' the doctor said. 'To tell you the truth,

I have a thick head after the celebrations last night and have had little chance to sleep it off.'

'You and me both, Doctor,' Ida said with a smile, 'and I think at least half of the adult population will be hung over in a couple of hours when the day really begins. I'll make the tea directly.'

Just minutes later, the doctor, after examining Rosie, looked into her white, strained face and said, 'You know I can't stop this.'

Rosie knew. She'd felt the blood seeping from her, the blood that should surround and protect the baby, and no amount of clamping her legs together or trying to ignore the drawing pains attacking her body could save this child. 'But why, Doctor?' she cried. 'I mean, last time I was ill and it was maybe understandable, but this time... Doctor, I've done nothing.'

'Hmm,' Doctor Patterson said, drawing up a chair beside the bed. 'I could say it's just one of those things, but I'm following a pet theory of my own here. You worked in a munitions factory, didn't you?'

'Aye, but not for long,' Rosie said. 'I mean, I got a cough that turned to bronchitis, you remember, and that put paid to it. My face didn't even get a chance to go yellow.'

'Even so,' the doctor said. 'You were in contact with the sulphur. Inhaling the sulphur dust was what, I should imagine, gave you the initial cough.'

'Maybe, but what's that to do with losing a child?'

'Sulphur is poisonous, Mrs Walsh,' the doctor said. 'I am conducting a private survey of my own on the number of miscarriages or still births amongst the women who worked in the munitions factories. There are others who seem fine and healthy, their husbands the same, who can't seem to get pregnant. I want to see if there is a connection.'

Dr Patterson knew the authorities were refusing to acknowledge this, but there were too many for it to be a coincidence and he wanted to force the Government to face up to this.

But he saw that this second tragedy was badly affecting Rosie. She'd answered his questions about the munitions works reasonably enough, but when he went on to voice his concerns her mouth had dropped open and she stared at him, her eyes wide and full of pain and the colour drained from her face.

The thoughts pounded in her head. It's my fault. I can't have any more children for they are poisoned by me in the body that should protect them. She wetted her lips and faced the doctor. She had to hear the words from the man's own lips. 'D'you mean to say the child I lost and this one I am losing could be due to the work I did in the munitions factory? That I brought it on myself?'

The doctor bitterly regretted telling Rosie straight out that she might have poisoned her child and might continue to poison subsequent children. What had he been thinking of? He knew had he been in his right mind and not so befuddled, he would never have done such a thing. But the damage was done now and the words could not be unsaid, and he saw the guilt that she'd been to blame stealing over Rosie's face. 'Mrs Walsh,' he said. 'None of this was your fault. You were not to know.'

'No,' Rosie said bitterly. 'Well I know now, all right. You've been honest with me so far and so I want you to answer another question honestly. Tell me straight, will I ever manage to carry a child full-term, Doctor?'

'I can't possibly say.'

'You could give me a bloody guess, for God's sake,' Rosie cried. 'I mean, will this bloody sulphur ever pass through my body, or what?'

'Mrs Walsh, this war was the first time women were exposed to dangers like this,' the doctor said, knowing Rosie deserved as much of the truth as he knew. 'No-one was really aware of the risks, and even if my theory is right I don't know how it will affect people long-term.'

'Tell me what you think, before I go mad altogether?' Rosie yelled at the man. 'Am I to go on and on trying to bear a child and losing them one after the other, like I've lost the previous two, for that I couldn't stand, Doctor.'

Dr Patterson bent his head, for the pain in Rosie's eyes was raw, and he castigated himself for his careless words, and yet. He knew if Rosie was to go on year after year, losing one child after another, she wouldn't be able to cope. Indeed, few women could cope with such an ordeal. She would go under, for she was that kind of woman. Maybe, he thought, it would be kinder to be as straight as he could. 'Mrs Walsh,' he said. 'As I said before, I know little of the long-term effects of sulphur, but with you losing two children like this, I would say the likelihood would be that at the present time you would not be able to carry a child full-term.'

'Thank you, Doctor,' Rosie said, and she turned her face to the wall. Danny would never have his son, she thought, and she would never hold another baby in the arms that ached to do so. She'd never feel another child tugging at her breasts and smiling at her in that special way. She cried hot, scalding tears at the pity of it, while her stomach continued to contract and push of its own violation, and before the day was really light, Rosie had miscarried another child.

The news flew around the streets and there was a troop of people coming in to express sympathy. Rosie wrote to Danny, she felt she owed him that, and told him not only of the miscarriage but also the doctor's prediction that she'd probably never be able to carry a child full-term because of the sulphur that had poisoned her body at the munitions works, and she received a heartbroken reply from Danny.

Rosie seemed sunk in lethargy, but it was really guilt. Both boys had died through her doing. 'You had to go,' Rita reminded her. 'You needed the money.'

'Danny warned me,' she said.

'He didn't know either,' Betty said. 'He just wanted you out of the place.'

'Well he was damned right.'

'Yeah, he was, but you can't be held responsible.'

'I've robbed him of his sons.'

'No you haven't.'

'It's how I see it,' Rosie said implacably and nothing either of the women said could shake Rosie's conviction that she was at fault.

'She'll get over it in time,' Ida said. 'Let's not keep at her now.'

'Oh yeah, you've got great faith in time being the great healer, ain't you?'

'That's cos it is.'

'Pity she ain't had no letters from Ireland and that,' Rita said. 'They always buck her up.'

'They won't know, will they?' Ida said. 'Any letters she gets now won't make her feel better. I mean, they'll probably go on about the baby and all.'

'Oh Christ, yeah.'

'I mean, has she told you she's written to them?' Ida asked.

'No, she just wrote to Danny, as far as I know.'

'We could do it for her,' Ida said. 'She wouldn't mind.'

'She don't seem to mind owt,' Rita said. 'That's half the bloody trouble. I'd better ask her.'

But Rosie had no objection and Rita and Ida wrote the short letters to Wicklow and to the nuns in Baggot Street and those in Handsworth. And back came letters of support, just as before.

A few weeks later, and not long before Christmas, Rosie had something to think about besides herself and the loss of her baby, because Rita arrived early one morning and told her Betty was far from well and insisted on getting up and going to work, and Rosie went down with Rita to play war with her. She found Betty as ill as Rita had said and she told her she wasn't to think of going any place except bed.

'I'll not be ordered about by you,' Betty snapped. 'A fine one you are to give medical advice, when you don't take it yourself.'

'All right,' Rosie said. 'I know I'm stubborn, but you're not getting any younger, Betty, and, face it, you're far from well.'

'I'll be worse if I starve to death.'

'You'll hardly do that.'

'You can smile, girl, but all I've got is me savings. I get the pension in three years' time. Fat lot of good it is, though, five bob a week when the rent's half a crown.'

'I know that, Betty,' Rosie said. 'But you must have saved a pretty penny at the munitions and your boys send you something when they can. You've told me that.'

'Ah, I know I did and they do, they're good lads, but savings don't last forever if you have to live on them, do they?'

'No, but...'

'Look, Rosie, you're a good girl and you know the same as me, jobs is like gold dust, and I need a job and before all the men start coming home from the war like, I'd only just got that job in the Sauce.'

It was true, that was the shame of it. After being off work for four weeks from Kynoch's works after the armistice, Betty had got a job at HP Sauce and only a few days after starting it, she'd been taken ill.

'It isn't your fault,' Rosie said.

'Won't be my fault if some other bugger has my job when I do go back, either,' Betty said morosely. 'And I've only got a bleeding cold.'

'Well, if you have it'll soon clear up,' Rosie said. 'But I don't like the sound of your chest and going out in the cold and fog will do you no good.'

'Oh that's all right then, I'll just live on fresh air, will I?'

'I've never known such an aggravating patient,' Rosie said, exasperated. 'If you've got so much energy, why don't you sit tucked up in bed and make some more of those rag dolls you've done since you left munitions. I told you, Cleggy down the Bull Ring nearly snapped the hands off me and Rita for the five we took down yesterday. He said they'd sell like hot cakes, especially with Christmas around the corner. You wouldn't have to go out in all weathers then. Danny always said you could make a fortune with those dolls.'

'I don't know.'

'Well I do. And I know something else. You're going no place today, so forget that idea. And you can either sit and do nothing and feel sorry for yourself or get on with another doll. The choice is yours. Do you want me to get your sewing box and bag of fabrics or not?'

Betty glared at Rosie mutinously and Rosie met the stare head on, and Betty thought she'd give in, for that day at least, for she acknowledged she didn't feel well. Not that she'd admit it openly, but her head was swimming and a throbbing ache had begun in her temple and her chest was tight and sore. She had a feeling she wouldn't be able to stand on her own two feet, for they didn't feel as if they belonged to her. She'd fall and make a fool of herself.

'If you're so determined to fuss and keep me in bed unnecessarily, you might as well fetch my things,' she said grudgingly and with a sigh, but Rosie allowed herself a secret smile of triumph.

Later, she discussed Betty with Ida and Rita, who also agreed to help care for her. 'I'm worried to death about her,' she said. 'She's a funny colour and her eyes are heavy. I just know it's something. She says it's a cold, but...'

'You don't think it's bloody flu?'

'I hope not.' All three women gazed at the ceiling where Bernadette, Georgie and Ida's three, now home for the Christmas holidays, were playing. This flu affected the young and old, wiped them off the face of the earth, and sometimes within a few short weeks. What if Betty had the flu and Rosie brought it back home to Bernadette, or indeed any of the youngsters. 'We'll have to be very careful,' she said, 'in case Betty has caught the flu, not to spread the infection.'

'I've heard you soak a sheet in disinfectant and hang it over the door opening,' Ida said.

'I've heard that too,' Rosie said. 'And we must wash our hands when we leave the sick room with warm water and carbolic soap. We must have plenty of water in so that we can heat it and hope to God the tap doesn't freeze over.'

'D'you think we should contact her sons at all?' Ida asked.

'You don't think we're overreacting?'

'Maybe, but if we don't...'

'I know,' Rosie said. 'I'll tell you what, if she doesn't rally in the next few days, we'll call the doctor and go on what he says.'

'I shouldn't think it would be easy to come home from America anyway,' Rita said. 'Not just after a war.'

'No, maybe not, but if Betty doesn't get better they ought to be told,' Rosie said. 'We owe that much to her.'

Betty didn't rally and by Christmas Eve, when she'd been ill for a week, Doctor Patterson was called in.

'Has she the flu, Doctor?' Rosie asked as he came down the stairs and entered the room where she was waiting.

'Yes, I think so,' the doctor said gravely. 'You're not related to her, are you?'

'No, Doctor,' Rosie said with a smile, 'just a neighbour. There's three of us seeing to her.'

'You know it's very infectious,' the doctor said.

Rosie lifted her head. 'I know that, Doctor, but Betty is my friend,' she said simply. 'And as I explained, I am not the only one that sees to her. We've tried to minimise the risk, pinning the sheet doused in disinfectant across the doorway, and we wash with warm water and carbolic soap when we come out of the room.'

'Both good measures,' the doctor said. 'But there is still a risk for there's no cure.'

'I know that. Isn't it down to your constitution?'

'It is,' the doctor said, writing on a prescription pad. 'Get this from the chemist, they'll make it

435

up. The quinine will stabilise the temperature and the medicine may help the cough, and keep on with the warmed camphorated oil on the chest. She probably won't eat much, try coddled egg, chicken soup and beef tea, and give her all the drinks she wants.'

'Doctor,' Rosie said suddenly. 'Betty has two sons in America. Shall we send for them?'

There was a few seconds' silence before the doctor nodded his head briefly. 'That would be wise, I feel,' he said, and Rosie promised to see to it.

Christmas passed in a blur. As there was no sign of Rosie's Danny coming home, and no word from America, the women and five children celebrated at Rita's because it was the nearest to Betty's, and they took turns to seeing to her over the holiday.

The doctor's medicine did little good and the women tried to bring Betty's temperature down by bathing her with tepid water, but it gave only limited relief and even that didn't last. They encouraged her to drink as the doctor had suggested and spent hours making appetising soups she would only sip at.

On New Year's Eve, when Rita went in to check on Betty in the morning, she found the pillow and bed soaked with blood, a scarlet stream of it still pouring from Betty's nose. It was the first of many bleeds that day and the following one, and even when the doctor was called in he was little help. 'Nosebleeds are one of the symptoms,' he said. 'Sit her upright and hold the nose until it stops. It's the only solution, dropping keys down the back is no good at all. I'm worried about her temperature. Can someone come to the surgery, I'll make up a stronger mixture that may help.'

'I think we should start sleeping in her room,' Rosie said. 'She might need us in the night. If one of you will have Bernadette, I'll take my turn.'

'I don't mind watching Bernadette,' Rita said. 'And I don't suppose Ida does, either, but do you think it's necessary?'

'Yes,' said Rosie, 'I do. She can't lift herself if she coughs and the nosebleeds must be terrifying.'

'I just wonder if we're taking too many risks,' Ida said. 'I mean, the women up the yard and in the streets are already treating us like bleeding lepers. They ask how Betty is, all right, but they shout it out from the bloody doorstep. They never come near.'

Ida was right. The other women from the yard were only too keen to help, they'd do any shopping needed and even wash the bedding to help a little, but they wouldn't go into the house any further than the threshold. They couldn't be blamed, the speed this flu spread was frightening and the death rate, if you caught it, was also rising at an alarming level.

Everyone knew of someone who'd caught it and everyone could talk of tragedies, children orphaned with the father killed in the war and their mother dying with the flu, or whole families wiped out. It was indiscriminate too, because your survival was determined by your ability to fight it and that alone. No money in the world was any good to you, but when Rosie said that, Ida put in, 'Yeah, but the rich have better food than the rest of us in the war, like. Stockpiling it they was, before rationing, and even then they could go out for dinner and things like that. All I'm saying is that they would be better nourished and that probably means better able to fight off the flu or any other damned thing.'

Rosie had to admit Ida had a point, for many around them were ill-nourished and inadequately clad for the elements. What chance would they have against a killer disease? She, like many mothers, would go without to make sure Bernadette hardly ever went hungry or cold, but mothers with more mouths to feed would be hard-pressed.

'I'm wondering whether we should ask the doctor about sending Betty to the hospital.'

Rosie stared at her friend, appalled. 'You know what manner of hospital the likes of us go into,' she said. 'And what care would she get there that we can't provide?'

Rita couldn't answer that, and they shelved the hospital idea. That night, despite her fears, Ida was glad to be there when Betty began being sick, for she was too weak and too disorientated to lift herself up. 'Leave me,' she cried when the spasm was over and Ida was gently wiping her face. 'You have a family to see to. Get away.'

'I'll do no such thing,' Ida said. 'Come on now, let's get you cleaned up first and then I'll see to the bed.'

And that night set the pattern of the next few days and nights. The nosebleeds continued and so did the vomiting, over and over again, even when there was nothing to bring up. The women were constantly changing and washing sheets and nightdresses, which were often damp with sweat, and the bedding was draped about the houses, for the January weather was not conducive to drying anything.

As well as this, there was their own work to do, their own washing and shopping and cooking for the family, despite help from the women around them.

It wasn't surprising that Rosie's head was often pounding so much that she felt sick, and she put it down to overtiredness. She also felt guilty about the little time she spent with Bernadette and the way she seemed to keep her at arm's-length. She seldom picked her up or tucked her in bed or sat down in a chair with her for a story. This was partly lack of time and also because she was afraid of infecting her with this killer flu. Danny, still nowhere near demob from the army, sent a censorious letter telling Rosie to take more care of herself and Bernadette. He liked Betty but didn't really want Rosie anywhere near her, risking all he held dear.

Rosie's reply was swift. Wouldn't he have put himself at risk for a comrade, injured or in trouble? she'd asked. What was the good of God giving us compassion and kindness if we turn our backs on our fellow human beings because of fear for ourselves?

Scared though he was for Rosie's well-being, Danny had to admit that she was right. He'd lost count of the times he'd dragged an injured man to the relative safety of the dugout. Then there was the time he'd freed his commanding officer from the barbed wire. Danny remembered he'd been so intent on his task he'd been almost unaware of the bombs and shells falling all around him, for the officer had already had his leg blown off and his lifeblood was seeping into the muddy field. Danny knew his only chance of survival was getting him to a field hospital and fast, but he couldn't have got himself free of the barbed wire without help.

Was that any different from what Rosie was doing? Weren't things done in the heat of the battle that you'd never attempt if you had time to think about it in peacetime?

He didn't know, but he knew of Rosie's stubbornness and also of her loyalty, so his next letter was more understanding. Rosie had little time to peruse it, for when she woke in Betty's room the following morning she found the woman had given up on the fight for life. She approached the bed quietly and looked down at the woman, who in such a relatively short space of time had become a staunch friend, easing her passage in the munitions factory and helping her in all ways, and she knew she would miss her greatly.

She closed Betty's eyes gently. She'd never done the laying out of a dead person until she helped Ida with Gertie, but now she began to remove Betty's clothes tenderly. She wished she'd had the benefit of a priest come to see her, to pray with her. The Catholic Church was comforting in that way, it somehow gave dignity to death. But Betty, like Gertie, had not been a churchgoer. She supposed she'd go back to Reverend Gilbert, he seemed a good man. God knows how they'd pay for it. Rita said Betty must have plenty stashed away in the Post Office, but none of the women had searched for the book. If they had found it they couldn't have cashed it and wouldn't think they had a right anyway. If only there was news from America.

The day before the funeral, arranged for the Monday 20th January, two strangers alighted from a petrol-driven taxi, an unfamiliar sight in those streets.

The men who stepped out of it were unfamiliar too. Little could be seen of their faces under the trilby hats they both wore except for the fact that one was clean-shaven and one sported a beard. Apart from that they were identical, and wore black, well-cut coats with dark grey trousers peeping beneath and shiny black shoes of the finest leather on their feet. They were dressed for the weather too, with mufflers at their neck, and everyone watching was amazed at their smart leather gloves. Gloves on a man, except for working gloves, was considered a sissy thing to wear, but these men looked anything but sissies.

The children not yet old enough for school stopped playing on the pavements and in the gutters and gawped openly at the strange men. But most of the women knew who they probably were, though they'd not seen them for many a year.

They came out onto the steps as the men

441

disappeared down the entry.

'Come at last, then?'

'Too late, though. Poor old sod's dead and gone.'

'Proper toffs, ain't they. Gloves and all.'

'Looked after Betty, though. Fair's fair,' another put in. 'Sent her dollars in every letter they did.'

No-one could argue with that, or with the fact you can't come from America in five minutes. And that's what the two men who introduced themselves as Hugh and Chris were explaining to the three women they found in their mother's house, who were startled to see them. 'We should have sent a telegram,' the younger man, Chris, said. 'But we thought it might frighten you to death.'

Rosie remembered how the sight of the telegraph boy through the war had reduced her to jelly. Even now, with the war over, telegrams seldom signalled good news. She looked at Ida and Rita and remembered the telegrams they'd both received and she shivered. 'It probably would have done,' she said.

'We came as quickly as we could,' Chris said. ''Course, both of us had to arrange time from work, and to tell you the truth it isn't a good time at the moment. Jobs are hard enough to come by and with the soldiers coming back too it will be worse.'

'I know,' Rosie said with feeling, for she knew whenever Danny was released from the army he would have a tough job finding anything.

'We decided to come as soon as we got the letter,' Hugh said. 'We knew no-one would have written that way if things hadn't been serious and so as soon as we were assured we could have the time off and our jobs were safe, we booked a passage straight away.'

'Aye, and we arrived too late,' Chris said.

'She wouldn't have known you,' Rosie said soothingly. 'She knew no-one at the end and you did your best. I'm glad you're here because there are things to sort out. We've arranged the funeral service to be held at St Paul's. That's in Park Road, but you may remember that. The vicar there is a Reverend Gilbert and he buried the old lady that lived in the house I have, and I found him very nice. We didn't know if Betty … I mean, I hope that is all right for you.'

'I'm sure that will be fine,' Hugh said. 'But may I ask how it was paid for?'

Rosie blushed. 'I'm afraid we haven't paid for everything. We had a whip-round and instead of buying flowers we put it to the funeral.'

'Hadn't our mother any money?' Chris asked. 'She told us she had a fair bit saved and we sent her more every week.'

'We don't know what she has,' Rosie said. 'We've never looked. Had we received no word after the funeral, I suppose we'd have had to go through her things. It isn't something I was relishing.'

Hugh and Chris had noted the poverty of the area and knew many husbands were away, or dead, and that money wouldn't be plentiful. 'We'll reimburse you, of course,' Hugh said.

'There's no need.'

'There is every need,' Chris said. 'She was our

mother, our responsibility.'

But in the end, when the two men investigated, they found Betty had an insurance policy that would more than pay the funeral expenses and a sizeable amount in the post office. 'You must have some of this for your trouble.'

'It was no trouble,' Ida said. 'Thank you, but it is just neighbourliness.'

'Even so.'

'We couldn't,' Rosie said. 'It wouldn't be right.'

'Yes it would,' Hugh insisted. 'It's what our mother would have wanted, I'm sure.'

In the end they agreed to accept ten pounds each and then fell to discussing the funeral arrangements for the morning. 'I can't go to the service,' Rosie said. 'It's because I am a Catholic, so I thought I would stay here and make up some sandwiches and such. I will go along to the graveside later and then we can all come back here if that's all right. Many would like to pay their respects; Betty was well-liked.'

'It seems perfect,' Hugh said, peeling notes off the roll he had in his hand. 'Lucky I changed to English money on the ship,' he said, handing a five-pound note to Rosie. 'Get what you need.'

'I won't need five pounds, nor anywhere near it,' she protested.

'Spoil yourselves,' Hugh said. 'That's just for food, mind. We'll get the booze in. Send my mother out with a big bash.'

'All right,' Rosie said. 'I will.'

Betty's funeral was talked about for days after, for Rosie spent the money Hugh gave her and the spread she made for the mourners was lavish, with food many of them hadn't seen for a long time. The men dealt with buying the drinks and it took on an air of a party and reminded Rosie of the wakes she'd attended in Ireland.

The older people who'd lived in the street for some years remembered Hugh and Chris growing up before America beckoned them, and some of the younger people had been with them at school and many seemed bent on renewing their acquaintances.

Watching the cluster of people around Betty's sons, Ida said wistfully, 'My Herbie always wanted to go to the States. I wouldn't go and leave our mam and dad, being the last like, and then we weren't married five minutes and the pair of them was took off with TB. Just a year married I was.'

'Why didn't you go then?'

'Oh, I dunno,' Ida said. 'I had their house then d'ain't I. I mean it ain't much, none of these houses are. Bloody awful if the truth were told, but I was brought up here like. I know all the neighbours. Betty was a sort of auntie to me when I was a nipper, she was to all the kids, and I was on with our Jack then and bloody terrified as to how I'd cope like. I didn't want to travel halfway across the world to strangers. Herbie could see that. He weren't a bad man and he d'ain't press me. But I can't help thinking, if I'd gone he'd probably be alive now.'

'America was in the war too in the end,' Rosie reminded Ida. 'You can't think that way.'

'You can't help it, can you. I mean, I know

America came in, in the end, but my Herbie was killed at the Somme in the summer of 1916, nearly a year before the Yanks came in, and Betty's Chris was telling me they didn't take married men unless they had to like.'

'That was what they said here, though, and they took them in the end, didn't they?'

Rosie looked across the room at the ease and charm of Hugh and Chris, talking to people they hadn't seen for years in their American drawl, recalling incidents and events from their childhood. It was as if they hadn't a care in the world. They'd been sorry for their mother's passing, there was no doubt, but they hadn't seen her for so long Rosie wondered if she was like a stranger to them.

'Why did they never come before?' Ida said. 'When Betty was alive and well?'

'I don't know,' Rosie said sadly. 'It's the way of it. Everyone turns up for the funeral when the person is dead and gone. I'll miss her like crazy. It's hard to believe I won't see her any more.'

'We'll all miss her,' Rita said, overhearing Rosie's comment as she passed. 'I'll tell you what though,' she added, poking her in the ribs. 'Wherever the poor old bugger is now, she'd approve of her send-off.'

Rosie, looking round at the chattering people with not a sad face amongst them, had to agree. 'Aye, Betty liked a good party right enough. Hugh and Chris always wanted Betty to go over to America to visit them, you know?' she went on. 'They told me yesterday.'

'Dad too,' Chris had said. 'He was alive then.

And then, after he died, we redoubled our efforts, but she always refused.'

Rosie had wondered why, certainly after her husband died, she wouldn't want to go to where two strapping sons could look after her? 'Neither of you married?'

'No,' Hugh said. 'First we were too busy working our way up and then, when we'd made it, there were no decent women left.'

'I don't believe that. In the whole of America?'

'I must confess I didn't search the entire continent,' Chris said with a grin.

'You weren't worried about being conscripted into the army as single men and all?' Rosie asked.

'Well, no,' Chris said. 'We were almost at the cut-off point due to our ages. Anyway, we manage quite a large engineering plant that made a lot for the war. We could have claimed exemption, but it never came to that.'

No wonder they looked so hale and hearty, Rosie thought.

'I bet Betty would have given her eye teeth just to cast her eyes on her sons, even if it was just the once,' Rita said, bringing Rosie's thoughts back to the present. 'I'd hate Georgie to go so far and me never to see him again.'

'Come on,' Rosie said. 'It's years before you have that to think of and worry about.'

It was almost four o'clock and the light was nearly gone from the day and Rosie had had enough. 'Come on, Bernadette,' she said, holding her hand out to her daughter. 'I'll not be long after you in bed tonight.'

'Why, aren't you feeling well?'

'I'm just tired,' Rosie said, and she was deathly tired. She also had a sore throat and it hurt to swallow, but she didn't say any of that.

Hugh and Chris, seeing the three women about to leave, came over to them. 'I've just come over to thank you again for looking after our mother so well, and at great risk to yourselves,' Hugh said.

'Yeah, and don't go all modest on us and say it was nothing,' Chris added. 'Because we heard how it was from the neighbours.'

Rosie was as embarrassed as the other two, but she recovered enough to say, 'We were glad to do it. We were truly fond of your mother and will miss her greatly. The women all helped, they did their bit too, for your mother was a favourite with many. You only have to see how many that came to the house.'

'You took the brunt of it,' Hugh insisted, 'and don't worry about the house, we're seeing the landlord tomorrow and taking the money out of the post office. I'll bring your share around in the morning, if that's all right?'

'It seems awful to be paid for what we'd do naturally for one of our own,' Ida said. 'But the children never seem to stop growing and I must confess I will be glad of it.'

'We know it's what our mother would have wanted,' Hugh said. 'Her letters to us used to bring the courts and the streets alive for us, and we'd often cast our minds back, and although the occasion is sad it's been a pleasure to meet with many friends we remembered. But there was always a reference to the three of you and what worthy friends to her you've all turned out to be.'

'Ooh, be quiet,' Rosie said. 'Enough's enough.'

'Are you all right?' Chris asked. 'You're very flushed.'

'Can you wonder at it?' Rosie said. 'With your brother embarrassing the life out of us.'

But she felt it was more than that for heat was spreading through her body and her head spun so that she staggered and it was Hugh's arm which steadied her. 'It's the unaccustomed drink,' Rosie said with a smile, though she'd drunk little. 'I must take more water with it.'

'You've done too much,' Rita admonished. 'I said you would. Bed's the best place for you. You go on now, I'll mind Bernadette and pop in and see you when I bring her back.'

Rosie wanted to argue, to say she felt fine, but she felt decidedly weak and knew if she didn't soon lie down she'd fall down and so she nodded her head and said thanks to Rita.

Outside Betty's and in the courtyard once more, Ida tucked her arm inside Rosie's. 'Come on,' she said. 'We'll go across the yard together. These cobbles are ice-rimed and the last thing you want is a fall just now.'

But Rita knew it wasn't the ice that was giving Rosie that unsteady gait as she leaned heavily against her own doorway and watched the two women. Rita never went to church and had only a vague belief in some benevolent person in the sky somewhere, but she well knew Rosie firmly believed in God, so she silently prayed to that God there in the darkening yard. 'Please, please let this just be a bout of tiredness. Don't do

449

anything to harm Rosie.'

'Mammy, what are you doing?' Georgie whined, pulling at her hand. 'I'm freezing and I bet Bernadette is too.'

'Sorry you two, I was day-dreaming,' Rita said. 'Let's go in and give the fire a good old poke to get the blaze going.' And with a child either side of her, she led the way inside.

TWENTY-FOUR

When Rita brought Bernadette home, after having her for tea with Georgie, she found Rosie in bed asleep. 'You must be as quiet as a little mouse,' she told Bernadette, 'so as not to wake your mammy. So you get undressed before the fire and I'll have you into bed in a jiffy.'

Bernadette was usually one to argue about bedtime, hating the drab, cold attic lit only by a candlestick on a saucer, and 'bed in a jiffy' didn't sound a particularly good idea. But she'd seen her mammy sick before. Maybe if she went to bed like a good girl her mammy would be better in the morning.

So she undressed and even folded the clothes she took off and laid them on a chair and with Rita's help struggled into the pyjamas warmed before the fire and drank the mug of cocoa Rita gave her without a word of complaint.

'You've been a really good girl tonight, Bernadette,' Rita said. 'Your mammy will be pleased when I tell her.'

'Will she be better tomorrow?'

'We must hope so.'

However, Rosie wasn't better, and when Bernadette trailed into her room the next morning it was to hear that dreaded grating cough again, and added to that her mother's eyes looked

451

funny. Rosie, though, got to her feet and began to dress.

'What in God's name are you doing up?' Ida said, calling in that morning to see how she was.

'I can't stay in bed because of a cough,' Rosie declared. 'And small wonder I have it at all for when all's said and done this cold weather would slice you in two.'

'Rosie,' Ida said warningly. 'Don't do this.'

'Stop it, Ida!' Rosie snapped back. 'You're a right old prophet of doom, you are. Stop fussing over a wee cough.'

Ida said nothing more though she was worried and knew Rosie was, for despite her staunch words her eyes looked scared.

However, she put a brave face on it, and when Hugh and Chris came with the promised money later that morning she brushed away their concerns.

'It's a touch of bronchitis I have,' she assured them. 'It's a weakness from working in the munitions I think, and then of course it is so bitterly cold and for all you do in these houses they are always damp and draughty. Maybe you well remember that?'

They did of course, and though Rosie looked far from fine in their opinion, she seemed unconcerned about her cough, saying she was well used to it, and so they gave her the two five-pound notes and took their leave.

Rosie leaned against the door when they'd left, for trying to pretend she was well when she felt far from it had taken it out of her, and she saw Bernadette's eyes upon her. She hated hearing her mother cough because she remembered the last time and she'd not been allowed to see her for ages because of it.

Rosie saw her daughter's fear and she smiled at her, though it took an effort, and said, 'Don't worry, Bernadette, I'll be as right as rain before you know it.'

She pushed herself away from the support of the door and stood holding on to it with one hand, waiting for the dizziness to pass and the room to stay still. Then she walked carefully across the room, put the money behind the clock on the mantelpiece and sank gratefully into the chair before the range.

'Mammy, I'm hungry,' Bernadette's voice roused her mother and she opened her bleary eyes. The clock said it was half past two. She had slept for hours. No wonder the child was hungry, and the sleep had done her little good for the room around her spun and she knew she'd be unable to stand without help for her legs felt like rubber. 'Get Ida,' she said in a hoarse whisper.

Bernadette nodded and went out into the bleak, icy yard and knocked on Ida's door. 'My mammy's poorly again,' she told Ida. 'And I'm hungry and I haven't had my dinner.'

'Oh dear,' Ida said, looking at the child's woebegone face. 'Now, how about if you go down to Rita's and ask her to give you a piece of summat while I pop in and see your mammy? Will that do?'

'Yeah, I think so,' Bernadette said, and Ida waited till she saw Rita's door open to admit the

453

child before she went into Rosie's.

She looked with horror and concern at the sweat standing out in globules on Rosie's furrowed brow and her unhealthy pink cheeks, despite the fact the fire in the range was nearly out. Rosie's breath was coming in short pants and the infernal cough doubling her up, and fear ran all through Ida. 'Oh my God, girl,' she cried. 'Come on. Bed's the best place for you and then we should have the doctor in.'

She helped Rosie to her feet as she spoke and held her tight as she swayed, taking her weight as they crossed the room and almost carrying her up the stairs. Ida was as glad as Rosie to reach the bedroom and she let Rosie down gently as she flopped back on the pillows. The sheets were like ice and Ida took Rosie's things off her and pulled a nightdress over her head, before saying, 'I'll bring you an oven shelf from my place wrapped in flannel to warm the bed before I go for the doctor, because there will be no heat in yours, the range is nearly out.'

'I don't need a doctor,' Rosie protested. 'It's just a bit of a cough. If I have a couple of days in bed I'll be as fit as a fiddle.'

'Please, Rosie, humour me,' Ida said. 'To put my mind at rest.'

Rosie knew Ida was frightened of the same thing that was sending spasms of terror running through her own body, yet she said, 'I can't. I haven't paid him yet for calling him out that time in November when I lost the baby and now this. I can't afford the doctor, Ida.'

'What about the money that you got from

Betty's sons? Where did you put it?'

Rosie had forgotten that. She could well pay what she owed. 'It's behind the clock,' she said, and then she looked Ida full in the face and said, 'Do you think I have the flu?'

Ida avoided Rosie's red-rimmed eyes. 'Let's have the doctor in,' she said again.

Rosie knew it was sensible and yet her mind shrank from hearing the truth. But then she remembered Bernadette, who was dependent on her, and she nodded her head briefly. 'All right, but pay him what we owe him. Let him know that straight away.'

'I will, don't fret.'

'And keep Bernadette away.'

Ida knew exactly how she felt. 'Of course. Rita has her at the moment.'

'I mean keep her with you. Either at yours or Rita's.'

'I know what you mean, Rosie, and why worry yourself over that. Between us we'll take care of her.'

When Ida left the room, tears of helplessness squeezed between Rosie's lashes and trickled down her cheeks. She could die if she had the flu. She knew that. What would Bernadette do then – and Danny too? How would he cope alone? How could he care for Bernadette and work too?

She could never recall feeling so ill or so weak and her throat was sore. She wished now she'd asked Ida to make a drink. She wondered how long it would take her to bring the doctor. Maybe if she shut her aching eyes awhile it would ease the throbbing in her head.

She never felt Ida slip the warm oven shelf between the sheets for she'd fallen asleep and in fact she heard or felt nothing until the light touch on her arm and she opened her eyes to see the sympathetic ones of Doctor Patterson. 'Hallo, Mrs Walsh.'

Rosie ran her tongue over her parched lips. 'Have I got the flu, Doctor?'

Doctor Patterson was sure she had. Everything spoke of it. The very thing he dreaded had happened and it had to happen to Rosie Walsh, who with her chest already weakened by bronchitis the previous year was the very one least able to fight it off. 'I must examine you first,' he said, and he pulled the bedclothes away gently. No-one spoke, not Rosie in the bed, Ida by the door, or the doctor, but Rosie's laboured breathing could be heard by them all.

In the end the doctor said, 'I'm afraid, Mrs Walsh, you have got the flu and I am so very, very sorry.'

He was dog-tired. The epidemic was so bad he was working around the clock and worn down by tragedy at almost every house. He wondered at the insidiousness of this virus, that after the carnage of four years that had effectively stripped villages, towns and cities of their young men, this flu seemed to be set on attacking the rest – the women, the old, the young and the vulnerable. He was existing and operating with little sleep and he often wondered in his blackest moments if there would be many left alive by the summer.

Ida followed him downstairs and he faced her across the room. 'Mrs Walsh is in a bad way,' he said. 'No doubt about it. Take all the precautions you took last time, the sheet soaked in disinfectant across the doorway and wash your hands and arms with hot water and carbolic soap every time you touch her, and, as well as that, scald every cup and plate she uses. This is to protect yourself and your children.'

'Yes, Doctor,' Ida said. 'I'll do it like you say, never fear.'

'Have you got the time to come to the surgery? I could give Mrs Walsh something for the cough and quinine might bring the temperature down.'

'No problem, Doctor,' Ida said. 'I'll come directly. And send in your bill and for that time in November. Rosie has the money to pay you because Betty's sons gave us all something and I know Rosie would want you paid, she mentioned it.'

The doctor had given up ever seeing money for that frantic dash through the night and Susie had harassed him about it and called him a fool for running to these people as soon as they crooked their little finger even when he was not receiving a penny piece for it. Maybe this payment would shut her up, and so he said, 'Are you sure she has the funds?'

'Quite sure, Doctor.'

'Then I'll bring the bill the next time I call,' Doctor Patterson promised.

The following day a horse-drawn cart took Betty's furniture away. 'D'ain't they offer you owt?' a woman at the top of the entry asked Rita.

'Yeah, but I needed nowt. Anyroad, I'd be

worried about infection spreading, like. I got a bed for Rosie, for Bernadette can't stay in a cot forever, but I'll scrub it all over with bleach before I give it her.'

'Best way. Can't be too careful.'

'You can say that again.'

'How is her, anyroad – Rosie, I mean?' the woman asked, moving slightly away from Rita as she spoke.

'Bad enough.'

'Poor sod. Never rains but it bleeding pours, do it?'

That was the sentiment most people expressed, but they stated it from the relative safety of their own doorstep. They thought Rita and Ida either saints or fools to go through nursing an influenza victim again, putting their lives and those of their children at risk.

But then what was the alternative? Some cramped hospital, no better than a workhouse, where the care was very basic. And there would still be the problem of Bernadette.

Ida and Rita didn't bother talking about it, they just got on with the job of looking after both Rosie and Bernadette and waited for a letter from Danny in response to the one they wrote to him, thinking he needed to know how sick Rosie was. But by the time the distraught reply came, Rosie was far too ill to know or care.

Danny's letter reduced Rita to tears. He said it was far too late for recriminations. All that mattered was that his woman, his beloved wife, was sick and could easily die. He wrote that his commanding officer wasn't the compassionate

458

type and told Danny he was just one out of the hundreds of men who had some relative affected the same way. They couldn't all be running home to hold hands and especially in the case of the flu, as they'd possibly bring the infection back to run riot about the camp. Hadn't they lost enough men at the hands of the Hun? No, he was afraid any leave was out of the question.

Thank you for what you are doing for Rosie. Please look after her, for she is everything to me. If I could be with her, I would and I'd hold her close and tell her I loved her and make her fight this illness and pray it would be enough. Give Bernadette a big kiss for me too and tell her I was asking after her.

'Poor man,' Rita said as she folded the letter up.

'Yeah,' Ida agreed. 'And let's hope she pulls through for Danny and all, because I don't know how he'd cope without her.'

'I know,' Rita said with a sigh, thinking of her own loss. 'Life's bloody hard.'

Rita and Ida took it in turns to stay by Rosie's side night and day, constantly rousing her to take a few sips of strained chicken soup or nourishing beef broth that the doctor recommended they make. When she cried out in delirium, threshing her arms this way and that, someone was always there to soothe or hold her tight. Even when she drenched the sheets with sweat, Ida and Rita remained calm, putting fresh sheets on the bed and dosing Rosie with quinine before sponging her down. Often Rosie didn't know the hands that ministered to her, didn't recognise her friends, and her vacant eyes worried them.

When the nosebleeds came, the bouts of nausea following on their heels, Rosie would be unable to lift herself and would feel herself drowning in her own emissions. But always there were hands to help, to hold the bowl out and lay cool flannels on her swollen nose.

By the end of three weeks, with January leading into mid-February and still no apparent change, Rita and Ida were dead beat. On Friday 14th February there was a knock at the door and the two women looked at one another for few knocked. It was Father Chattaway, who'd just heard word of Rosie's sickness, and he seemed to have no fear of catching the disease himself. Rita took him up to the bedroom and he was shocked by Rosie's condition. Unselfconsciously, he placed a stole around his neck and knelt by the side of the suffering woman and mumbled prayers into his hands.

Rita and Ida withdrew and left Rosie and the priest together. 'If it don't do no good, it can't do harm either,' Rita said. 'God knows Rosie has gone through the mill. That priest might make the Almighty listen at least. Didn't Rosie always say the priests were well in with God?'

'Yeah, she did,' Ida said with a ghost of a smile. She gave a sudden yawn and stretch. 'Christ, I'm tired.'

'Why don't you have a bit of a kip then?' Rita said. 'It's my turn with Rosie tonight, anyroad.'

'What about him?' Ida said, giving a jerk of her head upwards.

'Who, the priest?' Rita said. 'What about him? He's come to see Rosie, not us. I'll offer him a cup of tea when he's done like, and that'll be that. Then we'll wait and see if the mumbo-jumbo works.'

Ida's sleep was broken by the children home from school, and after seeing to them she popped next door to relieve Rita so she could have a break before taking over the night shift, passing Georgie and Bernadette playing in the yard. Rita was at the range when Ida went in, putting a stew on the hob.

'That priest was here hours,' she said. 'In fact, he's not that long gone. Wouldn't take time for a cup of tea, he said. Christ, Ida, he could have had a three-course meal.'

'How's Rosie after it all?'

'Well, I popped up just after he left, but Rosie was asleep, and I haven't been near since, not wanting to disturb her like.'

'I'll stay if you like and you can take a bit of a break,' Ida offered.

'I will in a minute. D'you want a cuppa?'

'When do I ever say no?' Ida said. 'You mash the tea and I'll creep up and have a look at Rosie.'

Ida crept up quietly enough, but her progress down the stairs was swifter and noisier and when she burst into the room, tears were raining down her face, which was aglow, and her mouth opened in a wide smile. 'Oh Sweet Jesus,' Ida cried, leaping across the room and clasping Rita's hands. 'The fever has broken. She's sleeping normally and naturally. Maybe the mumbo-

461

jumbo worked after all.'

Rita shrugged. 'Who cares what it was. She'll get better. Oh thank God,' and the two women held each other and cried in relief, mightily glad Georgie and Bernadette were out in the yard and not there to see the carry-on, for they could never have explained it to their satisfaction.

When Rosie opened her eyes the next morning she felt, if not better, certainly better than she'd felt for a long time. The doctor called that afternoon and Rosie started to press him about the bill and only when she was told everything had been paid up-to-date could she relax. He was delighted that Rosie was so much better, but told her that the road to full recovery could take many weeks. 'You're not very good at looking after yourself, Mrs Walsh,' he said sternly, though his eyes belied the stance he took. 'Nor at doing as you are told, but unless you are to find yourself dreadfully ill again you need to take care, and I will tell your stalwart neighbours the same.'

He went on to tell Rita and Ida too that Rosie had to have the best of food and when he'd gone Rita remarked that with the doctor's bill paid and the cost of the good food he said Rosie needed, she'd be lucky if she had much of that ten pounds left by the time Rosie was totally out of the woods.

However, the flu had frightened the life out of Rosie and for once she was prepared to follow the doctor's instructions to the letter, for she was aware how close she'd come to dying.

Rosie found the doctor to be right. She was incredibly weak and though she was impatient to get better quicker, Doctor Patterson said she was doing fine.

She was bored in bed, though, and there was little to inspire her when she looked out of the window onto the dingy yard. It was hard to believe it was nearly spring. By early March in Ireland, the ground would be filled and new plants sown, early spring flowers would be seen in the hedgerows and buds apparent on some trees, and new lambs would be gambolling beside their mothers in the lush green fields.

Here, the greyness and grime of everything depressed her and only Bernadette could cheer her in any way. As soon as she was deemed not to be infectious any more she demanded to see the child, though at first a few minutes of her company was all she could manage. But now Bernadette spent a long time in her mother's company and the more Rosie saw of her daughter, the more she realised how precious she was, because after the doctor's predictions she did not want to try for more children.

Rosie would have to make that clear to Danny. She couldn't go through the pain of losing them over and over. Danny had to see that.

But by the time he came home she wanted to be fully recovered and able to welcome him properly and join in planning his demob party, and so she began walking around the bedroom. She was unsteady at first and could only manage a few steps. But each day her strength improved and soon she was able to walk right around the bed. When she could walk the length of the room, she said she wanted to come downstairs.

There she was able to lend a hand. She could prepare vegetables in a bowl before the range, or watch a boiling pot and do any darning needed. She took up knitting again and spent hours unravelling woollies Rita and Ida would get from the rag market and remaking them into things for the children. She was not averse to amusing the children either and would often snuggle into the chair with Georgie one side of her and Bernadette the other and read or tell them a story, and she taught them both to play Snakes and Ladders and Snap.

By the time Danny came home on 31st March, Rosie was feeling much stronger. March had been a gusty, squally month.

Blasts of wind would lift the rubbish from the gutters to send it swirling and dancing down the streets, lift ash from the courtyard and splatter windows and brickwork, and seep into the draughty houses to cover everything with a thick layer of dust.

But when Danny stood in the door he didn't notice the dust-laden mantelpiece, or even the fire in the range in an attempt to drive the chill from the room. He didn't even see the table laid for a party and the 'Welcome Home' banner, which they'd put above the fireplace, for Rita had said there was no good putting anything outside for it would be blown away.

He had eyes only for Rosie and Bernadette standing beside the range, and he was so filled of

464

love for them both he felt as if his heart would burst. He threw his kitbag to the floor, crossed the room in two strides and, scooping Bernadette up with one arm, he put the other one around Rosie and felt her tears of joy dampening his shoulder.

Rosie loved having Danny home, although she tried not to show that too much in front of Ida and Rita. However, they had been marvellous about the party and shown no spark of resentment, only cautioned Rosie about spending so much on it. But, the euphoria of Danny coming home had driven all sense of reason from Rosie's head and by the time she'd bought all she wanted she only had a few shillings left from the ten pounds Betty's sons had left her. Rosie thought it worth it as she saw the look in Danny's eyes when she was able to draw his attention to the spread.

Soon, however, the realities of life took over. At first, Danny was optimistic about soon finding employment. 'I'll wear my greatcoat you see,' he told Rosie. 'It shows I've done my bit.'
    And to help him while he searched for work as an ex-serviceman, he was entitled to a special benefit called Out-of-Work Donations. This amounted to twenty-nine shillings for himself and Rosie, with a further shilling for Bernadette.
    It was riches to Rosie and she resolved to put anything she had over each week into the post office. 'How long will it be paid out for?' she asked Danny.
    'Not long,' he said. 'I'll not be unemployed

long, you'll see.'

This optimistic stance was taken towards the middle of April, when Danny had been out of work just a fortnight.

Grateful though Danny was for the Out-of-Work Donations, it made him feel less of a man to have to rely on it. Something else made him feel less of a man too, and that was Rosie's lack of sexual interest. He'd been patient and as kind and considerate as he knew how to be, but still Rosie spurned his advances upon her. 'I'm sorry, is it too soon?' he asked at first, and Rosie gave a brief nod.

The next time was almost a week later. 'I'm not ready,' Rosie had replied, and eventually, after the third time, he'd said, 'When will you be ready, Rosie?'

'Never.'

'You don't mean that?'

'I've never meant anything more.'

'But Rosie...'

'Don't "but Rosie" me,' Rosie had spat out. 'I can't risk becoming pregnant. Don't you see that?'

Danny hadn't argued further, because he did see, and as much as he wanted a son, after what the doctor had said he too didn't want to risk pregnancy. Rosie had been through enough already.

Over the next few months, as summer took hold in the city, Danny travelled the length and breadth of it searching for work. He went to the Gun Quarter and off to the BSA (Birmingham Small Arms) in Small Heath; he toured the Jewellery Quarter, knocking on every workshop door, and he visited all the brass foundries. He went to the numerous small factories making buckles and buttons, pen nibs, hair grips and safety pins; and the larger ones making bicycles, sewing machines, motorbikes and cars, and even Fort Dunlop in Holly Lane in Erdington which made tyres.

Each day he returned home footsore and frustrated. The soles on his army-issue boots grew paper thin and his feet blistered, and almost everywhere the answer was the same, they hadn't work for their regular people, they were taking no-one else on.

Danny's boots needed soling and heeling after tramping the city, but he was hesitant about spending money on himself when he was bringing none in. 'For God's sake, Danny, you'll be walking on the uppers if you don't get something done soon, and they let in so much water every piece of cardboard you put inside is soaked in minutes,' Rosie told him angrily one day. 'Give me the boots. If you get a job after all this tramping in wet feet you'll be in bed sick and not able for it.'

Danny handed over the boots to repair, but reluctantly, and Rosie took them to the cobbler. She felt so sorry for her husband, who was frantic that he could find no job. She knew what made it worse was that Jack, Ida's eldest, now twelve, had obtained work after school and on Saturdays at a greengrocer's on the Lozells Road, and that he proudly presented his modest pay-packet to his mother each Saturday evening. 'Just last year he could have been full-time,' Ida said, for they'd only put the school-leaving age to fourteen the previous year. 'But, still, we've got to be grateful for small mercies, eh?'

Rosie ached to hold Danny in her arms, to stroke his hair and smooth the worry lines from his brow. But she did none of these things, for she knew what they might lead to and knew Danny would think she was promising something she wasn't, and she couldn't do that to him. It was bad enough refusing him. Many men would have had the priest out to her by now, taking her to task about her duty and a man's conjugal rights. She wouldn't be the first Catholic woman it had happened to. But she doubted Danny would ever shame her in that way. He was a good man, no doubt about it.

But Danny was also an unhappy man. Inactivity had always hung uneasily on him and now Rosie seemed divorced from him too. There were no comforting hugs or lingering kisses and sex was just a memory. It was a God-awful life when you thought about it.

And the job situation would be laughable if it hadn't been so tragic. He'd once had high hopes for the National Federation of Discharged and Demobbed Sailors and Soldiers who campaigned all summer for 'Jobs not Dole', and he'd even been to some of the rallies. But when he read in the paper that as well as the three hundred and sixty thousand ex-servicemen claiming dole there were six hundred and fifty thousand civilians, the situation seemed hopeless. There just weren't the jobs for so many people and any he might have done would have been snatched up by the men released from duty before he was.

Then Danny learned that his entitlement to his Out-of-Work donations would cease in August, as it was only paid out for a maximum of twenty weeks. 'What happens now?' he asked.

'Have you looked for work?'

'Everywhere. I've toured the city,' Danny said. 'I've tried everything.'

'Well, you can be brought into the Unemployment Insurance,' the woman snapped and her mouth turned down disdainfully. 'You haven't paid the contributions, I know, but these are waived in the case of ex-servicemen and certain other groups. You will receive fifteen shillings.'

'I have a wife, a child. Dear Christ, fifteen shillings.'

'We have no provision for your wife,' the woman behind the desk told him coldly. 'If you can bring the birth certificate for your child you will be awarded an extra shilling a week.'

'I can't feed and provide for a family on sixteen shillings a week.'

The woman stared at him emotionlessly. 'Fifteen shillings might not be paid at all after fifteen weeks,' she snapped out. 'You will be assessed further then and the claim will be disallowed unless you are genuinely seeking work and you remain capable and available for employment at all times.'

Danny stared at her. It was as if she was made of stone, and he knew if he was to stay and plead with her till doomsday he'd get not a penny more. So he went home with a scant fifteen shillings to tell Rosie. He hoped to God he'd be in work of some sort at the end of the fifteen weeks,

469

for he had an idea that that ice-cold sod wouldn't bat an eyelid if he, Rosie and Bernadette starved to death, curled up together in the gutter. What was the point of the damned war, if not to have a better society at the end of it? What was the sense of those young, mutilated dead bodies in the fields of France and Belgium if not to make 'a land fit for heroes', for the survivors?

Well, some society this was, and not what any of the servicemen had been led to expect on their return. But when had the working man, let alone the non-working man, been given the power to change anything? Never, that's when.

Rosie received the news stoically, just as she had when the rent man, who'd called that morning, had told her the rent, pegged while the war was on, had been increased to three shillings a week. 'Rita and Ida have little more,' she reminded Danny. 'And little chance of changing that income, or at least till their children are older. They manage and so will we. While you were away in France I picked up a lot of thrifty tips on saving a penny or two here and there, and I have a little saved in the post office from when you were getting Out-of-Work Donations. I'll cope, don't fret.'

Danny was glad Rosie had taken the news so well. Many he knew would have reacted badly, but Rosie knew Danny felt the lack of money more than she did, because it reflected on him. She could make him feel better about himself, make him feel that he was important to her whether he could find a job or not, but if she did that it would involve holding him close, kissing him as she often longed to do, but she knew how it would end and what that would result in. She wasn't prepared to take that risk, but she could at least be reasonable about the dole money they could expect for the next fifteen weeks. God alone knew how little they'd be expected to manage on after that.

Rosie, knowing how Danny felt, didn't let on when her boots began to leak, nor tell him she seldom had a pair of stockings to wear. She also kept from Danny the little amount she was eating, though she always had a meal to put before him. 'Where's yours?' he would ask.

'I had mine earlier with Bernadette.'

'Are you sure?'

'Of course I'm sure. Eat away. I couldn't eat another mouthful myself.'

Danny would eat then and feel less guilty and Rosie would hope her stomach wouldn't rumble and betray the little she had in it, a couple of potatoes with salt or the heel of a loaf with a scraping of cheap margarine or lard. There was not enough money to feed them all adequately and so Bernadette had to be catered for first in Rosie's eyes. Bernadette was the only child she would ever have and so she reasoned she had to look after her well, keep her fit enough to fight off infections and suchlike. Then Danny had to be kept as healthy as possible, so that he'd be able to do a job when one did come up.

So she lived on a subsistence diet in order that Danny and Bernadette ate moderately well, and viewed the future with trepidation.

TWENTY-FIVE

'I went after a job myself you know,' Rosie confided to Ida in early September, 'because Danny ... well, there's nothing, is there? He isn't the only one. Once in the streets you nearly trip over the gangs and clusters of unemployed. Anyway, Rita told me Power's in Rocky Lane were setting on women enamellers. But all they're offering is twelve shillings and sixpence. We'd be worse off. God, it's hard enough to manage now.'

'Yeah, I know,' Ida said. 'Rita finds it a struggle too. Still, as she says, Georgie is five just before Christmas and starts school in January. She's going to do summat then, she says, and she don't care what it is. She's going to make sure they ain't living hand to mouth all their bleeding lives.'

'I can't blame her,' Rosie said. 'I blame no-one for trying to get a bit extra. I mean, food's bad enough, but clothes and shoes are a nightmare.'

'Yeah, have you seen the barefoot urchins running around?' Ida said. 'Bare arses some of them too. Wonder they don't all die of pneumonia.'

'Maybe that's what the Government's hoping for, kill a few off and there'll be less to worry over.'

'God,' Ida said with a sigh, 'It makes you think Herbie and Harry died for nowt, don't it?'

It did seem that way and both women fell silent, and then Ida said to Rosie, 'You still hell-bent on taking Bernadette to the Catholic School up Thimble Mill Lane when her's five?'

'Aye.'

'You're clean barmy. There's a school in Upper Thomas Street.'

'Not a Catholic one.'

'Who cares?' Ida cried. 'You don't want to be dragging the little one all that way in the winter, and what if you have a couple of babbies to see to as well?'

'She'll be grand,' Rosie said. 'And there won't be any babbies.'

'What d'you mean?'

'What I say.'

'Oh. Was Danny injured like?' Ida said, her eyes and voice sympathetic, and for a second or two Rosie was tempted to say he was. But she couldn't do that to Danny so she said, 'No, it's after what the doctor said, about me maybe doing something to myself by working in munitions. I mean, if I can't carry a baby, I don't want to risk another pregnancy.'

'You mean you don't do it?'

'No.'

'Good God, girl, you're piling up trouble for yourself,' Ida said. 'You can't just leave a man like that. God, he's been at war for months. What do you want, a bleeding monk?'

'It isn't like that.'

'Maybe not for you it ain't,' Ida said, and added warningly, 'But I'm telling you straight, men ain't like women. They can't do without it forever and if you won't oblige, one day he might find someone who will.'

'Danny would never do that.'

'If you were to have asked Danny just a couple of years ago if you'd ever refuse him, what would he have said?'

Rosie knew what he'd have said and that was that he could never imagine a time that she would ever do that. She hung her head, but still said defiantly, 'I want no more children. What's the good of it? I'd lose them anyway.'

Ida felt sorry for her and she laid her hand on Rosie's arm and said gently, 'That's between you and him, Rosie. There are things you can use, I think. Things you can do, like.'

'They'll all be against the Catholic Church, I bet.'

'Bugger the Catholic Church!' Ida burst out. 'All I'm saying is this: there's pressures enough between the two of you anyway, with Danny not able to get a job and grinding poverty that would bring anyone down. Surely you can bring a measure of comfort to one another? Think about it. Talk to Danny. See how he feels.'

There was no way Rosie could bring herself to talk to Danny of ways of preventing pregnancy. It was totally out of her understanding anyway, though she knew Ida had a point and so when just a few days later Danny's hand reached for her in the bed she was suddenly filled with desire for this man that she still loved with all her being, though her insides were knotted with fear and she stiffened.

Danny stifled a groan. 'Please, Rosie,' he pleaded. 'I know what you are frightened of, but

I can pull out before I… You don't need to know about it, but I'll make certain you're all right.'

'Oh, Danny, are you sure. I am so frightened.'

'I promise you,' Danny said. 'You will not become pregnant. I don't want to see you suffer that way any more than you do. We have Bernadette and I am content. This is something different and will bring pleasure to both of us.'

Rosie could deny him no longer and didn't want to.

'Relax, my darling girl,' Danny said gently as he ran his hands all over her body. 'I'll never hurt you.'

'Oh, Danny, oh…' Rosie got no further for Danny kissed her then, her lips, her neck, her throat, until she groaned and writhed and eventually cried out. 'Oh, please, Danny. Now, now.'

It was rapturous, the only word for it, Rosie thought, and a shame it had ended so abruptly. Danny lay beside her and hoped to God he'd pulled out in time. He'd been so carried away and it had been so long that he'd almost forgotten. He didn't want to make Rosie pregnant, not again. He had to face the fact that he'd never have a son to follow in his footsteps. The bloody munitions had seen to that. But then, he asked himself, what footsteps? He'd more or less lost his inheritance. All any child of his could hope to look forward to was joining a line at the unemployment offices.

'Danny, was it all right?'

'All right? My darling girl, it was much more than all right,' Danny said and his lips sought hers. And Rosie sighed in contentment.

When Rosie's period came the following week she was ecstatic, for she knew that Danny had spoken the truth and they could make love without repercussions. It got much easier after that and Ida noticed the difference in Rosie and guessed the reason for it, but decided against teasing her.

Then, one day, a month before Christmas, Danny came home in a buoyant mood, something Rosie had not seen in ages. He'd got work on one of the narrowboats. 'It's Ted Mason's. You mind I told you of him before?'

'Aye,' Rosie said. 'I always wanted to meet him and his wife, didn't I?'

'Yeah,' Danny said. 'But he has had it rough. His eldest son was killed in the closing months of that butchering war and then Mabel took ill a couple of days ago with severe bronchitis, and she's staying with a friend on land while she's so poorly because Ted said the air around the canal is too damp for her and fog lingers there too. Syd's stayed with her, to see to her, he says, but I have my doubts.'

'Why?'

'Because he doesn't like canal life,' Danny said. 'Well, let's say he didn't when he was sixteen, and two years on I can't see it will have altered any. Anyway, Ted can't cope and because I've helped him before he thought of me. It's just till Christmas, he thinks. By then, with the holiday and all, he reckons Mabel will be as right as rain again. But just think, Rosie,' he said, grabbing her waist and spinning her around. 'Just before

Christmas. It couldn't be better.'

'And think what will happen if the dole place gets to hear?'

'How would they? Who will know?'

'Oh, Danny, don't be silly. The whole street I should think,' Rosie said. 'How can you hope to keep a secret in this place?'

'It's only for a few weeks,' Danny said, and his tone was dejected and Rosie was cross with herself for pouring water on his news. Excluding the army and odd times he'd helped on the canal, this was the first job of work he'd had since leaving the farm. Small wonder he was excited.

So she forced a smile to her reluctant lips. 'I'm delighted for you anyway, Danny.'

'You are?'

'Sure I am. The extra money will be tremendous. How much is it, by the way?'

'Ted said it depends what we carry. But at least two pounds a week.'

'Oh, Danny, that's terrific.'

'I thought so,' Danny said, and allowed himself a smile, and Rosie stood on tiptoes and kissed him on the lips, but only lightly.

Danny thoroughly enjoyed his time on the narrowboat and Rosie was grateful for the money. His last day was Christmas Eve and Ted paid him two one-pound notes like he'd done every week, with an extra ten-shilling note for Christmas, and said he was delighted with him. 'You're a natural, man,' he said. 'Come on, I'll stand you a few drinks.'

Danny would rather have gone home, but he

felt it would have been churlish to refuse. Most of the other boaties were already in there and a couple besides Ted bought Danny a drink, and eventually he knew he'd have to break into the ten bob note for he couldn't just accept drinks and not stand his corner. He felt bad about it for he'd wanted to give the two pounds ten shillings to Rosie complete and see joy and relief flood over her face. But still, he told himself, he'd just have the one more and go home.

However, Danny found it wasn't that easy. Someone produced a mouth organ and another had a tin whistle and yet another a squeezebox and the tunes they began to play set his foot tapping. Someone pressed another pint into his hand and by the time he'd finished that he found the urge to go home, away from the music, the congenial company, the crackling fire and the pints of foamy beer, was not a good prospect at all.

Rosie had Danny's dinner ready, as she had every night, and she was surprised when he wasn't in by half past six. Eventually she put Bernadette to bed, who was in a very bad humour for she always had time with her daddy before she went up, and Rosie had to be quite sharp with her in the end.

By half past eight, Rosie was convinced something had happened to her husband, and with a shawl wrapped around her she went to the top of the entry to see if she could see him coming. She stood peering into the dark till the cold started to eat into her bones and then she went back to the door. But unable to stay in her

478

own house alone and hear the fire settling and the clock ticking, with worry eating into her, she gave a brief knock on Ida's door and went in.

'He'll be away for a drink,' Ida told her. 'Don't worry. It's Christmas Eve, after all.'

'He said nothing.'

'He probably didn't know. My Herbie always had a skinful Christmas Eve and New Year's Eve. The rest of the time he was more sensible. Don't fret, and don't expect him early or sober either,' Ida said. 'Sit down here and have a cup of tea and calm yourself.'

Later, Rosie was glad Ida had warned her. Danny was unused to drink, there was little to be had in the army and before that he'd no more take a penny piece from Rosie's hard-earned money in the munitions for a pint than he would cut off his right arm. All he'd had in the time he'd been in England was the odd pint offered when he'd helped a boatie through a lock or some such.

So the pints he was imbibing at the impromptu party at the pub were affecting him far more than many of the rest. It didn't bother him at the time. Nothing bothered him, he didn't have a worry in the world and everyone was happy.

When, eventually, 'Time' was called, Ted hauled Danny to his feet where he stood swaying. He staggered and would have fallen but for Ted's arms around him. 'You all right?'

Danny had an inane grin on his face and he tried to say, he was grand, that he'd never felt better, but what came out was nothing like that. Ted laughed. 'By God, man, you're hammered.'

'You best walk with him till he's off the towpath

at least,' one of the party advised. 'Silly bugger will fall in the canal else.'

'Aye, I will. Ta-ra then, and a Merry Christmas to you.'

'Christmas,' Danny remembered in his befuddled brain and he tried to wish the season's greetings to all his new friends, but it was beyond the capabilities of his tongue, which seemed to have swollen to twice its normal size in his mouth.

Without Ted, Danny wouldn't have made it that night, and Ted realised that when he had nearly got him to the clock at Aston Cross and Danny just sank to his knees. 'Come on you drunken old sod, you,' Ted said good-naturedly, hoisting Danny to his feet again and wrapping one of his arms around his own neck. 'Good job you don't live far,' he said as he was taking most of the weight, and Danny just nodded.

Rosie opened the door to see a man she didn't know holding Danny up, and she knew the man to be a boatie for he had on the cord trousers, waistcoat and cap they all wore. Danny was so drunk he was unable to stand. 'Sorry, missus,' Ted said. 'I'm Ted Mason and your husband's been working for me these last weeks, and tonight we had a bit of a party and he had one too many like.'

Rosie was embarrassed at the state Danny was in and furiously angry with him, but she remembered her manners. 'Thank you for bringing him home,' she said to Ted stiffly. 'Please, won't you come in?'

Ted went in with Danny hung around his neck

and he looked around the room. No settee, no-where to lay the man down, and that little woman would never be able to manhandle him upstairs. 'Shall I take him upstairs for you, missus?'

'Oh, no, it's too much trouble.'

'No trouble and better me than you,' Ted said.

'If you're sure,' Rosie said. 'I'll go and turn back the sheets.' And she ran up ahead.

The stairs were almost Ted's undoing and he nearly fell many a time. 'Come on, Danny,' he cried at last. 'Give us a hand, mate. We're on the stairs, for Christ's sake, and if you don't want us to arrive at the bottom you'll have to help a bit.'

What Ted said funnelled through to Danny and he tried in the uncoordinated way of the drunk to help as best he could, and they reached the bedroom without further mishap. Ted lowered Danny onto the bed Rosie had turned back and removed his boots. 'He's all yours, missus,' he said, and then, because he'd seen Rosie's mouth in a tight angry line and two spots of bright colour on her cheeks, he added, 'Don't be too hard on him, like. I think it's that he's not used to it, for he had no more than the rest of us.'

'No, he isn't used to it,' Rosie said grimly.

'Well, I think he'll have a head and a half tomorrow,' Ted said with a smile and then he touched his cap. 'I'll say good-night to you and a Merry Christmas.'

'Merry Christmas,' Rosie said through clenched lips and began to divest Danny of his working jacket and muffler before Ted had reached the door. She was so angry with Danny for getting into such a state that she rolled him from side to

481

side roughly in an effort to remove his clothes as quickly as possible.

But in doing so she roused Danny and the feeling of her hands on his body further aroused him, and as she leaned over him to remove his trousers he smelled the sweet smell of her. His Rosie! And his arms clasped her tight and he pulled her on top of him.

She twisted to get away from his stale beery breath and the action had the effect of arousing him further and when she felt him harden against her she was terrified, for she knew Danny drunk wouldn't be as considerate as Danny sober, and she cried, 'Danny, please don't do this!'

Danny was too drunk and too fired up to listen to pleas. He rolled Rosie onto her back with him above and when her arms flailed at him and her cries rose he held her arms above her head with one hand, pulled her bloomers down with the other, and stopped her cries with his mouth. And when Danny entered her he could no more have pulled out in time than he could have stopped the tide. When he eventually released Rosie's mouth she sobbed as he pummelled into her over and over for she knew with a dread certainty his actions would result in another pregnancy and another premature baby miscarried.

Rosie was roused on Christmas morning by the dulcet and totally tuneless tones of the mouth organ she'd put in Bernadette's stocking the evening before. She looked at her inert husband beside her and hoped he had some money left after the binge of the night before, for as well as the toys she'd bought special food for the festive season.

She sighed as she got to her feet. She ached all over, she realised, and her wrists were chapped and scratched where Danny had held her so roughly. But all that would matter little if there was no result from the previous night. Oh God! She had the urge to hit Danny across the head with something heavy, but instead she went to take Bernadette downstairs and get her ready for Mass.

Danny was up when the two returned from Church. He looked decidedly green, quite ill in fact. And he *was* ill. Many times that day he had to go running down the yard to the privy to be sick. He could stomach neither breakfast nor dinner and retired to bed in the afternoon, saying he felt bad.

It put a damper on Rosie's whole Christmas and she decided to go into Ida's rather than sit on her own. Rita and Georgie were already in there too, and the children shared the toys they had and the unaccustomed sweets that Ida gave them, and Rosie eventually began to relax. 'God,' she said to her two friends. 'You should have seen the state of Danny last night.'

'I heard,' Ida said. 'I heard *you* too.'

Rosie blushed and Rita said, 'Did he want sex? My Harry always did when he'd had a few.'

'Wanted it? He was like a wild animal.'

'Could he do owt?' Ida asked surprised. 'If Herbie had got like that he couldn't've done anything.'

'Oh, I don't think there's anything Danny could do that would disable him in that department,' Rosie said bitterly. 'I mean, it's Christmas Day and I might as well be living with a zombie.'

'Let him sleep it off,' Ida suggested. 'He'll be fine tomorrow. Anyroad, let's have a nip of sherry ourselves, it being the festive season and all.'

'Yeah,' Rita said, lifting her glass. 'If you can't beat the buggers, you have to join them.' And she downed the contents in one gulp and held out her glass for a top-up and all the women laughed together.

It was late into Christmas evening before Danny decided he wasn't going to die and now his stomach had stopped churning he wasn't going to be sick again. Gradually, flashes of the previous night came back to him and he got up and went downstairs. Rosie sat on her own, knitting something in red and blue, and he looked at her sheepishly and then was appalled as he noticed the chafing on her wrists. 'Rosie, Rosie, I'm so sorry about last night.'

Rosie shrugged. 'I was sorry too, and disappointed in the man I married for the first time,' she said. 'I pleaded with you to leave me alone. What if I become pregnant again now?'

Without giving him time to reply, she said, 'Not that it will matter to you. Fine figure of a father you are. Too ill from your drunkenness to attend Mass, or even give a greeting to your child on Christmas Day, the one you are supposed to adore. She's in bed now, and this is the worst Christmas Day Bernadette and I have ever had.

Do you hear?' she said, her voice rising in indignation, 'the very worst.'

Danny's head had begun to thump again. 'Please, Rosie,' he cried, his hands waving in the air.

'Your head sore, is it?' Rosie said scornfully. 'Good! It's no more than you deserve and I'll shout as much as I want in my own bloody house. And now I'm tired, I've been up since the crack of dawn, unlike some, and I'm away to my bed.' She stabbed her knitting needles into the balls of wool decisively and slammed the stair door on her way up, which caused Danny to put his hands to his head and moan.

It was February before Rosie acknowledged that she was once more pregnant. She was bitterly upset and furiously angry with Danny. She resolved to say nothing, there was little point when she'd lose the child eventually as she had done the other two.

She never allowed herself to imagine this child might live. Why should it? And she distanced herself from the whole experience to protect herself. After a while she didn't think of herself as carrying a child, but a leaden weight inside her that she would expel in time.

The pregnancy caused sickness, more violent than Rosie had ever experienced before, and not just in the morning either. She was eating no more than before, and even that often caused nausea, and so she began to look thin and unwell though she managed to hide the vomiting from Danny.

They were still getting unemployment benefit, but in February Danny was called in for assessment and they asked many questions of where he'd looked for work and so on. He was given the same amount for another fifteen weeks, but the thought that this handout might be snapped away from him at any time caused him to trawl the city once more for employment of any kind, and he also took part in rallies and marches to bring the predicament that thousands were in, before the Government.

Danny had noticed that Rosie looked unwell, but when he asked her if she was all right she curtly replied she was grand. He didn't think he could press it. He knew things hadn't been right since Christmas and that had been his fault. He only had a hazy recollection of it and even that was enough to cause him to bow his head in shame, and he wasn't surprised that Rosie hadn't let him near her since.

Her friends too were worried for Rosie, though they weren't aware how often she had to steal away to the lavatory, but her gaunt appearance couldn't be hidden. 'Go and see the chemist,' Ida advised. 'He'll make you up a tonic.'

'I need no tonic.'

'Well, you need summat all right,' Ida said. 'I'm surprised Danny hasn't noticed.'

'Huh, as if I'd take any notice of anything he said,' Rosie retorted.

'You ain't still mad at him about Christmas, are you?' Ida asked, and at Rosie's silence said, 'Christ, Rosie, he's a man. These things happen.'

'Aye, they happen all right,' Rosie snapped.

'Well, they'll not happen again in a hurry. Nearly three bloody shillings he spent in that pub when he knew we needed every penny, and then he comes at me like a raging beast. He'll not do that again in a hurry either.'

'Rosie!'

'Don't start on about how it's different for men and all that clap-trap. I'm not interested. He's not coming near me again.'

'Christ, girl, you can't do that. You're married to the man.'

'And don't I know it.'

'Come on, Rosie. This ain't like you. All right, so Danny let his hair down, getting rolling, stinking drunk, but only the once, Rosie. Give the man a break?'

'No!' Rosie stated emphatically, and neither Ida's urging nor Rita's entreaties, calling in to see her on her way home from her cleaning job, made the slightest bit of difference.

Rosie felt so alone during this pregnancy, although she knew she only had herself to blame, because by choice she'd not let on to a soul. She couldn't bear it, the excitement and false hopes, the knitting of little garments, choosing names, planning a future, and all for nothing. But it meant she felt isolated.

She barely spoke to Danny and hardened her heart against the sorrowful looks he gave her. What's he got to feel sorry about, she thought. It's me who has to bear the consequences of his actions.

Danny stayed out of the house as much as

possible. If he wasn't actively looking for work, or at a rally, he often took Bernadette with him. She, at least, had forgiven her father for his aberration on Christmas Day and loved him as much as ever. Rosie didn't mind that, and often wanted to scream at him to, 'Take joy in her, she's the only child you'll ever have, for even this one I have in my belly will not live.'

However, she said none of these things, not to her husband, her friends or her relatives in Ireland, and as one day followed another she waited for the show of blood on her bloomers, the rush of water from her body, or the familiar drawing pains in her stomach.

In mid-March, without a word about it to Danny, Rosie took Bernadette to put her name down at St Joseph's in Thimble Mill Lane. She was more than ready, and missed Georgie greatly because he'd begun at the school in Upper Thomas Street after Christmas.

Mother Dunston was the headmistress of the girls' school at St Joseph's and Sister Maria was head of the infants. Rosie was introduced to both as she filled in the forms to enrol Bernadette.

They were shown into the classroom where Bernadette would begin. The pupils were very industrious, Rosie noticed, writing laboriously on the slates they had in front of them on the desks. 'Formal work is done in the morning,' Sister Maria explained. 'The younger children have more play in the afternoon.'

'Would you like to come here, Bernadette?' Rosie asked.

Bernadette looked at the bent heads of the children and her hand tightened in her mother's. 'I don't know,' she said. 'Perhaps.'

Over the child's head, the eyes of Sister Maria and Rosie met and they smiled. Little did Bernadette know going back to school wasn't optional.

Back in the office, Sister Maria said, 'Bernadette's fifth birthday is not till July you said, but I think we may be able to take her after Easter if you'd prefer.'

'Oh yes,' Rosie said. 'Not that I won't miss her, but she gets bored at home, especially now her special little friend began school after Christmas.'

'Here?'

'No, he's not a Catholic, Sister,' Rosie said. 'He went to a school near us.'

'Well, here she will mix and play with Catholic children,' Sister Maria said, as if saying the non-Catholics were inferior, but Rosie was used to the way nuns went on and she said nothing. 'The fees are a penny to fourpence a week,' the nun went on, 'and in view of your husband's lack of employment, your contribution will be one penny.'

'Thank you, Sister.'

'Will Bernadette be going home to dinner?'

'Oh yes, certainly. Well, at first at least.'

'If later you want her to stay at school she must bring something with her to eat,' the nun said. 'We do not provide meals.'

'No, no, of course not.'

'So that is settled then,' Sister Maria said. She put her hand on Bernadette's blonde curls and said, 'I'll see you on 12 April, when the school reopens again after Easter.'

489

Bernadette's blue eyes, full of trepidation, sought her mother's deep brown ones. 'Will she?'

'Yes, Bernadette,' Rosie said. 'Indeed she will, and her name is Sister Maria. You must remember that. Say goodbye now.'

Bernadette told her father as they sat down to a meal that evening, as Rosie knew she would, and she also knew Danny was cross. 'Isn't this something we should have talked about?'

Rosie shrugged. 'What is there to say? The child's going on for five, she needs to go to school, and St Joseph's is the nearest Catholic one. So that's that, as far as I'm concerned.'

'Am I of no account in this house?'

The words were out before Rosie could clamp her lips together to prevent them. 'No, not really.'

The look Danny cast Rosie as he pushed back his chair, scraping it across the lino, should have struck her dead. He left his dinner barely half-eaten, and pulling his cap and greatcoat from the hook behind the door he went out into the darkening night and slammed the door with such force it juddered on the hinges.

'Is Daddy cross?'

'Aye.'

'Why's he cross?'

'It doesn't matter,' Rosie said, and was surprised how little Danny's bad humour bothered her.

'Is it because I'm going to school?'

'Och, no, not at all,' Rosie told her small daughter. 'Why ever should you have that idea? Come on and eat up your dinner like a good girl, and whatever ails your father, he'll get over it in time.'

But though Rosie could reassure Bernadette, she was sorry she'd spoken in that way to Danny. He didn't know he'd left her pregnant again and she had no intention of telling him, thinking he'd know soon enough when she miscarried. But it did no good for Bernadette to see her sniping at him this way, did no good for any of them. It wasn't as if Danny could do anything about the pregnancy now and going on and on blaming him would eventually eat into the fabric of their marriage.

Bernadette had very reluctantly gone to bed before Danny returned and when he came in hesitantly, as if not sure of his welcome, Rosie greeted him with a kiss. 'I'm sorry.'

'I don't blame you. I am useless.'

'You're not,' Rosie said. 'I was sorry the minute the words were out of my mouth and you are right of course, the matter should have been discussed. She's your daughter as much as mine.'

It gladdened Danny's heart to hear Rosie say those words. He had been so dispirited and depressed when he'd left the house. It was bad enough to feel he was on the scrap heap because he had no job, but to think Rosie too thought he was of no account, that had really hurt. He loved Bernadette totally and absolutely and wanted to be an important part of her life.

'Go up to her now,' Rosie advised. 'She won't be asleep. She went up protesting on every stair that she couldn't be put to bed without giving you a kiss. I'll warm the dinner you left over a pan. I'm sure you will have more appetite for it now.'

'Rosie, I don't know what I ever did to deserve you,' Danny said humbly.

A lump filled Rosie's throat and the look in his eyes meant she could barely speak and though she waved her hand dismissively as she managed to say huskily, 'Away with you, you bletherer,' Danny had seen the glisten of tears in her eyes. He kissed her before bounding up the stairs to bid goodnight to his daughter.

TWENTY-SIX

It was mid-June before Rita and Ida noticed that Rosie was putting on weight, hidden from them previously by her thin frame. 'It couldn't be a babby,' Ida said, 'cos she'd have told us.'

'Well, if it was, it would have to be a bleeding immaculate conception by all accounts,' Rita said. 'I mean, if she's telling the truth about not letting Danny near her, how would she be pregnant?'

'Could be a growth, that's what I'm worried about,' Ida said.

'You're right. Christ knows, she looks ill enough to have anything wrong with her. Here, Ida, I best be off or I'll get the sack. You gonna ask her?'

'I think I've got to. I don't think she'll say owt.'

'Well, go easy. She's as bad-tempered as a bear with a sore head these days.'

'It's all part of it, though, maybe,' Ida said. 'If she's ill, like.'

Later, Ida was to say to Rita, 'You could have knocked me down with a feather. Christ, I mean, I just asked her was there summat wrong or was she ill or owt and she said no, she weren't ill, she were expecting.'

'She's having a baby!'

'Like I told you, and nearly six months gone and she's said nowt to anyone, not even to Danny nor his people.'

'Don't Danny know anyway?'

'Not according to Rosie. She says she makes sure she's in bed when he comes up, with the covers pulled up, and is up before him in the morning to get Bernadette off to school and so he ain't noticed.'

'Must have been that time at Christmas.'

'Must have been.'

'Ain't she the slightest bit excited?'

'No,' Ida said. 'You know what I think. She's terrified. She says she doesn't think of it as a baby, she can't, cos she sort of expects it will die.'

'Oh Christ,' Rita said. 'And the awful thing is, it could.'

'Don't talk like that.'

'I'm talking facts Ida,' Rita said. 'I know what the poor sod's going through. She's terrified of miscarrying again and there ain't a bloody thing in the world we can do about it.'

'Ain't you going to tell his mother?' Ida asked Rosie a few days later.

'Ida, I've done that twice already,' Rosie answered wearily. 'You're having a grandchild, I write, and they rejoice with me, and then a few months later I write to tell them there will be no grandchild. Instead of knitted jackets and bootees, I get condolence cards.

'Anyway, Connie has enough on her plate at the moment, what with arranging Sarah's wedding to Sam, and she's worried to death that she's hurtling headfirst into heartache but Sarah won't listen and refuses to believe Sam has anything to do with that sort of thing any more.'

'Maybe he hasn't then?'

Rosie shook her head. 'Ida, one of the reasons that we are here is because Danny tried to leave that organisation. It's a lifetime commitment in the IRA, so if Sam was involved then, he is now. The violence has gone up a level now that the Black and Tans are there with their love of brutality, bent on keeping law and order and on any terms.

'Christ, you'd hardly credit the things Connie writes about, the people shot in their homes and in the street, the barracks ransacked. Catholics are attacked and beaten up in the North and Protestant houses set ablaze in the Free State.

'And, of course, the retaliation follows. The Black and Tans will torch whole villages or haul all the men from a place and stand them against a wall and shoot the lot of them. I mean, Connie wrote only last week about the young boy shot in a Dublin school because they couldn't get his brother. It's like something you'd read about gangland America and she is having to live through that and knows her daughter will be involved in it through Sam.

'The last thing I want to do is upset her further, upset any of them when there is no need for it. It will all be over any day now, I'm thinking, and none will be any the wiser.' And that was the fear that dogged her every day and so when Danny caught sight of Rosie standing sideways she responded to his open astonishment with scorn.

'So, now you know,' she said. 'You did your work well at Christmas.'

'Christmas!' But it had to be Christmas. It was

495

July now and he hadn't touched Rosie since. 'You'll be almost seven months?'

'Aye, well done,' Rosie said. 'I can count to nine too, but I'll never carry the child that far, nor do I want to any more. I don't want this child. I feel nothing for it.'

Danny looked at Rosie and saw her fear and understood it. God, if the child were to die... But she'd never carried a child so far, except for Bernadette, and he began to hope. Maybe even if the doctor was right and Rosie had been poisoned by the sulphur at the munitions works, it had worked its way out of her system now.

So he said gently, 'It's part of us, Rosie. You must feel something.'

But the memory of that dreadful fear-filled night still sickened Rosie and she spat back, 'Aye I do feel something. Revulsion, not for the baby, but for the way it was conceived. There was no love there, just carnal, alcohol-riddled lust.'

She felt sorry for her harsh words when she looked at Danny and saw the guilt and shame on his face. 'Rosie, please forgive me that one lapse,' he said. 'I've never had the least desire to hurt you and I wouldn't have done so that night if I had been in my right mind. If I could turn the clock back I would. I had no idea that there had been repercussions.'

Rosie sighed. 'I know you didn't,' she said more softly, and then in an effort to get Danny to understand she went on, 'Each time I have lost a baby, I die a little and I'm frightened that this time there will be nothing of me left and that I won't want to go on anymore.'

Danny felt sickened by what he put Rosie through and he drew her gently into his arms. 'What can I do?' he asked helplessly.

'Nothing,' Rosie answered. 'That's the terrible thing, no-one can do anything.'

'She'll come around when it's born, don't fret,' Rita told Danny when he'd been driven to ask her advice.

'She won't talk to me,' Danny said. 'I know what I did on Christmas Eve hurt her and upset her; I let her down, I've admitted it and said I'm sorry time and again, but she can neither forget nor forgive.'

And Rosie couldn't. In fact she didn't think much about Danny at all. Father Chattaway said a child was a gift from God. Some bloody gift that he snatched back before they'd taken their first breath of air, she thought. And now he'd given her another gift that she had no feelings for.

And despite the reassuring words spoken to Danny, Rita and Ida were desperately worried over Rosie as one day slid into the next. Her eyes looked almost vacant and softened only when they alighted on Bernadette. 'Have you thought of any names yet?' Rita asked one day.

'Names?' Rosie repeated, her brow puckered in puzzlement. 'What names?'

'Names for the baby,' Rita snapped irritably. 'Wake up, Rosie, for God's sake.'

'I am awake, very awake, thank you,' Rosie said. 'And I have no names for this child. Don't you understand anything?'

They did understand in a way. 'I have a feeling

she isn't herself,' Ida said. 'She's sort of ill. She may get over it when the child's born.'

'She might,' Rita said. 'And yet, oh God, if the child is to die, maybe this is the only way she'll be able to deal with it.'

Danny, feeling unwelcome in his own home, spent any free time away from it, usually accompanied by his daughter. But, with the school holidays in full swing, if he took Bernadette to the park he often had half the kids in the neighbourhood tagging along too. Their mothers were only too glad to get them from under their feet and away from the dirt and grime of the yard or street, and they would pack them bread smeared with jam and bottles of cold tea to keep body and soul together and wave them off cheerfully.

Danny didn't mind. The children were company for Bernadette, and if anyone had hold of a pig's bladder for use as a ball he could have a knockabout with some of the boys. He never took an army with him when he went down the cut, though. Lots of young children and deep scummy water didn't mix in his opinion, and he always kept a tight grip of Bernadette's hand.

After the Christmas debacle he'd returned sheepishly in the New Year. 'I'd just like to say sorry,' he said to Ted. 'Made a bit of a fool of myself Christmas Eve.'

'Not at all, man,' Ted said cheerfully. 'Happens to the best of us. Mind, I bet your missus was mad. She looked fit to burst. Then, what am I talking about? If I'd gone home in a state like that, my old lady would have laid me out with a rolling pin.

''Course, funny creatures, women. My old woman can get like a raging bull over nothing at all. Or else she near drowns me with floods of tears. Mind you, the old girl's not the worst ... and she was proper cut-up about our Len.

'She'd have loved a little girl like yours, always had a hankering, and yet after Syd there was nothing. Funny thing, life, some families have half a dozen or more but we just had the two, and now with Len gone there's only Syd and you know him, never stops carping and complaining. Len, now, was a proper boatie, and Syd, I brought up the same way and yet not liking the life at all. I tell you, Danny, kids would tear the very heart out of you. Wants his head examining, young Syd, because as I said, it's a living and that's more than a lot of poor souls have these days.'

'You can say that again,' Danny said fervently. He was glad, though, that Ted didn't seem to think any the less of him for the state he'd got into on Christmas Eve, for he knew without the canal people he would be more lonely and dispirited than he was. The canal and its people was a favourite with Bernadette too, and Ted's wife Mabel in particular loved to see her.

Mabel always had a little treat for Bernadette and few enough treats came her way for Danny to complain about it and she would watch her fondly and told Danny how very lucky he was. 'God, I would have given my eye teeth for a wee girl like that,' she said one day and added, 'Funny thing, life. There's some boats chock-a-block full of children, families of eight and ten. God alone knows where some of them sleep. But me and Ted just had the two lads and now Len is dead and gone. Daughters are more attached to their homes somehow. It's what they say ain't it – "a son's a son till he gets him a wife and a daughter's a daughter for all of her life". It's true and all, that is.'

Bernadette loved Mabel. She was like a substitute grandmother. She liked best to go aboard the narrowboat and Mabel liked nothing better than showing her round, delighted at her preoccupation with how the beds and tables were hidden away and so small it was like a house for a child to play in. Not that Bernadette ever played much in there but sometimes she helped Mabel make cakes or biscuits that she'd later eat, warm from the oven.

Ted told Danny the child was a godsend. 'Poor old girl weren't right over Len when Syd took off,' he said, 'and that really shook her, being the only one left, like. She was proper down, she were, and your little'un has put the spring back in her step again, right and proper.'

Danny was glad he was pleasing someone for he hadn't a clue how to please Rosie these days. With each passing day she became more nervous and fearful and Danny knew it was those feelings that caused her to snap and lash out at him and yet it was hard to take. Had Ted but known it, the canal and the boaties, and in particular the Masons, were a godsend to Danny too.

Danny wanted to at least tell his mother about the baby, but Rosie would have none of it. He could have defied her, but he didn't dare make the situation between them any worse than it was already, and anyway, he could understand her caution.

She never discussed the subject. She knitted nothing for the coming child either, though she would buy bedraggled woollies from the rag market if she had the few coppers needed and she'd unravel them and knit a jumper for Bernadette, or sew colourful squares together to make an extra blanket for her bed in the winter. But for the baby she made no preparation.

Danny told himself not to worry. Surely it would work itself out. In the meantime, he had plenty of things to fret over. He had another assessment in two weeks' time. Each one made him nervous, for he was aware that the people behind the desk looked at him as if he'd crawled from under a stone, and that they held the survival of his family in the palm of their hands.

In their attitude too, and the way they spoke, they stripped a person of any shred of self-esteem they might have the audacity still to have. They always made the decision that they would continue to pay unemployment pay grudgingly. Danny felt ashamed and humiliated as he picked up his weekly handout from the Government. He'd be willing to do any job rather than take it, but there were no jobs to be had.

When Rosie ever let herself think of the birth of the child, she estimated it should be due in September any time from the middle onwards, and by mid-August she marvelled that this child had hung on for so long. Didn't mean it would

501

survive of course, and she wished she'd miscarried it earlier. It was only her stubborn determination that prevented her from having a faint hope of giving birth to a living child.

On Wednesday, 18th August, Rosie was alone in the house when she felt the first twinges. She wasn't alarmed at first, estimating it would take some time before she'd have to call anyone. Rita was at work, but by the time she might be needed, Ida would surely be back from Cannon Hill Park where she had taken all the kids that wanted to go. 'Your Danny has done his share of minding the nippers this holiday,' she told Rosie. 'And God knows, they'll be cooped up long enough at school soon. A bit of fresh air might do me some good as well, and it will give you a chance to put your feet up.'

'If you're sure?'

'Course I am. Where's your Danny today anyway?'

'Oh, I don't know. Off to some rally or other, for all the bloody good it will do,' Rosie said without enthusiasm. 'He comes home and tells me proudly he's walked everywhere to save the tram fare and I have to use the saved tram fare and more to have his boots soled.'

'Pity you don't get yours done at the same time,' Ida said.

'I haven't the money,' Rosie replied testily. 'Bernadette needed new boots for school, the other ones pinched her feet, and anyway they'd been cobbled so often there was nothing left of them.'

Ida said nothing. She knew few children got new boots, but Rosie thought nothing too good for her daughter. Rosie had seen enough bare-foot, ragged children about the doors, their begrimed feet blue with cold and shivering in their thin, threadbare clothes. She'd rather do without food and walk barefoot herself than bring that fate on Bernadette.

However, she had no objection to Ida taking her out and was glad her daughter was well out of the way when the griping pains became stronger. She had thought she didn't want anyone near her when her contractions started, none to notice her shame when yet another child was stillborn, yet she thought now, as she prepared the bed for herself, she'd value company.

But there was no-one about and so she went back downstairs and waited as the contractions grew stronger.

She remembered Ida telling her about the woman who lived in Upper Thomas Street who'd helped out at numerous births and she wondered now if she should fetch her, in case Ida wasn't back. She'd never spoken to her herself, though she knew the woman and knew she lived at number 59. She sank down on a chair suddenly as another pain took hold of her, clutching her stomach protectively, and felt the familiar stick-iness and saw the blood staining her bloomers.

The pain intensified quite suddenly and as one contraction followed another, Rosie moaned in agony. She knew she needed help and panic clawed at her as she struggled up to her feet intent on getting to the street and maybe sending a child for the woman.

The room spun and tilted as Rosie stood holding on to the mantelshelf. She waited anxiously for her head to stop spinning, knowing she had to get help before another pain could overwhelm her. But even as she thought this, the rush of water took her unawares, and as the next pain began she felt a blackness descend on her. She didn't feel herself falling onto the sodden rug before the range, nor the crack of her head as it smacked into the fender.

She was semi-roused from her unconscious state by the contractions and she shuddered with the pain of it and then sank back into oblivion. And that is what Rita saw as she popped in to see Rosie on her way home from work.

Rita thought at first she was dead and sprang across the room just as another contraction began. Then she saw Rosie's face grimace in pain and the trembling of her limbs and knew what was happening.

But what had rendered her unconscious? 'Rosie,' she cried, shaking her gently, and then she saw the cut on her head and the blood seeping from it onto the floor. 'Dear Almighty Christ,' she cried, sinking to her knees over the inert form. The floor and rag rug were soaking and she knew if Rosie was to get through this she needed help and fast.

She raced up the entry and looked up and down the street. A group of little boys were playing marbles in the gutter and she pulled on the sleeve of the eldest one, who was about eight. 'D'you want to earn tuppence?' The boy's eyes widened. 'Yeah, missus,' he said, thinking, who wouldn't?

'You need to go and get the doctor,' she said.

'He'll probably be at his surgery in the Lichfield Road. Doctor Patterson, you know him?'

The boy nodded. 'My ma had to have him when our Maggie, Colin and Dougie was dying of TB.'

Of course, Rita hadn't recognised the boy, but she knew him as one of the Murrays. The whole area had supported the boy's mother when she had had three of her children die of TB the previous year, and her a widow after her man had been killed at Wipers in 1915. It had been a tragedy, and yet if she didn't soon get help, Rosie might add to the death toll of the street. She said to the child, 'If he is out, ask where he is, you understand?'

He nodded.

'Tell him Rosie Walsh has need of him. Say she is having her baby and she's in trouble. Can you do that?'

''Course I can, missus.'

Rita opened her purse. She had two pennies in her hand, but she dropped them back and extracted a silver sixpence instead. The boy's eyes opened wide in disbelief as Rita pressed the coin into his hand. 'A tanner,' he breathed. He'd never had a tanner in the whole of his young life and already he was wondering whether he should buy a little treat for his mother to take the sadness from her eyes for a minute, or give the whole sixpence into her hand. But that was a decision he could make later. 'Don't you worry, missus, I'll bring the doctor,' he told Rita firmly. 'I'll find him wherever he is and make him come.'

Rita returned to Rosie. She had to get her more

comfortable and at least try and ease the rug from beneath her. But when she returned it was to see Rosie twisting her head from side to side, her face contorted in pain, though her eyes were still shut. Rita was afraid to do anything that might add to her distress. Instead, she positioned herself at her head and took one of her cold hands in hers and began to stroke it gently. 'Come on, Rosie. Hold on there. You'll be fine, the doctor will be here in a minute,' she said over and over.

Doctor Patterson was on his rounds of the back-to-back houses when he was accosted by the little boy. While everybody about knew Rosie Walsh was pregnant, they also knew she'd actually told few people and didn't want to discuss it, and could quite understand that after losing two babbies. Doctor Patterson had no idea she was even expecting. He'd had no occasion to visit the street or neighbouring courts for some months and so hadn't caught sight of Rosie, so he said to the child, 'Rosie Walsh? Are you sure that was the name?' For there were other women he knew to be near their time.

'That's what her said,' the boy stated. 'Rosie Walsh, and her said she were in trouble and needs you like and quick.'

'I'm on my way,' Doctor Patterson said.

The boy ran beside him as they hurried along, as if to assure himself the doctor would go straight to the Walshes'. The doctor wondered how far gone Rosie was this time and if she'd give birth to another dead baby. Christ Almighty, life was a bugger all right.

The husband must be an insensitive brute to

put her through this again, he thought. He barely remembered when he'd last touched his wife intimately and at times he burned with frustration, but Rosie's husband must have known what he was doing and what she would go through. The times he'd met Rosie, he'd liked and admired her.

So when he saw her laid out comatose on the saturated floor with blood still trickling from a head wound and her face contorted in pain, he thought for a moment he might have been sent for too late.

'She's in a bad way, isn't she?' Rita said after the doctor's brief examination.

He nodded. 'She needs to go to hospital,' he said. 'I'd feel happier. Don't worry, I'll go along with her. Can you stay with her a while, while I arrange it?'

'As long as you like,' Rita said.

Doctor Patterson raced up the entry to where the boy still stood. 'Can you go down to the surgery?' he said. 'Tell the woman behind the desk to telephone for an ambulance to come here. Can you do that?'

'Yeah.'

'Here's sixpence for your trouble,' Doctor Patterson said, drawing it from his pocket.

The boy, who would have walked across hot coals for half as much, thought this an easy way to make money. He supposed he was sorry Rosie Walsh was sick and all, but his mam always said not to look a gift horse in the mouth, and so he pocketed the money, hearing it jangle against the tanner already there, and began to run.

'How is she, Doctor?' Danny asked Doctor Patterson, leaping from the hard bench where he'd sat for hours supported by Rita and Ida. Doctor Patterson, who'd also hung about in the hospital for some time, heedless of the patients probably waiting for him at evening surgery, looked at Danny in distaste. Here was the brute who'd put Rosie through this. 'Your wife is very poorly indeed,' he said. 'She has had to have a caesarean section, but is now out of immediate danger, and you have a son.'

He didn't add that he didn't know how long the child would survive, for he was very small and puny-looking and the doctor didn't think much of his chances. But the baby didn't concern him as much as Rosie, and what would happen to her if this baby died as well. God, it was a hard life for some of these people.

Danny didn't understand the doctor's attitude, but then thought it mattered little how he was spoken to, it was Rosie he was concerned about and he barely registered what he'd said about the baby. 'Can I see her?' he asked.

'There is little point, she's still unconscious and will be for some time yet. Maybe you can look through the window?'

Danny thought he'd never get over the sight of Rosie lying there, so still and as white as the bandage that encircled her head. He noticed how her thinness had semi-disguised her pregnancy and now he noted her sunken cheeks and her hands so thin that even from the window he could see the prominent veins.

The nurse was at the door. 'Are you the husband?' she said to Danny.

Danny gave a brief nod. 'Aye. Will she... Will she be all right?'

'Oh yes,' the nurse said. 'She's in no immediate danger now. Do you want to see your son?'

The baby barely mattered to Danny and as he peered through the nursery window he could see little of the child anyway, swaddled as he was and laid in a cradle filled with cotton wool and with a light shining down on him for warmth.

He heard Rita and Ida both gasp. 'D'you think he's going to make it?' Rita whispered to Ida.

'I bloody well hope so,' Ida answered grimly. 'Rosie will go off her rocker altogether if she loses this nipper and all.'

'He needs to be baptised quickly,' Danny said. 'But we haven't even discussed names.'

Ida and Rita knew that. 'You choose summat then,' Ida said.

'I don't know,' Danny said. 'Rosie's been funny about this baby all the way through. I'd like her to have some say in what we call him.'

'Well, you can't ask her.'

And Danny knew he couldn't hang about, the child might not survive the night. 'I must go for the priest anyway,' he said. 'Maybe he'll think of something. Will you see to Bernadette for me?'

'Of course,' Ida said. 'Don't give it a thought. I must make my way home myself. I left Jack minding all of them and our Billy plays him up shocking sometimes.'

They took the tram together up the Victoria Road, but while the two women got off at Upper

Thomas Street, Danny stayed on to the next stop where the road crossed the Lichfield Road and it was there he ran into Doctor Patterson leaving his surgery. 'Not many in tonight,' he remarked to Danny. 'I was so late beginning evening surgery, those not in immediate danger of dying got fed up waiting and went home.'

'Is that because you stayed on at the hospital?'

'Yes, I was concerned about your wife,' the doctor said curtly. 'That head wound looked nasty and I had no idea she was pregnant again, and with her history of miscarriage and stillbirth, I was worried about her.'

'I know,' Danny said. 'She didn't want to go through it again. It ... it was my fault. Came about through me taking a drop too much at Christmas.'

The doctor looked at Danny and saw the worry etched on his face. His hair stood on end as if he had run his fingers through it in agitation and he knew that this man would rather cut off his right arm than willingly hurt his wife. It took a big man to admit he had been in the wrong so openly. 'Don't fret too much,' he said, 'though I know it's easy to say that, but what's done is done and your wife and son are in the right place now at least. These things happen.'

'It shouldn't have happened, not to Rosie,' Danny said morosely. 'I knew how she felt, she'd told me and I'd agreed. I didn't want her to go through this sort of thing again. If anything happens to the baby, I'll never forgive myself.'

'He's alive at the moment,' the doctor said. 'Cling on to that. If he survives tonight, he'll have a better chance of making it. Where are you making for now? Can I drop you anywhere?'

'No, thanks all the same,' Danny said. 'I'm going for the priest and the presbytery is just along the way here. I should like the baby baptised tonight – just in case, you know. Point is, we never discussed names – Rosie wouldn't, thought the child wouldn't survive, see?'

The doctor nodded. He could quite understand that.

'Point is,' Danny said, 'she was against using family names for all it is the custom, that's why we called our daughter Bernadette. Rosie's parents are... Let's just say they are not people I could take to and they led Rosie one hell of a life. She definitely wouldn't call a child after them and they would expect it if we'd say called our daughter Constance after my mother. Of course, that was decided when we thought we'd be biding in Ireland all our days and have a host of children with no problems. But still, she might be angry with me if she comes round and I've called the wee child Matthew after my own father.' He thought for a minute and then asked, 'What's your name, Doctor Patterson, if you don't mind me asking?'

'Not at all,' the doctor said, pleased, thinking with Susie not liking 'that kind of thing' it was the only namesake he was ever likely to have. 'I'd be honoured. My name is Anthony, Anthony Luke.'

'Anthony Luke Walsh,' Danny said, and repeated it with satisfaction. 'I like it. It sounds good. I'd like to ask Rosie if she's agreeable but we can't risk waiting any longer than we have to.'

Rosie couldn't be told or asked anything till the next day and then she showed little emotion. 'It's the doctor's names,' Danny said. 'Do you like them?'

Rosie shrugged. 'They're all right. I don't care really, I'm surprised he's still alive.'

'He's lovely, Rosie. I could take you in a wheel-chair to the nursery to see him. The nurses said I could.'

'No,' Rosie said. 'I don't want that. I told you, I feel nothing for this child.'

Danny thought that she might just be pro-tecting herself in case the child should die, but she was the same a few days later when there was cautious optimism that the child might make it. She refused to see him or hold him or feed him, and Ida and Rita weren't surprised that Danny was worried for they had all thought she would be fine once the baby was born.

'Maybe we're being too hard on her, though,' Ida told Danny. 'After all, the baby might still die. I mean, what if she really took to him like and he was to be snatched away again?'

'I do think of that,' Danny said. 'And she's probably glad she can't feed him. Doctor Patterson explained that the trauma of the birth and all dried up her milk.'

'Does she give him the bottles?'

'No, I do, or one of the nurses.'

'Well, she'll have to get over that when she comes home,' Ida said. 'She won't have an army of nurses then. She'll have to buck up her ideas.'

But Rosie didn't. She came home after ten days

and though she kissed and cuddled Bernadette and was fine with Rita and Ida, she was distant with Danny and the baby might as well not have existed. And that set the pattern, Danny found. He was the one getting up in the middle of the night when the baby cried and through the day he fed him and changed him, helped by a willing Bernadette when she was home. She, at least, was entranced by her wee brother and would do anything for him.

Danny had gone for another fifteen-week assessment the day before Rosie was due home and told them his wife had just had another baby. He received their condemnation for being so irresponsible when he had no job but they eventually agreed to continue paying his unemployment pay. However, to qualify for the money, a person had to be actively seeking work, but all thoughts of looking for a job had gone by the board because Danny had to look after the baby. He hoped some neighbour didn't think it in the nation's interest to inform the authorities of that fact. It couldn't go on and Ida agreed.

'Why don't you leave Rosie alone with the baby a bit more?' she suggested. 'Then, she'd have to see to him.'

'I can't, I daren't,' Danny said. 'The baby is too small and frail to risk that.'

To make up for Rosie's neglect, Danny spent more time with Anthony than he'd ever spent with Bernadette at the same age, rocking his son for hours or crooning to him, and Rosie, watching him, knew her fears had been realised. He had no time for his daughter now he had his precious son.

It wasn't true, Danny loved Bernadette as much as ever. But he felt sorry for Anthony for he hadn't his mother's love as Bernadette had had almost as a right.

However, he knew the situation could not go on like that, and in desperation he wrote to his mother when Anthony was just over four weeks old.

TWENTY-SEVEN

Almost every week, Rosie had written to Connie and the family and to her own parents and her sisters and Dermot. When it came to replies, though, the McMullens had to go to Connie for her to send their letters back, for, despite all pleading, she refused to give them Danny and Rosie's address.

After Anthony's birth the letters stopped, but although no one knew of the existence of the child they were still worried and both families sent letters asking if things were all right. On Wednesday, 22nd September, Dermot was posting yet another letter to Rosie before school. He was annoyed he was still at school, for in another month he'd be thirteen and by rights should have left in the summer.

However, in 1918 the Government had raised the school-leaving age to fourteen, and while Dermot didn't mind school he didn't think two years' further learning would make him better at ploughing a field or milking a cow.

It didn't help either that he looked much older than his years and could have passed for a young man of sixteen or so. Even his voice had deepened, and the slight child had grown tall and broadened out, hardened by the work on the farm, which he found he enjoyed. His face had a healthy glow to it, brought about by good food and fresh air, and while he could still be calculating when he wanted to be, the petulance of childhood had gone. He still had the blond curls, no barber had managed to tame them, but now they just made him look incredibly handsome.

Minnie and Seamus were ridiculously proud of their son, but Rosie's disappearance had hit Dermot hard and he'd begun, as he grew up, to draw closer to Chrissie and Geraldine. He knew Chrissie was courting a man called Dennis Maloney, whose family owned the grocer's in Blessington, but she hadn't told her parents, fearing they might put a stop to it, and said she'd tell them all when she was ready, if and when it became serious. So, for now, she saw her young man sometimes in her lunch hour and on Sunday afternoons when she'd go for a walk with Geraldine and Dermot so that she could meet with Dennis. Geraldine and Dermot would then go off on their own and leave the young couple to their courting.

In this way, Dermot knew a lot about Geraldine, and he began to feel sorry for his sister. While he'd been a child he'd accepted the acclaim and attention given to him without thinking much about it, but as Geraldine spoke he began to think about the things she said and see for himself how unfair it was and how brutal his mother often was with both girls.

He saw Geraldine's life especially as one of drudgery. She seldom left the farm and Minnie kept her at it from morning till night, berating her for very little and usually following the tirade with a smack or clout. But, though Dermot often felt immensely sorry for her, he knew if he was to say too much about it, it could easily rebound and make things worse.

He wrote none of this to Rosie, who he missed terribly, and asked how things were with her and Danny and wee Bernadette. He'd been as sad as anyone when he heard of the babies Rosie had lost and though he'd mentioned it to no one he'd been worried about the tone of Rosie's letters before this silence. So he wrote another letter to Rosie, begging her to let him know if anything was the matter, and decided to call in to the Walshes' on the way to school and leave it for them to post with their own.

Coming around the side of the house, he waved to the postman as he mounted his bicycle at the head of the lane. He saw through the window as he passed that Matt and Phelan were at their breakfast after milking and Connie was holding a letter in her hand, and he made for the door, which was propped open.

When Dermot heard Connie suddenly burst out, 'Dear Lord, our Rosie has had a little boy,' Dermot stopped stock-still in the doorway and no-one noticed him.

Connie went on, 'He was premature, Danny says, so he's small, but thriving for all that, born more than four weeks ago. Good God!'

Matt and Phelan stopped their forks halfway to their mouths and stared at her. 'What in God's name... Why didn't she let anyone know?' Matt demanded.

Connie knew exactly why Rosie had told no-one, for she knew she'd gone through agonies when she'd lost the other two, and her heart went out to her for carrying this secret on her own for months. She scanned down the letter further.

'That's not all,' she burst out. 'Our Danny, he's ... well, I'll read the letter out and see what you think about it.'

I'm distracted with worry over Rosie, Mammy, and that's the truth. She shows no interest in the baby at all. She cannot feed him for the birth wasn't straightforward; she'd had a fall and cut her head and was rendered unconscious, and the child had to be born by something called caesarean section. The doctor said it had upset her and her milk was dried up. But she doesn't ever give him a bottle or change him or take notice of him at all. She seems not to hear him even when he cries.

She has two good friends here, but both are widows due to the war. Rita has taken a job now her son is at school and Ida has three children of her own to see to. The care of Anthony is mainly down to me and Bernadette is more of a help than Rosie. I can't do this indefinitely for it means I can neither look for a job nor take one up if it were offered.

Anthony had to be baptised within hours of his birth and is too small and frail to be left to indifferent and inadequate care. Rosie doesn't seem to be improving at all. I am at my wits' end.

I don't know what I expect you to do, but I had to tell someone how it is. I feel so alone and isolated.

When Connie laid down the letter there were tears in her eyes. Danny had never written before – any letter-writing had been left to Rosie, like Matt had always left it to her – but this letter was written from the heart. She could almost feel the pain sparking off the page, and what in God's name should she do? Could she do?

'God,' Matt said, clearing his voice. 'It's a terrible time they're having over there altogether.'

'Aye,' Connie said with a sigh. 'And what can I do about it? There's Sarah's wedding on Saturday, and even after it... God, I can't just up and fly to Birmingham. To tell you the truth, I'd be feared to go to such a place and not sure I'd be any use if I got there.

'What I'd like this minute, or at least after the wedding, is for Phelan to fetch Rosie home. Here she would get fit and well and over what ails her, for it's obvious she isn't well just now. But Ireland is too dangerous a place for that and with Sam still hanging about with his old cronies they'd soon get word that Rosie was here. And then again, how could we leave Danny all alone in that house?'

Matt saw the problems well enough. 'Write back to him,' he advised. 'Say we're thinking of him and praying for him and when the wedding is out of the way we'll have to give the matter some thought. I hate for our son to write for help and us to do naught about it.'

'Aye,' Connie said and added, 'And let's keep the news of the baby to ourselves for a wee while, till after the wedding. I don't want people asking the questions about the baby we are not able to answer yet. Anyway, Saturday is Sarah's day. After that's over, we'll tell people.'

Dermot had heard enough. He stuffed the letter into his pocket and made for the hills.

There would be no school for him that day, he had thinking to do, and there was no space in the school day for thinking.

By the time Dermot had pounded over the Wicklow Hills for an hour or two, taking care to keep well away from any inhabited cottages where he could be quizzed as to why he wasn't at school, he had decided what he must do about Rosie. As he ate the sandwiches Minnie had given him for his dinner he'd worked out how it was to be achieved.

He headed for home earlier than he would be expected, for though he hadn't a watch he could tell by the sun, and he lay in the hills above his home and watched the house. He needed to talk to Geraldine alone and though he could see his father in the fields there was no sign of either his mother or Geraldine outside the house and so he sat and waited.

The dairy led off the kitchen, down a short passage, and there was another door next to the barn that opened onto the yard. When Dermot saw Geraldine open this door and throw water into the gutter, he knew she was probably in the dairy alone – for their mother seldom went in – and had been scalding out the churns.

For all that, he made his way down cautiously and from the back of the house where there was less likelihood of him being seen. He slipped into the barn unobserved and rubbed the window into the dairy with his sleeve before peering through it. As he'd thought, Geraldine was alone, and Dermot tapped urgently on the window.

Geraldine lifted her head at the sound and looked about her, not sure where it had come from, and Dermot knocked again. This time she saw her brother's face pressed against the glass and went out of the door and into the barn. 'What are you doing here?' she demanded. 'Why aren't you at school?'

'Listen, Geraldine,' Dermot said. 'We haven't got long.'

'Too right we haven't,' Geraldine said. 'I have a churn full of cream to turn into butter before tea-time or I'll have the head beaten off me.'

'Listen,' Dermot commanded. 'This is more important than butter,' and he told Geraldine what he'd overheard at the Walshes'.

Geraldine's mouth had dropped open at the news that their Rosie had given birth to a baby boy and said nothing to any of them. And then Dermot went on to explain how Rosie took no notice of the baby and Geraldine could scarcely believe it, remembering the wonderful mother she'd been with Bernadette and the joy she took in rearing her. 'You don't think you're exaggerating?'

'I'm telling it as it was read out in the letter,' Dermot said indignantly. 'And Danny wouldn't have written that way for fun. Anyway, keep it to yourself about the baby. I mean, tell Chrissie, but no-one else.'

'Why? It isn't a secret, surely.'

'No, it's just... I heard Connie say that she'll start telling folk after the wedding. I mean, Rosie's not right. Danny's letter was really sad and I think she needs help, they both need help, and I'm going off to give them a hand.'

'You?'

'Who else?' Dermot said. 'Could you go, or Chrissie, and would Mammy be bothered about Rosie even if I were to tell her? And Connie, I mean Mrs Walsh, is too busy just now getting Sarah's wedding ready.'

Even as Geraldine conceded that what Dermot said was true, she still said, 'You can't go either. You're just a boy and anyway, Mammy wouldn't let you.'

'Mammy isn't going to know.'

'She'll be raging, Dermot.'

'I don't care,' Dermot said defiantly. 'Rosie is more important than Mammy's bad humour.'

'Well just how d'you think it is to be achieved?' Geraldine said scornfully, thinking this was a pipe dream of Dermot's. He was not yet thirteen years old, for heaven's sake.

But Dermot went on seriously, 'That is a problem, and I've thought about it all day. The only day to go is Saturday, as far as I can see.'

'That's the day of the wedding.'

'Aye, quite,' Dermot said. 'And they'll all be at the wedding, nearly the whole village, and I can creep into the Walshes' house and hopefully find a letter or something with Rosie's address on it.'

'And if you don't?'

'If I don't, I'll find that convent in Handsworth where Connie once let slip they went first. Any would know where that was, I would imagine.'

'You really mean this, don't you?'

'Every word. And once I get the address, I'll skirt around Blessington, though they'll all be too

522

busy at the wedding to see me, and catch the tram from Cross Chapel.'

'And how d'you hope to escape Mammy's clutches?'

'I have to sit at the back of the church, don't I, because I'm one of the ushers,' Dermot said. 'So, when everyone is in it will be easy to slip out without Mammy noticing. She won't know until the Mass is over and you know how Nuptial Mass can go on and on? Afterwards is where you and Chrissie come in. You tell Mammy when she asks that I felt ill and was going for a walk to clear my head.'

'Dermot, we'll have to live with her afterwards,' Geraldine cried. 'She'll kill the pair of us.'

'She won't. Claim you know nothing of the plans. I'll back you up when I write.'

Despite herself, Geraldine was thinking that Dermot's plan could work and if he was right about Rosie someone needed to go and find out what was what. So although she was frightened of what their mother might do, she nodded her head slowly. 'All right,' she said. 'We'll do our bit and I know I speak for Chrissie too, for when she knows Rosie's news she'll be as anxious to help as I am.'

By the day of the wedding, Dermot had managed to hide a haversack with a few changes of clothes and his jacket on top in the knoll of a tree not far from the church. He would travel in the new suit and jacket his mother had been to Dublin to buy, because he knew it made him look older, and anyway, he wouldn't take the time to change.

523

Everything went according to plan. He slipped from the church as the bride began her walk down the aisle in step with music from the organ, and as all eyes were on the bride, no-one noticed him go.

Once outside he wasted no time, and, stopping only to retrieve his haversack, he made for the Walshes'. The deserted farmhouse looked odd and he slipped through the door and looked about him. Where would a person keep letters – he presumed Connie had kept them. He knew she'd missed the family and maybe would read the letters over and over as a comfort, as he did.

Perhaps they would be in one of the drawers of the press. He hated the thought of searching through people's personal things, but needs must. In the end he had no need to, for a letter was pushed behind a plate on the delph rack and he pulled it out and opened it up and found it to be the one Connie had read aloud.

As he read the letter again, it strengthened his resolve. He was doing the right thing, the only thing, and he gave a sigh as he looked at the address. It seemed a funny address altogether: *6 Back of 42 Upper Thomas Street, Aston, Birmingham 6, England.*

Dermot felt the hairs on the back of his neck stiffen in apprehension of what lay before him. But there was no time for hesitation now. He copied the address onto the piece of paper he'd put in his jacket pocket for the purpose and patted his other pocket where all the money he'd prised from his piggy bank was knotted into a handkerchief. He replaced the letter, picked up his haversack and began his journey.

There was no-one about, for most were at the wedding, and even some shops were closed as he made his way to Cross Chapel without meeting a soul.

He thanked his lucky stars the conductor on the tram was not one he knew, and he asked for a single to Terenure with no hint of nervousness, for he'd taken the journey to Dublin more than once. But in the whole of his life he'd been no further than Dublin, and he couldn't help little frissons of excitement building up inside him that were mixed a little with fear.

He had time in Dublin to look around for things to eat on the boat and train for he wasn't sailing until the evening tide. He could have enjoyed himself more, knowing the city well, if he wasn't so frightened of being discovered and so nervous of what lay ahead. He hoped Chrissie and Geraldine would keep protesting they didn't know where he'd gone, because he'd hate for his mother to arrive on top of him now and haul him home like a naughty wean, and then, at the end of it all, who would be there to help Rosie?

Dermot had never been on a boat in his life and he had to admit it looked massive in the evening light that was just turning dusky. The boat was called the *Hibernian* and had he but known it, it was the same boat Rosie and Danny had taken nearly three and a half years before.

He pressed down any feelings of apprehension and boarded the gangplank as if he'd done it every day of his life. He was not a moment too soon, for just minutes after being aboard, the hooters suddenly screeched and black smoke billowed from the funnels as the engines throbbed into life. Dermot watched the lights of the harbour and the town twinkling through the gloom and he breathed a sigh that was relief mixed with trepidation, but he did know that once an expanse of water was between him and his home in Wicklow, he'd feel safer. He stayed on deck, watching the boat churn through the foaming water, till the darkness and the cold drove him into the saloon bar where he opened the food he'd bought in Dublin. But he left some for the train, for he knew that that too would be a long journey.

There was a train in the station to meet the boat and Dermot was glad of it, for he was starting to feel weary. He couldn't sleep deeply, though, for he knew he had to change trains at a place called Crewe; the man who'd clipped his ticket told him, so he'd have to keep his wits about him, and as it was now black night it was all rather unnerving.

He dozed fitfully and found himself jerked awake at each station and would peer through the dense darkness to find out the name. One of the carriage occupants, seeing his preoccupation with this said, 'Where you bound for?'

'Birmingham,' Dermot answered. 'I have to change at a place called Crewe, I believe?'

'Most people change there,' the man said. 'And it's a big place, you can't miss it.' And then he added, 'No need to ask where you've come from.'

'No,' Dermot said, and because there was

surely no harm in telling this man, this stranger, he said, 'I come from County Wicklow and I'm going to my sister's place in Birmingham.'

'Holiday?'

'Sort of.'

'You'll find it a sight different from Ireland.'

'I will, surely,' Dermot said. 'But that's the beauty of it. There's no point in going to a place just the same as your own.'

The man laughed. 'You're right there,' he said. 'How old are you?'

Dermot was prepared for this question and knew that for him to state his real age would be madness, and so he said, 'I'm fourteen and I'll be fifteen next month.'

'Now I'd have put you older,' the man said, and Dermot gave a secret smile of triumph, for the man hadn't doubted him in the slightest, and they chatted together amicably until they parted company at Crewe.

Crewe was a big place, bigger than Dermot had ever seen, and it was also confusing and nerve-racking, especially for someone who'd never left his native land before. A railway official helped Dermot find the right train for Birmingham and he reached New Street Station at nearly half past four in the morning, for the station clock showed the time.

He climbed stiffly from the train aching with tiredness and marvelling at the size of the trains and the station and the crowds of people, and feeling a little lost. He was also very hungry, but he'd finished all he had brought and so he sat down on a bench and tried to ignore the pangs of hunger gnawing at his stomach. He watched the station grow quiet after the train had left and the passengers dispersed and wondered what to do next.

He could see that it was dark as pitch outside, and he had no desire to traipse around an alien city at such an hour looking for lodgings, nor could he try and find his way to Rosie's, and anyway, he was too tired. He lay down on the bench and, despite the chilly wind funnelling through the station, decided to try and sleep for an hour or two. Using his haversack as a pillow, he closed his eyes.

When Minnie first missed Dermot outside the church, Geraldine had told her, as planned, that Dermot had been taken ill and had gone for a walk. The distracted Minnie would then do nothing but go home and see if he'd returned there.

There was, of course, no sign of him, and eventually Seamus prevailed on her to go to the reception at Conlan's Hotel in Blessington and she'd gone, feeling sure if Dermot wasn't there already he'd turn up in due course. But there was no sign of Dermot, and by the end of the meal, worry had begun to eat at Minnie. Her fear was that Dermot lay injured somewhere amongst the Wicklow Hills, and Seamus led a search party to look for him.

Chrissie and Geraldine watched these proceedings with trepidation, knowing that their mother's worry would turn in the end to anger, and the more she fretted, the greater would be her fury. As darkness rendered the search useless, Minnie informed the Guard and even in front of him, Chrissie and Geraldine still stuck to their story. The Guard, however, knowing the nature of young boys, asked if anything was missing.

That had given Minnie a jolt and she'd checked his room and found his haversack, jacket and numerous other clothes to be gone. The Guard then took a different view of it. He told Minnie the boy had gone off on some adventure of his own and would probably come back of his own accord, and so not to fret. 'Boys will be boys,' he said, and he wouldn't be at all surprised if he didn't just turn up in the morning as if nothing had happened.

But Minnie knew he wouldn't, for suddenly in a flash, she knew where he'd gone. At the wedding reception Connie had told her about Rosie and the premature baby and the letter Danny had sent. 'I'm not broadcasting it to the town until after the wedding,' she'd said. 'But you have a right to know as Rosie's mother and grandmother to the wee boy.'

Minnie somehow knew that Dermot had discovered the letter Danny had sent, and he'd gone running to Rosie as he used to do when he was small. She was even more certain of this when she found the piggy bank, that had been stuffed with money, to be empty. She knew too the girls must have been fully aware of where he'd gone. It didn't matter how much they protested ignorance of Dermot's intentions, Minnie's anger had to have some outlet.

She'd used the strap on her daughters before,

many times, but never with the intensity she wielded it that day. At first she fell upon the pair of them like a wild animal, kicking and punching them before lashing into them with the strap until their screams brought Seamus running from the fields where he was checking the stock before turning in.

'For God's sake, woman,' he cried, pulling his wife away and holding her arms. 'Enough is enough. What's done is done and nothing will be gained by this carry-on.'

Minnie's eyes were wild, her face was brick-red and her hair had sprung from the grips holding it in place. Strands of it hung about her face and she was out of breath and panting heavily. She appealed to Seamus. 'He's gone to Rosie, our Dermot. That's where he always used to go whenever he was missing.'

'He doesn't know her address.'

'How do we know that?' Minnie said. 'Connie may have given it to him. Anyway,' she went on, as Seamus shook his head, 'however and wherever he got it, that's what he's done. I know it, and I also know he wouldn't have been able to do it alone. These,' she said, indicating her cowering daughters, 'knew all about it. They must have known.'

Seamus regarded his daughters, no longer screaming but holding one another while they sobbed. He took in their bruised faces and the marks across their arms and their backs, where the strap had ripped into their smart wedding clothes, shredding them into strips, and he said to Minnie, 'If you're right and Dermot is away to

530

Rosie we shall hear soon enough and nothing is to be gained by beating the girls. There is to be no more of it and let us hope you haven't alerted half the county. Come away to the fire now.' And to his daughters he said curtly, 'If you had any knowledge of what Dermot was up to you have only yourselves to blame for your mother's chastisement. Get to bed now, the pair of you.'

Trembling with shock and distress, the girls were quick to do as their father bid. The tears still flowed and they silently helped one another where the clothes were stuck to their backs. The weals from the strap still bled and they lay on their stomachs, their backs being too sore, and eventually Chrissie rubbed at her eyes with the sleeve of her nightgown and whispered fiercely, 'I hate her!'

'Ssh.'

'I don't want to ssh,' Chrissie said. 'I hate her I tell you.'

'I know,' Geraldine whispered. 'And so do I.'

'She'll not lay a hand on me again,' Chrissie said. 'That I know, for I'll give her the same back.'

'Chrissie!' Geraldine said, shocked that Chrissie should talk of raising her hand to their mother.

'I will,' Chrissie maintained. 'I will. If we'd joined forces today she'd never have managed the two of us.'

Geraldine acknowledged this was true and that surely her mother hadn't the right to do what she had done. Every bit of her ached or throbbed, but what was the point of talking about it all now. Weariness suddenly caused her to yawn and she said, 'Let's try to sleep now. Things may look better in the morning, they often do.'

Chrissie shook her head. She'd never feel differently about this business, but she heard the tiredness in Geraldine's voice and gave her arm a little squeeze. 'All right.' And as Dermot landed on the shores of Holyhead, his sisters eventually slept fitfully.

Dermot was woken by an early morning train pulling into the station in a cloud of steam, with singing rails and the squeal of brakes. For a second or two he was disorientated, wondering where he was, and then he rolled off the bench thankfully enough for it was hard and knobbly and he was suddenly so cold his teeth chattered.

He was also wondering if he'd done the wrong thing, for although he looked older than his years he wasn't quite thirteen and he suddenly felt unequal to the task before him. Why and how did he think he was the one to help Rosie? Wouldn't one of the girls have been better?

Impetus had carried him so far, leaving little time to think, but no-one knew what was wrong with Rosie, so he didn't even know what he would be facing. He also wondered at the financial state of the family. Danny had no job, for if he had Rosie would have told them in her letters home. Wouldn't it add to their financial burden if he landed on their doorstep?

He had money with him for now. His parents had given him plenty each week, since almost the day of his birth, and he'd happily share that but it wouldn't last forever.

However he decided, he couldn't just give up and go home without even seeing Rosie after coming that far, and so he left the station and went out into the streets, quiet because it was Sunday so there wasn't one person around to ask for directions. He didn't quite know what to do, but he acknowledged that there was nothing to be gained by standing about and he decided to walk around a bit and see if he could find someone to ask how a person could get to this place called Aston.

Although used to Dublin, Dermot was amazed at the array of shops Birmingham had to offer, fine buildings too. He wandered through the city streets and didn't see a soul and he thanked his lucky stars it was at least dry and fine.

Eventually, he came to a road called Colmore Row and in the distance he could see the spire of a church, and he made for it, knowing that while Sunday was a quiet day for shoppers it was often a busy one for the churches.

It was a pleasant church called St Phillip's and set in a garden of sorts, where lawns were interwoven with paths. It was nice, Dermot thought, to find that little oasis of green in the city centre.

As he approached the church, a handful of people came out of the door from the early Holy Communion Service, the first people Dermot had seen, and he approached them with the address held in his hand.

'Well,' said the first man he asked. 'There are many trams to Aston, but as you are here now you'd best get to Steel House Lane and get on there.'

'Steel House Lane?' Dermot repeated.

'It's aptly named,' the man said. 'For the police station is there. I can tell from your accent you're not from these parts.'

'No, I'm over here to see my sister,' Dermot said. 'She's been ill and I didn't tell her I was coming. It's meant to be a surprise.'

'I trust a pleasant one?' the man said with a smile and Dermot smiled too. 'I hope so.'

The man's directions were easy to follow and Dermot went on down Colmore Row, passing Snow Hill Station on the opposite side and a large Picture House. Like Rosie he had a longing to see the moving pictures inside one of those places. He could only imagine it, but he didn't linger and strode on. Just as the man said, the police station was on one side of the road and the workhouse on the other. It had a plaque outside saying it was the General Hospital, but it was easy to see what it had originally been built for and, Dermot thought, was very like the work-house in Dublin that his mother had pointed out one time.

Outside it, though, were the tram stops, and the man said he could catch any tram for they all ran through Aston. Dermot then had quite a wait because it was Sunday service, and when he alighted from the tram at Aston Cross, as the conductor had advised, the big green clock showed him it was turned half past seven.

He looked around. The tram had continued along a main road, past the Ansell's Brewery and behind that was a large tower with HP Sauce written on it in big letters. There were streets and streets of houses, and like his sister Rosie he'd been shocked by them for in all his life he'd never seen the like of them. He'd been brought up on a spacious farm and even his trips to Dublin had been confined to the shopping areas. This was his first introduction to a city's back-to-back housing and he wasn't impressed by it one bit.

Nothing had prepared him for what he saw as he walked up Upper Thomas Street. Even that fine September morning the houses were so grim and dismal he couldn't imagine anyone living in them. And yet it was obvious they did. Rosie did for a start, and that fact depressed him totally. He wandered up the road in a sort of daze. He found Aston Park at the top of the road and was absurdly pleased about that, and he went through the open gates, needing a little time to himself before he had the courage to call on Rosie.

TWENTY-EIGHT

Although Dermot found 42 Upper Thomas Street with no trouble, he had no idea what '6 the back of 42' even meant. In fact, the whole place unnerved him. He wondered where the children played, for there was no space that he could see and it bothered him that Rosie was living amongst such grey drabness.

Eventually he asked a little boy playing with dust piles in the gutter where '6 the back of 42' was. 'Down the entry, mister,' the boy said, pointing into the darkness with a jerk of his thumb, and Dermot walked down the cobbles of the entry to the yard beyond, where he stood looking about him in horrified disbelief, much as Rosie had on her first visit.

Then he collected his wits about him. He'd come to help Rosie, not judge the place she lived in, and he approached number six and lifted the knocker.

Rosie had just finished removing the last of the rags from Bernadette's hair and was brushing it into beautiful golden ringlets, and Danny had gone up to fetch the baby, who'd just woken, when the knock came at the door. 'Who on earth can that be?' Rosie said to Bernadette. 'Knocking on the door and at this hour on a Sunday morning.' She moved her daughter away as she spoke, got to her feet, crossed the room and opened the door.

Three and a half years before, when Rosie left Ireland, Dermot had been a wee boy. Now she saw a young man and a well-dressed one too, for she could see the white shirt and tie beneath his thigh-length and well-cut coat. His trousers were navy pin-stripe with turn-ups and his shoes shiny black leather. And so she said questioningly, 'Dermot?' She could hardly believe it, and anyway, what would her young brother be doing here?

'Do you not know me?' Dermot said with a laugh, and even that was strange for Dermot had the voice of a man.

But man or boy, Rosie was overjoyed to see him. She led him inside eagerly and put her arms around him, realising in that moment how much she'd missed them all back home. Her head was teeming with questions, but they would be answered in time. For now it was enough to hold Dermot tight, though she could have wept for the lost years when this boy had grown to the edge of manhood without her.

At that moment Danny stepped through the door with the baby in his arms, and Bernadette, shy of the man she had no recollection of who was hugging her mammy, crossed to her father's side. Danny, though, had eyes only for the boy, who he had recognised immediately, and he wondered if his appearance had anything to do with the letter he'd sent. He approached Dermot with his one free arm outstretched. 'Dermot? Where the hell have you sprung from?'

Dermot broke away from the embrace to shake Danny's hand, but he didn't mention the letter.

He had an idea Danny wouldn't like him to and that it had probably been written without Rosie's knowledge, so he just said, 'I came over to see how you were doing. We'd heard nothing for weeks and were concerned.'

And then he looked at the baby. He was very small and he remembered that the letter had said he was premature. Danny put him over his shoulder as he began to howl again.

Bernadette put her hands over her ears. 'He's always doing that,' she said.

'So would you, miss, if you hadn't had your breakfast,' Rosie said, and then she said to Dermot, 'Take off your coat or you'll not feel the benefit when you go out.'

When Dermot removed his coat, Rosie just looked at him, for the suit he wore was the smartest she'd ever seen. 'God, Dermot, you look the business and about twenty years old.'

'It was Sarah's wedding yesterday.'

'Of course.' Rosie should have known. It was all Connie had talked about for weeks. If she'd been writing her weekly letter she'd have been well aware of it.

'Well, it's a grand suit all right,' Danny said. 'You'll be almost too well-dressed for Mass. Did the wedding go off all right?'

'I don't know. I wasn't there.'

'Wasn't there. But...?'

'I was supposed to be there. I was one of the ushers, but I was so worried when we hadn't heard from you. We all were. I knew when they were all at the wedding it would be my chance to slip away unnoticed. It was also my one chance to go into the Walshes' place and get your address, for your mammy wouldn't give me as much as a sniff of it, Danny. How did you think I found out where you lived?'

'I assumed Connie gave it to you.'

'Well, she didn't,' Dermot said. 'She wouldn't, and Birmingham is a big place to search for a body without a clue or two.'

Dermot looked at his sister now. He'd been shocked by her pasty face and the extreme thinness; he'd felt her bones as he'd held her. But it was her sorrow-filled eyes that troubled him most.

As Danny sat at the table to feed the baby, Dermot moved beside Rosie before the range and said, 'Why did you tell no-one of the baby, Rosie?'

Rosie stared at him. 'You know everything and you have to ask that question?' she said. 'You know of the first baby I lost, after carrying for nearly six months; that all our family in Ireland were awaiting the birth of it, praying for it, longing for it as much as we were. When I miscarried, the doctor said it was one of those things, and Father Chattaway said I had to accept the will of God and please God there'd be another child in due course.

'I packed away the baby things of Bernadette's that I had washed in preparation and the few garments I'd knitted, and returned the cradle Danny had fashioned from orange boxes to the top of the cupboard in the attic. I wrote letters telling everyone the sad news and received letters of condolence in reply.'

539

Dermot was silent, everyone was silent, even the baby had stopped sucking, and Dermot had the feeling he was listening to the outpouring of Rosie's very soul. He saw she was unaware of the tears trailing over her cheeks as she swallowed and went on. 'But life goes on. I got over my tragedy and in time, just as Danny was forced to enlist, I became pregnant again. This time those in Ireland went to town; there were Masses said, candles lit, novenas undertaken, the rosary said. I felt surrounded by the Catholic Church and I felt sure God would not punish me in such a way again.

'But on the morning after peace was declared, hostilities at an end, a day of jubilation and happiness, I began to lose my baby. Danny was still overseas and I coped alone and thanked God for my neighbours who helped me and sustained me and wrote to Ireland after it was over, when I was unable to.

'And then I found out that the munitions factory I'd worked in when I first came to England might be the cause. The sulphur could have got into my bloodstream and would probably poison any child I carried. The doctor was doing a study on the history of stillbirths and miscarriages in women who worked in such places, and also those who couldn't become pregnant at all, and I knew then, the deaths of those two wee babies could be laid at my door.'

Rosie gave a gulp at this point and more tears ran from her eyes, which she'd closed, as if in pain, while she bit agitatedly on her bottom lip. 'It wasn't your fault, Rosie,' Danny cried. 'I've told you over and over.'

He crossed the room and passed his son to Dermot without a word and took his wife in his arms. She didn't push him away but continued to talk, her words muffled now by Danny's arms, but Dermot caught them. 'I didn't want to try for any more children after that. What was the point, I thought, when I can't carry them, and, oh God, I nearly died from the pain each time. Anthony was the child I should never have had.

'I refused to believe I was pregnant at first, and each week, each day, I expected my baby to lose his tenuous hold on life. I waited to miscarry. I couldn't afford to let myself care. Even when the baby was born he was a month premature and hastily christened before I'd even recovered from the operation I had to have to give birth to him at all. His life hung in the balance for days. Don't you see how it was?'

'Of course I see,' Dermot said. 'And I see how you suffered when you lost the other babies, Rosie. It's written all over your face. But when you had the child you thought you'd never carry and he's here and alive and thriving, aren't you delighted so? Isn't it a sort of consolation?'

Rosie looked at her young brother and knew he loved her and admired her and found she couldn't tell him how she resented the baby and everything his father did for him. She told herself Danny cared for him far more than Bernadette, for he'd never taken so much notice of her when she was so small. A small but insistent voice continued to remind her that there was no need for Danny to do such things for Bernadette, for

541

Rosie had done them, and if ever Rosie couldn't there had been a host of relations ready and willing to take her place. She pressed these words down. She couldn't deal with that, for she needed the resentment to fester inside her, lest she start to feel anything for the wee mite she had given birth to. How could she say that to a young boy, and Dermot for all his size *was* a young boy, and expect him to understand something she found hard to comprehend herself? How could she take his condemnation if she was to admit this to him. No, she couldn't risk that.

So she parried. 'We haven't time to go into this all now, Dermot.'

'Time enough,' Danny said, taking his son back. 'This young man is not halfway through his breakfast yet.'

Rosie's eyes narrowed. She wouldn't play Danny's games. She wasn't ready to be harassed in this way and Danny should know that.

She turned to Dermot. 'Okay, Dermot, since there's time to talk, have you thought what will happen to the girls when Mammy finds you gone?'

'They are to say they knew nothing about it.'

'Come on, Dermot, you're not a wee boy any more. You know what Mammy is capable of and you know she'll never believe they knew nothing.' Rosie had suffered for years at the hands of her mother and knew the kind of thing her sisters would be subjected to.

Dermot knew too, but he didn't want to face it. 'They're to swear it. I said I'd write a letter claiming the idea was mine as soon as ever I could and say I'd told them not a word.'

'D'you think that will help any?' Rosie cried. 'Haven't you realised yet that our mother thinks the sun shines out of your bleeding arse, but she hasn't a morsel of feeling for the rest of us?'

Bernadette's eyes opened wide with shock. Bleeding and arse were bad words and her mammy had said she'd smack her legs if she heard her saying them. She was going to remind her mammy of it, but one look at her angry face convinced her it would be better to say nothing just at that moment.

'The fact that you disappeared without a word is bad enough, Dermot,' Rosie said. 'But when she realises you are here... God, Dermot, she'd kill the girls stone dead.'

Dermot digested all Rosie said and knew she was right. He knew his mother wouldn't take his flight to England in a controlled and rational manner. It wasn't her style. His sisters hadn't believed that either, though they'd gone along with it to please him, and he knew his sisters' trepidation and nervousness would betray their guilt. 'I'll write the letter today, directly we're home from Mass,' Dermot said. 'I'll make her see it was my idea and only mine.'

Rosie said nothing, for really there was nothing further she could say.

True to his word, Dermot wrote the letter to his mother, shouldering the entire blame, and another to Connie in which he admitted overhearing her reading the letter and the anxiety resulting from it that caused him to steal away on the day of Sarah's wedding. He also told of entering the empty house to find the address.

He told Connie and his sisters of other more positive things too: the charm and beauty of Bernadette, now a schoolgirl, and of the baby, so small and frail still, despite being almost six weeks old, and the warm welcome he'd received from Danny and Rosie who had been delighted to see him.

He never mentioned the concerns he had, like the way it was Danny not Rosie who carried Anthony to Mass, wrapped in a shawl, and that Danny took him outside when he became fractious, and Danny who amused the baby while Rosie made them all porridge for breakfast. It was thin porridge, made with water with no sugar or creamy milk to mix with it. 'Bernadette is the only one who gets sugar,' Rosie told Dermot when he asked. 'We take salt.'

Bernadette, not being Communion age yet, had already been given a slice of bread and dripping before Mass, but now she had porridge with everyone else on their return, but hers was sprinkled with one small teaspoon of sugar.

The porridge did nothing to fill Dermot but he didn't complain, knowing that they could probably afford no more, and resolved to go out the following morning and use his money to buy some decent food and give them a wee bit of a treat for once.

He went to bed after he'd written the letters, wearied by the journey and lack of sleep he'd had. But as he lay on the shakedown in the attic he was disturbed by the crush of people and noise all around him: the raucous voices of gossiping women and the deeper ones of the men; the clatter of boots and the screaming laughter of children, a baby crying, the odd bark of a dog, or yowl of a cat, all overridden by the clanking of the trams and rumble of the automobiles going along the Lichfield Road.

He fell to thinking about Rosie. He remembered how sad he'd felt when he read about the stillbirth and miscarriage. Her sisters had cried and Connie's eyes had been red-rimmed when he'd taken around their cards and letters to send. Even Danny's daddy and Phelan had been sad. How much worse had it been for Rosie?

And he understood why she'd told no-one this time. And the way she was with the baby now, wasn't that a habit she'd got into because she thought Anthony would go the way of the others? What had she said? She couldn't afford to care. And then, against all the odds, the baby is born but too soon, small and puny, and Rosie would still be afraid to let down her guard, to begin to love and cherish a baby she might yet lose.

Now she'd got into the habit of ignoring Anthony because she'd had months of doing just that. Somehow she had to break that cycle, to open her heart to love Anthony as she loved Bernadette. But how was that to be achieved?

He suddenly wished he had his sisters here. Maybe they could talk to Rosie a little better than he could. It wasn't something he could write in a letter, for all that would do would be to worry them further, and for nothing. They couldn't help from where they were.

Chrissie and Geraldine could have told Dermot that they had troubles enough of their own. The morning after their beatings, their faces were too battered and their backs too sore to risk being seen and they didn't attend Mass that morning.

Dennis Maloney usually snatched a word with Chrissie after Mass, unbeknownst to her parents, and often made arrangements for the afternoon. But when she wasn't there that morning, but her parents were, he wasn't suspicious. He thought maybe after the wedding the previous day the family might have overslept and the girls were kept back to finish any jobs which needed to be done and would be at the Mass at eleven. He knew Dermot intended to go and see the sister that Chrissie too had been concerned about, for Chrissie had told him, but he didn't connect that with the girls not turning up for the children's Mass at nine o'clock.

At twelve, he was once more outside the church, watching the parishioners all come out of Mass, and when neither girl was there he was puzzled and worried. He regretted he hadn't spoken to her parents earlier and he decided to go to the house and see for himself.

He scanned the farm as he approached and was glad that the fields were empty. He guessed the father was at dinner. He wondered if Dermot had made the dash to England, where their sister Rosie was. 'It's a long jaunt for such a young boy,' he'd said to Chrissie. 'It's likely just talk and he'll bottle out on the day itself.'

'Not Dermot,' Chrissie had said, 'And especially

not if it concerns Rosie. He usually carries out a thing if he's decided upon it, and he loves Rosie more than anyone.'

'More even than the mother who dotes on him?'

'Oh yes. Especially more than her.'

Dennis thought of this now as the farmhouse drew near. If the boy had done as he said, what had transpired after it? Chrissie, he imagined, would have a tale and a half to tell him, if she was well enough that was.

He wondered if they were all eating dinner together. If so he'd have to wait to catch sight of one of them coming out of doors for something. But then he reminded himself that if they were too ill to go to Mass they could still be in bed. It suddenly occurred to him that the girls could have been hungover, for neither girl was used to strong drink and he imagined much would have been flowing at the wedding, and he decided to take a look through the bedroom window.

What he saw nearly stopped the blood in his veins. Chrissie, her back to the window, was kneeling up in the bed applying something from a white dish to her sister, who lay on her stomach on the bed beside her. Chrissie was bare and he saw the blood-encrusted weals around her back and knew what had kept her away from Mass. He also knew that she was probably applying goose grease to her sister and she'd already had the same treatment, for her back was glistening with it.

His anger was like a white-hot rage coursing through him and without a thought for the girls' nakedness he tapped lightly on the window.

Chrissie's head flew around and he saw a couple of weals on the breasts her long brown hair almost covered. Then, when he looked into her face, with her discoloured eye, grazed cheek and split lip, he was almost speechless. Chrissie went across to the window, stopping only to take a shawl from the bedstead to cover herself.

'Who did this to you?' he demanded in an icy hiss as Chrissie opened the window. 'Your father?'

God, he'd drag the man from the house and trounce him, Dennis thought. He'd bounce him off the cobblestones and not give a tinker's cuss about the man's age at all. But he was staggered when Chrissie said, 'No, my father laid no hand on us. It was my mother.'

Dennis's mouth dropped open in shock. 'Has she done this before?'

'Aye,' Chrissie said. 'But never this bad. It was about Dermot this time. She didn't believe we knew nothing about his running away. She's clean mad where that lad's concerned.'

'She'll not touch a hair of your head ever again,' Dennis promised. 'How well can you walk?'

'At this moment I feel I could walk to the end of the earth to get away from that woman,' Chrissie said. 'Don't you?'

Geraldine was too surprised at the turn of events to speak, but she nodded her head vigorously enough.

'That's all right,' Dennis said soothingly. 'I intended taking the two of you, anyway, but walking might be too difficult. I'm away for the pony and trap. You two pack up all you can and I'll be back for you.'

'She'll never agree.'

'I'm not going to ask permission.'

'She'll not let you.'

'She'll have no choice.'

'And where will you take us?'

'To my sister's, and you will bide there while the banns are read for our wedding, and then we'll live above the grocery shop and your sister can live with us if she'd like to.'

'Banns read?' Chrissie repeated, and attempting jocularity she said, 'Do I take it you are proposing marriage, Mr Maloney?'

'Aye, that's right, Miss McMullen.'

'Well,' Chrissie said. 'I won't say it's the most romantic proposal I've ever received, not that I'm an expert on these sort of things you understand, but it is accepted nevertheless.'

'I'm away.' Dennis kissed Chrissie's lips lightly and then said, 'I'll be back directly.'

Geraldine was inclined to be disbelieving of Dennis's claims. 'Mammy will stop him,' she said.

'He says not.'

'Not for you,' Geraldine cried. 'You are over twenty-one, but I'm only nineteen. She'll never let me go, you'll see.'

And that was the argument Minnie tried to use. She had no idea Chrissie had been seeing anyone and Chrissie often wondered afterwards why no-one had told the McMullens. Although they'd been careful, some person surely had seen them clasping hands as they strode across the hills.

Maybe people had felt sorry for her, sorry for all the girls. But for whatever reason, no-one had mentioned a word to Minnie, and so it was a complete surprise when a pony and trap galloped down the lane at breathtaking speed and then hauled to a stop before their cottage door.

Seamus had gone to the door and opened it to see the commotion, and he was nearly knocked on his back by the man who burst past him after almost throwing himself out of the trap. They knew him of course, the whole family knew the Maloneys. Didn't they leave money in their shop every week? But neither Seamus nor Minnie had seen Dennis like this. 'What's the meaning of this?' Seamus demanded angrily. 'Nearly knocked over on my own threshold. What's got into you at all, Dennis?'

Dennis was a tall, broad-shouldered young man and now the fury, still coursing through him, made him seem to swell to look even more menacing. His face was brick-red and shiny with sweat and he felt the hairs on the back of his neck stand up as he faced Seamus and said, 'Knocked over, you say? Think yourself lucky you're not spread-eagled on the cobblestones this minute with your face bashed in with my own fists.'

'What talk is this?' Minnie demanded.

'No talk!' Dennis snapped. 'The time for talking was past when you lifted your hand to two young girls, to punch them and slap them and strike at them with a strap till their backs were covered with weals.'

Minnie was shaken and for a moment or two was silent, wondering how Dennis knew this. But then she flew at him. 'If I have reason to chastise my daughters, may I ask what concern it is of yours?' she asked icily.

'Chastise, is it?' Dennis asked sarcastically. 'Is that the name they have on it these days? Ah then, it's sorry I am. I was under the impression it was a brutal beating you gave them.'

'You don't know the reason,' Minnie spluttered. 'They lied to me. It was not to be borne. I...'

'That's true indeed,' Dennis said, nodding his head as if in a conciliatory way, though he longed to send Minnie's teeth down her throat. 'You can't have two daughters living in the house lying to you.'

'I'm glad you see that,' Minnie said, but cautiously for there was something in the air she didn't understand and surely the man had given in too easily.

Seamus didn't understand either, but he considered everything had now gone far enough and he wanted to get this threatening young man out of his house and quick. 'So,' he said, opening the door wide. 'If that little matter has been cleared up.'

The change was rapid. Gone was any resemblance to the man they knew. The kick he aimed at the cottage door tore it out of Seamus's grasp and shut it with a resounding crash. 'Now,' Dennis said. 'I want you to listen well to what I am going to say to you. I have been courting Chrissie for about six months and we are to be married.'

He watched in satisfaction as the blood drained from Minnie's face and Seamus's mouth dropped open in astonishment. 'She can't,' Minnie said. 'She's not asked.'

'She has no need to ask,' Dennis said. 'She is over twenty-one. She has little respect for you, and no wonder from what I've heard over the years and seen earlier today with my own eyes. There's only one important child in this house, and that is the boy that's apparently gone walkabout.'

'You don't know the whole of it. He'll have gone to Rosie. He was always running to Rosie.'

'And why should that worry you?' Dennis said. 'Isn't Rosie his sister? What harm will he come to if he is there? Good God, woman, look around you at the state the country is in. Many a mother would be glad their son went to a family member rather than for them to run away to join the IRA as so many are doing. We've heard the mothers crying about it in the shop a time or two.'

'That wouldn't involve Dermot. He is but a child,' Minnie said dismissively.

'He's not,' Dennis said. 'A few years ago he'd be working by now and he's right to care about his sisters. He was wrong not to ask you, but you'd never have agreed for him to go if you'd known. But whatever Dermot did or didn't do, it cannot reflect on either Chrissie or Geraldine and your treatment of them was inhuman. It's only the fact that you are a woman that is saving you from me giving you a taste of your own medicine.'

'Don't you dare threaten my wife,' Seamus said, stepping in front of Minnie.

'Who'll stop me – you?' Dennis said contemptuously and he gave Seamus a push that sent him

552

reeling into the dresser.

'Now,' he said, turning again to Minnie. 'I am taking Chrissie away from here.'

'You are not!'

'Oh yes I am,' Dennis said. 'As I said, Chrissie is twenty-one and can do as she pleases and will be delighted to leave this place. She has agreed to become my wife and will lodge with my sister in Blessington until the wedding might be arranged. Everything is in order and Geraldine too will be coming with us.'

'Oh no she's not. She is just nineteen,' Minnie said. 'I can stop you. You try that and I'll have the authorities on you.'

'Oh, would you indeed?' Dennis said. 'Let's have them here now, shall we? The Guards will do to start with. We'll bring them out and let them see the mess you made of the girls' backs. You might find yourself at the centre of a cruelty charge.'

'Don't be stupid,' Minnie cried. 'I am their mother and can do with them as I see fit.'

'I don't think so,' Dennis said. 'Others might take a very different view of the matter altogether. I am leaving here with those two girls and I'll just promise you this: You try and stop me and I will spread the news abroad of what you have done. You will be unable to hold your head up in the village and will certainly have to find yourself another grocery store.'

Minnie's legs began to shake and she felt for the kitchen chair and sat on it and willed her legs to stop trembling. She glared at Dennis but his own eyes staring back did not flicker and she

553

realised she had met a formidable adversary. This was a man who would get what he wanted and he wanted her daughter Chrissie.

Well, Minnie decided, he could have her and welcome. From a child, Chrissie had been troublesome and never as compliant as Rosie or Geraldine, and she'd had to chastise her many a time. This time she wasn't sorry she'd hit the girls, but she'd be sorry if anyone had to know about it. It would never do. Their standing in the community would be gone for good.

Pity about Geraldine. She thought she'd have her help for years yet and she always did what she was told, for she was too frightened to go against her. Still, she doubted that even if she attempted to stop Dennis leaving with her, the girl would stay. Should she trail after them it would cause more of a scandal.

Eventually, she had to look away from Dennis's steel-grey eyes. 'If you… If I let you take the girls, you will keep it to yourself about the beating and all?'

'You have my word,' Dennis said. 'But I wasn't the one beaten. I can't answer for your daughters.'

'They'll do as you tell them.'

'They will do as they see fit,' Dennis said. 'I have no intention of telling them what to say, and how, and to whom. They are people in their own right.'

But he was to find Chrissie and Geraldine just wanted to leave the farm and for good. They had no intention of reliving their ordeal by talking about it. Dennis found both girls cowering behind the door when he entered the bedroom.

'Away out of that,' he chided gently. 'The time for hiding in corners is past. Come on, a new life is to begin for you both. Hold your heads high and go out to meet it.'

Both girls knew then their torment was over and that with Dennis's protection they would leave unmolested. He picked up the bass hampers they had packed and they walked behind him out of the room, passing their parents without a word. Out in the yard, Dennis helped each one into the trap before leaping up beside them.

'Good day to you,' Dennis said, with a jerk of his head to Seamus and Minnie.

They didn't reply and the girls made no attempt to speak at all. Dennis flicked the reins over the horse's head and he turned and clattered up the drive. Chrissie and Geraldine never looked back. They were on the open road and about a mile from the farmhouse before they felt they could relax and drop their shoulders and smile at each other. 'We're free,' Geraldine said. 'Oh God, I can scarce believe it.'

'Nor I,' Chrissie said, and she hugged her sister in delight and Dennis laughed at the two of them and knew he'd made the right decision that day and could scarcely wait for the time to come when he could make the beautiful Chrissie his wife.

TWENTY-NINE

Unaware of the events in Ireland, that same evening Dermot turned to Danny and said, 'You have no need to stay in the house while I'm here. You can start looking for work again if you've a mind.'

'Do you mean it?' Danny said. 'I heard today after Mass that they were setting on at Dunlop's. I thought to try there early tomorrow.'

'Go for it,' Dermot said.

'You'll have to see to the child,' Rosie said.

'That's all right,' Dermot said. 'I know, and in case you think I'm going to be a financial drain on you, I'm not. I have money.'

'We'll not take your money, Dermot,' Rosie said.

'Well then, forget your chance of a job, Danny. If Rosie is too high-principled to accept help from a brother I will take the first train back home tomorrow.'

'It doesn't feel right,' Rosie said.

'No, no, it doesn't,' Dermot said. 'My God, Rosie, who d'you think you're fooling? You barely eat enough to keep a bird alive, and I know why, even if you won't admit it. I have no need of this money, but you have. Let me share it with you?'

'Rosie, for God's sake,' Danny pleaded.

'All right,' Rosie snapped. 'God in heaven, must you harass me like this?'

'Aye, we must,' Dermot said. 'Because you're so stubborn. All right, Danny, you go out as soon as you like and I'll be here to give Rosie a hand,' and boy and man shook hands on the deal.

Danny didn't get a job at Dunlop's, nor at the Austin works he tried on Tuesday. When the rumour went out that there were jobs going at Ansell's on Thursday, Danny joined the line of men that snaked out of the gates and way along the Lichfield Road, past the clock and Aston Cross and on into the distance, a line of desperation and despair. Each day, Dermot took on the care of the baby, feeding him and changing him while Rosie saw to Bernadette.

He wondered if he was doing any good and how long he could stay. He wished he could take them all back to Ireland where they belonged, but he knew it was far too risky. Danny would be pulled back into it all if he returned, or shot or kneecapped if he refused. Phelan had explained it to him. Danny thought Sam and Shay were mad to be so involved still. Sarah didn't know the half of it, and he knew she was heading for a life of heartache with Sam. But he could do little about that, and little about making Rosie and his own new life in England better, either, it seemed.

By the time Dermot's letters reached his mother's house on Tuesday morning, Minnie's anger against Dennis Maloney and her daughters had barely lessened. It was incomprehensible to her that Chrissie and Geraldine should just up and leave that way. She felt they'd shown her up,

557

shamed her, and she doubted she'd ever forgive them for it.

The news of Dermot's disappearance, and the rumour he'd made for England and his sister's place, was almost common knowledge and Minnie knew that wouldn't be the end of it. She knew the school would soon get involved. The boy would get her into trouble if he didn't return shortly.

But the letter she received from her son said nothing of returning. He wrote that after he over-heard Connie reading the letter she had received from Danny, he felt worried about Rosie and had a yen to see her. He stressed it was his own idea and he'd told not a soul about it, and that he was sorry that he'd felt bound to creep away like that. He knew his parents would have been worried, but he was determined to stay on a wee while to lend a hand and said he thought he was needed.

Minnie was furious. She sent a vitriolic letter back, demanding Dermot's immediate return. He had no right to leave his home and go flying to England just as the notion took him, and she expected him back speedily and before she had the law on her back for him not going to school.

Connie wrote to Dermot in a different vein entirely. She was glad that the boy had gone over there to see the set-up for himself and could quite understand his concern, for her own anxiety over Rosie and Danny had almost spoiled the wedding for her. She included two ten-shilling notes in the letter.

I know things can't be easy for them, but neither Rosie

nor Danny will accept financial help from me and I've offered often. Don't tell them this money is from me, just use it sensibly to make their lives a little easier.

You're a good boy, Dermot, to care so well for your sister. I don't know if Chrissie is very fine at the moment for Elizabeth said she hasn't been at the factory since the wedding, something about catching a chill. Maybe your mother will tell you more.

Dermot was grateful for the money for he'd noticed the coal was very low and resolved to pop along that morning and order a few bags, but the reference to his sister's health had bothered him, for his mother had said nothing. He resolved to write and ask them what was wrong.

But before he was able to, the very next day a letter came from Chrissie. As Dermot read it he burned in shame for putting his sisters through such an ordeal and he was glad they'd had a strong champion in the form of Dennis Maloney to stand against their parents. He was glad too that his sisters were away from the place and safe, and he read that part of the letter out to Rosie.

'God, Dermot, our mother is a vicious woman,' Rosie burst out. 'I mean, I've felt the power of her hand many a time, and aye, she used the strap on me, on all of us time and enough, but she must have nearly half-killed the girls for Chrissie to be unable to go to work.'

'I know,' Dermot said miserably. 'I've been made more aware of her unfairness and all since I've been growing up. I did try speaking out a few times, but it made things worse, not better.'

'It would,' Rosie said, nodding her head. 'I can see that, for Mammy would see it as you taking their part against her and she'd blame them for it.'

'I feel so guilty about it all.'

'It's too late for that, Dermot. What's done is done,' Rosie said. 'What else does Chrissie say?'

Geraldine and I are so happy here. There is no-one to berate us or raise a hand to us. Dennis's sister Pauline is kindness itself and it was her that said I couldn't go to work this week because of my face, and she went along herself and told them I had a chill.

I feel much better now and will return on Monday and ask if there is an opening for Geraldine. If there isn't now, there soon will be, for when I marry Dennis I'll be working in the grocery store and she can take my place. Now my face is nearly back to normal we are seeing the priest this Sunday about calling the banns.

The townsfolk are very curious about my living here, though I've taken care they've not seen myself or Geraldine till we were fit to be seen, though it was hard to keep our presence a secret. Dennis just told any who asked that with our impending marriage it was easier for me living in the town and Geraldine is keeping me company. I don't know what they are thinking, nor do I care much, and anyway, your disappearance caused far more of a stir.

Tell Rosie it's impossible for her to come home, but there's no reason at all why Geraldine and I couldn't come over for a few days and see them. Dennis wouldn't mind, he knows how much we've missed them, so maybe in a few months we'd manage that. It's something to look forward to. In the meantime, tell her to write. We all miss her letters.

When Dermot read that out to Rosie she felt her heart lighten. She'd been outraged when Dermot told her what had happened to her sisters, but the last two paragraphs cheered her. 'I'm glad Chrissie and Geraldine are out of such an atmosphere,' she said. 'But oh how I'd love to see them. This Dennis Maloney must be an understanding sort of man.'

'He's all right,' Dermot said.

'Thank God for him, then,' Rosie said. 'And thank God the girls had somewhere safe to go to.'

On Sunday evening, Rosie began to acknowledge how much more positive everything is when a person is warm and well fed. On Saturday they had had bacon and cabbage and potatoes in their jackets, and on Sunday a good beef stew with food Dermot bought and which he insisted Rosie ate too. And there was plenty of coal to drive the chill from the house. Not knowing of the money her mother-in-law had sent, she wondered how much Dermot had left. She wanted to ask him, but not yet. She'd live in fool's paradise a little longer and believe she would always have a full belly and a warm house.

She was happy and contented for a wee while at least, with Bernadette in bed and Anthony slumbering in the cradle. Dermot was sitting opposite her helping her unravel wool from a heap of knitted garments she'd bought at the rag market the previous day as they chatted amicably together.

561

Suddenly the door burst open and Danny, who'd been out for a stroll, burst out, 'There's talk of a new factory opening up at Quinton, one of the fellows said, and they're setting on tomorrow.'

Rosie chose her words with care. 'Danny, Quinton is miles away.'

Dermot said nothing, but he wondered what it was that kept the hope alive in Danny; the motivation that kept him job-hunting fruitlessly day after day, dashing after this or that and never even getting a sniff. But then, did he have to even wonder? The motivation surely was his wife and children, and the need Danny had to feed and clothe them decently and keep a roof above their heads.

And then hadn't he come upon the lines of men outside the Labour Exchange one day in the week when he was making for the shops. The sight of the long, long queue of dejected men, shambling along in greasy caps pulled down and often in ragged, threadbare clothes with boots so cobbled there was little boot left, had depressed him for days. It had been sleeting and he was almost ashamed of his good thick clothes and boots that kept him both warm and dry. He could see why Danny had described unemployment as a living death.

And now Danny said, 'It's a tidy step all right, Rosie, but it's a chance of a job. I have to go, pet. You see that?'

And for what? thought Rosie. For another glimmer of hope to be nailed into the coffin of despair that someday will engulf you, for no-one can go on day after day, week after week, and be constantly rejected without it having some effect.

But none of these thoughts did she betray in her voice and manner as she said, 'Of course I see, Danny. What is the place?'

'A new place called Cartwright's, a small engineering factory. I want to be there for at least seven. That means leaving here before six.'

'That's all right,' Dermot assured him. 'I'll be here and getting up early is no odds to me. Haven't I been doing it for years to do the milking with Daddy?'

Both Rosie and Dermot saw the relief flood Danny's face and the droop of his shoulders as he relaxed. With Dermot there he could go off and search for this job like any other man, and do the job too if he was able.

Dermot was concerned about this, for he knew he couldn't stay indefinitely with Rosie and Danny. He'd tried to get Rosie to talk about her feelings for the baby but she never would, though she'd chat away about any other item under the sun. What he'd picked up on was that Rosie was so used to holding herself back from the baby that she didn't know how to break that mould.

And something must break it, Dermot thought, before the family is destroyed.

Next morning, Dermot lay in the dark of the attic and heard the rain bouncing on the roof of the skylight like so many pebbles. He heard Danny open the door below him and he slid from his makeshift bed and, careful not to wake the sleeping Bernadette, he dressed quickly and stole down the stairs in his stocking feet, his boots in his hand.

Danny was jiggling a restless Anthony in his arms and trying to make himself something to eat at the same time. Dermot tied his boots up quickly and held out his arms for the child. 'Give him to me. What's he doing up anyway?'

'Search me,' Danny said. 'He's been restless all night. I've been up three or four times already. I lost count after a while. And he was too restless now to leave upstairs; he'd have woken Rosie and then Bernadette in short order.'

'I'll give him a feed, shall I?' Dermot said. 'And change his nappy. That might settle him.'

'Would you?'

''Course I would,' Dermot said. 'Isn't that what I'm here for. You get yourself away. D'you see the weather? You have a fine day for it.'

Danny listened to the rain and the billowing wind moaning in the yard and shrugged his shoulders. 'It can't be helped. I've travelled further in worse,' he said, but he was worried for he knew the rain would go through his paper-thin clothes in minutes and soak into his feet, for the boots lined with cardboard to extend their life would no longer keep water out.

But, he told himself, was he to be put off going for a job because of a drop of rain? 'Don't take Anthony out in this,' he continued, 'and don't let Rosie go either. She's not all that strong and has a tendency to coughs and colds. The last thing I want is for her to go down with something now. Ida will mind Anthony while you take Bernadette to school.'

'Aye,' Dermot said, testing the bottle he'd made

up for the baby on the back of his hand.

'Glad she has only to go in the morning and come back in the evening on days like these,' Danny said. It was a system he'd talked over with the nuns after Anthony's birth, to send Bernadette with her dinner rather than fetch her home. Though most children went home, there were some living even further away than the Walshes that took their dinner and the nuns readily agreed that Bernadette could do the same.

By the time Danny left, Dermot had changed Anthony and was halfway through feeding him. He watched the baby sucking in blissful contentment and snuggled him close, and wondered why Rosie couldn't do the same.

The baby went to sleep later over Dermot's shoulder and he laid him down in the cradle by the range and tucked the blankets around him. He knew he would leave this child with no-one but Rosie that morning, for he'd decided a stand had to be made somewhere.

'Danny doesn't want the baby taken out in this,' he said to Rosie later as she ladled porridge into bowls.

'Aye,' Rosie said. 'Leave him at Ida's.'

'He's fast asleep.'

'Even so.'

'No,' Dermot said. 'It's coming down in bucketfuls. He'd be drenched and he's already been disturbed half the night, Danny said. He'll likely sleep till I come back from taking Bernadette to school.'

Rosie bit her lip in consternation. 'Look, Rosie,' Dermot said. 'He's one small baby. Surely to

565

God you can see he can't go out in this? Even as far as Ida's.'

Of course she saw. She nodded her head. 'All right,' she said. 'I'll take Bernadette today.'

'No you won't,' Dermot said. 'Danny said you weren't to go either. He said you get a lot of coughs and colds.'

Rosie was about to protest when Bernadette burst in. 'She does,' she said, remembering how frightened she'd been when her mammy was ill. 'She coughs and coughs and has to stay in bed ages and I can't even see her and have to stay with Auntie Ida or Auntie Rita.'

Rosie stared at her daughter and realised for the first time how much the child hated her being unwell. She couldn't risk going out into that bleak morning after her child had spoken like that.

'Out of the mouths of babes,' Dermot said with a smile.

'I'm afraid so,' Rosie said. 'But be as quick as you can.'

'I will,' Dermot said. 'I'd hardly dawdle in this.'

However, barely had the door closed on Dermot and Bernadette when the baby began to stir. Rosie watched almost fearfully as the movements in the crib became more marked and the mewling noises turned to a plaintive cry. She sat almost rooted to the spot as the cries turned to wails. Surely, she thought, Dermot must be back soon, or ... she'd go for Ida. That's what she'd do.

But she found she couldn't go and admit, even to her friend, that she was afraid to pick up one small baby, her own small baby. She approached the crib and looked down, wondering why she couldn't love this child as she did Bernadette.

Anthony's arms were threshing from side to side and his face scarlet as his cries reached crescendo level. Gently, Rosie lifted him into her arms and held him against her shoulder, and he could have been anyone's child, a friend's, a stranger's, she felt so little for him. She patted his back rhythmically and automatically rocked from side to side. 'Ssh, ssh, ssh,' she said over and over, and eventually the baby's cries eased and became hiccupping little sobs. Rosie lifted the baby down and looked at him. She wasn't even sure what colour eyes he had and now she saw the newborn blue had turned to brown, and then his mouth worked suddenly and fearing he would continue to cry she rocked him while she sang a lullaby.

Anthony stopped struggling and listened, a pucker appearing between his eyes, which he screwed up in an attempt to focus. Then his eyes suddenly opened wide and he gazed at Rosie, and then a smile – a real and beautiful smile – lit up his whole face.

Rosie was struck with such unexpected and inexplicable love for the child and with such force she felt as if she'd been kicked in the stomach by a mule and her legs trembled so, she'd felt for a chair with her free hand and sat down on it, gazing at her child as if she couldn't get enough of him.

Ida, calling in to see how she was, saw her sitting cuddling Anthony as if it was the most natural thing in the world. 'Thank God!' she said, but silently and afterwards she said to Rita, who she waylaid on the way home from work, 'I made up a bottle for the babby and she gave it to him as nice as you like. Oh my God, it brought tears to my eyes, it did really.'

Rita was as delighted as Ida. 'I think our Rosie's out of the woods now all right,' she said. 'If Danny could only get a job their lives would be perfect.'

'Ah wouldn't it,' Ida said, 'but that's as far away as ever. Danny is just one of thousands of men in the same boat.'

When Dermot returned home wringing wet and saw Rosie with the baby in her arms, he stood dead still in the doorway. Rosie turned to see him there and said calmly, 'Come in Dermot, come up to the fire and get those wet things off before you catch a chill.'

Dermot went as if in a trance and took off his wet coat and cap and hung them on the rail above the range. He was unable to keep his eyes off a sight he was beginning to think he'd never see. Ida had not long gone and Anthony was finishing the bottle she'd made for him. But, even after it, winded and changed, Rosie held him, reluctant to lay him down. When Dermot suggested he put him in the crib, 'He's had weeks, months there,' she said. 'Denied of his birthright, my love.'

'Why!' Dermot said. 'I mean, what's changed?'

'I don't know,' Rosie said. 'It hit me like a ton of bricks and I don't have any explanation.'

She remembered telling Danny she couldn't

love a child begotten through drunkenness and lust, but it wasn't that really. She knew the child was just the innocent victim of something that had happened that previous Christmas Eve. But she wasn't sharing any of that with her young brother. She didn't want to blame him either or have him think she was blaming him, for none of it was his fault either, so she spoke cautiously, 'Things were different for us after you were born, Dermot.'

'Geraldine has often said something similar,' Dermot said. 'Of course I saw a lot myself as I grew. You accept things as they are when you're just a wean.'

'Aye,' Rosie said. 'Well I didn't want the same thing to happen to Bernadette.'

'That's not likely though is it?' Dermot said. 'You and Danny are different parents to ours.'

'I know. At least I see it now,' Rosie said. 'But if you add that fear to the one that I'd never be able to give birth to a healthy child and my reaction because of it, it probably explains why I felt as I did about Anthony initially.'

'And now?'

'Now. Oh God, I love him to pieces,' Rosie said. 'I can't imagine ever thinking otherwise, but I shall make it up to him.'

'I know one person who will be pleased,' Dermot said. 'And that will be Danny.'

'Aye,' Rosie said, and added with a sigh, 'God, he'll need something to cheer him.'

'You think he's not a chance of this job at Quinton then?'

'Not a snowball's chance in Hell,' Rosie said.

'And he'll be more dispirited than ever.'

So Rosie was very surprised to see a happy, smiling Danny at the door some hours later; just as he was to see his wife lifting Anthony from the crib, a made-up bottle already in her hand. Dermot had gone down for Bernadette and so there was just the two of them and the baby, and Rosie said, hardly daring to hope, 'You ... you got the job?'

'At Quinton, no,' Danny said. 'Men must have been queuing there from black night; the queues were three deep and spreading right down the road. The foreman came out at eight and told anyone from halfway down there was no point in us waiting and so I set off home again. I didn't come back straight away because I felt too disappointed to face you. I went down the cut instead. I helped a boatie leg it through the tunnel as he was pulling a load of coal behind him and he gave me a shilling and I earned another shilling and a double brandy for helping a narrowboat through the locks. Don't look like that, Rosie, it was only the one double brandy and that was only because we were so soaked. It was keeping the life in us.'

Rosie felt Danny's jacket and knew he told the truth; though the rain had stopped now, his jacket was soaking. 'Take that off and come up to the fire. I'll put the kettle on. A drink may warm you.'

'It will,' Danny said. 'But let me finish the tale first. When I came out of the pub, Ted was on the canal and he hailed me. He said I'd saved him a journey for he was coming here tonight. Syd has done a runner it seems. Young Syd and Ted had a set-to more than a week ago and the boy took off.

'Ted took no notice, thinking each day he'd be back. Then this morning he had a letter from the lad saying he'd joined the merchant navy as a cadet and signed on for seven years. Ted and his wife can't manage the narrowboat on their own and they've offered me a job, and won't I like it better than any factory?'

Rosie was hardly able to believe it. After all this time, Danny in work! 'Permanent?'

'Aye, permanent. Ah Jesus, Rosie, how good it feels.' He grabbed Rosie and held her tight and she was heedless of the sodden jacket, though she held Anthony away from it. 'I'm delighted for you,' she said. 'And now go and get out of those wet things before you get your death and I'll feed this young man. In the oven I have liver and onions cooking that Dermot went shopping for this morning, a fine meal for a celebration.'

'But… how…' Danny couldn't put into words what he wanted to say. 'You and Anthony?'

'Well, whatever it was that ailed me with regard to the child, I'm over it,' Rosie said. 'I think I know why I was unable to take to Anthony at his birth, but I don't know why all that was pushed to one side because he smiled at me. But it has been. You need have no worries, Danny, I love my son as well as my daughter.'

'And your husband?'

'I've never stopped loving my husband.'

'Ah Rosie,' Danny promised. 'You need have no worries either. I'll make you proud of me.'

'I've always been proud of you.'

'God, how can you say that? There have been times I haven't been able to live with myself.'

'Danny, that's in the past. Let's put that behind us and look to the future. And whatever that holds we'll face it together. Now go and take off those wet things before they stick to you.'

When Bernadette and Dermot came in a little later, both their cheeks were red as they'd run most of the way home. Dermot had said nothing to Bernadette about Rosie's changed attitude to the baby, and so she watched her mother feeding Anthony for a bit and said, 'Do you like Anthony now, Mammy?'

Rosie was flummoxed by the question. 'I've always liked Anthony, Bernadette.'

'No, you haven't,' Bernadette said emphatically. 'I'm glad you do now. He does get on your nerves when he cries all the time, though.'

'He doesn't cry all the time.'

'Well, a lot, then.'

Rosie thought it time to change the subject. 'Bernadette, I don't want to discuss Anthony's crying just now, Daddy has got good news. He has a job on a narrowboat. He'll be at work again.'

This was news to Dermot too and he went across the room and took Danny's hand and shook it.

'I'm so happy for you,' he said. 'I haven't words to tell you how much.'

It made life easier for Dermot too, for he knew soon he'd have to return home and he'd have hated to go with things unresolved. Now he could leave with an easier conscience, and later, with Bernadette in bed and Anthony asleep in the crib, he told Rosie and Danny he must think about going home.

Rosie was surprised. She'd never asked Dermot what his long-term plans were, but she'd assumed he would bide with them for some time. Now, she saw that could never be. 'You'll return to the farm?'

'Aye,' Dermot said. 'Daddy will never manage it on his own and after all it will be mine one day. For the time being, anyway. I have another year at school and there may be trouble if I stay away any longer. There are to be changes, though. For example, I will see the girls and not lie about it either, skulking about the village as if it's something to be ashamed of.

'I'll see Connie too. She'll be anxious for news of you. She's not the same woman since you left. Phelan does his best, but she misses all of you. She'd love to hear of Bernadette and wee Anthony, for she'll never come here, the very thought of the journey terrifies her, and she knows you cannot come home for years. Write to her, Rosie?'

'Aye, I will,' Rosie said. 'Now everything's all right, I will.'

Later in the bedroom, Rosie said, 'I'll write to your mother first thing tomorrow. There will be only good news to give her for a change.'

Danny took Rosie in his arms. His eyes saddened suddenly. 'I once told you I'd never let anyone hurt a hair on your head,' he said. 'And then, when we came to Birmingham, I promised I'd make it up to you, leaving Ireland and all. I often think all I brought you was a vale of tears and sadness.'

'In everyone's life there is sunshine and shadow,' Rosie said. 'No-one knows what the future holds. But at least we have a future. What future have those young men, from whichever side, whose bodies are littered over battlefields in a war they often didn't have choice of fighting in? Ordinary people often don't have a choice, but at least we have each other and we faced our shadows together. Let's go out into the sunshine hand in hand.' And she reached for Danny's hand and grasped it tight.

The publishers hope that this book has given you enjoyable reading. Large Print Books are especially designed to be as easy to see and hold as possible. If you wish a complete list of our books please ask at your local library or write directly to:

Magna Large Print Books
Magna House, Long Preston,
Skipton, North Yorkshire.
BD23 4ND

This Large Print Book for the partially sighted, who cannot read normal print, is published under the auspices of

THE ULVERSCROFT FOUNDATION